PENGUIN CLASSICS  DELUXE EDITION

PRESENCE: COLLECTED STORIES

ARTHUR MILLER (1915–2005) was born in New York City and studied at the University of Michigan. His plays include *All My Sons* (1947), *Death of a Salesman* (1949), *The Crucible* (1953), *A View from the Bridge* and *A Memory of Two Mondays* (1955), *After the Fall* and *Incident at Vichy* (1964), *The Price* (1968), *The Creation of the World and Other Business* (1972), and *The American Clock* (1980). His other works include *Focus*, a novel (1945); *The Misfits*, a cinema novel (1961); and the texts for *In Russia* (1969), *In the Country* (1977), and *Chinese Encounters* (1979), three books in collaboration with his wife, photographer Inge Morath. His memoirs include *Salesman in Beijing* (1984) and *Timebends*, an autobiography (1987). His short fiction includes the collection *I Don't Need You Any More* (1967), the novella *Homely Girl, A Life* (1995), and *Presence: Stories* (2007). His later work includes the plays *The Ride Down Mt. Morgan* (1991), *The Last Yankee* (1993), *Broken Glass* (1994), *Mr. Peters' Connections* (1999), and *Resurrection Blues* (2006); *Echoes Down the Corridor: Collected Essays, 1944–2000*; and *On Politics and the Art of Acting* (2001). Among numerous honors, he received the Pulitzer Prize for Drama and the John F. Kennedy Lifetime Achievement Award.

BY ARTHUR MILLER

PLAYS

The Golden Years
The Man Who Had All the Luck
All My Sons
Death of a Salesman
An Enemy of the People
The Crucible
A View from the Bridge
After the Fall
Incident at Vichy
The Price
The Creation of the World and
    Other Business
The Archbishop's Ceiling
The American Clock
Playing for Time
The Ride Down Mt. Morgan
Broken Glass
Mr. Peters' Connections
Resurrection Blues
Finishing the Picture

ONE-ACT PLAYS

A View from the Bridge (*one-act version*)
A Memory of Two Mondays
Fame
The Reason Why
Elegy for a Lady (*in* Two-Way Mirror)
Some Kind of Love Story
    (*in* Two-Way Mirror)
I Can't Remember Anything
    (*in* Danger: Memory!)
Clara (*in* Danger: Memory!)
The Last Yankee

SCREENPLAYS

The Misfits
Playing for Time
Everybody Wins
The Crucible

MUSICAL

Up from Paradise

AUTOBIOGRAPHY

Timebends: A Life

REPORTAGE

Situation Normal
In Russia (*with Inge Morath*)
In the Country (*with Inge Morath*)
Chinese Encounters (*with Inge Morath*)
Salesman in Beijing

FICTION

Focus (*a novel*)
Jane's Blanket (*a children's story*)
The Misfits (*a cinema novel*)
I Don't Need You Any More (*stories*)
Homely Girl, A Life
    (*a novella and stories*)
Presence: Collected Stories

COLLECTIONS

Arthur Miller's Collected Plays,
    Volumes I and II
The Portable Arthur Miller
Arthur Miller: Collected Plays
    1944–1961 (*Tony Kushner,
    editor*)
Arthur Miller: Collected Plays
    1964–1982 (*Tony Kushner,
    editor*)
Arthur Miller: Collected Plays
    1987–2004 with Stage and Radio
    Plays of the 1930s and '40s (*Tony
    Kushner, editor*)
The Penguin Arthur Miller: Collected
    Plays

ESSAYS

Collected Essays
The Theater Essays of Arthur Miller
    (*Robert A. Martin, editor*)
Echoes Down the Corridor: Collected
    Essays, 1944–2000
    (*Steven R. Centola, editor*)
On Politics and the Art of Acting

VIKING
CRITICAL LIBRARY EDITIONS

Death of a Salesman
    (*Gerald Weales, editor*)
The Crucible
    (*Gerald Weales, editor*)

ARTHUR MILLER

Presence

COLLECTED STORIES

PENGUIN BOOKS

PENGUIN BOOKS

An imprint of Penguin Random House LLC
375 Hudson Street
New York, New York 10014
penguin.com

Presence: Collected Stories first published in Great Britain by Bloomsbury Publishing Plc 2009
Published in Penguin Books 2016

LIBRARY OF CONGRESS CATALOGING-IN-PUBLICATION DATA
Names: Miller, Arthur, 1915-2005, author.
Title: Presence : collected stories / Arthur Miller.
Description: Penguin Classics deluxe edition. | New York : Penguin Books, [2016]
Identifiers: LCCN 2016030438 (print) | LCCN 2016030917 (ebook) | ISBN
9780143108474 (paperback) | ISBN 9781101992029
Subjects: | BISAC: FICTION / Short Stories (single author). | FICTION /
Literary. | FICTION / Jewish.
Classification: LCC PS3525.I5156 A6 2016 (print) | LCC PS3525.I5156 (ebook) |
DDC 813/.52—dc23
LC record available at https://lccn.loc.gov/2016030438

Printed in the United States of America
1 3 5 7 9 10 8 6 4 2

Set in Sabon LT Std

Contents

Foreword

About Distances

These stories were written over the past fifteen years; all but one, which is published in this book for the first time, appeared in magazines. They were not, of course, conceived as a series (although reading them together now I am surprised at a certain continuity). They were done for my own pleasure, if indeed that can be possible when one intends writing to be published at all. In comparison to playwriting, however, writing stories is undoubtedly more pleasurable if one connects that word to something done primarily for its own sake. After all, we in this country pay small attention to stories, which are squeezed in between the magazine ads, and are ranked more or less casual things at the lower end of the scale of magnitude, like bungalows in the architectural world.

But I would just as soon see that attitude remain unchanged. The premium on grandiosity leaves us this form of art in which a writer can still be as concise as his subject really requires him to be. Here he need not say more than he knows for form's sake. There is a short-story tone of voice which, amid the immodest heroics of the day, still invites whoever wishes to speak or blurt out his truth in a single breath. For a playwright it has certain affinities; its economy and formal decorum—at least it *can* have those qualities—offer a vessel for those feelings and tales which, unelaborated, are truer, and yet for one reason or another do not belong on stage.

Of course, a playwright is expected to say that he enjoys writing stories because he is rid of actors, directors, and the nuisance of the theatrical machinery, but in all truth I rather like actors and directors. What I have found, though, is that from time to time there is an urge not to speed up and condense events and character development, which is what one does in a play, but to hold them frozen and to see things isolated in stillness, which I think is the great strength of a good short story. The object, the place, weather, the look of a person's shift of posture—these things can have but secondary importance on the stage, where action makes truth evident; in life, however, and in the story, place itself and things seen, the mood of a moment, the errant flight of apprehension which leads nowhere, can all register and weigh.

Some of these stories could never be plays, but some perhaps could have been. The latter were not written as plays partly because they seemed to me to reject the theatrical tone of voice, which is always immodest, at bottom. The playwright, after all, is a performer *manqué*; thoroughly shy and self-effacing philosophers do not write plays—at least not playable ones. That is probably why playwrights at middle age so often turn to fiction and away from the unseemly masquerade. All the world's a stage, but the point comes when one would rather be real and at home. In my case, over the years I have found myself arriving at that point once or twice a week (although not always lucky enough to seize a subject at these ripe moments), and it is then that I have found short-story writing particularly fitting. The mask, in short, is of another kind when one sits down to write a tale. The adversary—audience and critic—will be taken off guard in the dentist's waiting room, on a train or plane, or in the bathroom. They have less to resent. It is paradoxical but true, for me at least, that even as the short story falls, so to speak, into a well of silence once published, while a play is always accompanied by every kind of human noise, it is in the story that I find myself feeling some connection with the reader, with strangers. There is an aggressiveness in playwriting; if there is a friendly and familiar form of art it is the story. I feel I know Chekhov better from his stories than from his plays, and Shakespeare through his sonnets, which analogously at least are his stories. Certainly Hemingway is more palpable in his stories than in his novels, less covered up and professional in the icy sense. There is less to sweep one away in "The Cossacks" or "The Death of Ivan Ilyich" than in *War and Peace,* to be sure, but there is also less that one cannot possibly believe. Maybe that is the attraction—one stretches truth a little less in a story if only because the connective arcs of interpretation are shorter, less remote from the concrete; one can more quickly catch wonder by surprise, which is after all why one writes—or reads, for that matter.

None of which is to denigrate drama or the theatre, but merely to point to some of the differences. It has always been a curious thing to me, for example, that I should find dialogue so much harder to write in a story than in a play, and from time to time I have imagined various explanations for this strangeness. Perhaps, I thought, I know that no actor is going to speak these lines, so there is an absurdity in writing them. Then, it seemed there might be some sort of half-conscious objection to putting dialogue into a form where it was not absolutely necessary, and thus a feeling of arbitrariness had intervened. But I think now that there is a conflict of masks, a clash of tonalities. The spoken line is "speech," it is something said to a crowd and must therefore be peculiarly emphatic and definite, and implicitly must call for reply; every line of stage dialogue is one half of a dialectical conflict. But this kind of pressure laid upon dialogue in a story distorts everything around it. It is as though one were being told an incident by a friend who suddenly stands up, and casting his gaze beyond the room, continues his tale by imitating the voices of the participants in it. The sudden injection of formality, of this kind of formality, is the threatening imminence of the actor. This, perhaps, is why it is impossible to lift scenes of dialogue and put them on the stage. They may seem perfectly stageworthy on paper, and on occasion they really are, but for the most part the novelist's dialogue is pitched toward the eye rather than the ear and falls flat when heard. Conversely, the dialogue in a story needs to sacrifice its sound in order to be convincing to the eye. And this is another enticement stories have for a playwright—as one writes dialogue for the eye, the stage becomes a wonderful thing all over again and the thirst returns for playwriting, and the "right" to tell a story through sounds once more. That is odd and ironical to me because as a schoolboy I was first taken with books in proportion to the amount of dialogue a quick flip of the pages revealed. It was for the sake of the dialogue, I supposed, that the rest of the book was written; certainly it was for the dialogue that the book was read. This was when the author, I thought, stopped chattering and got out of the way; his own comment was like opinion as opposed to fact.

A primitive notion, but it reflects a truth nevertheless. All these forms we have inherited—story, novel, play—are degrees of distance writers need to take between themselves and the dangerous audience which they must cajole, threaten, and, in one way or another, tame. The playwright is all but physically on stage, face to face with the monster; the writer of fiction, however meager his covering, is most safe in this sense, but out of hearing of the applause, out of sight of the mass of strangers sitting spellbound in a theatre, sucked out of themselves by his imaginings. Thus, when a novelist takes to writing a play, or a playwright a story, he is shifting his distance toward or away from the terrible heat at the center of the stage. Sometimes a Dickens, a Mark Twain, striving to rip clear all masks, will come forward in person to the lecture platform, and a Sinclair Lewis as a member of Actors' Equity, a Hemingway as a personality in his own right, his work to one side. But there is no end to masks; the one we put down only leaves the one we have on. The problem is, therefore, not one of sincerity—who can know that of himself? It is rather the rending of a particular vision at its proper distance, the discovery of the tone appropriate to one's feeling for a thing, a person, an event. No single form can do everything well; these stories are simply what I have seen, at another distance.

ARTHUR MILLER
NOVEMBER 1966

Presence

COLLECTED STORIES

I DON'T NEED YOU ANY MORE

To the memory of Pascal Covici

I Don't Need You Any More

Several times in the previous days he had been not exactly warned but instructed, in a certain thickly absolute way, that God forbade swimming on Friday this week. And this was Friday now. He had been watching the ocean many times a day, and sure enough it had been getting rougher and rougher all the time and the color of the water was getting funny. Not green or blue but kind of gray and even black in certain places, until now, when the water was running with sins, the waves were actually banging down on the sand so hard that the curb on which he was sitting shuddered up faintly through his spine. Some connection ran under the beach and came up here where the street ended.

The waves were skidding in like big buildings that swayed drunkenly and then toppled over on their faces and splattered all over the hard sand. He kept his watch along the curved faces of the breakers for a sign of the bearded sins he knew were floating around in there like seaweed, and for a second now and then he got a glimpse of them. They were like beards, except that they were yards long and you couldn't see the man's face from which they grew. Somehow there were several beards, but they all belonged to the same face. It was like a man in there floating just a foot or so underneath the water or sometimes moving as fast as a fish and then floating again in another spot. It was because today and tomorrow were Tishebuf or Rosh Hashonoh or Yom Kippur or one of those holidays which Grandpa and the other old men somehow knew had arrived—days when everybody got dressed up, and he had to wear this tweed suit and tie and new

shoes, and nobody was allowed to eat all day except him, because
he was still only five and had not had Hebrew lessons yet. He
would also have piano or violin lessons when he would be six,
and once he started playing the piano or the violin he would not
be allowed to eat on this holiday either, like his brother couldn't.
Meantime, though, he could go to the synagogue and visit with
his brother and father, but he didn't have to. It was better to, but
if he got impatient and wanted to go outside in the fresh air he
could and not be blamed or even noticed. He could do practically
anything because he was still only five.

This morning after he had finished breakfast, eating all alone
on the oilcloth-covered kitchen table after his father and his
brother had gone off to pray, he had decided not to eat a single
thing again the rest of the day. At eleven o'clock, though, his
mother, as always, had come out of the bungalow looking for him
with a piece of jam-spread rye bread, and at first he had refused to
eat it. But then she had said, "Next year . . ." and he had compro-
mised for her sake and eaten it. It tasted good but not delicious,
and he got angry a moment later remembering how she had forced
it on him. Then at lunchtime she had come out again looking for
him, and he had eaten lunch in the same frame of discontent. But
now he openly wished, as he sat staring at the ocean and listening
to its booming roar, that his father or his brother had forbidden
him outright to eat at all. He could have stood it. Side by side with
his great father and his good brother he would have been able to
go without even water all day. Just as he wouldn't dream of going
into the ocean now, for instance, even though his tweed suit was
scratching his neck and thighs, even though he could not stop
himself from imagining how fine the water would feel on his skin.
His mother had said it was all right if he got into a pair of cotton
shorts, but he would not think of taking off his itchy suit. A holiday was a holiday. He tried now to wipe out of his mind that he
had eaten lunch. He tried to make himself feel very hungry, but he
could not remember the feeling exactly. At least he had not gone
back into the bungalow since lunch for a glass of milk. He counted

and, half believing, assured himself that he had fasted three times today, and then brushed some sand off the top of his shoes to make himself perfect. But after a moment a vague restlessness returned; he could not believe in anything alone, and he wished his brother or his father were here to see his perfection. Suddenly he realized that without even trying to stop himself he had not picked his nose all day, and felt silvery at the knowledge. But there was not a soul around to see.

The ocean went on booming. The beach, white as salt, was deserted. There was no tinkle of the ice-cream-man's bell, hardly any cars were parked on the bungalow-lined street now that September was here, and the little front porches, each one exactly like the next, were almost all empty. Practically no garbage cans stood out on the curbs any more. He felt, pressing against his thigh inside his pocket, the rusted penknife he had found in the Levines' vacated bungalow last week. It was the best treasure he had ever found at the end of the season when he had followed the other boys to ransack. He wondered idly why the mothers always left so many bobby pins and hairy pieces of soap. Fathers left razor blades, but these were not hidden in the crevices of drawers and under the mattresses. He wondered why mothers stopped talking or changed the subject whenever he came into a room. Under their skirts it was dark. Fathers kept right on talking, hardly noticing a little boy coming in, and there was always more light around.

A new strangeness on the ocean scattered his memories. He saw its surface tilting up. Far, far out a crest was rising as wide as the sea itself, and a new rumbling, deeper than any he had heard before, was beginning to sound. He got to his feet, ecstatically frightened, ready to run. Higher and higher the crest rose up until it was a straight wall of blackish water. No one else was seeing it, he knew, only he and the sand and the empty porches. Now it leaned forward, hard as stone and compact, and he could hear it kind of screaming to itself as it pounded over on its head, the spray shooting upward like fifty garden hoses going at once. He turned, happy to have escaped death, and started for his house to tell it. Already the joyful words were forming in his mouth. "The water got like hard, like the street, and then it stood up in the air and I couldn't even see the sky, and then you know what? I saw the beard!" He halted.

He was not sure, suddenly, whether he had seen the beard. He remembered seeing it, but he was not sure he had really seen it. He visualized his mother; she would believe it if he told her, as she always believed everything he reported that happened to him. But a sadness crept into him now, an indecision, as he remembered that lately she was not as excited about the things he told her. Of course she didn't say he was lying, like his brother did, or question him the way Ben did so that contradictory details turned up to ruin everything. But there was something about her now that was not exactly listening, the way she always used to. So that even with her now he was finding himself having to add things he knew were not true in order to make her really pay attention. Like about the milkman's horse stepping on the fly. It really had stepped on that fly, but when she had merely nodded at the news he had gone on and told how it had raised its hoof again, looked down at the ground, waited, and then clomped down on another fly, and then a third. His sallow face frowned. If he went to her now with the news of the ocean he would probably have to say he had seen not only the beard but even the face under the water, and maybe even tell how the eyes looked. In his mind he could clearly see the eyes—they were blue with fat white lids, and they could stare up through the salt water without blinking; but that was not the same as knowing he had actually seen the eyes. If she believed it, then probably he had seen it, but if she merely nodded as she was doing lately, and without gasping and being full of astonishment, then he would end up feeling vagrant and bad that he had said a lie. It was getting to be almost the same as telling things to his brother. Anger against her grew in him as he paused there, aching to tell her at least about the wave. For him, nothing happened if he could not tell it, and lately it was so complicated to tell anything.

He went to his front door and entered the small living room, his uncertainty filling him now with bitterness. He saw her through the kitchen doorway working over the pots. She glanced out at him and said, "Have a glass of milk."

Milk! When his father and his brother were standing right now praying to God in the synagogue with parched lips, yellow with hunger. He did not answer. He could not even bring himself to go into the kitchen, that blessed place where he always loved to sit with his chin on the cool oilcloth tablecloth, watching her while she cooked, telling her all the amazing things he had seen in the world outside. He hoisted himself onto a chair at the living-room table where he had never sat alone before.

After a few moments of silence she turned and saw him there. Her eyebrows rose as though she had discovered him suspended from the ceiling. "What are you doing there?" she asked.

As if she didn't know! He bitterly lowered his eyes to the table top. Now she came out of the kitchen and stood a few feet from him, mystified. He was not looking at her but he could see her, and once more, as though for the first time, he recalled that she had a strange look lately, her face was somehow puffy. Yes, and she walked differently, as if she were always in a slowly moving line of people.

She kept looking down at him without speaking, her eyebrows creasing together, and he was suddenly aware that he was the only one in the whole family, including his cousins, whose ears stuck out. "Pull in your ears, Martin, we're going through a tunnel!" And his uncles looking down at him, grinning—"Where did *he* come from? Who does he take after?" He did not look like any-body, he recalled as he sat there with his mother before him. The sensation grew in him now that there was a space through which he and his mother were looking at each other all the time, and he did not remember it before. "Are you sick?" she said at last, laying a hand on his forehead.

He brushed her hand away, lightly striking her belly with the side of his finger. Instantly his finger felt hot, and fright stabbed his stomach like a sliver of glass. She covered her belly with a silent gasp, a deep contraction within her body that he could almost hear, and she turned to go back into the kitchen. He took the chance and looked up at her turning face. It was shut away in silence, and in silence she went back to the stove. She never even screamed at him lately, he realized, and she never dressed any more if he was in the bedroom but went into her closet and talked to him through the nearly closed door. He knew he was not supposed to notice that, just as Ben and Papa didn't. And now he knew that he was not supposed to notice that she was not screaming at him any more, and he slid down off the chair, not knowing where to go next, his secret knowledge frosting his skin.

"Why don't you get into your shorts?" she said from the kitchen.

A sob started to convulse his stomach. Shorts now! When Ben and Papa had to be standing up and sitting down in the synagogue a million times a day in their wool suits! If it was up to her, people would be allowed to do anything they wanted—and the long beard floating in the water and the ocean so rough! He would like to dare her to go and tell Papa or Ben to put on their shorts!

"Go ahead, dear," she said, "they're in your top drawer."

The chair he had been sitting on skidded away, squealing along the floor. He realized he had kicked it and glanced across to the kitchen doorway; she had turned, a frightened amusement in her eyes.

"What's the matter?" she asked. Her falseness buzzed like insects around his face.

He sluffed out the front door, flinging it wide so that the spring meowed.

"Martin?" She was coming through the living room faster than he had expected, and he moved across the porch, wanting to run but keeping to a prideful stroll. He felt a certain amount of rightness for somehow he had enforced the law on her. Behind him the door spring meowed, and he was starting adamantly down the stoop when she reached out and grasped his shoulder. "Martin!" Her voice was a complaint, but it was also accusing now, reaching and spreading into his most silent thoughts, blasting his rectitude. He tried to wriggle out of her grasp, but she held on to his jacket, pulling so that his jacket button was up to his chin. "Martin!" she screamed now into his face.

The indignity flamed up in him that she should be so disrespectful of his suit, which he wore so carefully, and he struck at her arm with all his might. "Let me go!" he screamed.

His blow unleashed her. She cracked his offending hand, holding it by the wrist, again and again, until it stung, and trying to get away he stumbled and landed on the porch, sitting up. "Papa'll take his strap to you!" she yelled down at him, tears in her eyes.

Papa! She was going to tell Papa! His contempt pushed her distorted, yelling face a mile away, and he felt a calm road of light opening before him. His jaw trembling, his black eyes edged with hatred, he screamed, "I don't need you any more!"

Her eyes seemed to spread open wider and wider, like scandal. He was astonished; even now it did not seem a bad thing to say, only the truth; she didn't need him so he didn't need her. But there she was, her mouth open, her hand to her cheek, looking down at him with a horror he had never dreamed a person could show. He did not understand; only lies were horrible. She stepped away from him, looking down at him like a strange thing, opened the door, and quietly went into the house.

He heard the sea crashing behind him, the sound hitting him in the back familiarly. He got up, strangely spent. He listened, but she was not making any noise or crying that he could hear. He walked down the stoop and along the few yards of sidewalk to the sand, hesitated about ruining his shine, and continued onto the beach. He knew he was bad, but he did not know why. He approached the forbidden water. It seemed to see him.

There was a privacy here. The brisk breeze would cut off her voice if she called to him, and, he remembered, she could not run after him any more. Just as she did not dance around the table with him or let him jump onto their bed in the mornings, and if he came up behind her any more to clasp her around she would slip quickly out of his embrace. And nobody but he had noticed these new ways, and the knowledge was somehow dangerous.

Papa didn't know, or Ben, and as he walked along the edge of the wet sand, his body wrapped in the roar of the falling waves, he pressed one ear against his head, silently speaking his wish. If only he *looked* like his father and his brother! Then he wouldn't know what he was not supposed to know. It was his ears' fault. Because he looked so different he saw different things than they saw, and he had knowledge of things a fine boy could never know. Like the dentist.

His breath turned to pebbles in his throat as he tried to fend off the memory of that terrible day. A sudden wash flowed up and lapped at his shoe, and he leaped away. He bent over, trying to concentrate on drying his shoe with his hand. Suddenly he realized that he had actually touched the evil water. He smelled his hand. It did not smell rotten. Or maybe it was God who was in the water today, and you must not get in with Him, so that the water was not stinking rotten even though it was forbidden. He moved back several yards and sat on the sand, the image of the dentist mingling with his thrill of fear at having touched the water, and he gave way to a certain frightening pleasure.

He clearly saw the sidewalk before their apartment house in the city—his mother walking home, he at her hip, hearing the creaking of the brown-paper grocery bag she was carrying. And he remembered the feeling of walking with her and not having to think where to turn next, when to stop, when to hurry, when to go slow. They were as though connected, and he was simply there. And then, suddenly, they had stopped. Looking up, he saw the strange man's face close to hers. And a tear fell from the man's cheek past Martin's nose. She was talking with such a strange laughter, a dense excitement, posing very straight. And he called her by her first name, the stranger. And afterward, in the lobby as they waited for the elevator, she laughed and said, still with that same high-breathing laughter, "Oh, he was so in love with me! I was ready to marry him, can you imagine? But Grandpa made him go away. He was only a student then. Oh, the books he brought me all the time!"

Through the waves' roar he could still hear her excited voice over his head exactly as it had sounded in the lobby. And he reddened again with embarrassment, a humiliation which did not come from any thought or even from the incident itself. He could not imagine her really being married to the dentist since she was Papa's wife, she was Mama. In fact, he barely remembered anything she had said that day, but simply her laughter and the excitement in her breath when she had left the dentist and entered the apartment house. He had never heard her voice that way and it had made him resolve instantly never to let on that he had noticed the new tone and the rather strange woman who had made it. And the horror which lay behind his embarrassment was that she had thoughts which Papa did not have. He had felt since that day like a small shepherd guarding big animals that must be kept from understanding their own strength, and if he played out of their sight for a moment or even joked or fought with them, he never forgot that his flute would really be no match for their unrealized violence if they once became aware that they were not the same person but separate, not joined in their minds as they thought they were but capable of talking and breathing differently when out of each other's sight. Only he knew this and only he was in charge of guarding them from this knowledge and keeping them unaware that they were not as they had been before the dentist had come up to Mama on the street.

As it always happened when he recalled the stranger, he thought now of the day following, a Sunday, when the whole family had gone for a walk, and as they approached that particular square of pavement he had held his breath, certain that when Papa's shoe came down on it a roaring and a crashing would break the air. But Papa had walked right over the concrete, noticing nothing, and Mama had noticed nothing either, so that Martin at that moment saw his duty clearly; it was that he alone had the vigil to keep. For even though Mama had actually acted that way with the stranger, she was somehow not aware of its real meaning, as he was aware of it. He must never let her know, in any conceivable way, the true meaning of what she had done; that instead of laughing excitedly when she said, "He was so in love with me, I almost married him," she should have howled and screamed and been horrified. He would never tell her this, though.

Now his mind trembled and flickered out as it always did when he came to the last part, when he imagined what would happen if Papa should ever find out not only what had happened, but that he knew this secret. Papa would look down at him from his height and roar with terrible hurt and horror, "Mama almost married the dentist? What kind of a boy are you to make up such a thing! Waaaaaahhh!" And he would be swallowed up in the roaring, and the agony raised him to his feet.

He walked beside the ocean, picking up tiny snail shells and crushing them to powder; he threw stones, broke sticks, but a threat would not leave him alone. Slowly it returned to him that he had never seen his mother as horrified as he had just left her. He had driven her crazy many times, but not like this, not with that look in her eyes. And her teeth had showed when she hit him. That had never happened—not with the teeth showing.

Her teeth showing and her widened eyes . . . He looked at the sea. Maybe it had to do with today being a holy day? He already believed that his badness sent out a sort of invisible ray, a communication that passed beyond his family and entered a darkness somewhere far away; it was not something he ever thought of, it was something he had always known. And the retribution would come out of that darkness as from an unalterable judgment, which could not be stopped or entertained or deflected. Her scandalized eyes seemed now to be frightened for him, for what he had drawn down upon himself from the darkness. She hadn't been merely mad at him on the porch, she had been afraid with him. He must have said something to her that was not only an insult to her but a sin. And he could not remember what it was that he had said. His failure to remember frightened him in itself; it opened up some awful possibilities.

The dentist! His heart contracted; by mistake had he told her that he knew she had acted that way with the strange man? Or maybe she believed he had already told Papa? He wanted to run home and tell her, "Mama, I never told Papa about the dentist!" But as soon as he envisioned it he was stopped, realizing he could not tell her either that he knew. And if he told Ben, Ben would be horrified that he could even say such a thing. He sluffed along the empty beach as lonely as his duty, unknowingly sharing his secret with the bearded sea in whose forbidden depths there were eyes that saw, and saw him, and saw through his skull. And, walking, he remembered how it would be to lose his visibility; if Papa should ever discover what he knew, and roared, he would gradually disappear. But that was not the end. He would actually be there, hearing everything and seeing them all the time, except that they would not see him. He suddenly felt he would burst out weeping for them at having lost him, and he quickly corrected his vision. The fact is, he would be visible when they looked at him, but as soon as they turned their backs he would disappear. It was very fine. At night, for instance, he might get up out of bed and invisibly go into their bedroom and just sit there comfortably, and they would never know he was there. And if he got tired when it got very late, he could just lie down in bed between them and everybody would have a good sleep. Except—he carefully amended—he must remember not to wet the bed, or they would wake in the morning and see it and accuse each other and fight.

He found himself standing still, facing the ocean. As if it were a very old thought that never went away, he saw that he could walk into the water and drown. For the moment there was no fear in it, and no hope, but only the pleasure of not longing. And now he recalled the time earlier in the summer when he and his brother had gone in before breakfast when no one was on the beach. And they had played around in the water for a while, and then it came time to go back, and he could not. The undertow pushed him out as hard as he tried to swim against it. And then he had turned himself around in the water, already vomiting, and started to swim with the current. How easy it was, how fast! And soon he would have got to Europe. Then he was lying in his bed all bundled up, with the doctor there, and everybody saying he would have drowned except that the milkman happened to notice him.

He had never openly denied it to them. But, standing there now, he knew he had not nearly drowned at all. He would have made it to Europe, because he had a secret strength nobody knew he had.

And suddenly he remembered: "I don't need you any more!" His own words came back, shrill and red with fury. Why was that so terrible? He didn't need her. He could tie his laces now, he could walk forever without getting tired. . . . She didn't want him, why did he have to pretend he wanted her? The horror in it escaped him. Still, it probably was horrible anyway, only he didn't understand why. If only he could know what was horrible and what was only terrible! How fine it would be to sink into the ocean now, he thought. How she would plead with his dead, shut-eyed face to say something. Ben would be frantic too, and Papa . . . Papa would probably be waiting in the background not wanting to interfere with the doctor, waiting to be told what had happened. And then his lips would move a little, and they would all gasp. "He's going to speak!" she would cry. And he would open up his eyes and say, "I was by the ocean, walking. I saw a wave, and in the wave I saw the beard. It was a whole block long. All gray. And then I saw the face. It had blue eyes, like Grandpa, only much bigger. And it has a very, very deep voice, like whales hooting in the bottom of the ocean. It's God."

"It's God," his mother gasps, clapping her hands together the way she used to.

"How can it be God?" Ben asks, disgusted with his lies.

"Because He kissed me."

"Prove it!" Ben says, laughing warmly.

And he opens his mouth, and they look in, the way they all did when he had a toothache New Year's Eve and had to call up so many dentists. And in his mouth they see the whole ocean, and just beneath the surface they see the blue eyes and the floating beard, and then from his mouth comes a deep, gigantic roar, just like the ocean. In the corners of his eyes he saw a movement. A man was there, dressed in black.

He did not dare to turn fully, but even in that first instant he saw that the man had on black shined shoes, a white satin prayer shawl over his shoulders, and a black skullcap on top of his head.

Now he forced himself to face the man; a terror sucked his tongue an inch back into his throat, but quickly he was relieved—the man was really there, because there were other men standing behind him in a little crowd. They were as far away as he could throw a ball. The wind was whipping the white fringes of their prayer shawls. They were facing the sea, praying aloud from the black prayer books they held, and they were swaying backward and forward a little more urgently, he thought, than he had ever seen them do in the synagogue, and he saw his father and brother among them. Did they know he was standing here? Nobody even glanced at him; they kept addressing the air over the sea.

He had never seen so many men with shined black shoes on the beach. He had never seen prayer shawls in open sunlight. It was out of order to him, pulsing in a vague alarm. He feared for them, doing this, as though the roof had been lifted off the synagogue and God might really appear and not just the Scrolls of the Ark. They were facing Him, and He must be very near, and it was terrible. Seeing their inward stares, he wondered if they maybe did not realize they were out on the beach only a yard from the rough ocean. Maybe he should sneak quietly over to Papa and tell him, and then Papa would look up from his book, see where he was, and yell, "What did we do! How did we get out of shul!" And they would all turn around and run back, with prayer shawls flying, to the synagogue and then thank him for saving them from having looked into God's naked face.

Or maybe he wasn't even supposed to watch this, like the time last year in the synagogue when his grandfather had said, "You mustn't look now," and had made him cover his eyes. But for one second he had peeked through his fingers, and there up front on the raised platform he had seen a terrible sight. The cantor, or the rabbi, or somebody with a long beard, with three or four other old men, was covering his face with his silk prayer shawl. He had no shoes on, only white socks. All of them had white socks, and they started singing crazily and then they were *dancing*! And not a beautiful dance but an old man's dance, mainly up and down and rocking stiffly from foot to foot like a group of moving tents, and from under the shawls came squawking and crying and sudden shouts. Then they all faced the closet where the Scrolls of the

Ark were kept and got down on one knee, then on the other knee, and, like buildings bending over, they lay down right on their faces, all stretched out. Right up there on the altar, where usually the rabbi or the cantor or whoever he was always stood so stiff and didn't even look directly down at anybody. He was embarrassed at the thought of grave old men dancing.

Nobody in the little crowd was looking at him, not even Ben for a second, and not Papa either. "They know that I peeked that time at the cantor dancing," Martin thought, and they knew that he could not be saved any more; it did not matter whether he watched this now because he was not good. In fact, they might all have come here to mourn him, that he was such a bandit. If a good boy like one of his cousins with regular ears were here now, they would probably rush over and make him close his eyes and not watch. He turned his face from the men to concentrate on the roar of the sea, trying not even to hear them praying. But there was no reward, and still no reward, and suddenly the voice of the cantor, the man he had seen first, rose high and then higher in the wind, until it was like a girl's voice, and Martin had to look.

They all were praying louder now and crying out frighteningly toward the waves, the cantor and then the other men with him hitting themselves on the chest with their fists. The blows sounded like separate drums in the ground, making them grunt or cry out across the water again and again, and Martin saw some sparkling thing fly out of the cantor's hand and arch into a wave. A dead sardine? Or was it a speck of spray glistening? Now there was silence. No one moved. All their lips opened and closed, but there was only a deep humming that merged into the roaring of the waves.

Martin waited, and suddenly he felt fright at the thought that the cantor, as he had done in the synagogue last week, would draw out the curved ram's horn and blow on it. "Ahoooo-yah!" Martin's flesh moved at the memory of the raw, animal cry, which he prayed would not happen now, not now when God was so close that the noise would go right into His ear and drive Him up out of the ocean to burn them all in His blue-eyed gaze. Oh, what a clashing pillar of foam would break the surface of the sea, rivers of green water pouring down the great fall of beard!

Without warning, everybody started shaking hands. Now they were talking, so relieved and familiarly, and laughing, nodding, folding up their satin prayer shawls, closing their books, sounding like neighbors. Martin felt a singing in him that God had stayed where He belonged. Thank God He hadn't come out! He hurried over and squeezed through the crowd toward his father, forgetting all about whether he was supposed to have watched. He saw Ben first and called him excitedly as he tried to get through to him. Ben, seeing him, pulled his father's sleeve, and Papa turned and saw him, and both of them smiled down at him proudly, he felt. And before he could think he cried out, "Ben! I saw it! I saw him throw it in the water!" How fine it was to have seen a wonder, and not alone! "I saw it fly into the waves!" He felt as clear and fine as Ben, with nothing at all hidden inside him.

"What, in the water?" Ben asked, puzzled.

Terror snapped its nail lightly on Martin's eye. He blushed at the rebuff, but his desire would not be stopped. "The cantor—what he threw just before." He looked up quickly for corroboration at his father, who laughed down at him warmly and surprised, not understanding, but only loving him.

Ben shook his head to their father. "Boy," he said, "what he can make up!"

Papa laughed, but kind of crediting him, Martin thought, and he lived on the credit for a few moments as he walked with them across the beach toward the bungalow. At least he had made Papa laugh. But he *had* seen something arching into the sea—why wouldn't they admit it? A sallowness was creeping into him. He could feel his ears sticking out farther and farther, and he could not bear his loneliness, being thrown back into the arms of his secrets. "I *saw* it, Ben," he insisted, trying to stop Ben with his hand. "Pa? I saw him throw, I swear!" he yelled suddenly.

His father, alarmed, it seemed, looked down at him with his

kind incomprehension and his wish for happy behavior. "He just
throws out his hand, Marty. When he hits himself."

That was something anyway. "But what's in his hand, though?
He threw, I saw him."

"He throws his sins, dopey," Ben said.

"Sure," Papa said, "the sins get thrown in the ocean."

Martin sensed a shy humor in his father's tone. He wondered if
it was because this was not supposed to be talked about. And then
he wondered if it was that Papa did not absolutely believe they
were sins in the cantor's hand.

"And they shine, don't they, Pa?" he asked avidly. More than
anything, he wanted Papa to say yes, so that they could have seen
something together, and he would no longer be alone with what
he knew.

"Well—" Papa broke off. He sighed. He did not laugh but he
wasn't serious enough.

"Don't they shine?" Martin repeated anxiously.

Papa seemed about to answer but he didn't, and Martin could
not bear for it to end in silence. "I saw like"—his inner warnings
rattled but he could not stop—"like a sardine fly out and go in."

"A sardine!" His father burst out laughing.

"Oh, God!" Ben groaned, knocking himself on the head with
his fist.

"Well, it wasn't live! I mean dead!" Martin amended desperately.

"Dead yet!" Ben laughed. "You know what he said last week, Pa?"

"Shut up!" Martin yelled, knowing well what was coming.

"The milkman's horse—"

Martin grabbed his brother's sleeve and started to pull him
down to the sand, but Ben went on.

"—kills flies with his foot!"

With all his strength Martin beat his brother's back, pummel-
ing him with his fists.

"Hey, hey!" Papa called in his reedy voice that was just like Ben's.

"I saw him!" Martin tore at his brother's arms, kicked at his
legs, while their father tried to separate them.

"All right, you saw him, you saw him!" Ben yelled.

Papa pulled Martin gently clear of his brother. "All right, cut it out now. Be a man," he said and let him go. And Martin struck his father's arm as he was released, but his father said nothing.

They walked on across the beach. Martin tried to quell his throat, which kept squeezing upward to cry out. Before he knew he would speak he said with a sob, "There's a lot of flies on a horse."

"Okay," Ben said, disgusted with him but saying no more.

Martin walked on beside him, and his anger pumped in him. A woman in an apron was at the end of their street, looking off toward the dispersing crowd of men, probably for her husband. Seeing her there, Martin moved closer to his father so that maybe she would think he too had been fasting all day in the synagogue and praying on the beach with the others. She glanced at them as they approached the macadam and respectfully said, "*Gut Yontef.*"

"*Gut Yontef,*" Papa and Ben said together, weightily. Then Martin started to say it, but it was too late; it would sound naked, his voice all by itself, and maybe laughable since he had eaten so many times all day. They mounted the steps of their bungalow, and suddenly he was weak with uneasiness at not being one of them.

The door spring meowed, and his innocent father held the door open for Ben to go in and then pressed his great hand on Martin's back, warming it with pride. It was only when the door banged shut behind him that he remembered his mother's bared teeth and scandalized eyes.

"Ma?" Ben called.

There was no answer.

The stove was steaming, unattended. Martin's father went into the kitchen, calling her name in a questioning voice, and came back into the living room, and Martin saw the perplexity, the beginning of alarm in his face. Martin blushed, afraid of being aware of what his father did not know. And he envisioned that she had gone away forever, disappeared, so that they, the three men, could sit down quietly and eat in peace. And then Ben would go away and only he and Papa would be left, and how he would obey! How perfectly grave he would always be with his father, who would discuss with him seriously the way he did with Ben, making him get a shine the way Ben had to every Saturday, and conversing with him about holidays so he would always know way in advance, and not just suddenly the day before, that it was Rosh Hashonoh or Tishebuf or whatever it was, and sharing together the knowledge of what was or was not against the Law at all times.

The bathroom door opened and Mama came out. He saw at once that she had not forgotten. Her eyes were red, like after Uncle Karl had died from bending over to pick up a telephone book. Martin's neck prickled at the relentlessness of her present grief. It was no joke, he saw—Papa was really frightened and Ben's eyes were big.

"What happened?" they asked her, already astounded.

She looked from them down to Martin, powerless incomprehension, dried grief, glazing her eyes. "I shouldn't have lived to hear it," she said and turned back to Martin's father.

Even now Martin could not believe she was going to tell on him to Papa. Again he could not remember exactly what there was to tell, but for her to reveal anything that passed between them was obscurely horrifying and would leave him all alone to face his father's and Ben's awakening eyes and a crashing and screaming that would crush him out of sight.

"You know what he said to me?"

"What?"

"'I don't need you any more.' That's what he says to me!"

It seemed that no one could breathe. Ben's face looked so hurt and astonished he seemed about to faint. And Martin waited for her to go on, to set forth some final fact about him that would fall like a stone or a small animal from her mouth; and, looking at it, they would all know, and he would know, what he was.

But she was not going on. That was all! Martin had no clear idea what more she might say, but the final, sea-roaring evil was not brought into the room, and his heart lifted. She was talking again, but only about how he had hit her. And although Papa was standing there shaking his head, Martin saw that he was abstracted already.

"You shouldn't say a thing like that, Marty," he said and went into the bedroom, taking off his jacket. "Let's eat," he said from in there.

He wanted to run and kiss his father, but something kept him: a certain disappointment, a yearning for and a fear of a final showdown.

And suddenly his mother yelled, "Didn't you hear what I told you? He's driving me crazy every day!"

Papa's footsteps approached from the bedroom. Now, now maybe it would come, his thunderstruck roar of down-looking disgust. He appeared in the doorway in his shirt sleeves, enormous, immovable. "I'll take my strap to you, young fella," he said and touched his belt buckle.

Martin thrilled and got set to run around the table. Papa sometimes took his belt off—and Martin would have to dodge out of his way, keeping the dining-room table between them for a minute or two. But Papa never actually hit him, and one time his pants had started to fall down and everybody had laughed, including Mama and Papa himself.

But now he was unbuckling his belt, and a surge of pity for his father brought tears to Martin's eyes. He pitied his father for having so unworthy a son, and he knew why he was going to be beaten and felt it was right, for it was disgusting that a boy should know what he knew. He backed away from his father, not because he feared being hurt but to save him the pain of having to be cruel.

"I didn't mean it, Mama!" he pleaded. Maybe she would let Papa go, he hoped.

"You'll kill me!" she cried.

But instantly Martin knew it was his release. Papa's having unbuckled his belt was enough for her, and she went into the kitchen with her hand on her belly to stop a pot cover from rattling.

"Be a man," Papa said, buckling his belt again, and he went to the sideboard and filled a tiny glass with whisky and carried it over to the rocker by the window and, with a sigh, sat down.

The tablecloth and silverware sparkled. Martin noticed suddenly that Ben had gone out of the room, and he wondered if he had gone outside to cry. This wasn't finished yet, he knew.

Papa raised his glass toward the kitchen and said, "Well? A New Year!"

Mama called out from the stove, "*Mit glick!*" And she closed her eyes for an instant. Martin never made any noise at these times because they were addressing some unseen ear.

Papa swallowed the glassful in one gulp and exhaled. "I tell you," he said toward the kitchen doorway, "that cantor is a horse." Martin saw the cantor with his long beard harnessed to the milkman's wagon. "Never sat down all day. The man didn't stop for five minutes."

"Because he's not one of those fakers. He's a religious man."

"Well, say," Papa grudgingly agreed, "he's got all year to rest up."

"Oh, stop that."

"If I had two days' work a year I'd stand up too." Martin saw the warm humor in his father's eyes, his peaceful blinking.

"What are you talking about?" Mama said. "They could drop dead that way, singing all day with nothing in their bodies, not even a glass of water."

"He won't drop dead," Papa said. He always knew the evenness of things, Martin felt, the real way it always was going to turn out, and he prayed to be good. "His boss takes good care of him."

"Don't be so smart," Mama said, and she raised her eyebrows and closed her eyes for a second to ask God to pay no attention to what He had just heard.

"I wouldn't mind that either—a two-day year."

"That's enough already," Mama said with a little unwilling smile. She brought in Papa's big, gold-bordered soup plate filled with yellow chicken soup in which matzoh balls floated. "Eat," she said and returned to the kitchen.

Papa got up and hoisted up his pants, letting out his long brown belt two holes. Quickly Martin went to his place, climbed onto his chair, and put his skullcap on. Papa sat down at the head of the table and put his cap on. Mama brought Ben's soup and went back into the kitchen.

"Who's his boss?" Martin asked.

"Who?"

"The cantor's."

Papa shrugged. "God. Who knows?" Then, dipping his spoon into his soup, he stirred it and mumbled a prayer.

"Does he see God?" Martin asked. The hope was flying through his heart that the cantor and possibly Papa too had seen the beard in the ocean, and then he would be able to tell how he also had seen it floating there, and with this secret wiped out it would somehow take all secrets with it.

"Where's Ben?" Papa asked. The spoon was not quite to his lips.

Mama instantly came out of the kitchen. "Why? Where's Ben?" She looked at Martin with alarm, and his mouth hung open and he blushed.

"I don't know. I didn't do anything to him," he said.

"Ben?" Mama called, hurrying to the bedroom and looking in. "Ben?"

Papa watched her, his spoon still raised and dripping. "Take it easy, for God's sake," he said, irritated. But he was awakening to trouble too, and Martin felt alarmed that he maybe had done something to Ben which he had forgotten.

"What do you mean?" she said indignantly. "He's not in here!" And she hurried to the bathroom and found the door locked. "Ben? Ben!" she commanded an answer in fright, and with a shock Martin saw what a loss Ben would be.

The turning of the lock was heard, and the door opened. Ben came out, his hair wet and freshly combed, his blue tie still in place even though Papa had taken his off. Martin saw the hurt in his brother's face and that he was still not looking at him and that he had been crying for Mama's sake as a good son should.

"There!" Papa said. "*Now* what've you got to cry about?" And he gulped his soup, spoonful after spoonful.

"I thought something happened," she queried Ben.

"I was just in the bathroom," Ben said, his voice husky.

"Why didn't you report to her that you were going to the bathroom?" Papa said.

"All right, all right," Mama warned.

Ben tried to smile and sat down in his place.

"If you don't report," Papa went on, "you might've got killed—"

"Stop it," Mama said, grinning and angry.

"You could've got run over. After all, there's a lot of traffic in this house."

"Will you stop it?" she asked him, losing her grin.

"Place is full of trucks," Papa continued, as he ate his soup. "Person should ask her permission before they go to the bathroom." Then he looked up at her and shook his head, ready to laugh. "I'm telling you, young lady—" He broke off with a weary laugh and went back to his soup.

Ben adjusted his satin cap on his head and stared meaningfully at the silver centerpiece, which was full of fruit, and Papa stopped eating. Now there was quiet. "*Boruch ahto adonai . . .*" Ben monotoned, and without faltering or moving at all he went into the blessing. Mama stood there listening in the doorway, caught by his gravity, her hands clasped together, her face raised toward the air overhead, where Martin knew her secret wishes floated, aroused to life by Ben's power of prayer and his immaculate memory, which never left out a single holy word. Martin pressed one ear against his head, pretending he had a slight itch, while Ben continued unswervingly to the prayer's end. Only then did Papa resume eating and Ben, without rushing to break his terrible fast, selected his spoon, stirred his soup so long that it seemed he was even reluctant to eat at all, and finally he ate in grief. Mama took his grave permission to move and went silently into the kitchen and in a moment came out with her plate and sat down opposite Papa.

Martin's hand was still sticky from the salt water with which he had cleaned off his shoe, but he knew it was invisible, and he drank his soup, his chin just clearing the rim of his bowl. It was quiet in the room. He drew the soup through his lips with the same soft sound his father made, sniffing the way Papa did after each swallow. Now he calculated his matzoh ball. The edge of the spoon had to cut it exactly down the middle or it would slip out from under, spring out of the bowl, and his hand would come down sharply and spill the soup. He set the edge of his spoon on top of the matzoh ball, knowing his mother was watching him from the end of the table. With his left hand gripping the bowl he started to press down. The matzoh ball began to slide under the pressure.

"Martin," his mother began, "let me—"

Surprised at his own sharpness, he shot back, "I can do it!" Ben seemed stabbed but said nothing. Papa glanced up but went on eating.

He lifted his spoon and set its edge on the hard-packed ball again, slightly to one side of the previous mark. He knew that now Papa and Ben were also watching, even though they were not looking up. His face was getting rigid and red, his raised elbow trembling with his effort as he started to press down to cut the ball. Again it began to slide, but he knew that sometimes a sudden, swift, downward push could slice through before it flew out of the bowl, although sometimes this only sent it spinning out onto the table or into his lap. He hesitated, struggling with his dignity, which might collapse if he should start still a third cut, and he was about to raise the spoon to try again when he saw his mother's hand reaching toward his own to take the spoon away.

With all his might and anger he pushed the spoon down, drawing together his powers of mystic command to make the matzoh ball stand still and obey as it did for Papa and Ben, and at the same instant Mama's hand grabbed his. The ball shot out of the bowl and his hand banged down on the bowl's edge. The soup first warmed, then suddenly burned into his thighs through his good tweed pants, the smoky smell of wet wool alarming his nostrils. Out of the screaming he heard Ben's yell—the ball had toppled one of the candles into Ben's wine and he had knocked over the glass trying to save it. The tablecloth was bleeding through a red wound spreading down its middle. Martin was jumping up and down, hitting his hands against his burning thighs and trying at the same time to keep his mother's hands away from him, for she was trying to loosen his belt in order to get his pants off.

"You made me do it!" he screamed at her.

"He's burning! Get your pants off!" she yelled.

Ben was now in front of him, pulling at his pants to lower them.

This further indignity infuriated him. "Don't do that!" he screamed, but he could feel his pants being drawn down past his hips and he kicked out. Mama gasped, and Ben fell back to a sitting position on the floor. It was quiet. From somewhere up high he could hear Papa's reedy, questioning voice.

Mama was straightening up, her hand cupping one of her breasts, her alarmed eyes looking into the future over Martin's head. He heard the ocean booming as if it were underneath the floor and felt the house trembling as the waves struck. Papa, murmuring questions, followed Mama into their bedroom. Her breath was coming in short gasps. The door closed.

Ben stood facing the closed bedroom door. Fright and concern were rigid in his eyes.

"Why is she that way?" Martin asked softly.

"You kicked her!" Ben shouted in a whisper, glancing at Martin with contempt, then turned back to the door to listen.

Martin had no memory of kicking her. He knew he had kicked, but he had not hit anything, he thought. But it was impossible to explain, and shame gathered in him, and he saw a blackened sky.

"Pa?" Ben called softly through the door. There was no answer, and Ben's breathing quickened, close to sobbing, as he listened. Now Ben turned down to his brother, disbelief and disgust in his face. "How could you ever *say* that to her?"

"What?"

"What you said. You don't need her any more. To your own mother!"

Martin sobbed aloud but softly, standing there.

"You have to go to her and apologize. You have to beg her pardon," Ben said, as though Martin did not know anything at all about behaving. "Did you even apologize?"

Martin shook his head, sobbing.

"You didn't even apologize?"

Martin wept, covering his face with his hands. He wept because he had hurt his mother and did not understand anything and was alone outside the circle of a fine family. His pants were getting cold now.

"Pa?" Ben called again, more insistently now. Then he carefully turned the knob and peeked inside. "Pa?" he asked. Papa's deeper voice spoke from within, and Ben entered the room, closing the door behind him. Martin listened for any sound of the window being opened and all of them climbing out to leave him forever. But they were still talking in there.

He waited. His soup bowl lay overturned on the floor; the wreckage of the table seemed to make a screeching, disorderly noise at him; one candle still burned its holy light while the wick of the other lay in Ben's overturned glass, and all the chairs stood facing in odd directions. He took a step toward his bowl to pick it up, but his thigh touching his cold wet pants stopped him, and he busied himself trying to re-form the vanished crease. Again he tried to walk, but the coldness of the tweed clinging to his skin disgusted him and brought tears to his eyes. It was like waking up between wet sheets, and it brought the same resentment and mystification into his heart. Vaguely he felt it was his mother's fault, and he felt stronger, having blamed her, and walked stiff-legged into his and Ben's room.

Using his fingertips, he unbuttoned his pants and let them down, then sat on the floor to slip them over his shoes. They smelled like a wet dog. He stood up, trying to decide what to do with them, and he started to cry. He went about the room crying softly, the pants hanging heavily from his fingertips. He draped them over the back of the only chair in the room and stepped away, but their weight pulled them down to the floor. Then he started to lay them on his bed but feared they would wet the blanket; he had not wet his bed in a long time, maybe two weeks ago or a month or three months, and he did not want to give them any new ideas now. He crossed the room to the closet, but the hangers were impossibly high; and, besides, he vaguely recalled a time when he had been scolded for having put his wet bathing suit in the closet. Standing there sobbing softly, he looked around the room for a place to leave his pants, and a hand seemed to reach in and squeeze his stomach. "Ma!" he called softly, careful not to let his call penetrate the wall to her room. But he was really crying now, and in raising his hands to wipe his eyes he dropped the pants on the floor; he looked at them there and, giving himself up to his fate, walked out into the living room.

The bedroom door was still shut. He walked over to it, still sobbing, and said, "Ma?" and tried to stifle his sobs in order to hear. But it was silent in there now. They had left him! "Mama!" he called louder and stamped his foot. Maybe they had wet his pants so he would go into his bedroom, giving them time to get away. For the first time in his life he did not dare turn the door-knob without first hearing permission; he dared not open it and find an empty room. He banged on the door, calling his mother, his shouts blinding him. A sudden rage flung itself up into his head, the way the ocean sometimes spews a wave deep onto the beach. "I didn't kick that baby!" he yelled, the skin on his temples crawling, "I didn't see it!"

As though in reply a chair scraped angrily inside the room and the door opened, and Martin was already half across the living room in flight. Papa appeared in the doorway. His fair face was darker than Martin had ever seen it. He was frowning, with no trace of a smile even in his eyes. It was no joke. He looked down at Martin. He was going to say, "Nobody's ears stick out in this family but yours! Nobody in this family stands around trying to see the beard in the ocean! Nobody peeks through his fingers at the cantor dancing in his white socks! Nobody goes around with his shoelaces opening all the time and throwing matzoh balls all over the clean tablecloth and wetting his pants from McCreery's and making up about dentists! And nobody knows anything about babies! *Nothing is happening at any time in this house, Martin!*"

And then Martin would disappear. He saw, with great relief, how he would vanish, like that time when he had accidentally turned the electric fan on the egg-white his mother had whipped, and it flew off the dish into the air and was not there any more. He would always be around watching, but they would not see him, and he could sit with his mother or Papa or lie down between them in bed on Sunday mornings the way he used to, and they wouldn't know.

"Sit down," his father said, partly to him and partly to Ben, who was coming out of the bedroom, red-eyed.

Martin went and picked his bowl off the floor, carefully avoiding the puddle, and set it neatly at his place and climbed up onto his chair. Everything was far away. Ben sat at his place, righted his wineglass, and put back the fallen candle in its silver holder, handling it as though it stood for his mourning. But Papa, instead of sitting, went into the kitchen. Martin could hear dishes being moved in there. Ben stared down at the red gash in the tablecloth. Mama's empty chair twisted Martin's heart, and he began to sob softly again, trying not to attract either sympathy or blame or any notice at all. Papa came out of the kitchen and gave them each a plate of chicken piled on top of the peas and carrots. Martin never ate white meat but he did not complain. In a moment Papa came out again with his own plate and sat down.

Martin ate through his sobs, but the chicken was being wetted by his tears, the water from his cold nose, and the saliva flowing loosely inside his mouth. Papa reached into his back pocket, drew out his great handkerchief, and reached over and held it under Martin's nose. It was warm. He blew. "Again," Papa said. Martin's pleasure started his sobs pulsating again, but he adamantly controlled himself and blew for Papa's sake.

"Should I cut your chicken?" Papa asked.

Martin hesitated; Papa's newly respectful tone freshened his memory of the pain he had caused him, his treason, and he did not want to go even further now and turn down his kindness. But he could not bear the injustice of having his chicken cut when Ben was cutting his so easily. "I can do it, Papa," he whispered apologetically.

"Okay. Be a man."

Papa ate rapidly for a few minutes, thinking. Ben kept his eyes on his plate. Now the table looked even worse than before, like a desecration of a holiday. There was no sound from the bedroom. At last Papa put down his knife and fork, drank some wine, and tilted his body to one side with his hand gripping his chair arm. He was going to talk. He looked at Martin with a clear look, a shyness and an unspoken pride in him. "So you're going to go to school soon, eh?"

"I think next week," Martin said, glancing toward Ben for correction. But Ben was not looking up and would not give way to Papa's lightness.

"You going to go with the gentleman together?" he asked Ben.

"I'll take him in the beginning," Ben said after a moment.

Papa nodded. Martin had not known Ben was to take him to school in the mornings. Again he realized that Ben and Mama must be having secret talks when he was not around—when he slept, maybe. In that thought he felt the warmth of being cared for, but uneasy again at finding things out only after they had happened.

"So now you'll have to wash your face in the morning and get your shoes shined. You going to have to tend to your business now."

"Yes, Pa," Martin said, elated, hoping Papa would continue on with further commands. But there were none. "I think I have to have my own fountain pen," he suggested, knowing how carefully a fountain pen had to be taken care of. Oh, how he would care for his pen!

"You don't need a fountain pen in the first grade," Ben said.

"Well, I mean in the second grade." Martin blushed.

"As long as you don't need a secretary," Papa said. Then he added, "Third grade you can have a secretary." He laughed, but Ben would not be fooled, and Martin laughed with his father, feeling how fine it would be to keep him just like this. But Ben was immovable, and his mind searched rapidly for a marvel to distract his brother's judgment. "You know what?" he said, avidly now, his brown eyes darting back and forth between them. He had no idea what he was going to say yet, but he was adamant—he was going to keep Papa amused even if Ben refused to forget his sins.

"What?" Papa asked.

"They're going to have Indian's summer!"

"You don't say! Who?"

He saw that Ben was starting to turn pink trying not to laugh, and he felt a strange power over his brother that he could force him out of his condemning sulk, a power that was evil because it could bedazzle Ben's righteous condemnation. He kept his eyes on his father, feeling close to him now because Papa was listening, yet somehow traitorous as he sensed he was about to astound him. "I think in the hotel," he said.

"Oh," Papa said, throwing his head up overmuch, "in the hotel they going to have Indian summer?"

Martin nodded eagerly. Now there was nothing but the pleasure of his vision. "The milkman told me."

Ben went "Ts" and turned his head away.

"He did!" Martin shouted angrily, yet happy that Ben was coming out to oppose him openly and not mourning remotely any more.

"Every time he can't think what to say he blames it on the milkman," Ben said scoffingly, but his eyes were amused and interested to hear more.

Martin reddened. "He told me! They didn't have it last year, but they're going to have it this year. So they have to have more milk."

"To feed the Indians," Papa said.

"He told me," Martin said.

"Well, sure." Papa turned to Ben. "They're probably expecting a lot of Indians."

"From the country," Martin added, clearly seeing a file of feathered Indians emerging from the woods near the railroad station.

"In other words," Papa said, "country Indians."

With a spray of spittle flying from his burst-open mouth, Ben laughed helplessly.

"Well, they are!" Martin yelled indignantly, but strangely happy that he was making them laugh at his lies and not at something worse.

"Hey, hey!" Papa frowned at Ben, but with laughter in his eyes. "Cut it out, don't laugh."

"Country Ind—" Ben choked hysterically.

Martin giggled, infected. "It's when everybody goes back to the city," he explained, desperately meticulous. "That's how come nobody sees them."

Ben's arms suddenly flew up as he slipped off his chair onto the floor, and his fall made Martin burst out in clear, victorious laughter.

He jumped down, thrilling with love for his brother's laughter, and he ran around the table and flung himself on Ben, tickling him under the arms with all the strength in his fingers. Ben fell back on the floor helplessly, pleading for Martin to stop, but his suffocating gasps were like soft wet sand to dig into, and Martin kneaded his brother's flesh, straddling him now, darting from his ribs to his belly to his neck until Ben was not laughing any more. But Martin kept on, feeling a delightful fury and a victorious power. Ben's neck was stretched and his face contorted, tears on his cheeks, unable to take a breath. Martin struggled against being lifted into the air and heard his father calling, "Ben? Ben?" And then, "Ben!" And Ben at last drew a breath and lay there gasping, laughing with tears in his eyes, and he wasn't dead.

Papa put Martin down. "Okay, Indian, that's enough. Go and say good night to your mother and go to sleep. We've got to start the packing tomorrow early. Ben, you too."

Ben, still breathing heavily, got to his feet, his expression sobering as he brushed off the seat of his pants and inspected his shoes. Martin happily began to brush his pants too, his brother's equal, but discovered he was in his underwear, and his mind darkened with the memory of his wet pants still lying in the middle of his and Ben's bedroom. Papa had already gone into the other bedroom where Mama lay.

"You have to apologize to her," Ben whispered.

"Why?" Martin asked in all innocence. Anger stirred in him again as he felt himself slipping back.

"For what you did, you nut," Ben whispered. "Before." Then he went into their parents' bedroom. He always knew exactly what had to be apologized for.

Martin followed, moving toward his parents' bedroom as slowly as he could without actually coming to a halt. First he moved one foot an inch or two and then the other. He searched in his mind for a clue to sadness; he was inwardly still happy. He thought of his Uncle Karl dying and it sobered his face, but he could not precisely recall what he was to apologize about, and his forgetting left voids that frightened him. He knew it was not

about his pants lying in the middle of his room, because nobody
had seen them yet, and the memory of his mother standing up
holding her breast had splintered in his mind; he could see her
doing that and gasping, but he could not quite recall what had
caused her pain. The fear he felt as he approached the open doorway of her bedroom was that he had done something he did not
even know about. Things were always being remembered that he
had forgotten. Only Ben never forgot; Ben remembered everything.

He entered the bedroom, feeling his ears growing foolishly bigger and heavier; his mother was looking at him from her pillow,
and Papa and Ben, standing on either side of the bed, turned to
look at him as though they had all been discussing him for an
hour and knew what he was supposed to do.

At the foot of the bed he stopped, trying not to let his eyes be
caught by the hill over her stomach. In the silence the ocean's hiss
and boom came into the room, surprising him with its sudden
presence. He could smell the water in here and see the bearded
thing floating just beneath the heaving water like seaweed.

She smiled at him now, tiredly; his lips parted tentatively in
reply. His father, he saw, was crooking his arms to stand with his
hands bracing his back, elbows out. Martin's hands slipped down
off his hips when he tried it, so he lowered his hands and rested
one on the soft yellow blanket.

"So?" she asked, without turning from him, but smiling. "He
ate—my bandit?"

"Sure he ate," Papa said, "he's a big man. Leave him alone,
he eats."

Hearing her call him her bandit—which she never called Ben—
he lowered his eyes with pleasure, distinguished by his crimes. He
knew exactly where he was now, and he loved all of them.

"You ate your peas too?"

"Uh-huh."

"And the carrots?"

"Yeah." In this expectancy he saw his recognition, his unique-
ness expanding before his mother, and Papa too, and even Ben
seemed magnanimously vanquished and kind of showing him to

her. But he kept his eyes on the blanket, not knowing why he was beginning to feel embarrassed.

"So now you're going to be good, heh?" she said.

"Uh-huh." He glanced at her face; she was serious and still hurt. Then he looked down at the blanket and plucked at it, growing wary about the next five minutes, for he knew once again that something was still unfinished.

"You bother him too much," Papa said. "He's practically a professor and you still—"

"He's going to cut his own matzoh balls? You crazy?"

"A man is got a right to cut his own matzoh balls."

"Oh, shut up."

"Specially a professor with his own fountain pen."

"What do you know about it?" she said. Martin glanced at her and saw that she was angry but smiling. Fear moved into him. "I slave like a dog all day and you come home and he should do whatever he wants!" Papa looked up high to make little of it, but she was going toward an underlying darkness, and dread flew into Martin's chest, so he grinned. "I don't bother him," she denied. "I'm just trying to help him. A boy five years old can't—"

"A boy five years old! I was six I was out selling newspapers."

"Sure," she said, "that's why you got such a good education!" She turned to Ben, as she always did at this point in the story. "Not even to let a boy go to school so he could maybe read a book in his life."

Papa sat there slightly blushing for his upbringing, his family, and Martin kept grinning and plucking in agony at the blanket. Through the corners of his eyes he saw the three books on her bed table, and his heart got cold; were these the books the weeping dentist had given her? "Oh, the books he used to bring me!" Her voice in the lobby sang over his head with all its longing, and the memory reddened his face. Oh, Papa must never know! "When I grow up—" he said.

They turned to him, smiling at his sudden statement. "What, when you grow up?" his mother asked, still flushed with her feelings.

He lowered his eyes to the blanket; he had not meant to say

anything aloud, and his face burned with shame. "What, dar-ling?" his mother persisted. He did not know if he wanted to say that he would teach Papa so he could read books in a chair the way she did, or whether he would grow up and bring her books himself, so she would not remember the dentist, and then they wouldn't argue any more, she and Papa. He only knew for certain that he wanted her never to make Papa ashamed.

She kept asking what would happen when he grew up, and he knew he had to say something quick. "Papa gave us chicken," he said. They all laughed in surprise, and he felt relieved, and he laughed although he did not know what was funny about it. "Right on top of the peas and carrots!" he added.

"Some waiter!" Mama laughed. They all laughed louder, but Papa was blushing, and Martin wanted to run to him and apologize.

She was proud of Martin now, and he knew she ought not to be. "Come here, give me a kiss," she said, holding out her arms. He lingered in place, crunching his toes inside his shoes. "Come!" she smiled.

Fearing to affront her again, he moved an inch toward her out-stretched arms and writhed to a halt, pulling at the blanket with his fingertips. "Ben's taking me to school," he said, keeping out of her reach.

"He can't wait to go to school, you see?" she boasted directly to Papa, and in the instant Martin glowed under her pride in his tak-ing after her. But when he saw how pleased and innocently Papa nodded, his mind quickly darkened; he only knew she must not so blatantly make him her own in front of Papa, and in the air between his mother and himself he felt an evil compact growing, a collusive understanding, which he lusted for and could not bear.

"I can spell 'beach'!" he said suddenly and immediately felt afraid.

"Oh, you! You'll spell everything!" She waved the words at him with her hand. "Go—spell, 'beach.'"

"'Beach,'" he said, in the approved way of saying the word before starting to spell it. He saw Ben grinning; was it because he was proud of him or doubtful he could really spell the word? Martin's memory sharpened around each letter. "'B' . . ."

"Right!" she said, nodding with satisfaction.

"'e' . . ."

"Very good!" she said, glancing with pride at Papa.

"'a' . . ." he said less strongly.

She seemed to sense a wavering in him and kept silent. He was looking at his father now, his warm, magnanimous smile, his wholly selfless gaze—and he knew in that instant that Papa did not know how to spell "beach." He and Ben and Mama knew how, but Papa was sitting out there all alone with his patient ignorance.

"'B-e-a' what?" his mother prompted. He could feel the embracing power of her demand like a wind on his back, and he dug in his heels against it. But Papa saw nothing, only the wonder that was about to come out of his son's mouth, and the sense of his own treason burned in him.

"What, darling? 'B-e-a' . . ."

"'B-e-a' . . ." Martin began again, slowly, to make more time. He lowered his eyes as though searching for the final letters, but the realization stuck to him that he was teaching his father. How dare he teach Papa! She must shut up or something terrible would come down upon them. Because . . . he did not know why, but he did not want to be standing there in front of Papa, teaching him what he had learned from her or . . . His mind drowned in the consequences as in the trough of an incoming wave. "I can spell 'telephone,'" he said. They all laughed. Somehow "beach" was forbidden now. He remembered suddenly that he had once spelled "telephone" off the cover of the phone book to Papa. He wanted deeply to spell "telephone" for him again and to wipe out the memory of "beach."

"First spell 'beach,'" she lightly complained. "You can spell it."

Ben spoke. "It's the same as 'teach.'"

"I know!" Martin shot out at his brother. His heart quickened at the fear that Ben was about to spell "beach" himself.

"Or 'reach,'" Ben said.

"Shut up!" Martin yelled, and both his father and mother were starting to laugh.

"I can spell it!" he shouted at his father and mother.

"Well, go, spell it," his mother said.

He got himself set, but now it was he who was alone, pleading with them, all three of them, to be allowed to show what he could spell. And he could not bear the indignity, the danger, that lay in having to produce something in exchange for their giving him a place among them. The golden aura was gone from his head; he was merely standing there stripped of his position, and he started to sob, and he did not know why, except that he hated them all, as though he had been somehow betrayed and mocked.

"What's the matter, darling?" she asked and reached toward him. He struck at her falseness, and she withdrew her hand.

"Come on, let's go to sleep," his father said, coming over to him. He pushed his father's belly away but not with his full force. "I don't want to go to sleep!" Something, some battle, remained unfought, and he lusted for it now as for peace.

The feel of his father's belt buckle remained impressed on his hand. He looked up at Papa's perplexed, fading grin. Now, now he would take his belt off and whip him! Through the red webbing of his anger Martin saw the promise of an end, of peace. Swiftly he saw that now he would be really whipped, and then the thoughts of the dentist would be driven out of his mind and he would never again hear the sound of his mother's high and excited laughter that day. Oh, yes—it would all be cracked away by the snap of that leather and Papa in fury roaring out, "I . . . I . . . I . . . I!" Now, now he would do it! And then Papa would turn and knock Mama against the wall, and she would never dare to make him teach Papa anything again.

But Papa was bending over him, patting his back, saying, "It's late, professor, come on," and Martin felt his father's great hand folding around the back of his neck and allowed himself to be walked to the doorway of the room. And as he was going out into the living room he heard his brother's voice, weighted down by the responsibility for teaching him. "It's 'b-e-a-c-h,' Marty."

The injustice fell on his head like a shower of nails. He heard the crash first, then saw the tablecloth cascading down over his feet, the dishes rushing toward him and smashing on the floor, fruit rolling across the room, the falling arc of the lighted candle, a smack of a palm across his forehead, another on his behind, and he was running, running into Ben first and dodging out of his grasp, then into Mama's thigh, and then he was high in the air, his legs kicking beneath him, his face toward the ceiling where the marks of three flies his father had once squashed still showed. Everything was red, as though he were looking through his own blood, and he could feel the thuds of his toes inside his shoes as he kicked against his father's body. "Hey!" He was let down, dropped to his feet, and he glimpsed his father's hand going to his belly as though it hurt, and the pain he had caused his father caught at his throat but he was strangely free, full of himself— bad, agile, swiftly glancing at them at bay, knowing he could never be caught and held if he did not want himself to be. For an instant no one moved, and he could only hear himself gasping.

He ran into his room, picked up his crumpled pants, rushed back into the living room and flung them down on the floor before his family. The next thing, he knew, would be that he would run out the door and down the street and never come back. No—he corrected—he would run across the beach and go swimming! Into the bearded ocean where he belonged—he was not afraid like they were! His mother moved one foot to approach him and he stiffened, gasping for his breath. The words pitched upward from his stomach—*I don't need you any more!* His mouth was open and he was yelling, but nothing came out because his tongue was crouching flat in the back of his throat.

"Martin!"

He yelled again. "Aaahhg!" came out. The root of his tongue felt cold now. He felt frightened. They were all coming closer to him, carefully. He swallowed, but his tongue would not come up to where it belonged. He felt himself being carried, and his pillow came up under his head.

His bedroom was dark, and their faces were cut in half by the moonlight coming through the window. For a long time he did not see them, but he could hear their talking and worried mur- murings. He could not move his mind out of his mouth, where it groped and felt for his tongue. He felt a hand on his arm and turned to his bedside, expecting his mother to be there, but it was his father who was seated in the chair. He looked toward where Mama's voice was coming from, and she was down at the foot of his bed with Ben. It was strange; Papa always stood at the foot of the bed when he was sick, and Mama sat at his side. Turning back to his father, he felt helpless and grateful, striving to understand their novel positions.

"Say something, Martin," his mother said fearfully from her distance.

He kept his eyes on the half-dark face of his father, waiting. But his father, alarmed as he looked, did not speak; he was there merely holding on to Martin's arm, communicating some new, unfathomable thought. And Martin in his silence pleaded with his father to speak, but his father did not.

"What's the matter, darling? It's all right. Nothing happened. Say something. Say 'boy.' Can you say 'boy'?"

The root of his tongue was turning icy. With his mind groping inside his mouth he could hear her voice only distantly, and her far-away quality made it easier for him not to answer her. Unable to answer back, he felt strangely relieved of all thought and strategy. A remoteness from all of them, and from his own feelings, set him afloat, and unawares he grasped the powers of invisibility—he had no doubt he was on his bed, but nobody could get mad at him when he could not reply to their demands, and his enforced silence gave him a new, smoothed-out view that was cleared of the necessity to be thinking at every instant what he should or should not say next. All of a sudden in his life nothing seemed to be happening, and everything was about to happen. Beauty seemed to be forming around him, all of them gently rising and falling together in an imminence, an about-to-be that was like an unsung but audible singing. The distance his mother fearfully kept struck him as vaguely respectful, and his father's hand on his arm held some kind of new promise he could not understand. His mother continued asking him to speak, and he heard Ben's voice too, and under their words a pleasantly steady astonishment at him that carried no blame. Had he broken his tongue? he wondered. Oddly it did not terrify him but only held him in suspense, and there was no pain.

He felt time passing and passing, and there was still no anger in them, only a worried curiosity, which he felt was gradually bringing him a little closer to them—until there was something quite new for him in this half darkness, a new sense forming in him of his own truthfulness. The fact was spreading through his mind that this was a wonder they had all discovered at the same moment as he had. It was not something he had half made up and half believed, it was a real happening that had overcome him and yet was astounding to them too. They were all sharing the single belief together, and this sudden unity, fusing them without warning, burned away his sense of having secrets. He felt supported in space, with them suspended around him, and in this moment there was no Mama or Papa or Ben but three congealments of warmth embracing him with no thoughts of their own. And it seemed to him now that this was all he had been trying to find, this was actual and perfect, while everything else, the whole past of arguments and fights and smiles and shouts, was a dream.

She was telling him to try to close his lips now and say "b." But a secret winter seemed to have frozen his upper lip, and he could not bring it down. Something strange moved in the moonlight, and he peered to see his father biting on his lower lip. He had never seen him distort his face like that. He watched. Papa, half green in the moonlight, was looking down at him, biting hard on his lip, and his one illuminated eye was oddly widened with fury. The rising and falling steadied and then stopped. Warmth began to flow into Martin's tongue, and his own lip was getting less stiff. He felt fear flowing into his chest. Papa's hand was now gripping his arm, through which he could sense a living power in his father's great body. A thunder seemed to be gathering, expanding his father, infuriating him, like a whole sky suddenly drawing a storm into itself. A popping sound burst from Martin's lips, and his neck prickled with a sudden sweat. He saw himself swept away now, flung outward into the night like a lump of cloth. "Papa!" he cried, backing into his pillow.

"He's all right!" his mother's voice screamed, startling him. He could hear her hurrying toward him alongside the bed, saw her arms reaching toward him, and fright broke his silence. "Mama!" he sobbed, and she fell on him, kissing him frantically, calling into his face, "Yes, yes, speak, my baby, speak! He's all right!" Her thankfulness, so unexpectedly pure, swept him out of the reach of the punishment he had expected a moment before; her oneness with him blotted out his last thought, and he seemed to swim with her effortlessly through light. She was weeping now and stood erect, looking down at him, her hands clasped prayerfully together.

And once again now Martin saw his father, and he saw that he was not happy, not thankful, but just as he had been a moment before. And he heard his father's voice before he heard his words, like thunder rumbling before it speaks with a crash. "Gaaaaooodammit!"

Mama swerved to look at him.

"When are you going to stop bothering him!" he bellowed into her face.

"I—?" she started to defend herself.

"You bother him and bother him till you drive him crazy!" The rumbling was sharpening now, forming the burning white crash, and Martin stiffened against its burst, his brain thrilling to the howl of winds that seemed to be hurling across the darkened air. "So he spills a little soup! Goddammit, how's he gonna learn if he don't spill something!"

"I only—" she started weakly.

"You 'only'!" Oh, he wouldn't let her even explain! He saw, astonished, that Papa's anger was not at all against him! And how frightened she was, standing there, facing him with her hands still clasped in prayer. His father's thunder hit the earth now, and he could not hear the words, but his mother's fright gave him their message—her fright and Ben's lowered eyes. Both of them were getting it now, both of them being pressed farther and farther from Papa's love.

"You can't treat a boy that way," he was saying more quietly now, more sternly. "If he can't eat, don't give him a spoon; if he can eat, stop bothering him." She did not dare answer now. Papa moved about, towering over her. "I'm no professor, but that's no way," he said. "No way. You're killing yourself and everybody else."

"I was only trying to—"

"Stop trying so much!" he roared out, with the moon over his ear. "Now, come. Let him sleep. Come on." Breathing angrily, he made a commanding gesture with his open hand, and she started for the door. She hesitated, wanting, Martin knew, to kiss him good night, but instead she obediently walked past Papa and went out of the room, and Martin felt her chastised happiness as she silently vanished.

Now Papa turned to him and said sternly as before, "Less tricks now. Listen to her when she tells you, y'hear?"

"Yes, Papa," Martin whispered, his love choking off his voice.

Papa reached down. Martin stiffened against a blow, but his father gently straightened his blanket a little and walked out of the room.

For a moment Martin forgot entirely that Ben was still there at the end of his bed. A conviction of valor had come alive in his soul; it felt almost as though he had fasted all day at his father's side, and he was braced by the echoes of that deep voice which had so suddenly smashed the air in his defense. And in a moment he almost believed that he had been the roarer himself; in his mind he imitated the sounds and the expression in his angry father's face and quickly had them exactly for his own. Purified and wanting to act anew, he wished for morning and the chance to walk in daylight beside his father and possibly meet someone and hear his father say, "This is my son." His son! For the first time in his life he had the hard, imperishable awareness of descent, and with it the powers of one who knows he is being watched over and so receives a trust he must never lay down. In his mind's eye there rushed past the image of his angry father, and behind Papa was Grandpa and then other men, all grave and bearded, watching over him and somehow expecting and being gratified at the renewal of their righteousness and bravery in him. And in the warmth of their commending nods he began to slide into sleep.

A loud sob woke him. He raised up quickly. Ben! He looked into the darkness for his brother, whom he had forgotten, wanting to tell him—it didn't matter what he would tell him—he merely had nothing to hide any more and he wanted to reach out to his brother.

"Ben?" Unaccountably Ben was not at the end of the bed any more. Martin waited. Again, but softly now, he heard him weeping. How could Ben be sad? he wondered.

"Ben?" he called again. The weeping continued, remote, self-sufficient, and it reached Martin, who felt himself being pushed away. Suddenly he saw that Ben was sitting right next to him, facing him from across the aisle that separated their beds. He was fully dressed.

"What's the matter?" Martin asked.

Moonlight illuminated one cheek and the corner of an eye; the rest of Ben's face was lost in the darkness. Martin could not tell what expression Ben had, and he waited for Ben to speak with only curiosity and no fear. But now he could hear his brother's irregular breathing, and even though he could not remember any sin he had done he felt condemnation gathering in the long silence.

"What happened?" he asked.

In a voice broken by mourning Ben said, "How could you say a thing like that?"

"Don't cry," Martin began to plead. But Ben sat there crying into his hands. "They're *sleeping*!" he cautioned nobly. But Ben wept even more strongly at the mention of their parents, and Martin's fear found him again; and his old sense of his secrets came evilly alive in him once more.

"Don't cry like that!"

He quickly slid off his bed and bent over to see up into his brother's face. Panic was opening a space at his elbows. "I didn't mean it, Ben. Please!" And yet he still did not know what had been so terrible in what he had said, and his not knowing in itself was a mark of his badness.

Suddenly he reached out to draw Ben's hands down from his face, but Ben pulled himself away and lay over on his bed with his back to Martin. A swirl of clouds, ocean depths, and bearded secrets flowed out of Ben's back and swept around Martin's head. Soundlessly he crept back into his bed. "I'll never say it again. I promise," he offered.

But Ben did not reply. Even his sobs were quieting. He waited, but Ben did not accept his promise, and in his brother's silence he saw that he had been cast away. Lying there with his eyes open to the darkness, he saw that even though Papa had yelled out for his sake, it was because Papa did not understand, as Ben did, how bad he was. Papa was innocent so he defended him. But Ben knew.

He could not lie there. He sat up and sniffed loudly to see if Ben would turn to him, but Ben was motionless, quiet. Was he falling asleep in his clothes? This disruption of age-old order spread Martin's vision, and he remembered that the dining room must still be full of his wreckage. How wonderful it would be if he slipped out there and cleaned up without a sound, and in the morning they would all be amazed and love him!

His feet were on the floor. Ben still did not move. He bent low and tiptoed out of the bedroom, his hands stretched out in the empty black air.

In the dining room there was no moonlight, and he moved inch by inch for fear of noise. His hand touched the table, and he stretched his hands out. It was all bare. Only now he remembered it precisely as it had been, and he heard the great crashing for the first time, and the reality of his badness was like a blow on his face. He got down on his knees, fiercely resolved to clean up. His knee descended on a pear and squashed it, repelling him. He sat down to clean off his knee and felt cold meat under him and jumped; it was a chicken leg. Keeping his knees off the floor, he went on all fours away from the table to escape a rising feeling of disgust. At the front window he stood up and looked out and saw a wonder. A silvery greenish glow was hanging over the mac-adam street.

He had never seen such bright moonlight. It even glistened on windows across the street. In the silence he heard a faint high ringing in his ears, like insects. His eyes swallowed the mysterious glow outside, and in a moment he no longer knew what had brought him out here. A sense of newness was upon him; things to do that he had never done before. It was a secret moment suddenly; with no one watching everything was up to him. No one knew he was standing here, and he had never before been walking around when everyone was asleep. He could even go outside! The illicit freedom exhilarated him—to go outside and be the only one awake in the world! His hand reached up and turned the key in the front door and it opened, surprising him a little. Looking out through the screening, he felt how warm the air was. Now he heard the new gentleness of the falling surf, and he opened the screen door enough to look out to the left, and then he walked onto the porch and faced the ocean. It was flattened out, all the roughness of the preceding days melted away. God was gone?

The magical new calm of the ocean sucked at his mind. When no one was looking God had shot up out of the water with a rush of foam; and when the water had fallen back the waves flattened out and the sea was at rest. God had waited there until they had thrown in their sins, and He had taken them up with Him, leaving the water clean and hairless. How wonderful it was that Papa and the other men knew what to do about God! How to pray to Him and when to throw their sins to Him and when to go home and eat. Papa, and Ben too, with the others, had an understanding with Him and knew what was supposed to happen next and what He wanted them to do.

Facing the glistening beach, the salt-white sand that stretched before him like a sky to walk on and the moon's green river flowing on the ocean toward his eyes, he yearned to know what he should do for God, as the others knew. His body stretched as with a mute vow, a pure wish that quickly changed to fact; as when he had stood up and sat down with the congregation in the synagogue, not knowing why but satisfied to be joined with others in sheer obedience, he now vowed obedience to the sea, the moon, the starry beach, and the sky, and the silence that stretched its emptiness all around him. What exactly its command was he did not know, but an order was coming to him from the night, and he was grateful, and it made him better and no longer quite alone. He felt, without any sense of the details, that secretly, unknown to anyone but known to the night, he was the guardian of Ben's and his parents' innocence. Vaguely he felt that with some words which he knew were somewhere in his head he had almost sent them all screaming and roaring at one another and at him, so that—had he said what he could say, they would all be horrified at the mere sight of one another and there would be a terror of crashing. He must keep them from that knowledge, and he knew this and received it like water when he was thirsty, with placid eyes and an inner attention and pleasure, with a yearning that was more than knowledge.

Suddenly he felt exhausted. Sleep was felling him as he stood there holding on to the railing. He held his hand out past the eaves of the porch roof and felt the moonlight. It wasn't warm! Now, washing both his hands in it, he searched for its heat and texture, but it felt no different than darkness. He put his moon-touched hands to his face to feel, but no warmth came out of them. He raised up and tried to lean out over the rail to put his face into the moonlight, but he couldn't reach. With his eyelids heavy he walked unsteadily to the low stoop and went down and walked to the corner of the house, where the beach began, and moved out of the house's shadow into the open moonlight. As he looked up, the light blinded him, and he sat suddenly, falling back on his stiffened arms; then his elbows gave way, and he lay down on the sand.

With the last darkening corner of his mind he sought to feel his face warming, and slowly it was. His eyelids first, then the bridge of his nose, then his mouth, were feeling the spread of the moon's heat. He saw his brother and his father and his mother and how he would tell that the moonlight was so warm!—and he heard their laughter at the impossibility, their laughter that was like a gate keeping him out of their world, and even as he felt angry and ashamed and big-eared he was their protector now. He would let them laugh and not believe him, while secretly, unknown to anyone but the eyes that watched everything from the sea, he would by the power of his silence keep them from badness and harm. In league with rule, in charge of the troubled peace, he slept in the strength of his ministry.

The breeze cooled him, and soon the sand chilled his back, but he summoned more heat from the moonlight and quickly he was warmed. Sinking down, he swam through the deepest sea and held his breath so long that as he came up with the sunlight bursting from his hair he knew he would astonish everybody.

[1959]

Monte Sant' Angelo

The driver, who had been sitting up ahead in perfect silence for nearly an hour as they crossed the monotonous green plain of Foggia, now said something. Appello quickly leaned forward in the back seat and asked him what he had said. "That is Monte Sant' Angelo before you." Appello lowered his head to see through the windshield of the rattling little Fiat. Then he nudged Bernstein, who awoke resentfully, as though his friend had intruded. "That's the town up there," Appello said. Bernstein's annoyance vanished, and he bent forward. They both sat that way for several minutes, watching the approach of what seemed to them a comically situated town, even more comic than any they had seen in the four weeks they had spent moving from place to place in the country. It was like a tiny old lady living on a high roof for fear of thieves.

The plain remained as flat as a table for a quarter of a mile ahead. Then out of it, like a pillar, rose the butte; squarely and rigidly skyward it towered, only narrowing as it reached its very top. And there, barely visible now, the town crouched, momentarily obscured by white clouds, then appearing again tiny and safe, like a mountain port looming at the end of the sea. From their distance they could make out no road, no approach at all up the side of the pillar.

"Whoever built that was awfully frightened of something," Bernstein said, pulling his coat closer around him. "How do they get up there? Or do they?"

Appello, in Italian, asked the driver about the town. The driver, who had been there only once before in his life and knew no other who had made the trip—despite his being a resident of Lucera, which was not far away—told Appello with some amusement that they would soon see how rarely anyone goes up or comes down Monte Sant' Angelo. "The donkeys will kick and run away as we ascend, and when we come into the town everyone will come out to see. They are very far from everything. They all look like brothers up there. They don't know very much either." He laughed.

"What does the Princeton chap say?" Bernstein asked.

The driver had a crew haircut, a turned-up nose, and a red round face with blue eyes. He owned the car, and although he spoke like any Italian when his feet were on the ground, behind his wheel with two Americans riding behind him he had only the most amused and superior attitude toward everything outside the windshield. Appello, having translated for Bernstein, asked him how long it would take to ascend. "Perhaps three quarters of an hour—as long as the mountain is," he amended.

Bernstein and Appello settled back and watched the butte's approach. Now they could see that its sides were crumbled white stone. At this closer vantage it seemed as though it had been struck a terrible blow by some monstrous hammer that had split its structure into millions of seams. They were beginning to climb now, on a road of sharp broken rocks.

"The road is Roman," the driver remarked. He knew how much Americans made of anything Roman. Then he added, "The car, however, is from Milan." He and Appello laughed.

And now the white chalk began drifting into the car. At their elbows the altitude began to seem threatening. There was no railing on the road, and it turned back on itself every two hundred yards in order to climb again. The Fiat's doors were wavering in their frames; the seat on which they sat kept inching forward onto the floor. A fine film of white talc settled onto their clothing and covered their eyebrows. Both together began to cough. When they were finished Bernstein said, "Just so I understand it clearly and without prejudice, will you explain again in words of one syllable why the hell we are climbing this lump of dust, old man?"

Appello laughed and mocked a punch at him.

"No kidding," Bernstein said, trying to smile.

"I want to see this aunt of mine, that's all." Appello began taking it seriously.

"You're crazy, you know that? You've got some kind of ancestor complex. All we've done in this country is look for your relatives."

"Well, Jesus, I'm finally in the country, I want to see all the places I came from. You realize that two of my relatives are buried in a crypt in the church up there? In eleven hundred something."

"Oh, is this where the monks came from?"

"Sure, the two Appello brothers. They helped build that church. It's very famous, that church. Supposed to be Saint Michael appeared in a vision or something."

"I never thought I'd know anybody with monks in his family. But I still think you're cracked on the whole subject."

"Well, don't you have any feeling about your ancestors? Wouldn't you like to go back to Austria or wherever you came from and see where the old folks lived? Maybe find a family that belongs to your line, or something like that?"

Bernstein did not answer for a moment. He did not know quite what he felt and wondered dimly whether he kept ragging his friend a little because of envy. When they had been in the country courthouse where Appello's grandfather's portrait and his great-grandfather's hung—both renowned provincial magistrates; when they had spent the night in Lucera where the name Appello meant something distinctly honorable, and where his friend Vinny was taken in hand and greeted in that intimate way because he was an Appello—in all these moments Bernstein had felt left out and somehow deficient. At first he had taken the attitude that all the fuss was childish, and yet as incident after incident, landmark after old landmark, turned up echoing the name Appello, he gradually began to feel his friend combining with this history, and it seemed to him that it made Vinny stronger, somehow less dead when the time would come for him to die.

"I have no relatives that I know of in Europe," he said to Vinny. "And if I had they'd have all been wiped out by now."

"Is that why you don't like my visiting this way?"

"I don't say I don't like it," Bernstein said and smiled by will. He wished he could open himself as Vinny could; it would give him ease and strength, he felt. They stared down at the plain below and spoke little.

The chalk dust had lightened Appello's black eyebrows. For a fleeting moment it occurred to Appello that they resembled each other. Both were over six feet tall, both broad-shouldered and dark men. Bernstein was thinner, quite gaunt and long-armed. Appello was stronger in his arms and stooped a little, as though he had not wanted to be tall. But their eyes were not the same. Appello seemed a little Chinese around the eyes, and they glistened black, direct, and, for women, passionately. Bernstein gazed rather than looked; for him the eyes were dangerous when they could be fathomed, and so he turned them away often, or downward, and there seemed to be something defensively cruel and yet gentle there.

They liked each other not for reasons so much as for possibilities; it was as though they both had sensed they were opposites. And they were lured to each other's failings. With Bernstein around him Appello felt diverted from his irresponsible sensuality, and on this trip Bernstein often had the pleasure and pain of resolving to deny himself no more.

The car turned a hairpin curve with a cloud below on the right, when suddenly the main street of the town arched up before them. There was no one about. It had been true, what the driver had predicted—in the few handkerchiefs of grass that they had passed on the way up the donkeys had bolted, and they had seen shepherds with hard mustaches and black shakos and long black cloaks who had regarded them with the silent inspection of those who live far away. But here in the town there was no one. The car climbed onto the main street, which flattened now, and all at once they were being surrounded by people who were coming out of their doors, putting on their jackets and caps. They did look strangely related, and more Irish than Italian.

The two got out of the Fiat and inspected the baggage strapped to the car's roof, while the driver kept edging protectively around and around the car. Appello talked laughingly with the people, who kept asking why he had come so far, what he had to sell, what he wanted to buy, until he at last made it clear that he was looking only for his aunt. When he said the name the men (the women remained at home, watching from the windows) looked blank, until an old man wearing rope sandals and a knitted skating cap came forward and said that he remembered such a woman. He then turned, and Appello and Bernstein followed up the main street with what was now perhaps a hundred men behind them.

"How come nobody knows her?" Bernstein asked.

"She's a widow. I guess she stays home most of the time. The men in the line died out here twenty years ago. Her husband was the last Appello up here. They don't go much by women; I bet this old guy remembered the name because he knew her husband by it, not her."

The wind, steady and hard, blew through the town, washing it, laving its stones white. The sun was cool as a lemon, the sky purely blue, and the clouds so close their keels seemed to be sailing through the next street. The two Americans began to walk with the joy of it in their long strides. They came to a two-story stone house and went up a dark corridor and knocked. The guide remained respectfully on the sidewalk.

There was no sound within for a few moments. Then there was—short scrapes, like a mouse that started, stopped, looked about, started again. Appello knocked once more. The doorknob turned, and the door opened a foot. A pale little woman, not very old at all, held the door wide enough for her face to be seen. She seemed very worried.

"Ha?" she asked.

"I am Vincent Georgio."

"Ha?" she repeated.

"Vicenzo Giorgio Appello."

Her hand slid off the knob, and she stepped back. Appello, smiling in his friendly way, entered, with Bernstein behind him closing the door. A window let the sun flood the room, which was nevertheless stone cold. The woman's mouth was open, her hands were pressed together as in prayer, and the tips of her fingers were pointing at Vinny. She seemed crouched, as though about to kneel, and she could not speak.

Vinny went over to her and touched her bony shoulder and pressed her into a chair. He and Bernstein sat down too. He told her their relationship, saying names of men and women, some of whom were dead, others whom she had only heard of and never met in this sky place. She spoke at last, and Appello could not understand what she said. She ran out of the room suddenly.

"I think she thinks I'm a ghost or something. My uncle said she hadn't seen any of the family in twenty or twenty-five years. I bet she doesn't think there are any left."

She returned with a bottle that had an inch of wine at the bottom of it. She ignored Bernstein and gave Appello the bottle. He drank. It was vinegar. Then she started to whimper and kept wiping the tears out of her eyes in order to see Appello. She never finished a sentence, and Appello kept asking her what she meant. She kept running from one corner of the room to another. The rhythm of her departures and returns to the chair was getting so wild that Appello raised his voice and commanded her to sit.

"I'm not a ghost, Aunty. I came here from America—" He stopped. It was clear from the look in her bewildered, frightened eyes that she had not thought him a ghost at all, but what was just as bad—if nobody had ever come to see her from Lucera, how could anybody have so much as thought of her in America, a place that did exist, she knew, just as heaven existed and in exactly the same way. There was no way to hold a conversation with her.

They finally made their exit, and she had not said a coherent word except a blessing, which was her way of expressing her relief that Appello was leaving, for despite the unutterable joy at having seen with her own eyes another of her husband's blood, the sight was itself too terrible in its associations, and in the responsibility it laid upon her to welcome him and make him comfortable.

They walked toward the church now. Bernstein had not been able to say anything. The woman's emotion, so pure and violent and wild, had scared him. And yet, glancing at Appello, he was amazed to see that his friend had drawn nothing but a calm sort of satisfaction from it, as though his aunt had only behaved correctly. Dimly he remembered himself as a boy visiting an aunt of his in the Bronx, a woman who had not been in touch with the family and had never seen him. He remembered how forcefully she had fed him, pinched his cheeks, and smiled and smiled every time he looked up at her, but he knew that there was nothing of this blood in that encounter; nor could there be for him now if on the next corner he should meet a woman who said she was of his family. If anything, he would want to get away from her, even though he had always gotten along with his people and hadn't even the usual snobbery about them. As they entered the church he said to himself that some part of him was not plugged in, but why he should be disturbed about it mystified him and even made him irritated with Appello, who now was asking the priest where the tombs of the Appellos were.

They descended into the vault of the church, where the stone floor was partly covered with water. Along the walls, and down twisting corridors running out of a central arched hall, were tombs so old no candle could illuminate most of the worn inscriptions. The priest vaguely remembered an Appello vault but had no idea where it was. Vinny moved from one crypt to another with the candle he had bought from the priest. Bernstein waited at the opening of the corridor, his neck bent to avoid touching the roof with his hat. Appello, stooped even more than usual, looked like a monk himself, an antiquary, a gradually disappearing figure squinting down the long darkness of the ages for his name on a stone. He could not find it. Their feet were getting soaked. After half an hour they left the church and outside fought off shivering small boys selling grimy religious postcards, which the wind kept taking from their fists.

"I'm sure it's there," Appello said with fascinated excitement. "But you wouldn't want to stick out a search, would you?" he asked hopefully.

"This is no place for me to get pneumonia," Bernstein said.

They had come to the end of a side street. They had passed

shops in front of which pink lambs hung head down with their legs stiffly jutting out over the sidewalk. Bernstein shook hands with one and imagined for Vinny a scene for Chaplin in which a monsignor would meet him here, reach out to shake his hand, and find the cold lamb's foot in his grip, and Chaplin would be mortified. At the street's end they scanned the endless sky and looked over the precipice upon Italy.

"They might even have ridden horseback down there, in armor— Appellos." Vinny spoke raptly.

"Yeah, they probably did," Bernstein said. The vision of Appello in armor wiped away any desire to kid his friend. He felt alone, desolate as the dried-out chalk sides of this broken pillar he stood upon. Certainly there had been no knights in his family.

He remembered his father's telling of his town in Europe, a common barrel of water, a town idiot, a baron nearby. That was all he had of it, and no pride, no pride in it at all. Then I am an American, he said to himself. And yet in that there was not the power of Appello's narrow passion. He looked at Appello's profile and felt the warmth of that gaze upon Italy and wondered if any American had ever really felt like this in the States. He had never in his life sensed so strongly that the past could be so peopled, so vivid with generations, as it had been with Vinny's aunt an hour ago. A common water barrel, a town idiot, a baron who lived nearby. . . . It had nothing to do with *him*. And standing there he sensed a broken part of himself and wondered with a slight amusement if this was what a child felt on discovering that the parents who brought him up were not his own and that he entered his house not from warmth but from the street, from a public and disordered place. . . .

They sought and found a restaurant for lunch. It was at the other edge of the town and overhung the precipice. Inside, it was one immense room with fifteen or twenty tables; the front wall was lined with windows overlooking the plain below. They sat at a table and waited for someone to appear. The restaurant was cold. They could hear the wind surging against the window-panes, and yet the clouds at eye level moved serenely and slow. A young girl, the daughter of the family, came out of the kitchen,

and Appello was questioning her about food when the door to the
street opened and a man came in.

For Bernstein there was an abrupt impression of familiarity with
the man, although he could not fathom the reason for his feeling.
The man's face looked Sicilian, round, dark as earth, high cheekbones, broad jaw. He almost laughed aloud as it instantly occurred
to him that he could converse with this man in Italian. When the
waitress had gone, he told this to Vinny, who now joined in watching the man.

Sensing their stares, the man looked at them with a merry flicker
of his cheeks and said, *"Buon giorno."*

"Buon giorno," Bernstein replied across the four tables between
them, and then to Vinny, "Why do I feel that about him?"

"I'll be damned if I know," Vinny said, glad now that he could
join his friend in a mutually interesting occupation.

They watched the man, who obviously ate here often. He had
already set a large package down on another table and now put his
hat on a chair, his jacket on another chair, and his vest on a third.
It was as though he were making companions of his clothing. He
was in the prime of middle age and very rugged. And to the Americans there was something mixed up about his clothing. His jacket
might have been worn by a local man; it was tight and black and
wrinkled and chalkdust-covered. His trousers were dark brown
and very thick, like a peasant's, and his shoes were snubbed up at
the ends and of heavy leather. But he wore a black hat, which was
unusual up here where all had caps, and he had a tie. He wiped his
hands before loosening the knot; it was a striped tie, yellow and
blue, of silk, and no tie to be bought in this part of the world, or
worn by these people. And there was a look in his eyes that was
not a peasant's inward stare; nor did it have the innocence of the
other men who had looked at them on the streets here.

The waitress came with two dishes of lamb for the Americans.
The man was interested and looked across his table at the meat
and at the strangers. Bernstein glanced at the barely cooked flesh
and said, "There's hair on it."

Vinny called the girl back just as she was going to the new-comer and pointed at the hair.

"But it's lamb's hair," she explained simply.

They said, "Oh," and pretended to begin to cut into the faintly pink flesh.

"You ought to know better, signor, than to order meat today."

The man looked amused, and yet it was unclear whether he might not be a trifle offended.

"Why not?" Vinny asked.

"It's Friday, signor," and he smiled sympathetically.

"That's right!" Vinny said although he had known all along.

"Give me fish," the man said to the girl and asked with inti-macy about her mother, who was ill these days.

Bernstein had not been able to turn his eyes from the man. He could not eat the meat and sat chewing bread and feeling a rising urge to go over to the man, to speak to him. It struck him as being insane. The whole place—the town, the clouds in the streets, the thin air—was turning into a hallucination. He knew this man. He was sure he knew him. Quite clearly that was impossible. Still, there was a thing beyond the impossibility of which he was drunk-enly sure, and it was that if he dared he could start speaking Ital-ian fluently with this man. This was the first moment since leaving America that he had not felt the ill-ease of traveling and of being a traveler. He felt as comfortable as Vinny now, it seemed to him. In his mind's eye he could envisage the inside of the kitchen; he had a startlingly clear image of what the cook's face must look like, and he knew where a certain kind of soiled apron was hung.

"What's the matter with you?" Appello asked.

"Why?"

"The way you're looking at him."

"I want to talk to him."

"Well, talk to him." Vinny smiled.

"I can't speak Italian, you know that."

"Well, I'll ask him. What do you want to say?"

"Vinny—" Bernstein started to speak and stopped.

"What?" Appello asked, leaning his head closer and looking down at the tablecloth.

"Get him to talk. Anything. Go ahead."

Vinny, enjoying his friend's strange emotionalism, looked across at the man, who now was eating with careful but immense satisfaction. "*Scusi*, signor."

The man looked up.

"I am a son of Italy from America. I would like to talk to you. We're strange here."

The man, chewing deliciously, nodded with his amiable and amused smile and adjusted the hang of his jacket on the nearby chair.

"Do you come from around here?"

"Not very far."

"How is everything here?"

"Poor. It is always poor."

"What do you work at, if I may ask?"

The man had now finished his food. He took a last long drag of his wine and got up and proceeded to dress and pull his tie up tightly. When he walked it was with a slow, wide sway, as though each step had to be conserved.

"I sell cloth here to the people and the stores, such as they are," he said. And he walked over to the bundle and set it carefully on a table and began untying it.

"He sells cloth," Vinny said to Bernstein.

Bernstein's cheeks began to redden. From where he sat he could see the man's broad back, ever so slightly bent over the bundle. He could see the man's hands working at the knot and just a corner of the man's left eye. Now the man was laying the paper away from the two bolts of cloth, carefully pressing the wrinkles flat against the table. It was as though the brown paper were valuable leather that must not be cracked or rudely bent. The waitress came out of the kitchen with a tremendous round loaf of bread at least two feet in diameter. She gave it to him, and he placed it flat on top of the cloth, and the faintest feather of a smile curled up on Bernstein's lips. Now the man folded the paper back and brought

the string around the bundle and tied the knot, and Bernstein
uttered a little laugh, a laugh of relief.

Vinny looked at him, already smiling, ready to join the laughter, but mystified. "What's the matter?" he asked.

Bernstein took a breath. There was something a little triumphant, a new air of confidence and superiority in his face and
voice. "He's Jewish, Vinny," he said.

Vinny turned to look at the man. "Why?"

"The way he works that bundle. It's exactly the way my father
used to tie a bundle—and my grandfather. The whole history is
packing bundles and getting away. Nobody else can be as tender
and delicate with bundles. That's a Jewish man tying a bundle.
Ask him his name."

Vinny was delighted. "Signor," he called with that warmth
reserved in his nature for members of families, any families.

The man, tucking the end of the string into the edge of the
paper, turned to them with his kind smile.

"May I ask your name, signor?"

"My name? Mauro di Benedetto."

"Mauro di Benedetto. Sure!" Vinny laughed, looking at Bernstein. "That's Morris of the Blessed. Moses."

"Tell him I'm Jewish," Bernstein said, a driving eagerness
charging his eyes.

"My friend is Jewish," Vinny said to the man, who now was
hoisting the bundle onto his shoulder.

"Heh?" the man asked, confused by their sudden vivacity. As
though wondering if there were some sophisticated American
point he should have understood, he stood there smiling blankly,
politely, ready to join in this mood.

"*Judeo*, my friend."

"*Judeo*?" he asked, the willingness to get the joke still holding
the smile on his face.

Vinny hesitated before this steady gaze of incomprehension.
"*Judeo*. The people of the Bible," he said.

"Oh, yes, yes!" The man nodded now, relieved that he was not to be caught in ignorance. "*Ebreo*," he corrected. And he nodded affably to Bernstein and seemed a little at a loss for what they expected him to do next.

"Does he know what you mean?" Bernstein asked.

"Yeah, he said, 'Hebrew,' but it doesn't seem to connect. Signor," he addressed the man, "why don't you have a glass of wine with us? Come, sit down."

"Thank you, signor," he replied appreciatively, "but I must be home by sundown and I'm already a little late."

Vinny translated, and Bernstein told him to ask why he had to be home by sundown.

The man apparently had never considered the question before. He shrugged and laughed and said, "I don't know. All my life I get home for dinner on Friday night, and I like to come into the house before sundown. I suppose it's a habit; my father—you see, I have a route I walk, which is this route. I first did it with my father, and he did it with his father. We are known here for many generations past. And my father always got home on Friday night before sundown. It's a manner of the family I guess."

"*Shabbas* begins at sundown on Friday night," Bernstein said when Vinny had translated. "He's even taking home the fresh bread for the Sabbath. The man is a Jew, I tell you. Ask him, will you?"

"*Scusi*, signor." Vinny smiled. "My friend is curious to know whether you are Jewish."

The man raised his thick eyebrows not only in surprise but as though he felt somewhat honored by being identified with something exotic. "Me?" he asked.

"I don't mean American," Vinny said, believing he had caught the meaning of the man's glance at Bernstein. "*Ebreo*," he repeated.

The man shook his head, seeming a little sorry he could not oblige Vinny. "No," he said. He was ready to go but wanted to pursue what obviously was his most interesting conversation in weeks. "Are they Catholics? The Hebrews?"

"He's asking me if Jews are Catholics," Vinny said.

Bernstein sat back in his chair, a knotted look of wonder in his eyes. Vinny replied to the man, who looked once again at Bernstein as though wanting to investigate this strangeness further, but his mission drew him up and he wished them good fortune and said goodbye. He walked to the kitchen door and called thanks to the girl inside, saying the loaf would warm his back all the way down the mountain, and he opened the door and went out into the wind of the street and the sunshine, waving to them as he walked away.

They kept repeating their amazement on the way back to the car, and Bernstein told again how his father wrapped bundles. "Maybe he doesn't know he's a Jew, but how could he not know what Jews are?" he said.

"Well, remember my aunt in Lucera?" Vinny asked. "She's a schoolteacher, and she asked me if you believed in Christ. She didn't know the first thing about it. I think the ones in these small towns who ever heard of Jews think they're a Christian sect of some kind. I knew an old Italian once who thought all Negroes were Jews and white Jews were only converts."

"But his name . . ."

"'Benedetto' is an Italian name too. I never heard of 'Mauro' though. 'Mauro' is strictly from the old sod."

"But if he had a name like that, wouldn't it lead him to wonder if . . . ?"

"I don't think so. In New York the name 'Salvatore' is turned into 'Sam.' Italians are great for nicknames; the first name never means much. 'Vicenzo' is 'Enzo,' or 'Vinny' or even 'Chico.' Nobody would think twice about 'Mauro' or damn near any other first name. He's obviously a Jew, but I'm sure he doesn't know it. You could tell, couldn't you? He was baffled."

"But, my God, bringing home a bread for *Shabbas*!" Bernstein laughed, wide-eyed.

They reached the car, and Bernstein had his hand on the door but stopped before opening it and turned to Vinny. He looked heated; his eyelids seemed puffed. "It's early—if you still want to I'll go back to the church with you. You can look for the boys."

Vinny began to smile, and then they both laughed together, and Vinny slapped him on the back and gripped his shoulder as though to hug him. "Goddam, now you're starting to enjoy this trip!"

As they walked briskly toward the church the conversation returned always to the same point, when Bernstein would say, "I don't know why, but it gets me. He's not only acting like a Jew, but an Orthodox Jew. And doesn't even know—I mean it's strange as hell to me."

"You look different, you know that?" Vinny said.

"Why?"

"You do."

"You know a funny thing?" Bernstein said quietly as they entered the church and descended into the vault beneath it. "I feel like—at home in this place. I can't describe it."

Beneath the church, they picked their way through the shallower puddles on the stone floor, looking into vestibules, opening doors, searching for the priest. He appeared at last—they could not imagine from where—and Appello bought another candle from him and was gone in the shadows of the corridors where the vaults were.

Bernstein stood—everything was wet, dripping. Behind him, flat and wide, rose the stairway of stones bent with the tread of millions. Vapor steamed from his nostrils. There was nothing to look at but shadow. It was dank and black and low, an entrance to hell. Now and then in the very far distance he could hear a step echoing, another, then silence. He did not move, seeking the root of an ecstasy he had not dreamed was part of his nature; he saw the amiable man trudging down the mountains, across the plains, on routes marked out for him by generations of men, a nameless traveler carrying home a warm bread on Friday night—and kneeling in church on Sunday. There was an irony in it he could not name. And yet pride was running through him. Of what he should be proud he had no clear idea; perhaps it was only that beneath the brainless crush of history a Jew had secretly survived, shorn of his consciousness but forever caught by that final impudence of a Saturday Sabbath in a Catholic country; so that his very unawareness was proof, a proof as mute as stones, that a past lived. A past for me, Bernstein thought, astounded by its importance for him, when in fact he had never had a religion or even, he realized now, a history.

He could see Vinny's form approaching in the narrow corridor of crypts, the candle flame flattening in the cold draft. He felt he would look differently into Vinny's eyes; his condescension had gone and with it a certain embarrassment. He felt loose, somehow the equal of his friend—and how odd that was when, if anything, he had thought of himself as superior. Suddenly, with Vinny a yard away, he saw that his life had been covered with an unrecognized shame.

"I found it! It's back there!" Vinny was laughing like a young boy, pointing back toward the dark corridor.

"That's great, Vinny," Bernstein said. "I'm glad."

They were both stooping slightly under the low, wet ceiling, their voices fleeing from their mouths in echoed whispers. Vinny held still for an instant, catching Bernstein's respectful happiness, and saw there that his search was not worthless sentiment. He raised the candle to see Bernstein's face better, and then he laughed and gripped Bernstein's wrist and led the way toward the flight of steps that rose to the surface. Bernstein had never liked anyone grasping him, but from this touch of a hand in the darkness, strangely, there was no implication of a hateful weakness.

They walked side by side down the steep street away from the church. The town was empty again. The air smelled of burning charcoal and olive oil. A few pale stars had come out. The shops were all shut. Bernstein thought of Mauro di Benedetto going down the winding, rocky road, hurrying against the setting of the sun.

[1951]

Please Don't Kill Anything

That beach was golden toward sundown. The bathers had all gone home when the wind got brisk. Gulls were diving just beyond the breakers. On the horizon they could see four stubby fishing boats moving in a line. Then she turned toward the right and saw the two parked trucks and the fishermen hauling on a net. "Let's see if they caught anything," she said, with the swift surge of wonder that swept through her at any new sight.

The trucks were battered and rusty, with open backs, and the one they came upon had about twenty-five big, sand-sprinkled bass and small bluefish piled at the tailgate. A man in his sixties was sitting on the truck, holding a rope that was wound around a winch at his side. He nodded to them pleasantly and drew on the rope to keep it wound tightly around the turning winch. At the water's edge another man kept watch over the net, piling it in a heap as it was drawn out of the water.

Sam glanced at the fish as they arrived at the truck and knew she would be startled. She saw them, and her eyes widened, but she even tried to smile in congratulation to the old man who drew on the rope, and she said, "You catch all these?"

"Yup," he said, and his eyes warmed at her beauty.

"These are all dead, aren't they," she said.

"Oh, ya," the old man said.

She had an excitement in her eyes as she looked, it seemed, at each individual fish to be sure it wasn't moving. Sam started talking to the old man about the probability of a good catch in the net now coming into shore, and she was drawn into the conversation, and he was relieved that her eyes, the color of the blue sea, were calmed.

But now the old man moved a lever, and the winch speeded up with a rising whine, and he was exerting himself to keep the rope taut. The winch on the other truck also turned faster, and the two net-tenders on the beach moved rapidly from the trucks to the edge of the water, hurriedly piling up the incoming net. Now they could see the curving line of cork floats only a few yards away in the water.

"Why do you pull so fast?" Sam asked the old man. "Are they fighting the net?"

"Naw," the old man said, "just want to keep her taut so they mightn't jump over and git away."

The waves were breaking into the net now, but they could not yet see any fish. She put her two hands up to her cheeks and said, "Oh, now they know they're caught!" She laughed. "Each one is wondering what happened!" He was glad she was making fun of herself even if her eyes were fixed in fear on the submerged net. She glanced up at her husband and said, "Oh, dear, they're going to be caught now."

He started to explain, but she quickly went on, "I know it's all right as long as they're eaten. They're going to eat them, aren't they?"

"They'll sell them to the fish stores," he said softly, so the old man at the winch wouldn't hear. "They'll feed people."

"Yes," she said, like a child reassured. "I'll watch it. I'm watching it," she almost announced to him. But in her something was holding its breath.

A wave receded then, and with one pull the bag of the net was drawn out of the surf. Voices sounded from both trucks; it wasn't much of a catch. She saw the tails of small bluefish writhing up through the net ("They're standing on their heads!"), and a great bass flopping, and sea robins trying to stretch their curved umber wings, and one flounder lying in the midst of this tangled rubble of the sea. She kept pointing here and there at a fish that had suddenly jerked or flopped over, and called out, "There's one! There's another one!"—meaning they were not dead yet and, he knew, must be rescued.

The men opened the net and pulled out the bass and some blue-fish, tossing the sea robins onto the sand and the flounder, and two blowfish, which immediately began to swell. She turned to the old man on the truck and, trying to smile, she called to him with a sharpness in her voice, almost a cry, "Don't you take those?"

He drew an old man's warmth from the glow of her face and the startling shape of her body under the striped jersey and the beige slacks. "They're no good, ma'am," he said.

"Well, don't you put them back?"

The old man seemed to hesitate as though some memory of guilt had crossed his mind. "Sure. We put them back"—and sat there watching his partner, who was picking good fish out of the net and tossing the winged fish right and left onto the sand.

There were now about fifty sea robins on the beach, some of them gulping, some perfectly still. Sam could feel the tension rising in her, and he walked over to the nearest fish and, feeling a tremor of repugnance, picked it up and threw it into the waves and came back to her. The pulse of its life was still in his fingers. "If I had something to hold them with," she began.

"You can't throw all those fish back," he said.

"But they're alive!" she said, desperately trying to smile and not to separate herself from him.

"No, they're dead. Most of them are dead, sweet."

"Are they dead?" she turned and asked the old man.

"No, they ain't dead. Most."

"Would they live again if they had water?"

"Oh, sure, they come to," he said, trying to assuage her but not moving from his place.

She took off one sandal and went to a fish that was writhing and tried to flip it into the water, but it slipped away. Sam came over and picked it up and flung it into the sea. He was laughing now, and she kept saying, "I'm sorry. But if they're alive . . . !"

"It's all right," he said, "but they're mostly dead by now. Look." And he picked up one that was motionless; it felt flabby. He threw it into the water, and it arched itself as it struck, and she cried out, "There! It's swimming!"

Defeated and grinning, now that he saw the fishermen watching him with smiles on their faces, he went about throwing all the sea robins back into the water. He sensed that even with their smiles the men were somehow held by her insistence, and as he threw the slimy fish in one by one he saw each fish separately, each straining for its quart of sea, and he was no longer ashamed. And there were two fish left, both sea robins with white bellies and stiff umber wings and the beginnings of legs sprouting from both sides of their necks. They were motionless on their backs. He did not bend to pick them up because she seemed prepared to sacrifice them, and he went back to her, feeling, somehow, that if he let those two die on the beach she might come to terms with this kind of waste. For he had had to open the window at home, once, to let out a moth, which ordinarily he would have swatted, and while part of his heart worshiped her fierce tenderness toward all that lived, another part knew that she must come to understand that she did not die with the moths and the spiders and the fledgling birds and, now, with these fish. But it was also that he wished the fishermen to see that she was not quite so fanatic as to require these two last, obviously dead, sea robins to be given their chance.

He stood beside her again, waiting. He smiled and said, "You got a job cut out for yourself. There's twenty-five miles of beach we can cruise, throwing back fish." She laughed and drew his head down and kissed him, and he hugged her, and she said, "Just those two. Go on, Sam. They might be alive."

He laughed again and picked up one of the fish, knowing that it was even more unjust for two to die when fifty had been saved, and as he tossed it to the waves a dog appeared. It was a big, brown retriever with sea-matted hair, and it leaped into the waves and dipped its head into the water, raised up with the sea robin gently cradled in its mouth, and came back with great pride to lay it carefully at Sam's feet. "God, look how gently he brings it back!" Sam said.

"Oh, dear!" She laughed and bent toward the stern face of the buff-eyed dog. The dog returned her a look of athletic determination. "You mustn't do that!" Helplessly she looked at Sam, who picked up the fish and threw it back. Again the dog leaped in and retrieved it and now with enormous élan and pride nearly danced back to Sam, laid it at his feet, and stood waiting for the next throw, its legs trembling with eagerness.

"Well?" he said to her. "There you are. There's a whole conspiracy against these two fish. This guy was trained to help man; man has to eat and something's got to die, puss . . ."

As he spoke a silvery minnow slid out of the mouth of the sea robin at his feet. "Look at that now!" he yelled. "See? What about *that* little fish?"

"Yes!" she said, like an admission.

"You see? The victims make other victims."

"Well, hurry, throw it back anyway."

"But this character keeps bringing it back. This fish is doomed," he said, and they were both laughing, but she had in her head a clock which was telling her that every second counted, and she started to bend toward the fish at his feet despite her repugnance at touching it. He moved her hand away and picked it up, threw it, and when the dog turned and went into the water for it, he ran a few yards along the beach to the other fish and threw it in.

"Now," he said a little breathlessly as the dog returned with the first fish, "now there's one. This is a positively doomed fish on the principle that man has to eat and this dog is part of the scheme to feed him." But now even he could not take his eyes from the fish, which had taken to breathing rapidly, what with the shocks of being thrown into the water and being picked up by the dog and flying through the brisk wind. "This fish wishes you'd let it die in peace!" He laughed.

She looked around almost frantically, still smiling and laughing with him, and saw a stick and ran, ran with the dancer's leaping stride, and the dog glanced at her, then watched her as she waved the stick and called to him. She threw it into the sea, and the dog streaked into the water after it; and Sam picked up the last fish quickly and flung it, and it arched with life as it slid into a wave.

The beach was now clean, and the fishermen were busy stowing their nets, and the two walked away toward the road. "I'm sorry, Sam, but they were alive, and if nobody's going to eat them . . ."

"Well, the tide would have taken them out dead, puss, and they'd have been eaten by other fish. They wouldn't have been wasted."

"Yes," she said.

They walked, holding each other by the hand, and she was silent. He felt a great happiness opening in him that she had laid his hand on the fish which were now swimming in the sea because he had lifted them. Now she looked up at him like a little girl, with that naked wonder in her face, even as she was smiling in the way of a grown woman, and she said, "But some of them might live now till they're old."

"And then they'll die," he said.

"But at least they'll live as long as they can." And she laughed with the woman part of her that knew of absurdities.

"That's right," he said, "they'll live to a ripe old age and grow prosperous and dignified . . ."

She burst out laughing. "And see their children grown up!"

He kissed her on her lips, blessing her and her wish. "Oh, how I love you," she said with tears in her eyes. Then they walked home.

[1960]

The Misfits

Wind blew down from the mountains all night. A wild river of air swept and swirled across the dark sky and struck down against the blue desert and hissed back into the hills. The three cowboys slept under their blankets, their backs against the first upward curve of the circling mountains, their faces toward the desert of sage. The wind and its tidal washing seethed through their dreams, and when it stopped there was a lunar silence that caused Gay Langland to open his eyes. For the first time in three nights he could hear his own breathing, and in the new hush he looked up at the stars and saw how clear and bright they were. He felt happy and slid himself out of his blankets and stood up fully dressed.

On the silent plateau between the two mountain ranges Gay Langland was the only moving thing. He turned his head and then his body in a full circle, looking into the deep blue sky for sign of storm. He saw that it would be a good day and a quiet one. He walked a few yards from the two other sleepers and wet the sandy ground. The excitement of the stillness was awakening his body. He returned and lit the bundle of dry sage he had gathered last night, dropped some heavier wood on the quick flames, perched the blackened coffeepot on the stones surrounding the fire bed, and sat on one heel, staring at the fresh orange embers.

Gay Langland was forty-five years old but as limber as he had ever been in his life. The light of his face brightened when there were things to do, a nail to straighten, an animal to size up, and it dimmed when there was nothing in his hands, and his eyes then went sleepy. When there was something to be done in a place he stayed there, and when there was nothing to be done he went from it. He had a wife and two children less than a hundred miles from here whom he had not seen in more than three years. She had betrayed him and did not want him, but the children were naturally better off with their mother. When he felt lonely for them all he thought of them longingly, and when the feeling passed he was left without any question as to what he might do to bring them all back together again. He had been born and raised on rangeland, and he did not know that anything could be undone that was done, any more than falling rain could be stopped in midair. And he had a smile and a look on his face that was in accordance. His forehead was evenly tracked with deep ridges, as though his brows were always raised a little expectantly, slightly surprised, a little amused, and his mouth friendly. His ears stuck out, as they often do with little boys or young calves, and he had a boy's turned-up snub nose. But his skin was browned by the wind, and his small eyes looked and saw and, above all, were trained against showing fear.

Gay Langland looked up from the fire at the sky and saw the first delicate stain of pink. He went over to the sleepers and shook Guido Racanelli's arm. A grunt of salutation sounded in Guido's head, but he remained on his side with his eyes shut. "The sumbitch died off," Gay said to him. Guido listened, motionless, his eyes shut against the firelight, his bones warm in his fat. Gay wanted to shake him again and wake him, but in the last two days he had come to wonder whether Guido was not secretly considering not flying at all. The plane's engine was rattling its valves and one shock absorber was weak. Gay had known the pilot for years and he knew and respected his moods. Flying up and down these mountain gorges within feet of the rock walls was nothing you could pressure a man to do. But now that the wind had died Gay hoped very much that Guido would take off this morning and let them begin their work.

He got to his feet and again glanced skyward. Then he stood there thinking of Roslyn. And he had a strong desire to have money in his pocket that he had earned himself when he came to her tonight. The feeling had been returning again and again that he had somehow passed the kidding point and that he had to work again and earn his way as he always had before he met her. Not that he didn't work for her, but it wasn't the same. Driving her car, repairing her house, running errands—all that stuff wasn't what you would call work. Still, he thought, it was too. Yet, it wasn't either.

He stepped over to the other sleeper and shook him. Perce Howland opened his eyes.

"The sumbitch died, Perce," Gay said.

Perce's eyes looked toward the heavens and he nodded. Then he slid out of his blankets and walked past Gay and stood wetting the sand, breathing deeply as in sleep. Gay always found him humorous to watch when he woke up. Perce walked into things and sometimes stood wetting his own boots. He was a little like a child waking up, and his eyes now were still dreamy and soft.

Gay called over to him, "Better'n wages, huh, Perce?"

"Damn right," Perce muttered and returned to the fire, rubbing his skin against his clothes.

Gay kneeled by the fire again, scraping hot coals into a pile and setting the frying pan over them on stones. He could pick up hot things without feeling pain. Now he moved an ember with his finger.

"You make me nervous doing that," Perce said, looking down over his shoulder.

"Nothin' but fire," Gay said, pleased.

They were in silence for a moment, both of them enjoying the brightening air. "Guido goin' up?" Perce asked.

"Didn't say. I guess he's thinkin' about it."

"Be light pretty soon," Perce warned.

He glanced off to the closest range and saw the purple rocks rising in their mystery toward the faintly glowing stars. Perce Howland was twenty-two, hipless and tall, and he stood there as effortlessly as the mountains he was looking at, as though he had been created there in his dungarees, with the tight plaid shirt and the three-button cuffs, the broad-brimmed beige hat set back on his blond head, and his thumbs tucked into his belt so his fingers could touch the engraved belt buckle with his name spelled out under the raised figure of the bucking horse. It was his first

bucking-horse prize, and he loved to touch it when he stood waiting, and he liked to wait.

Perce had known Gay Langland for only five weeks, and Guido
for three days. He had met Gay in a Bowie bar, and Gay had
asked him where he was from and what he was doing, and he had
told Gay his story, which was the usual for most of the rodeo riders. He had come on down from Nevada, as he had done since he
was sixteen, to follow the local rodeos and win some money riding bucking horses, but this trip had been different, because he
had lost the desire to go back home again.

They had become good friends that night when Gay took him to
Roslyn's house to sleep, and when he woke in the morning he had
been surprised that an educated eastern woman should have been
so regular and humorous and interested in his opinions. So he had
been floating around with Roslyn and Gay Langland, and they
were comfortable to be with; Gay mostly, because Gay never
thought to say he ought to be making something of his life. Gay
made him feel it was all right to go from day to day and week to
week. Perce Howland did not trust anybody too far, and it was not
necessary to trust Gay because Gay did not want anything of him
or try to manipulate him. He just wanted a partner to go mustang-
ing, and Perce had never done anything like that and he wanted to
see how it was. And now he was here, sixty miles from the nearest
town, seven thousand feet up in the air, and for two days waiting
for the wind to die so the pilot could take off into the mountains
where the wild horses lived.

Perce looked out toward the desert, which was beginning to
show its silent horizon. "Bet the moon looks like this if anybody
could get there."

Gay Langland did not answer. In his mind he could feel the wild
horses grazing and moving about in the nearby mountains and he
wanted to get to them. Indicating Guido Racanelli, he said, "Give
him a shake, Perce. The sun's about up."

Perce started over to Guido, who moved before Perce reached
him. "Gettin' light, Guido," Perce said.

Guido Racanelli rolled upright on his great behind, his belly slung over his belt, and he inspected the brightening sky in the distance as though some personal message were out there for him. The pink reflected light brightened his face. The flesh around his eyes was white where the goggles protected his face, and the rest of his skin was burned brown by wind. His silences were more profound than the silences of others because his cheeks were so deep, like the melon-half cheeks of a baboon that curve forward from the mouth. Yet they were hard cheeks, as hard as his great belly. He looked like a jungle bird now, slowly turning his head to inspect the faraway sky, a serious bird with a brown face and white eyes. His head was entirely bald. He took off his khaki army cap and rubbed his fingers into his scalp.

Gay Langland stood up and walked to him and gave him his eggs and thick bacon on a tin plate. "Wind died, Guido," Gay said, standing there and looking down at the pilot.

"It doesn't mean much what it did down here." Guido pointed skyward with his thumb. "Up there's where it counts."

"Ain't no sign of wind up there," Gay said. Gay's eyes seemed amused. He did not want to seem committed to a real argument. "We got no more eggs, Guido," he warned.

Guido ate.

Now the sky flared with true dawn, like damp paper suddenly catching fire. Perce and Gay sat down on the ground facing Guido, and they all ate their eggs.

The shroud of darkness quickly slipped off the red truck which stood a few yards away. Then, behind it, the little plane showed itself. Guido Racanelli ate and sipped his coffee, and Gay Langland watched him with a weak smile and without speaking. Perce blinked contentedly at the brightening sky, slightly detached from the other two. He finished his coffee and slipped a chew of tobacco into his mouth and sucked on it.

It was a pink day now all around the sky.

Gay Langland made a line in the sand between his thighs and said, "You goin' up, Guido?" He looked at Guido directly and he was still smiling.

Guido thought for a moment. He was older, about fifty. His pronunciation was unaccountably eastern, with sharp r's. He sounded educated sometimes. He stared off toward the squat little plane. "Every once in a while I wonder what the hell it's all about," he said.

"What is?" Gay asked.

Perce watched Guido's face, thoroughly listening.

Guido felt their attention and spoke with pleasurable ease. He still stared past them at the plane. "I got a lousy valve. I know it, Gay."

"Been that way a long time, Guido," Gay said with sympathy.

"I know," Guido said. They were not arguing but searching now. "And we won't hardly get twenty dollars apiece out of it—there's only four or five horses back in there."

"We knew that, Guido," Gay said. They were in sympathy with each other.

"I might just get myself killed, for twenty dollars."

"Hell, you know them mountains," Gay said.

"You can't see wind, Gay," the pilot said.

Gay knew now that Guido was going up right away. He saw that Guido had just wanted to get all the dangers straight in his mind so he could see them and count them; then he would go out against them.

"You're flying along in and out of those passes and then you dive for the sons of bitches, and just when you're pulling up, some goddam gust presses you down and there you are."

"I know," Gay said.

There was silence. Guido sipped his coffee, staring off at the plane. "I just wonder about it every once in a while," the pilot said.

"Well, hell," Perce Howland said, "it's better than wages."

"You damn right it is, Perce," the pilot said thoughtfully.

"I seen guys get killed who never left the ground," Perce said.

The two older men knew that his father had been killed by a bull long ago and that he had seen his father die. He had had his own arms broken in rodeos and a Brahma bull had stepped on his chest.

"One rodeo near Salinas I see a fella get his head snapped right clear off his chest by a cable busted. They had this cable drawin' horses up onto a truck. I seen his head rollin' away like a bowlin' ball. Must've roll twenty-five yards before it hit a fence post and stopped." He spat tobacco juice and turned back to look at Guido. "It had a mustache. Funny thing, I never knowed that guy had a mustache. Never noticed it. Till I see it stop rolling and there it was, dust all over the mustache."

"That was a dusty mustache," Gay said, grinning against their deepening morbidity.

They all smiled. Then time hung for a moment as they waited. And at last Guido shifted onto one buttock and said, "Well, let's get gassed up."

Guido leaned himself to one side with his palm on the ground, then got to his feet by moving in a circle around this palm, and stood up. Gay and Perce Howland were already moving off toward the truck, Perce heisting up his dungarees over his breakfast-full stomach, and the older Gay more sprightly and intent. Guido stood holding one hand open over the fire, watching them loading the six enormous truck tires onto the bed of the truck. Each tire had a twenty-foot length of rope wired to it, and at the end of each rope was a loop. Before they swung the tires onto the truck Gay inspected the ropes to be sure they were securely knotted to the tires, and the loops open and ready for throwing.

Guido blinked against the warming sun, watching the other two, then he looked off to his right where the passes were, and the fingers of his mind felt around beyond those passes into the bowls and hollows of the mountains where last week he had spotted the small herd of wild horses grazing. Now he felt the lightness he had been hoping to feel for three days, the bodiless urge to fly. For three days he had kept away from the plane because a certain carelessness had been itching at him, a feeling that he always thought would lead him to his death. About five weeks ago he had come up to this desert with Gay Langland and he had chased seven mustangs out of the mountains. But this time he had dived to within a foot of the mountainside, and afterward, as they sat around the fire eating dinner, Guido had had the feeling that he had made that deep dive so he could die. And the thought of his dead wife had come to him again, and the other thought that always came into his mind with her dead face. It was the wonderment, the quiet pressing-in of the awareness that he had never wanted a woman after she had been buried with the still-born baby beside her in the graveyard outside Bowie. Seven years now he had waited for some real yearning for a woman, and nothing at all had come to him. It pleasured him to know that he was free of that, and it sometimes made him careless in the plane, as though some great bang and a wreckage would make him again what he had been. By now he could go around in Bowie for a week and only in an odd moment recall that he hadn't even looked at a girl walking by, and the feeling of carelessness would come on him, a kind of loose gaiety, as though everything was comical. Until he had made that dive and pulled out with his nose almost scraping the grass, and he had climbed upward with his mouth hanging open and his body in a sweat. So that through these past three days up here he had refused to let himself take off until the wind had utterly died, and he had clung to moroseness. He wanted to take off in the absolute grip of his own wits, leaving nothing to chance. Now there was no wind at all, and he felt he had pressed the sinister gaiety out of his mind. He left the dying fire and walked past Gay and Perce and down the gentle slope to the plane, looking like a stout, serious football coach before the kick-off.

He glanced over the fuselage and at the bald doughnut tires and he loved the plane. Again, as always, he looked at the weakened starboard shock absorber, which no longer held its spread so that the plane stood tilted a little to one side, and told himself that it was not serious. He heard the truck motor starting and he unfastened the knots of the ropes holding the plane to the spikes driven into the desert floor. Then the truck pulled up, and young Perce Howland dropped off and went over to the tail handle, gripped it, lifted the tail off the ground, and swung the plane around so she faced out across the endless desert and away from the mountains. Then they unwound the rubber hose from the gas drum on the truck and stuck the nozzle into the gas tank behind the engine, and Perce turned the pump crank.

Guido then walked around the wing and over to the cockpit, whose right door was folded down, leaving the inside open to the air. He reached in and took out his ripped leather flight jacket and got into it.

Perce stood leaning against the truck fender now, grinning. "That sure is a ventilated type jacket, Guido," he said.

Then Guido said, "I can't get my size any more." The jacket had one sleeve off at the elbow, and the dried leather was split open down the back, showing the lamb's-wool lining. He had bombed Germany in this jacket long ago. He reached in behind the seat and took out a goggle case, slipped his goggles out, replaced the case, set his goggles securely on his face, and reached in again and took out a shotgun pistol and four shells from a little wooden box beside his seat. He loaded the pistol and laid it carefully under his seat. Then he got into the cockpit, sat in his seat, drew the strap over his belly and buckled it. Meantime Gay had taken his position before the propeller.

Guido called through the open doorway of the cockpit, "Turn her over, Gay-boy!"

Gay stepped up to the propeller, glanced down behind his heels to be sure no stone waited to trip him when he stepped back, pulled down on the blade, and hopped back watchfully.

"Give her another!" Guido called in the silence.

Gay stepped up again, again glancing around his heels, and pulled the blade down. The engine inhaled and exhaled, and they could all hear the oily clank of her inner shafts turning loosely.

"Ignition on, Gay-boy!" Guido called and threw the switch.

This time Gay inspected the ground around him even more carefully and pulled his hatbrim down tighter on his head. Perce stood leaning on the truck's front fender, spitting and chewing, his eyes softly squinted against the brazen sun. Gay reached up and pulled the propeller down and jumped back. A puff of smoke floated up from the engine ports.

"Goddam car gas," Guido said. "Ignition on. Go again, Gay-boy!" They were buying low octane to save money.

Gay again stepped up to the propeller, swung the blade down, and the engine said its "Chaaahh!" and the ports breathed white smoke into the morning air. Gay walked over to Perce and stood beside him, watching. The fuselage shuddered and the propeller turned into a wheel, and the dust blew pleasantly from behind the plane and toward the mountains. Guido gunned her, and she tumbled toward the open desert, bumping along over the sage clumps and crunching whitened skeletons of cattle killed by the winter. The stiff-backed plane grew smaller, shouldering its way over the broken ground, and then its nose turned upward and there was space between the doughnut tires and the desert, and lazily it climbed, turning back the way it had come. It flew over the heads of Perce and Gay, and Guido waved down, a stranger now, fiercely goggled and wrapped in leather, and they could see him exposed to the waist, turning from them to look through the windshield at the mountains ahead of him. The plane flew away, climbing smoothly, losing itself against the orange and purple walls that vaulted up from the desert to hide from the cowboys' eyes the wild animals they wanted for themselves.

They would have at least two hours before the plane flew out of the mountains driving the horses before it, so they washed the three tin plates and the cups and stored them in the aluminum grub box. If Guido did find horses they would break camp and return to Bowie tonight, so they packed up their bedrolls with sailors' tidiness and laid them neatly side by side on the ground. The six great truck tires, each with its looped rope coiled within, lay in two piles on the bed of the truck. Gay Langland looked them over and touched them with his hand and stood for a moment trying to think if there was anything they were leaving behind. He jumped up on the truck to see that the cap was screwed tight on the gas drum, which was lashed to the back of the cab up front, and it was. Then he hopped down to the ground and got into the cab and started the engine. Perce was already sitting there with his hat tipped forward against the yellow sunlight pouring through the windshield. A thin and concerned border collie came trotting up as Gay started to close his door, and he invited her into the cab. She leaped up, and he snugged her into the space between the clutch and the left wall of the cab. "Damn near forgot Belle," he said, and they started off.

Gay owned the truck and he wanted to preserve the front end, which he knew could be twisted out of line on broken ground. So he started off slowly. They could hear the gas sloshing in the drum behind them outside. It was getting warm now. They rode in silence, staring ahead at the two-track trail they were following across the bone-cluttered sagebrush. Thirty miles ahead stood the lava mountains that were the northern border of this desert, the bed of a bowl seven thousand feet up, a place no one ever saw except the few cowboys searching for stray cattle every few months. People in Bowie, sixty miles away, did not know of this place. There were the two of them and the truck and the dog, and now that they were on the move they felt between them the comfort of purpose and their isolation, and Perce slumped in his seat, blinking as though he would go to sleep again, and Gay smoked a cigarette and let his body flow from side to side with the pitching of the truck.

There was a moving cloud of dust in the distance toward the left, and Gay said, "Antelope," and Perce tipped his hat back and looked. "Must be doin' sixty," he said, and Gay said, "More. I chased one once and I was doin' more than sixty and he lost me." Perce shook his head in wonder, and they turned to look ahead again.

After he had thought awhile Perce said, "We better get over to Largo by tomorrow if we're gonna get into that rodeo. They's gonna be a crowd trying to sign up for that one."

"We'll drive down in the morning," Gay said.

"I'll have to see about gettin' me some stock."

"We'll get there early tomorrow; you'll get stock if you come in early."

"Like to win some money," Perce said. "I just wish I get me a good horse down there."

"They be glad to fix you up, Perce. You're known pretty good around there now. They'll fix you up with some good stock," Gay said. Perce was one of the best bronc riders, and the rodeos liked to have it known he would appear.

Then there was silence. Gay had to hold the gear-shift lever in high or it would slip out into neutral when they hit bumps. The transmission fork was worn out, he knew, and the front tires were going too. He dropped one hand to his pants pocket and felt the four silver dollars he had from the ten Roslyn had given him when they had left her days ago.

As though he had read Gay's mind, Perce said, "Roslyn would've liked it up here. She'd liked to have seen that antelope, I bet." Perce grinned as both of them usually did at Roslyn's eastern surprise at everything they did and saw and said.

"Yeah," Gay said, "she likes to see things." Through the corners of his eyes he watched the younger man, who was looking ahead with a little grin on his face. "She's damned good sport, old Roslyn," Gay said.

"Sure is," Perce Howland said. And Gay watched him for any sign of guile, but there was only a look of glad appreciation. "First woman like that I ever met," the younger man said.

"They's more," Gay said. "Some of them eastern women fool you sometimes. They got education but they're good sports. And damn good *women* too, some of them."

There was a silence. Then the younger man asked, "You get to know a lot of them? Eastern women?"

"Ah, I get one once in a while," Gay said.

"Only educated women I ever know, they was back home near Teachers College. Students. Y'know," he said, warming to the memory, "I used to think, hell, education's everything. But when I saw the husbands some of them got married to—schoolteachers and everything, why I don't give them much credit. And they just as soon climb on a man as tell him good morning. I was teachin' them to ride for a while near home."

"Just because a woman's educated don't mean much. Woman's a woman," Gay said. The image of his wife came into his mind. For a moment he wondered if she was still living with the same man he had beaten up when he discovered them together in a parked car six years ago.

"You divorced?" Perce asked.

"No. I never bothered with it," Gay said. It always surprised him how Perce said just what was on his mind sometimes. "How'd you know I was thinkin' of that?" he asked, grinning with embarrassment. But he was too curious to keep silent.

"Hell, I didn't know," Perce said.

"You're always doin' that. I think of somethin' and you go ahead and say it."

"That's funny," Perce said.

They rode on in silence. They were nearing the middle of the desert, where they would turn east. Gay was driving faster now because he wanted to get to the rendezvous and sit quietly waiting for the plane to appear. He held on to the gear-shift lever and felt it trying to spring out of high and into neutral. It would have to be fixed. The time was coming fast when he would need about fifty dollars or have to sell the truck, because it would be useless without repairs. Without a truck and without a horse he would be down to what was in his pocket.

Perce spoke out of the silence. "If I don't win Saturday I'm gonna have to do somethin' for money."

"Goddam, you always say what's in my mind."

Perce laughed. His face looked very young and pink. "Why?"

"I was just now thinkin'," Gay said, "what I'm gonna do for money."

"Well, Roslyn give you some," Perce said.

He said it innocently, and Gay knew it was innocent, and yet he felt angry blood moving into his neck. Something had happened in these five weeks, and Gay did not know for sure what it was. Roslyn had taken to calling Perce cute, and now and again she would bend over and kiss him on the back of the neck when he was sitting in the living-room chair, drinking with them.

Not that that meant anything in itself, because he'd known eastern women before who'd do something like that and it was just their way. Especially college-graduate divorced women. What he wondered at was Perce's way of hardly even noticing what she did to him. Sometimes it was like he'd already had her and could ignore her, the way a man will who knows he's boss. But then

Gay thought it might just be that he really wasn't interested, or maybe that he was keeping cool in deference to Gay.

Again Gay felt a terrible longing to earn money working. He sensed the bottom of his life falling if it turned out Roslyn had really been loving this boy beside him. It had happened to him once before with his wife, but this frightened him more and he did not know exactly why. Not that he couldn't do without Roslyn. There wasn't anybody or anything he couldn't do without. She was about his age and full of laughter that was not laughter and gaiety that was not gaiety and adventurousness that was labored, and he knew all this perfectly well even as he laughed with her and was high with her in the bars and rodeos. He had only lived once, and that was when he had had his house and his wife and his children. He knew the difference, but you never kept anything, and he had never particularly thought about keeping anything or losing anything. He had been all his life like Perce Howland, sitting beside him now, a man moving on or ready to. It was only when he discovered his wife with a stranger that he knew he had had a stake to which he had been pleasurably tethered. He had not seen her or his children for years and only rarely thought about any of them. Any more than his father had thought of him very much after the day he had gotten on his pony, when he was fourteen, to go to town from the ranch, and had kept going into Montana and stayed there for three years. He lived in this country as his father did, and it was the same endless range wherever he went, and it connected him sufficiently with his father and his wife and his children. All might turn up sometime in some town or at some rodeo, where he might happen to look over his shoulder and see his daughter or one of his sons, or they might never turn up. He had neither left anyone nor not-left as long as they were all alive on these ranges, for everything here was always beyond the farthest shot of vision and far away, and mostly he had worked alone or with one or two men, between distant mountains anyway.

In the distance now he could see the shimmering wall of the

heat waves rising from the clay flatland they wanted to get to. Now they were approaching closer, and it opened to them beyond the heat waves, and they could see once again how vast it was, a prehistoric lake bed thirty miles long by seventeen miles wide, couched between the two mountain ranges. It was a flat, beige waste without grass or bush or stone, where a man might drive a car at a hundred miles an hour with his hands off the wheel and never hit anything at all. They drove in silence. The truck stopped bouncing as the tires rolled over harder ground where there were fewer sage clumps. The waves of heat were dense before them, nearly touchable. Now the truck rolled smoothly and they were on the clay lake bed, and when they had gone a few hundred yards onto it Gay pulled up and shut off the engine. The air was still in a dead, sunlit silence. When he opened his door he could hear a squeak in the hinge he had never noticed before. When they walked around they could hear their shirts rasping against their backs and the brush of a sleeve against their trousers.

They stood on the clay ground, which was as hard as concrete, and turned to look the way they had come. They looked back toward the mountains at whose feet they had camped and slept, and scanned their ridges for Guido's plane. It was too early for him, and they made themselves busy, taking the gas drum off the truck and setting it a few yards away on the ground, because they would want the truck bed clear when the time came to run the horses down. Then they climbed up and sat inside the tires with their necks against the tire beads and their legs hanging over.

Perce said, "I sure hope they's five up in there."

"Guido saw five, he said."

"He said he wasn't sure if one wasn't only a colt," Perce said.

Gay let himself keep silent. He felt he was going to argue with Perce. He watched Perce through the corners of his eyes, saw the flat, blond cheeks and the strong, lean neck, and there was something tricky about Perce now. "How long you think you'll be stayin' around here, Perce?" he asked.

They were both watching the distant ridges for a sign of the plane.

"Don't know," Perce said and spat over the side of the truck. "I'm gettin' a little tired of this, though."

"Well, it's better than wages, Perce."

"Hell, yes. Anything's better than wages."

Gay's eyes crinkled. "You're a real misfit, boy."

"That suits me fine," Perce said. They often had this conversation and savored it. "Better than workin' for some goddam cow outfit buckarooin' so somebody else can buy gas for his Cadillac."

"Damn right," Gay said.

"Hell, Gay, you are the most misfitted man I ever saw and you done all right."

"I got no complaints," Gay said.

"I don't want nothin' and I don't want to want nothin'."

"That's the way, boy."

Gay felt closer to him again and he was glad for it. He kept his eyes on the ridges far away. The sun felt good on his shoulders. "I think he's havin' trouble with them sumbitches up in there."

Perce stared out at the ridges. "Ain't two hours yet." Then he turned to Gay. "These mountains must be cleaned out by now, ain't they?"

"Just about," Gay said. "Just a couple small herds left. Can't do much more around here."

"What you goin' to do when you got these cleaned out?"

"Might go north, I think. Supposed to be some big herds in around Thighbone Mountain and that range up in there."

"How far's that?"

"North about a hundred miles. If I can get Guido interested."

Perce smiled. "He don't like movin' around much, does he?"

"He's just misfitted like the rest of us," Gay said. "He don't want nothin'." Then he added, "They wanted him for an airline pilot flyin' up into Montana and back. Good pay too."

"Wouldn't do it, huh?"

"Not Guido," Gay said, grinning. "Might not like some of the passengers, he told them."

Both men laughed, and Perce shook his head in admiration of

Guido. Then he said, "They wanted me take over the ridin' academy up home. I thought about that. Two hundred a month and board. Easy work too. You don't hardly have to ride at all. Just stand around and see the customers get satisfied and put them girls off and on."

He fell silent. Gay knew the rest. It was the same story always. It brought him closer to Perce, and it was what he had liked about Perce in the first place. Perce didn't like wages either. He had come on Perce in a bar where the boy was buying drinks for everybody with his rodeo winnings, and his hair still clotted with blood from a bucking horse's kick an hour earlier. Roslyn had offered to get a doctor for him and he had said, "Thank you kindly. But I ain't bad hurt. If you're bad hurt you gonna die and the doctor can't do nothin', and if you ain't bad hurt you get better anyway without no doctor."

Now it suddenly came upon Gay that Perce had known Roslyn before they had met in the bar. He stared at the boy's profile. "Want to come up north with me if I go?" he asked.

Perce thought a moment. "Think I'll stay around here. Not much rodeoin' up north."

"I might find a pilot up there, maybe. And Roslyn drive us up in her car."

Perce turned to him, a little surprised. "Would she go up there?"

"Sure. She's a damn good sport," Gay said. He watched Perce's eyes, which had turned interested and warm.

Perce said, "Well, maybe; except to tell you the truth, Gay, I never feel comfortable takin' these horses for chicken feed."

"Somebody's goin' to take them if we don't."

"I know," Perce said. He turned to watch the far ridges again. "Just seems to me they belong up there."

"They ain't doin' nothin' up there but eatin' out good cattle range. The cow outfits shoot them down if they see them."

"I know," Perce said.

"They don't even bother takin' them to slaughter. They just rot up there if the cow outfits get to them."

"I know," Perce said.

There was silence. Neither bug nor lizard nor rabbit moved on the great basin around them, and the sun warmed their necks and their thighs. Gay said, "I'd as soon sell them for riding horses but they ain't big enough, except for a kid. And the freight on them's more than they're worth. You saw them—they ain't nothin' but skinny horses."

"I just don't know if I'd want to see like a hundred of them goin' for chicken feed, though. I don't mind like five or six, but a hundred's a lot of horses. I don't know."

Gay thought. "Well, if it ain't this it's wages. Around here anyway." He was speaking of himself and explaining himself.

"I'd just as soon ride buckin' horses and make out that way, Gay." Perce turned to him. "Although I might go up north with you. I don't know."

"Roslyn wouldn't come out here at first," Gay said, "but soon as she saw what they looked like she stopped complainin' about it. You didn't hear her complainin' about it."

"I ain't complainin', Gay. I just don't know. Seems to me God put them up there and they belong up there. But I'm doin' it and I guess I'd go on doin' it. I don't know."

"Sounds to me like the newspapers. They want their steaks, them people in town, but they don't want castration or branding or cleanin' wild horses off the ranges."

"Hell, man, I castrated more bulls than I got hairs on my head," Perce said.

"I better get the glasses," Gay said and slid out of the tire in which he had been lounging and off the truck. He went to the cab and reached in and brought out a pair of binoculars, blew on the lenses, mounted the truck, and sat on a tire with his elbows resting on his knees. He put the glasses to his eyes and focused them. The mountains came up close with their pocked blue hides. He found the pass through which he believed the plane would come and studied its slopes and scanned the air above it. Anger was still warming him. "God put them up there!" Why, Christ, God put everything everywhere. Did that mean you couldn't eat chickens, for instance, or beef? His dislike for Perce was flowing into him again.

They heard the shotgun off in the sky somewhere and they

stopped moving. Gay narrowed his eyes and held the binoculars perfectly still.

"See anything?" Perce asked.

"He's still in the pass, I guess," Gay said.

They sat still, watching the sky over the pass. The moments went by. The sun was making them perspire now, and Gay wiped his wet eyebrows with the back of one hand. They heard the shotgun again from the general sky. Gay spoke without lowering the glasses. "He's probably blasting them out of some corner."

Perce quickly arched out of his tire. "I see him," he said quickly. "I see him glintin', I see the plane."

It angered Gay that Perce had seen the plane first without glasses. In the glasses Gay could see it clearly now. It was flying out of the pass, circling back, and disappearing into the pass again. "He's got them in the pass now. Just goin' back in for them."

"Can you see them?" Perce asked.

"He ain't got them in the clear yet. He just went back in for them."

Now through his glasses he could see moving specks on the ground where the pass opened onto the desert table. "I see them," he said. He counted, moving his lips. "One, two, three, four. Four and a colt."

"We gonna take the colt?" Perce asked.

"Hell, can't take the mare without the colt."

Perce said nothing. Then Gay handed him the glasses. "Take a look."

Gay slid off the truck bed and went forward to the cab and opened its door. His dog lay shivering on the floor under the pedals. He snapped his fingers, and she warily got up and leaped down to the ground and stood there quivering, as she always did when wild horses were coming. He watched her sit and wet the ground, and how she moved with such care and concern and fear, sniffing the ground and moving her head in slow motion and setting her paws down as though the ground had hidden explosives everywhere. He left her there and climbed onto the truck and sat on a tire beside Perce, who was still looking through the glasses.

"He's divin' down on them. God, they sure can run!"

"Let's have a look," Gay said and reached out, and Perce handed him the glasses, saying, "They're comin' on fast."

Gay watched the horses in the glasses. The plane was starting down toward them from the arc of its climb. They swerved as the roaring motor came down over them, lifted their heads, and galloped faster. They had been running now for over an hour and would slow down when the plane had to climb after a dive and the motor's noise grew quieter. As Guido climbed again Gay and Perce heard a shot, distant and harmless, and the shot sped the horses on again as the plane took time to bank and turn. Then, as they slowed, the plane returned over them, diving down over their backs, and their heads shot up again and they galloped until the engine's roar receded over them. The sky was clear and lightly blue, and only the little plane swung back and forth across the desert like the glinting tip of a magic wand, and the horses came on toward the vast stripped clay bed where the truck was parked.

The two men on the truck exchanged the glasses from time to time. Now they sat upright on the tires, waiting for the horses to reach the edge of the lake bed, when Guido would land the plane and they would take off with the truck. And now the horses stopped.

"They see the heat waves," Gay said, looking through the glasses. He could see the horses trotting with raised, alarmed heads along the edge of the barren lake bed, which they feared because the heat waves rose from it like liquid in the air and yet their nostrils did not smell water, and they dared not move ahead onto unknowable territory. The plane dived down on them, and they scattered but would not go forward onto the lake bed from the cooler, sage-dotted desert behind them. Now the plane banked high in the air and circled out behind them over the desert and banked again and came down within yards of the ground and roared in behind them almost at the height of their heads, and as it passed over them, rising, the men on the truck could hear the shotgun. Now the horses leaped forward onto the lake bed, all scattered and heading in different directions, and they were only trotting, exploring the ground under their feet and the strange, superheated air in their nostrils. Gradually, as the plane wound

around the sky to dive again, they closed ranks and slowly galloped shoulder to shoulder out onto the borderless lake bed. The
colt galloped a length behind with its nose nearly touching the
mare's long silky tail.

"That's a big mare," Perce said. His eyes were still dreamy and
his face was calm, but his skin had reddened.

"She's a bigger mare than usual up here, ya," Gay said.

Both men watched the little herd now, even as they got to their
feet on the truck. There was the big mare, as large as any full-
grown horse, and both of them downed their surprise at the sight
of her. They knew the mustang herds lived in total isolation and
that inbreeding had reduced them to the size of large ponies. The
herd swerved now and they saw the stallion. He was smaller than
the mare but still larger than any Gay had brought down before.
The other two horses were small, the way mustangs ought to be.

The plane was coming down for a landing now. Gay and Perce
Howland moved to the forward edge of the truck's bed where a
strap of white webbing was strung at hip height between two stan-
chions stuck into sockets at the corners of the truck. They drew
another web strap from one stanchion to the other and stood inside
the two. Perce tied the back strap to his stanchion. Then they
turned around inside their harnesses and each reached into a tire
behind him and drew out a coil of rope whose end hung in a loop.
They glanced out on the lake bed and saw Guido taxiing toward
them, and they stood waiting for him. He cut the engine twenty
yards from the truck and leaped out of the open cockpit before the
plane had halted. He lashed the tail of the plane to a rope that was
attached to a spike driven into the clay and trotted over to the
truck, lifting his goggles off and stuffing them into his torn jacket
pocket. Perce and Gay called out laughingly to him, but he seemed
hardly to have seen them. His face was puffed with preoccupation.
He jumped into the cab of the truck, and the collie dog jumped in
after him and sat on the floor, quivering. He started the truck and
roared ahead across the flat clay into the watery waves of heat.

They could see the herd standing still in a small clot of dots more
than two miles off. The truck rolled smoothly, and in the cab Guido

glanced at the speedometer and saw it was past sixty. He had to be careful not to turn over and he dropped back to fifty-five. Gay, on the right front corner of the truck bed, and Perce Howland on the left, pulled their hats down to their eyebrows and hefted the looped ropes, which the wind was threatening to coil and foul in their palms. Guido knew that Gay Langland was a good roper and that Perce was unsure, so he headed for the herd's left in order to come up to them on Gay's side of the truck if he could. This whole method—the truck, the tires, the ropes, and the plane—was Guido's invention, and once again he felt the joy of having thought of it all. He drove with both heavy hands on the wheel and his left foot ready over the brake pedal. He reached for the shift lever to feel if it was going to spring out of gear and into neutral, but it felt tight, and if they did not hit a bump he could rely on it. The herd had started to walk but stopped again now, and the horses were looking at the truck, ears raised, necks stretched up and forward. Guido smiled a little. They looked silly to him standing there, but he knew and pitied them their ignorance.

The wind smashed against the faces of Perce and Gay standing on the truck bed. The brims of their hats flowed up and back from a low point in front, and their faces were dark red. They saw the horses watching their approach at a standstill. And as they roared closer and closer they saw that this herd was beautiful.

Perce Howland turned his head to Gay, who glanced at him at the same time. There had been much rain this spring, and this herd must have found good pasture. They were well rounded and shining. The mare was almost black, and the stallion and the two others were deep brown. The colt was curly-coated and had a gray sheen. The stallion dipped his head suddenly and turned his back on the truck and galloped. The others turned and clattered after him, with the colt running alongside the mare. Guido pressed down on the gas and the truck surged forward, whining. They were a few yards behind the animals now and they could see the bottoms of their hoofs, fresh hoofs that had never been shod. They could see the full manes flying and the thick and long black tails that would hang down to their fetlocks when they were still.

The truck was coming abreast of the mare now, and beside her the others galloped with only a loud ticking noise on the clay. It was a gentle tacking clatter for they were light-footed and unshod. They were slim-legged and wet after running almost two hours in this alarm, but as the truck drew alongside the mare and Gay began twirling his loop above his head the whole herd wheeled away to the right, and Guido jammed the gas pedal down and swung with them, but they kept galloping in a circle, and he did not have the speed to keep abreast of them so he slowed down and fell behind them a few yards until they would straighten out and move ahead again. And they wheeled like circus horses, slower now, for they were at the edge of their strength, and suddenly Guido saw a breadth between the stallion and the two browns and he sped in between, cutting the mare off at the left with her colt. Now the horses stretched, the clatter quickened. Their hind legs flew straight back and their necks stretched low and forward. Gay whirled his loop over his head, and the truck came up alongside the stallion, whose lungs were hoarsely screaming with exhaustion, and Gay flung the noose. It fell on the stallion's head, and with a whipping of the lead Gay made it fall over his neck. The horse swerved away to the right and stretched the rope until the tire was pulled off the truck bed and dragged along the hard clay. The three men watched from the slowing truck as the stallion, with startled eyes, pulled the giant tire for a few yards, then leaped up with his forelegs in the air and came down facing the tire and trying to back away from it. Then he stood still, heaving, his hind legs dancing in an arc from right to left and back again as he shook his head in the remorseless noose.

As soon as he was sure the stallion was secure Guido scanned the lake bed and without stopping turned sharply left toward the mare and the colt, which were trotting idly together by themselves. The two browns were already disappearing toward the north, but Guido knew they would halt soon because they were tired, while the mare might continue to the edge of the lake bed and back into her familiar hills where the truck could not follow. He straightened the truck and jammed down the gas pedal. In a minute he was straight on behind her, and he drew up on her left side because the colt was running on her right. She was very heavy, he saw, and he wondered now if she was a mustang at all. As he drove alongside her his eyes ran across her flanks, seeking out a brand, but she seemed unmarked. Then through his right window he saw the loop flying out and down over her head, and he saw her head fly up, and then she fell back. He turned to the right, braking with his left boot, and he saw her dragging a tire and coming to a halt, with the free colt watching her and trotting very close beside her. Then he headed straight ahead across the flat toward two specks, which rapidly enlarged until they became the two browns, which were at a standstill and watching the oncoming truck. He came in between them, and as they galloped Perce on the left roped one, and Gay roped the other almost at the same time. And Guido leaned his head out of his window and yelled up at Perce, who was on the truck bed on his side. "Good boy!" he hollered, and Perce let himself return an excited grin, although there seemed to be some trouble in his eyes.

Guido made an easy half circle and headed back to the mare and the colt, and in a few minutes he slowed to a halt some twenty yards away and got out of the cab. The dog remained sitting on the floor of the cab, her body shaking all over.

The three men approached the mare. She had never seen a man, and her eyes were wide with fear. Her rib cage stretched and collapsed very rapidly, and there was a trickle of blood coming out of her nostrils. She had a heavy dark brown mane, and her tail nearly touched the ground. The colt with dumb eyes shifted about on its silly bent legs, trying to keep the mare between itself and the men, and the mare kept shifting her rump to shield the colt from them.

They wanted now to move the noose higher up on the mare's neck because it had fallen on her from the rear and was tight around the middle of her neck, where it could choke her if she kept pulling against the weight of the tire. They had learned from previous forays that they could not leave a horse tied that way without the danger of suffocation, and they wanted them alive until they could bring a larger truck from Bowie and load them on it.

Gay was the best roper so Perce and Guido stood by as he twirled a noose over his head, then let it fall open softly, just behind the forefeet of the mare. They waited for a moment, then approached her, and she backed a step. Then Gay pulled sharply on the rope, and her forefeet were tied together. Then with another rope Gay lass'd her hind feet, and she swayed and fell to the ground on her side. Her body swelled and contracted, but she seemed resigned. The colt stretched its nose to her tail and stood there as the men came to the mare and spoke quietly to her, and Guido bent down and opened the noose and slipped it up under her jaw. They inspected her for a brand, but she was clean.

"Never see a horse that size up here," Gay said to Guido.

Guido stood there looking down at the great mare.

Perce said, "Maybe wild horses was all big once," and he looked to Guido for confirmation.

Guido bent and sat on his heels and opened the mare's mouth, and the other two looked in with him. "She's fifteen if she's a day," Gay said, and to Perce he said, "She wouldn't be around much longer anyway."

"Ya, she's old," Perce agreed, and his eyes were filled with thought.

Guido stood up, and the three went back to the truck. Perce hopped up and sat on the truck bed with his legs dangling, and Gay sat in the cab with Guido. They drove across the lake bed to the stallion and stopped, and the three of them walked toward him.

"Ain't a bad-lookin' horse," Perce said.

They stood inspecting the horse for a moment. He was standing still now, heaving for breath and bleeding from the nostrils. His head was down, holding the rope taut, and he was looking at them with his deep brown eyes that were like the lenses of enormous binoculars. Gay got his rope ready in his hand. "He ain't nothin' but a misfit," he said, "except for some kid. You couldn't run cattle with him, and he's too small for a riding horse."

"He is small," Perce conceded. "Got a nice neck, though."

"Oh, they're nice-*lookin'* horses, some of them," Guido said. "What the hell you goin' to do with them, though? Cost more to ship them anywhere than they'd bring."

Gay twirled the loop over his head, and they spread out around the stallion. "They're just old misfit horses, that's all," he said, and he flung the rope behind the stallion's forelegs, and the horse backed a step, and he drew the rope and the noose bit into the horse's lower legs, drawing them together, and the horse swayed but would not fall.

"Take hold," Gay called to Perce, who ran around the horse and grabbed onto the rope and held it taut. Then Gay went back to the truck, got another rope, returned to the rear of the horse, and looped the hind legs. But the stallion would not fall.

Guido stepped closer to push him over, but the horse swung his head and showed his teeth, and Guido stepped back. "Pull on it!" Guido yelled to Gay and Perce, and they pulled on their ropes to trip the stallion, but he righted himself and stood there bound by the head to the tire and his feet by the two ropes the men held. Then Guido hurried over to Perce and took the rope from him and walked with it toward the rear of the horse and pulled hard. The stallion's forefeet slipped back, and he came down on his knees and his nose struck the clay ground and he snorted as he struck, but he would not topple over and stayed there on his knees as though he were bowing to something, with his nose propping up his head against the ground and his sharp bursts of breath blowing up dust in little clouds under his nostrils.

Now Guido gave the rope back to young Perce Howland, who held it taut, and he came up alongside the stallion's neck and laid his hands on the side of the neck and pushed, and the horse fell over onto his flank and lay there; and, like the mare, when he felt the ground against his body he seemed to let himself out, and for the first time his eye blinked and his breath came now in sighs and no longer fiercely. Guido shifted the noose up under the jaw, and they opened the ropes around the hoofs, and when the horse felt his legs free he first raised his head curiously and then clattered up and stood there looking at them, from one to the other, blood dripping from his nostrils and a stain of deep red on both dusty knees.

For a moment the three men stood watching him to be sure he was tightly noosed around the neck. Only the clacking of the truck's engine sounded on the enormous floor between the mountains, and the wheezing inhale of the horse and his blowing out of air. Then the men moved without hurrying to the truck, and Gay stored his two extra ropes behind the seat of the cab and got behind the wheel with Guido beside him, and Perce climbed onto the back of the truck and lay down facing the sky, his palms under his head.

Gay headed the truck south toward where they knew the plane was, although it was still beyond their vision. Guido was slowly catching his breath, and now he lighted a cigarette, puffed it, and rubbed his left hand into his bare scalp. He sat gazing out the windshield and the side window. "I'm sleepy," he said.

"What you reckon?" Gay asked.

"What you?" Guido said. He had dust in his throat, and his voice sounded high and almost girlish.

"That mare might be six hundred pounds."

"I'd say about that, Gay," Guido agreed.

"About four hundred apiece for the browns and a little more for the stallion."

"That's about the way I figured."

"What's that come to?"

Guido thought. "Nineteen hundred, maybe two thousand," he said.

They fell silent, figuring the money. Two thousand pounds at six cents a pound came to a hundred and twenty dollars. The colt might make it a few dollars more, but not much. Figuring the gas for the plane and the truck, and twelve dollars for their groceries, they came to the figure of a hundred dollars for the three of them. Guido would get forty-five dollars, since he had used his plane, and Gay would get thirty-five including the use of his truck, and Perce Howland, if he agreed, as he undoubtedly would, would have the remaining twenty.

They fell silent after they had said the figures, and Gay drove in thought. Then he said, "We should've watered them the last time. They can pick up a lot of weight if you let them water."

"Yeah, let's be sure to do that," Guido said.

They knew they would as likely as not forget to water the horses before they unloaded them at the dealer's lot in Bowie. They would be in a hurry to unload and to be free of the horses, and only later, as they were doing now, would they remind themselves that by letting the horses drink their fill they could pick up another fifteen or twenty dollars in added weight. They were not thinking of the money any more, once they had figured it, and if Perce were to object to his smaller share they would both hand him a five- or ten-dollar bill or more if he wanted it.

Gay stopped the truck beside the plane at the edge of the lake bed. The tethered horses were far away now, except for the mare and her colt, which stood in clear view less than half a mile off. Guido opened his door and said to Gay, "See you in town. Let's get the other truck tomorrow morning."

"Perce wants to go over to Largo and sign up for the rodeo tomorrow," Gay said. "Tell ya—we'll go in and get the truck and come back here this afternoon maybe. Maybe we bring them in tonight."

"All right, if you want to. I'll see you boys tomorrow," Guido said, and he got out and stopped for a moment to talk to Perce.

"Perce?" he said. Perce propped himself up on one elbow and looked down at him. He looked very sleepy. Guido smiled. "You sleeping?"

Perce's eyelids almost seemed swollen, and his face was indrawn and troubled. "I was about to," he said.

Guido let the reprimand pass. "We figure about a hundred dollars clear. Twenty all right for you?"

"Ya, twenty's all right," Perce said, blinking heavily. He hardly seemed to be listening.

"See you in town," Guido said and turned and waddled off to the plane, where Gay was already standing with his hands on the propeller blade. Guido got in, and Gay swung the blade down and the engine started immediately. Guido waved to Gay and Perce, who raised one hand slightly from the truck bed. Guido gunned the plane, and it trundled off and into the sky, and the two men on the ground watched as it flew toward the mountains and away.

Gay returned to the truck, and as he started to climb in behind the wheel he looked at Perce, who was still propped up on one elbow, and he said, "Twenty all right?" And he said this because he thought Perce looked hurt.

"Heh? Ya, twenty's all right," Perce answered. Then he let himself down from the truck bed, and Gay got behind the wheel. Perce stood beside the truck and wet the ground while Gay waited for him. Then Perce got into the cab, and they drove off.

The mare and her colt stood between them and the sage desert toward which they were heading. Perce stared out the window at the mare, and he saw that she was watching them apprehensively but not in real alarm, and the colt was lying upright on the clay, its head nodding slightly as though it would soon fall asleep. Perce looked long at the colt as they approached, and he thought about how it waited there beside the mare, unbound and free to go off, and he said to Gay, "Ever hear of a colt leave a mare?"

"Not that young a colt," Gay said. "He ain't goin' nowhere." And he glanced to look at Perce.

They passed the mare and colt and left them behind, and Perce laid his head back and closed his eyes. His tobacco swelled out his left cheek, and he let it soak there.

Now the truck left the clay lake bed, and it pitched and rolled on the sage desert. They would return to their camp and pick up their bedrolls and cooking implements and then drive to the road, which was almost fifteen miles beyond the camp across the desert.

"Think I'll go back to Roslyn's tonight," Gay said.

"Okay," Perce said and did not open his eyes.

"We can pick them up in the morning and then take you down to Largo."

"Okay," Perce said.

Gay thought about Roslyn. She would probably razz them about all the work they had done for a few dollars, saying they were too dumb to figure in their labor time and other hidden expenses. To hear her, sometimes they hadn't made any profit at all. "Roslyn goin' to feel sorry for the colt," Gay said, "so might as well not mention it."

Perce opened his eyes, and with his head resting on the back of the seat he looked out the window at the mountains. "Hell, she feeds that dog of hers canned dogfood, doesn't she?"

Gay felt closer to Perce again and he smiled. "Sure does."

"Well, what's she think is in the can?"

"She knows what's in the can."

"There's wild horses in the can," Perce said, almost to himself.

They drove in silence for a while. Then Perce said, "That's what beats me."

After a few moments Gay said, "You comin' back to Roslyn's with me or you gonna stay in town?"

"I'd just as soon go back with you."

"Okay," Gay said. He felt good about going into her cabin now. There would be her books on the shelves he had built for her, and they would have some drinks, and Perce would fall asleep on the couch, and they would go into the bedroom together. He liked to come back to her after he had worked, more than when he had only driven her here and there or just stayed around her place. He liked his own money in his pocket. And he tried harder to visualize how it would be with her, and he thought of himself being forty-six soon, and then nearing fifty. She would go back East one day, he knew, maybe this year, maybe next. He wondered again when he would begin turning gray and how he would look with gray hair, and he set his jaw against the picture of himself gray and an old man.

Perce spoke, sitting up in his seat. "I want to phone my mother. Damn, I haven't called her all year." He stared out the window at the mountains. He had the memory of how the colt looked, and he wished it would be gone when they returned in the morning. Then he said, "I got to get to Largo tomorrow and register."

"We'll go," Gay said.

"I could use a good win," he said. He thought of five hundred dollars now, and of the many times he had won five hundred dollars. "You know something, Gay?" he said.

"Huh?"

"I'm never goin' to amount to a damn thing." Then he laughed.

He was hungry, and he laughed without restraint for a moment and then laid his head back and closed his eyes.

"I told you that first time I met you, didn't I?" Gay grinned. He felt the mood coming on for some drinks at Roslyn's.

Then Perce spoke. "That colt won't bring two dollars anyway. What you say we just left him there?"

"Why, you know what he'd do?" Gay said. "He'd just follow the truck right into town."

"I guess he would at that," Perce said. He spat a stream of juice out the window.

They reached the camp in twenty minutes and loaded the gasoline drum onto three bedrolls and the aluminum grub box in the truck and drove on toward Bowie. After they had driven for fifteen minutes without speaking, Gay said he wanted to go north very soon for the hundreds of horses that were supposed to be in the mountains there. But Perce Howland had fallen fast asleep beside him. Gay wanted to talk about that expedition because as they neared Bowie he began to visualize Roslyn razzing them again, and it was clear to him that he had somehow failed to settle anything for himself; he had put in three days for thirty-five dollars, and there would be no way to explain it so it made sense, and it would be embarrassing. And yet he knew that it had all been the way it ought to be even if he could never explain it to her or anyone else. He reached out and nudged Perce, who opened his eyes and lolled his head over to face him. "You comin' up to Thighbone with me, ain't you?"

"Okay," Perce said and went back to sleep.

Gay felt more peaceful now that the younger man would not be leaving him. He drove in contentment.

The sun shone hot on the beige plain all day. Neither fly nor bug nor snake ventured out on the waste to molest the four horses tethered there, or the colt. They had run nearly two hours at a gallop, and as the afternoon settled upon them they pawed the hard ground for water, but there was none. Toward evening the wind came up, and they backed into it and faced the mountains from which they had come. From time to time the stallion caught the smell of the pastures up there, and he started to walk toward the vaulted fields in which he had grazed; but the tire bent his neck around, and after a few steps he would turn to face it and leap into the air with his forelegs striking at the sky, and then he would come down and be still again.

With the deep blue darkness the wind blew faster, tossing their manes and flinging their long tails in between their legs. The cold of night raised the colt onto its legs, and it stood close to the mare for warmth. Facing the southern range, five horses blinked under the green glow of the risen moon, and they closed their eyes and slept. The colt settled again on the hard ground and lay under the mare.

In the high hollows of the mountains the grass they had cropped this morning straightened in the darkness. On the lusher swards, which were still damp with the rains of spring, their hoofprints had begun to disappear. When the first pink glow of another morning lit the sky the colt stood up, and as it had always done at dawn it walked waywardly for water. The mare shifted and her bone hoofs ticked the clay. The colt turned its head and returned to her and stood at her side with vacant eyes, its nostrils sniffing the warming air.

[1957]

Glimpse at a Jockey

It's like this saloon, it's the best in New York, right? You can't even sit down in the can here without a hundred-dollar bill in each ear, look over there at that gray-hair loafer with the broad, getting himself loaded to put the wife out of his mind and for what? So he can make it with that Sue he paid anyway. I love them all. I bequeath myself to this world, life, the whole skam.

I'm happy here talking to you. Why is that? Who knows why you cross the bridge to some people and not to others? I'm absolutely happy right now. They underrate the whole nature of loyalty between men, it's different than with a woman, the kind of challenge. I'd win sometimes and be ashamed because the friggin' horse had me bobbling around coming over the finish line, instead of stylish. I could get down closer to the horse than any son of a bitch ordinarily, but sometimes you draw some broken-legged horse and you bump in like a trussed flounder on a no-spring truck. You ride for the other jocks, for their admiration, the style. My last race I went through the fence in Argentina, wired, screwed, and welded twenty-two bones, and after three months in the hospital the flowers stopped. A jock is like a movie star, the whole skam's night and day, the broads drooling your name printed on your friggin' forehead. Nothin'. Except two guys, mostly Virgil, that loyal son of a bitch, I'd die for the bastard.

Who understands that any more? I went to see this Doctor Hapic last year, what a sweet old starch, the greatest according to what you hear. And I lay down on the broken-down old couch and

he looks around in the bins and comes up with a racing form! I figure I'm in for homosexuality because that's the hinge if men move
you so much, and here's old Al diggin' me for a line on the sixth
race, askin' me who's an honest bookie and all. I put in three hours
with him, he canceled one appointment after another, and when I
left he charged me for half an hour! But how the hell do I know
who's goin' to win? Even when I was riding I didn't know. Chrissake, the horse didn't know! Why can't they leave it alone, I mean
the analyzing? Everybody I know who went come out a friggin'
judge. I admit it, the whole skam is pistils and stamens, all right I
surrender. But Jesus, give me room, let me die laughing if I'm goin'
to die. I'm ready. If I slide off a snowbank under a cab outside
there I'll cheer death. I love her, my wife, married eighteen years,
and my kids, but you draw a line somewhere, someplace, before
there's no room left for the chalk down in the corner. The men are
scared, did you see it where you been around? They keep makin'
little teeny marks but they can't draw the line. Nobody knows any
more where he begins or ends, it's like they pied the maps and put
Chicago in Latvia. They don't allow nobody to die for loyalty any
more, there's nothin' in it to steal.

What the hell do I know, ignorant, accordion-pleated mind that
I have, but I know style in anything. The great thing is not winning, it's riding the friggin' horse nobody else could stay onto.
That's the bastard you want to ride. Where the other jocks look
and know the horse wants to kill you. That's when the flag
stretches out and your corpuscles start laughing. Once I went to
see my father.

I never told this to anybody, and you know how much I talk.
Honest, I never told this. I made this television thing, interviewing
ugly authors about their books, the line was that a jockey could
actually read words, and it went over big till I threw myself in the
Jag and drove to Mexico, I couldn't stand it. I'm all for stealing but
not pickpocketing, these authors weren't any goddam good authors,
but every week you got to make over them like it's Man O'War did
the mile in nothin' pissing all the way and a blind jock on top.

Anyway the station gets this letter from Duluth asking if I was born in Frankfort, Kentucky, and my mother's name is so and so, and if I was all them things he's probably my old man. This silly old handwriting like he wrote it on a tractor. So I throw myself into a plane and drive up to the door and he's a house painter.

I just wanted to see, you know? I wanted to lay my both eyes on him. And there he was, about seventy or a hundred. He left when I was one. I never saw him. Now I'd always dreamed of him like he was a high roller or some kind of elegant thief or maybe a Kentucky Rousseau or somebody stylish with broads, and left to seek his fortune. Some goddam thing interesting. But there he is, a house painter. And lives in the nigger section. I'm the last of the holdouts, I can't stand them. But there's this one next door, a real nice guy, and his wife was nice too. You could see they loved him. And I'm standing there. What did I come for? Who is he? Who am I if he's my father? But the crazy thing is I knew I belonged to him. It's like you said, I'm the son of my father. I knew it even if he was a total stranger. I just wanted to do something for him. Anything. I was ready to lay down my life for him. After all, who knows the situation? Maybe my old lady drove him out. Who knows the inside of the outside? So I ask him, what do you want?

I'll get you anything, I said, that is within my means, although I was loaded, it was after the Derby. He was small too, although not as small as me. I'm so small I'm almost un-American, but he was small too, and he says, The grass in the back yard gets so high and thick I can't push the mower through it. So if I had one of them mowers with an engine on it.

So I grab the phone and they send over a truckload of all the kinds. And he was all afternoon goin' over each one and finally he picks out one with a motor bigger than this friggin' table, and I buy it for him. I had to leave to make the plane back because I promised Virgil I'd be in San Pedro to guard some broad he had to leave there a whole night, so I go into the back yard to say goodbye. And he wouldn't even turn the motor off so we could talk quietly. And I left him enjoying himself, joggling around that yard behind that friggin' mower.

Christ, how did I get so drunk! Those two broads across there have been lookin' at us. What do you say? What's the difference what they look like, they're all the same, I love 'em all.

[1962]

The Prophecy

Not all, but some winters in those parts are almost unendurable. A fog settles into the old Dutch valleys toward the end of November and never really goes away until April. Some nights it suddenly appears on the ridge tops, leaving the lowlands clear, and no one knows why it moves about, but it does, sometimes settling around a particular house for days at a time and nowhere else. Then it goes away and reappears around another house. And some winters the sun never properly comes out for two months at a time. A grayness like water drowns all the views, and the trees drip all day when their branches are not covered with creaking ice.

At the start of winter there is always hope, of course, that it will be a decent one. But when, day after day and week after week, the same monotonous wind sucks the heat out of the house, and there is never even a momentary break in the iron sky, the old people first and then everyone else gradually change their temperaments. There are unaccountable arguments in the supermarkets and at the gas station, lifelong enmities are started, people decide to move away and do, forever, and there is always a rash of unnecessary road accidents. People break arms, hitting trees whose locations they know by heart; there are always one or two who get run over by their own cars rolling back down the driveways; and decisions are made out of desperation, which permanently change the course of many lives.

Toward the end of December of such a winter Stowey Rummel decided to supervise personally the hanging of his architectural drawings and the display of his models for a permanent exhibition of his work in a new Florida university whose campus he had designed a few years before. He was in his mid-fifties at this time, long past the establishment of his name and the wish to be lionized yet once again, and it was almost a decade since he had sworn off lecturing. There was never a doubt any more how his structures would be received; it was always the same unqualified success now. He could no longer build anything, whether a private residence in his Pennsylvania county or a church in Brazil, without its being obvious that he had done it, and while here and there he was taken to task for repeating the same airy technique, they were such fanciful and sometimes even playful buildings that after a time the public's sense of recognition overwhelmed any dispute as to their other values. Stowey Rummel was internationally famous, a crafter of a genuine Americana in foreign eyes, an original designer whose inventive childishness with steel and concrete was made even more believably sincere by his personality.

He had lived for almost thirty years in this same stone farmhouse with the same wife, a remarkably childish thing in itself; he rose at half-past six every morning, made himself some French coffee, had his corn flakes and more coffee, smoked four cigarettes while reading last Sunday's *Herald Tribune* and yesterday's *Pittsburgh Gazette*, then put on his high-topped farmer's shoes and walked under a vine bower to his workshop. This was an enormously long building whose walls were made of rocks, some of them brought home from every continent during his six years as an oil geologist. The debris of his other careers was piled everywhere; a stack of wire cages for mice from his time as a geneticist and a microscope lying on its side on the window sill; vertical steel columns wired for support to the open ceiling beams with spidery steel cantilevers jutting out into the air; masonry constructions on the floor from the time he was inventing his disastrous fireplace, whose smoke would pass through a whole house, visible all the way up through wire gratings on each floor. His files, desk, drafting board, and a high stool formed the only clean island in the chaos. Everywhere else his ideas lay or hung in visible form—his models, drawings, ten-foot canvases in monochromes from his painting days—and underfoot a windfall of broken-backed books that looked as though their insides had been ransacked by a maniac. Bicycle gear sets he had once used as the basis of a design for the Camden Cycle Company plant hung on a rope in one corner, and over his desk, next to several old and dusty hats, was a clean pair of roller skates, which he occasionally used up and down in front of his house. He worked standing, with his left hand in his pocket, as though he were merely stopping for a moment, sketching with the surprised stare of one who was watching another person's hand. Sometimes he would grunt softly to some invisible onlooker beside him; sometimes he would look stern and moralistic as his pencil did what he disapproved. It all seemed—if one could have peeked in at him through one of his windows—as though this broken-nosed man with the muscular arms and wrestler's neck was merely the caretaker trying his hand at the boss's work. This air of disengagement carried over to his apparent attitude toward his things, and people often mistook it for boredom in him or a surrender to repetitive routine. But he was not bored at all; he had found his style quite early in his career, and he thought it quite wonderful that the world admired it, and he could not imagine why he should alter it. There are, after all, fortunate souls who hear everything but know how to listen only to what is good for them, and Stowey was, as things go, a fortunate man.

He left his home the day after New Year's, wearing a mackinaw and sheepskin mittens and without a hat. He would wear this same costume in Florida, despite his wife Cleota's reminders over the past five days that he must take some cool clothes with him. But he was too busy to hear what she was saying. So they parted when she was in an impatient humor. When he was bent over behind the wheel of the station wagon, feeling in his trouser cuffs for the ignition key he had dropped a moment before, she came out of the house with an enormous Romanian shawl over her head, which she had bought in that country during one of their trips abroad, and handed him a clean handkerchief through the window. Having found the key under his shoe, he started the engine, and while it warmed up he turned to her standing there in the dripping fog and said, "Defrost the refrigerator."

He saw the surprise in her face and laughed as though it were the funniest expression he had ever seen. He kept on laughing until she started laughing with him. He had a deep voice, which was full of good food she had cooked, and good humor; an explosive laugh that always carried everything before it. He would settle himself into his seat to laugh. Whenever he laughed it was all he was doing. And she was made to fall in love with him again, there in the rutted dirt driveway, standing in the cold fog, mad as she was at his going away when he really didn't have to, mad at their both having got older in a life that seemed to have taken no more than a week to go by. She was forty-nine at this time, a lanky woman of breeding, with an austere, narrow face that had the distinction of a steeple or some architecture designed long ago for a stubborn sort of prayer. Her eyebrows were definite and heavy and formed two lines moving upward toward a high forehead and a great head of brown hair that fell to her shoulders. There was an air of blindness in her gray eyes, the startled-horse look that ultimately comes to some women who are born at the end of an ancestral line long since divorced from moneymaking, which, besides, has kept its estate intact. She was personally sloppy, and when she had colds would blow her nose in the same handkerchief all day and keep it, soaking wet, dangling from her waist, and when she gardened she would eat dinner with dirt on her calves. But just when she seemed to have sunk into some depravity of peasanthood she would disappear and come down bathed, brushed, and taking deep breaths of air, and even with her broken nails her hands would come to rest on a table or a leaf with a thoughtless delicacy, a grace of history, so to speak, and for an instant one saw how ferociously proud she was and adamant on certain questions of personal value. She even spoke differently when she was clean, and she was clean now for his departure, and her voice clear and rather sharp.

"Now drive carefully, for God's sake!" she called, trying to attain

a half-humorous resentment at his departure. But he did not notice
and was already backing the car down to the road, saying "Toot-
toot!" to the stump of a tree as he passed it, the same stump that
had impaled the car of many a guest in the past thirty years and
that he refused to have removed. She stood clutching her shawl
around her shoulders until he had swung the car onto the road.
Then, when he had it pointed down the hill, he stopped to gaze at
her through the window. She had begun to turn back toward the
house, but his look caught her and she stood still, waiting there for
what his expression indicated would be a serious word of farewell.
He looked at her out of himself, she thought, as he did only for an
instant at a time, the look that always surprised her even now, when
his uncombable hair was yellowing a little and his breath came hard
through his nicotine-choked lungs, the look of the gaunt youth she
had suddenly found herself staring at in the Louvre on a Thursday
once. Now she kept herself protectively ready to laugh again, and
sure enough he pointed at her with his index finger and said "Toot!"
once more and roared off into the fog, his foot evidently surprising
him with the suddenness with which it pressed the accelerator, just
as his hand did when he worked. She walked back to the house and
entered, feeling herself returning, sensing some kind of opportunity
in the empty building. There is a death in all partings, she knew,
and promptly put it out of her mind.

She enjoyed great parties when she would sit up talking and dancing and drinking all night, but it always seemed to her that being
alone, especially alone in her house, was the most real part of life.
Now she could let out the three parakeets without fear they would
be stepped on or that Stowey would let them out one of the doors;
she could dust the plants, then break off suddenly and pick up an
old novel and read from the middle on; improvise cha-chas on the
harp; and finally, the best part of all, simply sit at the plank table in
the kitchen with a bottle of wine and the newspapers, reading the
ads as well as the news, registering nothing on her mind but letting
her soul suspend itself above all wishing and desire. She did this
now, comfortably aware of the mist running down the windows, of
the silence outside, of the dark afternoon it was getting to be.

She fell asleep leaning on her hand, hearing the house creaking as though it were living a private life of its own these two hundred years, hearing the birds rustling in their cages and the occasional whirring of wings as one of them landed on the table and walked across the newspaper to perch in the crook of her arm. Every few minutes she would awaken for a moment to review things: Stowey, yes, was on his way south, and the two boys were away in school, and nothing was burning on the stove, and Lucretia was coming for dinner and bringing three guests of hers. Then she fell asleep again as soddenly as a person with fever, and when she awoke it was dark outside and the clarity was back in her eyes. She stood up, smoothing her hair down, straightening her clothes, feeling a thankfulness for the enveloping darkness outside, and, above everything else, for the absence of the need to answer, to respond, to be aware even of Stowey coming in or going out, and yet, now that she was beginning to cook, she glimpsed a future without him, a future alone like this, and the pain made her head writhe, and in a moment she found it hard to wait for Lucretia to come with her guests.

She went into the living room and turned on three lamps, then back into the kitchen, where she turned on the ceiling light and the switch that lit the floods on the barn, illuminating the driveway. She knew she was feeling afraid and inwardly laughed at herself. They were both so young, after all, so unready for any final parting. How could it have been thirty years already? she wondered. But yes, nineteen plus thirty was forty-nine, and she was forty-nine and she had been married at nineteen. She stood still over the leg of lamb, rubbing herbs into it, quite suddenly conscious of a nausea in her stomach and a feeling of wrath, a sensation of violence that started her shivering. She heard the back door opening and immediately went through the pantry toward it, knowing it must be Alice.

The old woman met her, having already entered, and was unhooking her yellow slicker with her stiff white fingers. "Something's wrong with my phone," she said, proving at once that she had come with a purpose and not to intrude.

"What do you want to do?" Cleota asked, not moving from the

center of the pantry, her position barring the way to the kitchen door. Her anger astounded even her; she would never have dared bar the way if Stowey were here, and she thrilled at her aggressiveness toward his old sister.

"I'd better call the company, hadn't I?" Alice asked, already indicating in her tone that she recognized the outlandish barrier and was not prepared to go out at once.

"Well, you can certainly use the phone," Cleota said and turned her back on the old woman and went to her leg of lamb on the table.

Alice, wearing calf-height rubber boots and a fisherman's drooping-brim rubber hat, got to the phone and held it away from her ear, blinking papery eyelids and avidly inspecting the kitchen as she waited for the operator to come on. Beside the instrument— between it and a flour canister—stood a Fiji mask, a carved, elongated face. She turned it absent-mindedly.

"*Please* don't, Alice!"

The old lady turned in such quick shock that her deep-brimmed hat slid and remained sideways on her head. Cleota, her face swollen with feeling, bent to the oven and put in the meat.

"It was facing toward the wall a little," Alice started to explain.

Cleota stood erect, her cheeks red now. The house was hit by a slap of wind, a push that shuddered it. "I *have* asked you not to touch my things, Alice. I'm having guests and I've a lot to do. So will you please do what you have to and let me get on with it!"

She went to the refrigerator, opened it, and stood half bent over, looking into it, trying to concentrate on what she had thought to take from it.

The old lady put down the phone. "Yours is out too, I guess."

Cleota did not answer, remaining before the open refrigerator, unable to think.

For a moment they stood there waiting, one for the other, as they had waited at odd moments since Alice had moved into the house down the road nine years before. Now the old woman hooked up her slicker, her watery eyes glancing hungrily about the kitchen as though for some new detail she might not have seen before. She had no thought to ask what the matter was, not because she clearly knew but because she took for granted she was hated by this woman with a reasonless hatred that nothing could ever dissolve. In her autobiography, which she wrote at every day in her kitchen and in good weather under the apple tree behind her house, she was developing the concept of human types, unchangeable personalities created by a primeval spirit, each of which had the function of testing others who were equally unchangeable. Cleota, in her book, was the Eternally Dissatisfied. She did not blame Cleota for her personality; indeed she pitied her and knew that nothing she could say or do would ever mitigate her need for an opponent, an enemy. Cleota, like so many other perversely incomprehensible phenomena, was Necessary.

Alice dawdled at the pantry door. She would not leave in too much of a hurry. She had a right, she felt, to have been invited tonight; certainly she would have been if Stowe had been at home. Besides she was hungry, having neglected her lunch today, and the few morsels she did eat would hardly matter to the dinner that was to be served. And if there were to be any men here, they would certainly be—as they always were—interested in her views, as so many of her brother's guests had told him after they had met her.

She reached the back door and turned back to her sister-in-law. "Good night," she said. The first tremors of her hurt quavered the words and stiffened Cleota, who barely glanced at her to return the farewell. Alice grasped the doorknob. She felt the question rising to her mouth and tried to escape before it came out, but it was too late. She heard herself asking, "Who are you having?"

The ladle in Cleota's hand struck the stove and slid along the floor. "I can't have this, Alice. You know exactly what I am talking about, so there is nothing more to say about it."

The old lady shook her head, just once, turned the knob and went out, softly closing the door behind her.

Cleota picked up the ladle and stood there shaking. Once again the house was no longer hers. The indignity of the visit made her clench her teeth; Alice knew perfectly well that if her phone was out, then theirs was too, since they were on the same line. She had come simply, purely, to demonstrate that she had the freedom of the premises, to show once again that whatever else he may have become and whomever he might have married, Stowey was her baby brother first.

Cleota, who did not believe in a definite god, looked toward the ceiling despite herself, with a longing for an ear that would hear, and whispered, "Why doesn't she die?" Alice was seventy-three, after all, and was nothing any longer but a smell, a pair of watery eyes, and, above all, a coiled power secreted in that house down the road which Stowe had bought for her when her husband had died. She felt now, as she often did, that the old woman lived on only to laugh secretly at her. She knew how unreasonable this idea was; the woman survived falls on the ice, broken hips, and cold and pneumonia last winter because she wanted to live for her own sake, but this stubborn refusal to succumb was somehow obscene to Cleota, quite as though the woman had something illicit in her unabashed craving for a life that would never end.

Cleota went to the Fiji mask and turned it as it had been before, as though this would cancel out Alice's having moved it. She touched the hard brown wood, and her finger rested on a rough spot under the lower lip. This had always felt like a wart and made the image seem alive, and the touching of the spot recalled her father's hands on it when he gave it to her. As foolish a man as he had been, he had known how to disappear from the lives of those he could not help. She felt a rising pride in her father now; with his own bizarre dignity he had assembled his lunatic expeditions, read the wrong books, learned outmoded anthropological theories, sailed to the unmeaningful islands, spent years studying tribes that had been categorized many times before, and had succeeded only in cluttering the homes of his children with the bric-a-brac of the South Seas. Now, however, now that he could never return, she sensed in his career a certain hidden purpose, which she felt he must have secretly followed. It had been his will to declare himself even in his inanity, and to keep on declaring himself until the idiotic end, his ankle caught in a rope and his bald head in the water, discovered hanging over the side of his sloop off San Francisco harbor. How strange it was that this fool had slowly taken on—for many besides herself—an air of respect! And it was not wrong that this should be, she thought. He had had a passion, and that, she felt now, was everything.

Returning to her stove, she saw that she was separated from herself as her father had not been from himself. The gaunt image of Stowey appeared before her, enraging her mind; why could she not *have* him! They were like two planets circling each other, held in their orbits by an invisible force that forbade their juncture, the force coming out of those two watery eyes, those clawed white fingers, that put-on stupidity, that selfish arrogance which sat in the house down the road, grinning and enthroned. A burst of wind against the house reminded her that guests would be here. She turned her mind to the food and sought once more the soft suspension of all desire. One of the parakeets flew up from the floor and perched on her wrist. She stopped working and moved it to her lips and kissed its glistening head, and as always it bowed and plucked at her flesh with its talons.

To Cleota it was faintly ill-mannered to ask biographical data of a guest. What people did for a living, whether they were married or divorced, had mistresses or lovers, had been to jail or Princeton or in one of the wars—the ordinary pegs on which to drape the growing tapestry of an evening's conversation did not exist for her mind. Until she was sixteen she had not met, or at least had not had to cope with, anyone whose background and attitudes were different from her own. Her uncles, aunts, and cousins had all been of a piece and of a place, even if they had gone all over the world to live, and it was—or seemed—quite the same for the other girls who attended her schools. Her life had taken her, at Stowe's side, into many countries, the *palaz-zos* of financiers, the hovels of artists, the Harlems of the world, the apartments of *nouveaux riches* and university trustees, and the furnished rooms of doped musicians, but rich or poor, famous or infamous, genius or dilettante, they were all greeted and listened to with her same blind stare, her inattention to details, her total absence of discrimination. She seemed not to realize that people ordinarily judged others; not that she liked everyone equally, but so long as they were in some way amusing, or sincere, or something at least definite, she was happy to have them in her house. What did arouse her was to be put upon—or ever to be told what to think or to feel. It was simply an absurdity that anyone should impose on anyone else. Beyond this prohibition, which her manner made it unnecessary to enforce very often, she was not troubled by people. Unexpectedly, however, she did not disapprove of moralists. It was simply that moralizing for them was, or must surely be, somehow necessary, just as some people hated the outdoors and others never ate peppery food. There were things, of course, of which she disapproved, and she often appeared to verge on moral indignation, as toward people being denied passports by the government or being kept out of restaurants because they were colored. But it soon became clear she was not speaking of any moral situation; it was simply that her sense of her own person had been inflamed by the idea of some blind, general will being imposed upon an individual. And then it was not indignation she felt so much as bewilderment, an incomprehension similar to her father's when he traveled around the world three different times at his own expense to present petitions to the League of Nations protesting the oppression of various tribes, one of which had come close to eating him, and failed to get any response.

Lucretia had called this morning and among other things had said that John Trudeau had stopped by the night before on his way to New York, and when the two women had decided to have dinner together Trudeau was inevitably included, along with another guest of Lucretia's, a Madame something who was also visiting her. Cleota had known Trudeau and especially his wife Betty until last year, when he quit his job teaching at Pemmerton School in Hanock, a few miles from her house, and went to live in Baltimore. She had been less impressed with him than with his wife, a tall young beauty, yet sensible. Some six years ago their wedding party had spilled over into the Rummel house, and Cleota still connected Trudeau with that evening, when with Betty at his side he seemed a promising, deeply serious fellow who she hoped would become the poet he had set his heart on being. There had seemed to be a touching faith between them, like hers in Stowe when young. They had had four children and lived poorly in an unremodeled farmhouse near the school, and Cleota had often dropped in there in the hope she could draw them out of a deepening seclusion, which gave her the feeling that they were perhaps ashamed of their poverty. She had made sure to invite them whenever there was anything going at her house, and they had come more often than not, but toward the end of their years here she could not help seeing that they were cool to each other and that Trudeau had gotten gray quite suddenly, and she could not tell why their failure had left her feeling an angry frustration, especially when they had never been close friends.

So she was not entirely surprised to see Trudeau tonight with a girl who was not his wife, but that it should be a girl like this! He was still a handsome man in a conventional way, tall, white-haired at the temples, a rather long face with a Byronic nose, but, she thought now, somewhat on the weak side overall. She saw now that she had met his face on many a sailing boat long ago, the perpetual sportsmen who remained Princeton boys forever. How had she misjudged him so? Yet he still had something serious, some suffering in his eyes, which she fancied looked at her now with a tinge of nervous shame, whose cause she quickly concluded was the physical appearance of this girl who obviously was his mistress.

All through dinner Cleota could neither look at her directly nor take her eyes from her profile. The girl hardly spoke but stared over the others' heads in seeming judgment upon the not brilliant conversation, straining her brows, which were penciled nearly into her hair, blinking her enormous brown eyes whose lids were blackened like a ballerina's in a witches' dance. She wore a black sweater and a black felt skirt, both tightened over enormous breasts and weighty but well-made thighs, and her shoes were spike-heeled and black too. There was no make-up on her olive skin, not even lipstick. Her arms jangled with bracelets and her name was Eve Saint Bleu. Trudeau, incredibly, called her "Saint" and from time to time tried to draw her into the talk, but she would only turn her morose eyes toward him instead of the walls and windows. At each of his slavish attempts to engage the girl, Cleota would turn quickly to hear what remark would fall from Saint's full lips, to witness Saint when she might leave off with what to Cleota was an incredibly rude attempt to appear bored and disapproving of everything. Or was she merely as stupid as she looked? After twenty minutes of this silent sparring Cleota refused any further interest in Saint and did what she always did with people in her house—left out whoever did not appeal to her and attended to those who did.

She had always liked Lucretia, her friend since their schooldays, and Madame . . . "I don't think I heard your name, Madame," she said to the woman who sat across the table from her, eating the lamb in large chunks and chewing with a full mouth.

"Lhevine. Manisette-Lhevine. Ish shpelled with an aish," the lady said, trying to swallow at the same time.

Cleota laughed at her attempt and liked this ugly woman who was so small she had to sit on a cushion at the table. She had the face of a man, the skin of a mulatto, with a blob of a nose that seemed to have been deboned, it hung so unsupported and unshaped. Her eyes were black like her kinky hair, which was bobbed high and showed her manly ears, which stuck out from her head. She had a large mouth and well-filled teeth. Her hands were bulb-knuckled and veined, and when she laughed, which she did often, deep creases cut parentheses into her tight cheeks. She had asked permission to remove the jacket of her gray suit, exposing her skinny, muscular arms, which sprouted from a sleeveless blouse like the twisted branches of an old apple tree. Cleota, as though to compensate Madame for the sensuous form of her other guests, kept placing fresh slices of bread and meat before her alone as they talked.

"I want Madame to do you," Lucretia said, and only now Cleota recalled her having mentioned on the phone that this woman told fortunes. An oddly suspended smile was hanging on Lucretia's face as Cleota turned to her. Lucretia sat there as though she were going to brazen out an embarrassing but true confession, for she had always been a severely practical, scientifically minded woman with no patience whatsoever for any kind of mysticism. During the first years of her marriage she had even returned to school for her master's degree in bacteriology and had worked in laboratories until the children came. She knew exactly how many calories, proteins, and carbohydrates there were in every food, used pressure cookers to preserve the vitamins, kept instruments in her kitchen with which she could predict humidity and weather, and dealt with everyone, including her own children, with a well-scrubbed avoidance of sentimentality and muddle.

But there she sat, not half as embarrassed as Cleota thought she would surely be at having admitted this intense interest in fortune-telling, and Cleota could not absorb such a violent contradiction of her old friend's character, and for a moment her mouth went from a smile to a serious expression as she wondered if she were the victim of a joke.

"She's wonderful, Cleota," Lucretia insisted. "I haven't told her anything about you, but you wait and see what she finds out."

Quite suddenly Saint spoke. "I had an aunt who did that." It was her first remark unprompted by a question from Trudeau, and everyone turned to her, waiting for more. And she momentarily looked so eager to tell them something, her supercilious air gone, that she seemed merely a shy girl who had been intimidated to find herself in Stowe Rummel's actual house. Trudeau relaxed and smiled for the first time and encouraged her with happier eyes to go on. She opened her lips to speak.

"Your aunt didn't do *this*, dear," Madame Lhevine cut her off, grinning across the table at her with clear resentment and giving the table one significant pat.

Saint looked hurt, and Trudeau put a hand on her thigh under the table and said, "Honey . . ." But Madame Lhevine was going on now to Cleota, to whom she looked with softened eyes, as though she shared a secret understanding with her alone. "There's no need to do you," she said.

"Why not?" Cleota blushed.

"You're there already."

Cleota laughed high. "Where?"

"Where it all begins," Madame said, and her persistent calm, absurd to Cleota at first, gave her an authority that now caused all to watch her every movement.

Cleota's high, hawking laugh burst from her; it was followed by a sip of red wine and a wondering glance at Lucretia, for it suddenly swept in upon her that to have become so intensely involved with this woman her long-time friend must be in some great personal trouble. But she quickly turned back to Madame Lhevine.

"I'm not laughing at you, Madame," she said, busying her hands with sweeping crumbs toward herself. "It's just that I don't know where *anything* begins. Or ends." She laughed again, blushing. "Or anything at all."

Madame Lhevine's eyes did not stir. "I know that, dear," she said.

A blow seemed to have struck Cleota from somewhere; she felt herself pierced by the fanatic but oddly kind eyes of the fortune-teller. A new need for this woman's attention and even for her care pressed upon Cleota, who suddenly felt herself lonely. She lowered her gaze to the last crumbs, saying, "I suppose it's just as real as anything else, though."

"Neither more nor less," Madame Lhevine said with the quiet joy of those who believe and are saved.

Cleota could not sit there any longer. "I'll get some coffee," she said and went out into the kitchen.

Her hand unaccountably shook as she held the kettle under the faucet. Her cheeks were hot. The faces in the living room revolved before her until Lucretia's expression hung in her mind, the close-set eyes so strangely eager for Cleota to accept Madame Lhevine. All at once it was obvious to her that Lucretia and her husband had broken.

She stared at the flame, still, quiet. Bud Trussel was home only weekends this year not because he had to be traveling all over the state on business. They were effectually separated.

This knowledge was like something sliding out of her that she had not known was in her at all. How could she have been so blind to what was so obvious! She felt frightened. Her kitchen itself began to seem strange. What else, she wondered, was lying in her mind, unknown to her? Again she thought of Lucretia's new, almost lascivious manner tonight, the same Lucretia who had always sat with one leg entwined about the other, always blushing before she even dared to laugh! And now so . . . immoral. But what had she done or said that was immoral? It was all silly!

A coldness spread through her body, and she glanced toward the pantry to see if the door had opened. She sensed Alice outside, listened, but it was quiet out there. Still, it was not beneath Stowe's sister to peek through the windows. She strode to the back door and opened it brusquely, already infuriated. No one was there. The swift wind was wracking the trees, and through their waving branches her eyes caught a distant, unaccustomed light. She stopped moving, tracing the geography of the roads in her mind until she decided it was Joseph's house, a surprise since he and his wife rarely came up in winter, although he did alone sometimes, to write. Had she known she would have called him tonight.

Already there was a smile on her face as she returned to the stove, thinking of Joseph confronting Madame Lhevine. "A fortune-*what*?" he would ask, poker-faced—or some such half-joke that would make her laugh with embarrassment. There was always something on the verge of the inappropriate about what he said, on the verge of . . . of the truth. She went to the phone and held it absently to her ear, waiting for the tone. And still, she thought, visualizing this man, he is also a believer. So many Jews were, she thought for the first time. And his image came strongly to her mind as she stared at the mask beside the phone—he was like her father that way, he had some torturing statement in him that was always seeming to come out but never quite did. Like Stowe too! Now she became aware of the receiver's silence and put it down in pique, half blaming Alice for having damaged it somehow. When she turned back to the stove Lucretia walked in and stood without speaking in the middle of the kitchen, slumping her long, wide-shouldered body onto one hip. And Cleota saw the willed smile on her shy face.

"Is it upsetting you?" Lucretia's voice was deep; she always seemed to imitate a man when she had to perform a duty.

"No!" Cleota laughed, surprised at her own sharpness. And instantly the feeling came over her that for some reason she was being got at by Lucretia tonight—she had brought the fortune-teller for a reason. What? If only they would both leave! Now, before this dreadful intimacy thickened! It had never been like this, not even in their beds at school when they had talked into the nights—from the beginning there had been an unspoken agreement to leave truly private matters untouched. It had been not a relation through words, but something like the silent passage of light from sun to moon, as when Lucretia had let her hair grow after Cleota stopped cutting hers, or took to wearing rings when Cleota returned with some for herself from Mexico. Facing her lifelong friend now, seeing the oddly broken smile on her face—was it a cynical smile?—she felt the fear of one who has wielded the power of example without having known it and must now deal with the revolt of the unwittingly oppressed. It flashed through her mind that Lucretia had moved to the country only because she had, and would never, never straighten out the chaos of her house because it was only an imitation of this house, and that her chains of projects—starting her shrub nursery, then designing shoes, now breeding horses—were not the good and natural blossoms of her joyous energy, as she always tried to imply, but abortive distractions in a life without a form, a life, Cleota saw now, that had been shaded by her own and Stowe's. Cleota stared at the seemingly guilty and dangerous eyes, sensing—what she had always known!—that a disaster had been spreading roots through her friend's life this last thirty years and now had burst it apart.

Lucretia took a swallow of her drink and said, "Bud's left me, Cleota," and smiled.

Cleota's spine quivered at her prophecy come true. She cocked her head like a dog that has been summoned and does not know whether to approach or flee. "When?" she asked, merely to fill the silence until she could think what to say.

"I don't know when. He's been on his way a long time, I guess." And now she raised her arms, put them around Cleota's neck, and—much the taller—rested her head awkwardly on Cleota's shoulders. In a moment Cleota pressed her lightly away, and they looked at one another, changed.

"Are you divorcing?" she asked Lucretia. How dreamily unfeeling that embrace had been!

"Yes," Lucretia said, red-faced but grinning.

"Is it another—?"

"No," Lucretia cut her off. "At least I don't think there's anybody else." And, glancing at the pot, she said, "Coffee'll be cold, won't it?"

The coffee? Cleota only now remembered why she had come into the kitchen. She got the cups down and set them on the tray.

"It won't be much of an adjustment anyway," Lucretia said, behind her.

"You don't seem very upset. Are you?" Cleota turned to her, picked up the tray, thinking that she had never before asked anyone such absurdly personal questions. Some dangerously obscene thing had invaded her person, she felt, and her house, and it must be stopped. And yet Lucretia appeared not to notice. It suddenly seemed ages ago since Stowe had been here.

"I've been miserable for a long time, Clee," Lucretia answered.

"I didn't know."

"Yes."

They stood in the middle of the kitchen under the hanging bulb, looking at each other.

"He's actually moved out?"

"Yes."

"What are you going to do?"

"Look for a job, I guess. I think I've had it up here anyway."

"Oh," Cleota said.

"I'm glad I could tell you alone. Without Stowe."

"Really? Why?"

"He likes Bud so." Lucretia laughed dryly. "I'd feel ashamed to tell him."

"Oh, Stowe won't mind. I mean," she corrected, "he's never surprised at anything." She laughed at Stowe's childish insulation of mind, his somehow irritating ignorance of people's relations, and said, "*You* know—" and broke off when Lucretia smiled as though celebrating Stowe's trouble-blind charm.

Cleota picked up the loaded tray. "Have you known her long? Madame?"

"Only since yesterday. She came up to buy the horses. She has a place near Harrisburg or somewhere. She's fabulous, Clee. Let her do you."

Lucretia's persistence again pressed down upon Cleota, like some sort of need for her complicity. Trudeau walked in, bowing a little to both women to apologize for interrupting them. "We'll have to leave, Cleota."

He gripped her hand, which she offered him under the tray, and held it under some terrific pressure, which only leaving her house would evidently alleviate. She felt she could not ask him what the matter was because it was obviously the girl's insisting he must take her away even without coffee. Cleota reddened at his embarrassment, telling him, "It was nice to see you again, John. I think the driveway light is still on."

Trudeau nodded thankfully for her unquestioning farewell, but his honor seemed to forbid him to turn away too soon from the openly bewildered look in her face.

"Tell Stowe I left my best," he said, letting go of her hand.

"Yes."

Now he turned away, a slight shift in his eyes confessing to her that his life was misery. The three entered the living room together.

Saint was already in her coat, a black pile, and wore a black gauze veil over her head. She was looking out at the driveway through the pane in the door and turned to Trudeau, who immediately got his coat and joined her. She glanced once at Cleota, who had hardly time to put the tray on the table when both of them were gone.

"Well!" She laughed, blushing but relieved. "What happened?"

"She got mad at me," Madame Lhevine said.

"Why?" Cleota asked, still tingling from Saint's hatred of her. What a weird night it was! From out of nowhere a strange girl comes to hate her! And yet everything seemed to be somehow in order and as it had to be, all around her the broken cliffs of people's lives sliding so deftly into the sea.

"Her aunt *couldn't* have been a gypsy. A gypsy is a gypsy, not somebody you just call a gypsy. I told her her aunt was not a gypsy."

"Oh," Cleota said, her eyes very wide as she tried to understand what was so serious about Madame Lhevine's point. "Are you a gypsy?" she asked innocently.

"Me? No, I'm Jewish."

Lucretia nodded in confirmation. Evidently she also thought these identities important. Cleota felt that the two of them had the secret of some closed world, which gave them some assurance, some belonging sense. She swallowed whisky. Madame lit a cigarette and squinted her eyes in the smoke. Lucretia looked at the table and played with a match. A moment passed in total silence. Cleota realized that she was now supposed to ask Madame to tell her fortune. It was, she began to feel, a matter of their dignity that she ask. To refuse to ask would be to question their authenticity. And a feeling rose in Cleota again that she was being put upon, pressured toward a discipleship of some vague sort.

"I can't understand John," she said to Lucretia. "Do you?"

"It's just sex," Lucretia said, implying a surfeit of experience that Cleota knew she did not have. Or did she?

"But that girl," Cleota said, "she's not very pretty, is she?"

Lucretia was strangely excited and suddenly reached across what seemed like half the room to drag a small table over to herself with a pack of cigarettes on it. "What's pretty got to do with sex?" she said.

"Well, I don't understand it. He must have his reasons, but his wife is much more beautiful than this one."

Cleota was perfectly aware that Lucretia was playing toward Madame Lhevine, acting out some new familiarity with degradation, but she still could not help feeling on the outside, looking in at an underwater world. *The* world? She prayed Stowe had forgotten something and would suddenly walk in.

Madame Lhevine spoke with certainty, an elder who was used to waiting for the issue to be joined before moving in to resolve it along the right lines. "The spirit doesn't always love what the person loves," she said.

Oh, how true that was! Cleota sensed a stirring in her own depths, a delight in the quickening of her own mind.

"It's a difficult thing," Madame went on. "Not many people know how to listen to the inner voice. Everything distracts us. Even though we know it's the only thing that can guide us."

She squinted into the ashtray and truly listened as Cleota spoke. "But how can one hear? Or know what to believe? One senses so many things."

"How do you know your body? Your hands feel it, your eyes see it every day in the mirror. It is practice, that's all. Every day we inspect our bodies, do we not? But how often do we set time aside to inspect our souls? To listen to what it can tell us? Hardly ever. People," she said with some protest now, "scoff at such things, but they accept that one cannot sit down at a piano and play the first time. Even though it is much more difficult, and requires much more technique, to hear one's own inner voice. And to understand its signs— this is even more difficult. But one can do it. I promise you."

With enormous relief Cleota saw that Madame Lhevine was serious and not a fool.

"She's marvelous," Lucretia said, without any reserve now that she saw the impression made on Cleota.

"I don't tell fortunes," Madame went on, "because there is really no future in the vulgar sense."

How kind she was! How her certainty even loaned her a loveliness now! To have lost touch with oneself, Cleota thought, was what made women seem unattractive. "I don't understand that," Cleota said, "about the future."

"Perhaps you would tell me more about what you don't understand," Madame said.

Cleota was reached by this invitation; she felt understood suddenly, for she did want to speak of her idea of the future. She settled more comfortably in her chair and sought her thoughts. "I don't really know. I suppose I never used to think about it at all, but—well, I suppose when one gets to a certain point, and there's more behind than ahead, it just somehow . . . doesn't seem to have been quite worth it. I don't mean," she added quickly, for she noted that Lucretia seemed oddly gratified with this implication of her failure, "I don't say that I've had a bad time of it, really. I haven't. It's really got nothing to do—my idea—with happiness or unhappiness. It's more that you . . . you wonder if it wasn't all a little too"—she laughed, blushing—"small." And before Madame could speak she added without any emphasis, "I suppose when the children aren't around any more one thinks of that." It struck her that she would never have shown such doubt with Stowe around, and she felt freed by his absence.

"It's more than the children not being around," Lucretia said.

"It's that too," Madame reminded Lucretia. "We must not underestimate the physical, but"—she turned back to Cleota—"it is also the climax inside."

Cleota waited. She felt she was being perceived, but not any longer by a merely curious mind. Madame, she felt, was seeing something within her with which the word climax was connected.

"One sees that there will be no ecstasy," Madame Lhevine said. "And that is when the crisis comes. It comes, you might say, when we see the future too clearly, and we see that it is a plain, an endless plain, and not what we had thought—a mountain with a glory at the top."

"Oh, I never thought of any glory."

"I am not speaking of accomplishment. I am speaking of oneness. The glory is only the moment when we are at one."

Death burst into Cleota's mind, the complete sense of a dying; not any particular person, not herself, but some unidentifiable person lying dead. Then her oneness would be in her, and a glory, a beneficent peace.

A quick joyousness raised her to her feet and she went to the sideboard and got a new bottle of whisky and returned to the table and, without asking, poured. Then she looked across at Madame Lhevine, her face flushed.

"What do you do?" she asked, forbearing to say "now." She did not want to impute any formal routine to Madame, any cheap ritual. Some truth was closing in, some singular announcement, which, she felt, must not be spoiled.

"If you wish, you can simply put your hands on the table."

Stowe would laugh; her father would have looked at the ceiling and stalked out of the room. She raised her hands, and when she set them on the table it felt as though they had been thrust into a cold wind. Now Madame's hands glided and came to rest with her middle fingers touching Cleota's. They were old hands, much older than Madame's face. The four hands looked like separate living animals facing one another on the table.

Cleota awaited her next instruction, but there was none. She raised her eyes to Madame's.

The woman's great age struck her anew. Her cheeks seemed to have sunk, she looked Slavic now, her skin cracked like milk skim, the veins in her eyeballs twisted like a map of jungle rivers.

"Look in my eyes, please," Madame Lhevine said.

Cleota shuddered. "I am," she said. Was it possible the woman had gone blind? Looking more sharply, Cleota saw in fact that Madame was not seeing, that her gaze had died, gone within. It was too appropriate, and for a moment she thought to break off, but a feeling came that she would lose by mocking; whatever her distrust, she felt she must continue to look into these black eyes if she ever was to hope again for a connection to herself.

Now Madame Lhevine lifted her hands and patted Cleota's and breathed. Cleota put her hands back in her lap. Madame Lhevine blinked at nothing, seeming to be putting together what she had heard or seen.

"Is there an older woman—?" Madame broke off. "Is there an old woman?" she corrected.

"My husband's sister. She lives nearby."

"Oh." Madame raised her chin. She seemed to be steeling herself. "She will live longer than he."

A tremor shook Cleota's head; she looked stupidly at Madame Lhevine, her mind shocked by the picture of Stowe in his casket and Alice standing over it, while she must wait forever by herself in a corner, a stranger again. It seemed to her she had always had this picture in her head and the only news was that now someone else had seen it too.

Cleota was agonized by the relief she felt at the image of Alice's outliving Stowe. Simply, it wiped out her entire life with him. She had met him first in the gallery with Alice at his side, the air between them thickened by a too dense, too heavy communication. She had never broken into it herself, never stood alone in the center of his vision. Thirty years vanished, nullified. She was now where she had come in, with nothing to show.

"I'm sorry I had to—" Madame broke off as she laid her hand on Cleota's. The touch brought Cleota back to the room and an awareness of Alice hovering somewhere near the house. Anger puffed her eyelids. What Madame and Lucretia saw was the furious look that was sweeping up into her face.

A car, driven fast, squealed to a halt in the driveway. The three women turned together toward the door, hearing the approaching footsteps outside, the steps of a man. Cleota went toward it as the knocking began and opened it.

"Joseph!" she almost shouted.

The young man threw up his hands in mock fright. "What'd I do?" he called.

Cleota laughed. "Come in!"

Now he entered, grinning at her and speaking the drollery that had always served best between them. "Am I too late?"

"For what!" Cleota heard the girlish crack in her voice.

"Whatever it is," he said, taking off his zipper jacket and tossing it to a chair. "I mean it's late and I didn't want to wake you."

"We're obviously awake," she taunted him, feeling a new cruelty torn loose within her.

He felt hung up, facing the other two women, and so he shouted, "I mean will I be in the way if I come in for a few minutes because I'm not ready to go to sleep yet and I thought it would be nice to say hello! Is what I mean!"

Lucretia also laughed. There was something aboriginal about him, in her opinion, as she had once told Cleota.

"So hello!" he said and drew a chair up to the table, combed his fingers through his thick brown hair, and lit a cigar.

"Have you had dinner?" Cleota asked.

"I ate once at five and again at nine," he said. Cleota seemed oddly charged up. He did not know if it was because he was intruding or because he was very welcome as the only man.

He glanced toward Madame Lhevine, who gave him a nodding smile, and only now did Cleota realize, and she introduced them.

"How long will you stay up here?"

"I don't know. Few days." He drank what she put before him. "How's Stowey?"

"Oh, all right," and she gave a quick, deprecating laugh. This had always given him a smoky sense of an understanding with her, about what precisely he did not know. But now she added seriously, "He's having a show in Florida."

"Oh, that's nice."

She laughed again.

"Well, I meant it!" he protested.

Her face turned instantly grave. "I know you did."

To Madame Lhevine and Lucretia he said, "Between us it's always a battle of half-wits."

The women's laughter relieved him; he was some ten years younger than Cleota and Lucretia, a rolling-gaited, hands-in-pockets novelist whose vast inexperience with women had given him a curiosity about them so intense as to approach understanding. With women, he usually found himself behind any one of various masks, depending on the situation; at the moment it was that of the raffish youth, the younger poet, perhaps, for it was never possible to arrive—especially before Cleota—as himself. She was, he always sensed, an unhappy woman who perhaps did not even know her unhappiness; she therefore sought something, some sensuous reassurance, which he could distract her from by simulating this carefree artist's bantering. Not that Cleota herself attracted him; that she was a wife was enough to place her in a vaguely sacred area. Unless he should strike out toward another sort of life and character for himself, a life, as he visualized it, of truthful relations—which is to say, personal relations of a confessional sort. But somewhere in his mind he knew that real truths only came out of disaster, and he would do his best to avoid disaster in all the departments of his life. He had to, he felt, out of decency. For the true terror of living in a false position was that the love of others became attached to it and so would be betrayed if one were to strike for the truth. And treason to others—to Joseph Kersh— was the ultimate destruction, worse even than treason to himself, living with a wife he could not love.

By the time he was seated at the table he was already chafing at the boyish role Cleota had thrust upon him these six or seven years of their acquaintance. He made his manner grave and seemingly even troubled, and since, as the only man present, attention was centered on him for the moment and he had to speak, he looked directly into Lucretia's eyes and asked, "How's your husband?"

Lucretia lowered her gaze to her cigarette and, tapping it impatiently, she said, "He's all right."

He heard her door clap shut. Women discovered alone, he believed, must have been talking about sex. He had believed this since his childhood, when his mother's bridge parties had always gone from screaming hilarity to matronly silence as soon as he appeared. He knew then, as he knew now, that there was something illicit here, something prohibited in the air. Knowing was no problem to him; it was admitting that he knew. For it tore at his sense of good, of right, and of the proper nature of things that wives should betray the smallest contempt for their husbands. And yet, he felt, contempt was around this table now. And he was dismayed that this flattered him and gave him a joyous feeling of fitness. "Just a half," he said to Cleota, who was pouring more whisky into his glass. "I've got to get to sleep soon."

"Oh, don't go!" she said strongly, and he saw that she was flushed with whisky. "Are you writing up here?"

"No." Gratified, he saw how she was waiting for serious news of him. Lucretia too was curious. "I'm just worrying."

"*You?*"

"Why not?" he asked, genuinely surprised.

"Just that you seem to do everything you want to do."

Her admiration, he believed, was for some strength she seemed to think he had, and he accepted with pleasure. But a distant alarm was ringing for him tonight; something intimate was happening here, and he should not have come.

"I don't know," he answered Cleota. "Maybe I do do what I want to. The trouble is I don't know I'm doing it." And he resolved, in the name of some distant truthfulness, to reveal a little of his own bewilderment. "I really go from moment to moment, despite appearances. I don't know what I'm doing any more than anybody else."

"Ah, but you do know," said Madame Lhevine, narrowing her eyes. He looked at her with surprise. "I have read your books. You do know. Within yourself you know."

He found himself liking this ugly woman. Her tone reminded him of his mother's when she would look at him after he had knocked over a vase and say, "You will be a great man."

"You follow your spirit, Mr. Kersh," she went on, "so it is not necessary to know anything more."

"I suppose I do," he said, "but it would save a lot of trouble if I could believe it."

"But I'm sure you understand," Madame pressed on, "that the sense you have of not knowing is what makes your art. When an artist knows what he is doing he can no longer do it, don't you think?"

This so matched the license Joseph secretly claimed for himself, and the blessed freedom from responsibility he longed for, that he could not in good conscience accept it. "Well, I wouldn't go that far," he said. "It's romantic to think an artist is unconscious." And now he broadened his shoulders and his right hand closed in a fist. "A work of art must work, like a good machine—"

"But a machine made by a blind man," Madame said in an experienced tone.

"I deny that," he said, shaking his head, helpless to dam up this flood of certainty. "I have to think through a form before I can write. I have to engineer a structure. I have to know what I am doing."

"Of course," Madame cut in, "but at a certain point you must know nothing and allow yourself only your feelings. In fact, that is my only—my only reservation about your work."

"What?" he asked. He did not like her. Women ought not to criticize. She was repulsively ugly, like a dwarf.

"They are a bit overconstructed," she said. "I hope you will not think me presumptuous, but I do not have that feeling even though I admire enormously what you say."

He hoped that the heat he felt rising in his face would be attributed to the whisky. Crossing his knees suddenly, he knocked the table against Madame and quickly set it back in place, laughing. "I'm sorry, I didn't mean to cripple you."

He saw, with near shock, that Cleota was openly staring at him—with admiration. It was most noticeable. Why was Stowe gone, alone?

Lucretia was deep in thought, looking at the ashtray and tapping her cigarette on it. "But really, Joe"—she faced him with her over-puzzled look—"don't you think that people are really much more disoriented than you portray them? I mean—"

"My characters are pretty disoriented, Lucretia," he said and made Cleota laugh.

"No, seriously; your people always seem to *learn* something," she complained.

"Don't you think people learn?" he asked and wondered what they were secretly arguing about. There was, in fact, something dense about Lucretia, he had always thought. The first time he had met her she had just come from mating two horses and was feverish with her success, and it had seemed so clear that she had had a sexual interest in the procedure herself, yet was unaware of it, and this had given her a dull quality in his eyes—a musky one too, however.

"Of course they learn," she said—and it was clear she was matching intellects with him, which a woman ought not do, he felt—"but they learn geometry and the necessary dates. Not . . ." She sought the word, and Madame supplied it.

"Not spirit."

"Yes!" Lucretia agreed but deferred to Madame to continue.

"I'm sure you agree," said Madame, "that essentially the spirit is formed quite early. Actually it knows all it will ever know from the beginning."

"Then what's the point in living?"

"Because we must live. That is all."

"I wouldn't call that much of a point," Joseph said.

"Maybe there isn't much of a point," Cleota suddenly put in.

Joseph turned to her, struck by her sad gravity. He wondered whether Stowe had any idea she was so hopeless. But he checked himself—she was only talking and being her usual tolerant self. That was what he could never understand—she and Stowe could feel deeply about some issue and yet be perfectly friendly with people who stood for everything they opposed. Life to them was some kind of game, whereas one ought to believe something to the point of suffering for it. He wished he could find a way of leaving now instead of sitting here with these three crocked lunks arguing about spirits!

"Although I do think we learn," Cleota went on, with an open glance of support for Joseph. "I don't know if we learn only what we unconsciously knew before, or whether it's all continuously new, but I think we learn."

How admirably direct she was! Joseph caught this flower she had surprisingly tossed him and with it charged against the other two women. "What always gets me is how people will scoff at science and conscious wisdom and the whole rational approach to life, but when they go to the more "profound" places, like Mexico or Sicily or some other spiritual-type country, they never forget to take their typhoid shots!"

The mocking voices of Madame Lhevine and Lucretia were in the air, and he reddened with anger. Lucretia yelled, "That's got nothing to do with—"

"It's only the exact point! If you believe something you have to live by it or it's just talk! You can't say we don't learn and then blithely accept the fruits of what we've learned. That's—it's—" He wanted to say, "Lying."

"Oh, now, Joe," Lucretia drawled, looking at him with toleration—he sounded like her husband proving to her on engineering principles that she was not unhappy—"what we're talking about is simply not on that *plane*. You're ten years behind the times. Nobody's underrating science and conscious wisdom; it's simply that it doesn't provide an inner aim, a point to live for. It still leaves man essentially alone."

"Except that the only people I ever met who feel part of an international, a world community are scientists. They're the only ones who aren't alone."

"Now, Joe, really—what does a sentence like that *mean?*"

He was furious. "It means that they don't live for themselves only, they live in the service of a greater thing."

"*What*, for heaven's sake?"

"What? The alleviation of human pain and the wiping out of human poverty."

"We can't all be wiping out poverty, Joseph. What do *we* do? We're simply not talking about the same things." She turned to Cleota. "Do you sense the difference, Clee?"

"Of course there's a difference," Cleota said, her eyes avoiding Lucretia's, "but why can't you both be right?" And she glanced at Joseph for confirmation of this, to him, total absurdity.

"I don't care about being right," he said quietly now. But his hopes for Cleota had again subsided; she was a total mystery to him. Nothing ever came to an issue for her. The idea came sharply to his mind that every time he came here it was an anticlimax. This was why he always left feeling he had wasted his time—they were people who simply lived in an oblong hum and did not strive for some apotheosis, some climax in life, either a great accomplishment or a discovery or any blast of light and sound that would fling them into a new speed, a further orbit.

Yet, inexplicably, when he had been fired from the university for his refusal to disavow the Left-wing youth, she had gone on for months indignantly talking about it, phoning to see how he was, and for a while even spoke of living abroad to protest the oppressive American atmosphere.

Madame and Lucretia evidently felt he had been put down successfully, and the ugly woman allowed him a kind look and said, "It doesn't matter anyway—you are a very good writer."

This outstretching of a finger instead of a whole hand made

Joseph and Cleota laugh, and he said, "I'm not knocking intuition." Cleota laughed louder, but he had meant this as a compromise with Madame and said to Cleota, "Wait a minute, I'm
making up to her," and Cleota laughed louder still. His abrupt-
ness always entertained her, but it was something more now; in
his passion for his ideas, ideas she understood but did not find
irreplaceable, she sensed a fleshed connection with an outside
force, an unseen imperative directing his life. He *had* to say what
he said, believe what he believed, was helpless to compromise,
and this spoke a dedication not different from love in him.

She drank three inches of whisky straight, observing a bright
stain of green moonlight through the wet windows over her guests'
heads. A planetary silence seemed to surround the continuing argument; she felt herself floating away. Her only alarm was that the
talk was dying and they would all soon leave. She poured whisky
for Joseph, who was pounding the table with his open hand. "I am
not knocking intuition," he was saying again, "I work with it, I
make my living by it." Out of nowhere an idea hit him. "I'll tell you
something, Madame Lhevine. I come from a long line of superstitious idiots. I once had an aunt, see, and she told fortunes—"

Cleota exploded, throwing her hands up in the air and turning
from the table doubled over by laughter. Lucretia first smiled, trying to resist for Madame's sake, but she caught the infection, and
then Madame herself unwillingly joined, and Joseph, smiling stupidly, looked at the three women laughing hysterically around
him, asking, "What? What!" but no one was able to answer, until
he too was carried into the waves; and, as always happens in such
cases, one of them had only to look at the other to begin insanely
laughing all over again. And when they had quieted enough for
him to be heard he explained to Cleota, "But she did. In fact, she
was part gypsy!"

At this Cleota screamed, and she and Lucretia bent across the
table, grasping each other's arms, gasping and laughing with their
faces hidden by their shoulders, and Madame kept slapping the
table and shaking her head and going, "Ho, ho, ho."

Joseph, without understanding what it was all about, could not help feeling their hysteria was at his expense. His soberness returned before theirs, and he sat patiently smiling, on the verge of feeling the fool, and lit his cigar and took a drink, waiting for them to come to.

At last Cleota explained with kindness that Saint had said precisely the same things, and that . . . But now it was hard to reconstruct the earlier situation, especially Madame's resentment at the girl's presumptuous claim of an aunt who could do what Madame did—at least it could not be explained, Cleota realized, without characterizing Madame Lhevine as being extremely jealous and even petty about her talent for fortune-telling; and, besides, Cleota was aware that Madame was not happy with the title of fortune-teller and yet she did not know what else to call her without invoking words like spiritualist or seer or whatever— words that embarrassed Cleota and might in the bargain again offend the lady. The net of the explanation was a muddle, a confusion which confirmed in Joseph his recurring notion that the Rummels were in fact trivial and their minds disoriented, while for Cleota her inability to conclusively describe Madame left her—however hilariously amused she still appeared—with the feeling that Madame was perhaps a fraud. This was not at all a distasteful idea to Cleota; it was simply Madame's character. What did disturb her under her flushed smile, and prevented her from detaining Madame, who now said it was getting late, was the thought of being left alone. The image surged up of Stowe lying dead in his casket, and it stiffened her a little toward Lucretia as she helped her into her coat, quite as though Lucretia had borne her this prophecy in part, carrying it from her own blasted home where nothing ever went right.

Cleota returned from the driveway and removed her Romanian shawl and poured herself a new drink, still enjoying the exhilaration that follows helpless laughter, the physical cleanliness and strength that it leaves behind in healthy people, and at the same time her eyes had the indrawn look that the discomposing news had left there, and Joseph watched her, bewildered by her double mood.

Without asking him she handed him a drink, and they faced each other at the fire, which she had just fanned to life. "I'll go soon," he said. "I have to work tomorrow."

He saw that she was drunk, much drunker than she had seemed with the other two women present. In one continuous motion she sat down and let her knees spread apart, staring over his head. Then she leaned over heavily and set her drink on the floor between her feet and fell back into the chair again, blowing out air and turning her face toward the fire. Her breathing was still deep, and her hands hung limply from the arms of the wicker chair. Her seeming abandon was not a sign of sensuousness to him at first. He thought she was even indicating such trust in him that she need not look composed.

Drunken women made Joseph nervous. He spoke, trying for their customary bantering tone. "Now what was *that* all about?" he asked, grinning.

She did not answer, seemed hardly to have heard. Her staring eyes suggested some vast preoccupation and finally a despair that he had never before seen in her. An engagement, a moment of personal confrontation, seemed to be approaching, and to ward it off Joseph said, "I did have an aunt like that. She read my palm the night before I left home for college and predicted I'd flunk out after one semester."

He had hardly started his remark when it sounded to him like chatter unworthy of the moment. And now Cleota turned her head, still resting on the rim of the chair's back, and looked at him. With a shock he felt the challenge in her eyes. She was looking at him as a man, and for the first time. Her challenge kept growing in him, and to throw her off he lazily put his arm over the back of his chair and turned to the fire as though he too were preoccupied with other thoughts. Was it possible? Cleota Rummel?

"Do you remember John Trudeau?" she asked.

He turned to her, relieved; it would be gossip after all. "I think so. That tall guy used to teach up at—"

"Why—do you know why—?" She broke off, her face drawn together in mystification. She was seeing past him and around him, staring. "Why do they all end in sex?"

He was relieved at the genuinely questioning note; she was not being coy. He damned his evil mind of a moment before. "What do you mean?" he asked.

"He has a perfectly beautiful wife. Those children too. He was here tonight. With a girl. A perfectly ghastly girl." And once again she demanded of him, as though he must certainly know, being a man, "Do you know why that is happening? To everybody?"

Her driving need for an answer pierced him because the question was his obsession these days. It seemed very strange she had reached into him and had grasped precisely what bewildered him.

"It seems to me," she went on, "that almost everyone I know is going crazy. There doesn't seem to be any other subject any more. Any other *thing*—" She broke off again and drew in a long breath and wiped a strand of hair out of her eyes. Then she turned back to the fire, unable for the moment to continue looking at Joseph's resolute face. She wanted to weep, to laugh, to dance—anything but to sit here at this disadvantage. For an instant she remembered the warmth in Madame Lhevine's eyes, the feeling she was being enfolded by one more powerful, and she longed desperately to be taken up and held.

Her tone of supplication told Joseph that he was moving into a false position, for he dared not betray his own feelings of bewilderment. If they were both at a loss they would join in their miseries, and he could not, on even larger grounds, declare himself dumbfounded by life. "I know what you mean," he said, careful to direct his mournful tone toward unspecified others and away from himself and Cleota. "I see it myself all the time."

She looked at him from the fire. "Do you?" she asked, demanding he go on.

"I don't know the answer," he said and only glanced at her with this. "I guess it's that there is no larger aim in life any more. Everything has become personal relations and nothing more."

The blurred sensuousness drained out of her eyes, and she seemed alert to him again. "Is there something more?"

"Sure. That is, there might be."

"What?"

"Well . . ." he felt like a schoolboy, having to say that the welfare of mankind, the fight for justice, caring for the oppressed, were the something more. But as he began to evoke these thoughts their irrelevancy choked off his words, their distance from the suffering he saw in this woman lying back in the wicker chair with her knees fallen outward and the drink at her feet. She was lusting for a truth beyond what he possessed, yet he had to go on. "It's a law of history. When a society no longer knows its aims, when it's no longer dominated by the struggle to get food and safety, the private life is all there is. And we are all anarchists at heart when there is no greater aim. So we jump into each other's beds." God, what a fraud all ideas were—all anyone wanted was love!

"Joseph," she began, her voice very soft, her eyes on the fire, "why is it happening?"

He felt her proposal stretching out its wings, testing the air. He finished his drink and stood up. "I'll go, Cleota," he said.

She looked up at him, blinking lazily. "That woman said Stowe would die before his sister."

He could not speak; her belief in the prophecy shocked and persuaded him. He saw Stowe dead. He reached down and pressed his hand on hers awkwardly. "You can't believe that nonsense, can you?"

"Why are you going?" she asked.

Her simplicity terrified him. "I'll have one more drink," he said and got the bottle and set it on the floor beside his chair and sat again, taking as long as he could with the business. And again he damned his suspicious mind—she was simply frightened for Stowe, for God's sake! He would stay until she either fell asleep or came out of her fright.

Through the warm haze that surrounded her she saw that Joseph had suddenly come to life. How young he really was! His hair was not even graying, his skin was tight, and there was no judgment coming to her from him, no orders, no husband's impatience; her body felt new and unknown. "A larger aim," she said, her words muffled.

"What?" he asked.

She stood up and thrust her fingers into her hair and, breathing deeply, walked to the door. He sat still, watching her. She stopped at the pane and looked out through the mist, like a prisoner, he thought. He took a long swallow of his drink, resolved to leave. She stood there ten yards away with her hands in her hair, and he admired the angled backthrust of her torso secreted in her gray woolen dress. He saw her in bed, but all he could feel was her suffering. And then Stowe would return sometime, and the three of them in this room? The weedy morass of that scene shuddered him.

Moments went by and she did not turn from the door. She was waiting for him, he saw. Goddam! Why had he stayed? He saw that he had acted falsely, a role, the protector's part. Beneath his character and hers, beneath their very powers of speech, was the anarchy of need, the lust for oblivion and its comfort. He sat there reddening with shame at having misled her, his manhood spurious to him and thought itself a pretense.

She turned to him, still at the door, lowering her arms. The amateurishness of her seduction pained him for her sake as she stood there openly staring at him. "Don't you like me?"

"Sure I do."

Her brows came together densely as she walked to him and stood over him, her hands hanging at her sides, her head thrust forward a little, and as she spoke her open hands turned ever so slightly toward him. "What's the matter with you?"

He stood up and faced her, unable to speak at the sight of the animal fury in her face.

"What's the matter with you!" she screamed.

"Good night," he said, walking around her toward the door.

"What did you stay for?" she screamed at his back.

She came toward him unsteadily, a smile of mockery spreading on her face. She could feel, almost touch, his trembling, and she clenched her teeth together with the wish to tear with them. She felt her hands opening and closing and an amazing strength across her back. "You . . . ! You . . . !"

She stood up close to him, saw his eyes widening with surprise and fear. The taste of her stomach came into her mouth; her disgust for him and his broken promise brought tears to her eyes. But he did not move a hand to her; he was pitiless, like Stowe when he stared through her toward Alice, and like Alice moving in and out of this house. She wept.

Joseph touched her shoulder with his hand and instantly saw Stowe's laughing face before him. She neither accepted his touch nor rejected it. As though he had no importance for her any more. So he raised the immense weight of his arms and held her. The stairs to the second floor were a few yards away; he would almost have to carry her. She would be half conscious on the pillow; toward dawn the countryside from the bedroom window would be littered with hair, with bones, with the remnants of his search for an order in his life. Holding her to him, he feared her offering was an accusation of his complicity, a sign of their equal pointlessness. But he tightened his arms around her to squash out of her any inkling she might have of his unwillingness to share her world's derangement.

She encircled his waist and pressed her body against him. To love! To know nothing but love!

He took hold of her head and turned her face up to forestall the next moment. Her eyes were shut and tears were squeezing out of their corners, her skin hot in his hands. Cleota! Cleota Rummel! But without love? he thought, without even desire? He once again saw Stowe in this room, saw himself bantering with him, discussing, felt Stowe's bumbling warmth. How easy to ruin a man! From tomorrow on he could ruin Stowe with their usual handshake and the clap on the back. The power to destroy shaped itself in his mind like a rising rocket, astounding him with its frightfulness and its beauty, an automatic force given to him like a brand-new character, a new power that would somehow finish a struggle against the meaninglessness of life, joining him at his ease with that sightless legion riding the trains and driving the cars and filling the restaurants, a power to breathe the evil in the world and thus at last to love life. She pressed her lips against his throat, surprisingly soft lips. Disastrous contempt if he should try to leave her now, but to take her upstairs—his practical mind saw the engineering that would entail. A willed concussion of skeletons. He knew it was not virtue loosening his embrace but an older lust for a high heart uncondemned, a niggardly ambition it seemed to him now as he summoned his powers to say, "Good night, Cleota," and in such a tone as would convince her that he did not dislike her in his arms.

She opened her eyes. God, he thought, she could kill! "Whaz a matter with you?" she asked him.

"Nothing's the matter with me," he said, dropping his hands to his sides but blushing.

"What?" She swayed, peering at him through bewildered eyes, genuinely asking, "Whad you stay for?"

A good question, he thought, damning his naïveté. "I thought you didn't want to be alone," he said.

"Yez. You don't like me. I'm old. Older and older."

He reached out his hand to her, afraid she would fall, and she slapped it away, sending herself stumbling sideways, banging against the wall, where she held herself upright, her hair fallen over half her face. "Whaz a matter with all of you! All of you and all of you!" She was sobbing but seemed not to know it. "And if he dies before she does? Doesn't someone have to . . . have to win before the end?" She bent over, thrusting out her hands in a strangely theatrical gesture of supplication—how awkward she had become! How false all gracefulness is! And dredging up her arms from near the floor, her fingers wide, she called, weeping, a furious grimace stretching the two tendons of her throat, "Don't you have to win before it's over? Before . . . it's *overrrr!*"

He could not stop the tears in his eyes. "Yes," he whispered. The attempt to speak loosened some muscle in his stomach, and he fled weeping from the house.

The thumping resounded through his dreamless sleep. Boom, boom, boom. He opened his eyes. Boom. Again. He got out of bed and staggered. The whisky, he thought. He was dizzy and held on to the window sill. The booming sounded again below. He pulled up the shade. The sun! A clear day at last! The sun was just starting to come up at the far edges of the valley. The booming sounded again below. He pulled the window up and started to lean out but his head hit the screen. Now he saw Cleota's car in the road before the house, parked askew as though it had been left there in an emergency. The booming noise went on, now violently. He called out, "Yes!" then ran to the bed as though it were a dream and he could go back to sleep now that he had realized it.

But it was truly dawn and the noise was a knocking on his door, a dreadful emergency knocking. He called out "Yes!" again and got into his pants, which were lying on the floor, and struggled into his shirt and ran down the stairs barefoot and opened the door.

She was standing there, morning-fresh except for the exhaustion in her eyes. But her hair was brushed and she stood tall, herself again, if one did not know that she had never looked so frightened, so pleadingly at anyone in all her life. Suddenly he thought her beautiful with the sparkling air around her head. He was still passing up through the webs of his sleep, and she was part dream standing there in his doorway in a fox-collared coat of deep, rich brown, looking at him as though she had sprung from the grass without a history except that of earth and the immense trees on the road behind her. He reached out his hand, and she took it and stepped into the hallway. He was freezing in the icy breeze and started to close the door, but she held it and looked desperately up at him, wanting back what she had given him.

"I beg your pardon for last night," she said.

It was entirely askew to her; he was standing there trying to keep his eyes open, obviously undisturbed, she felt, by what she had done. Obviously, she saw now, he had had many women, and her coming here now was idiotically naïve to him. She felt such shame at her naïveté that she turned abruptly and pulled open the partly closed door, but he caught her arm and turned her to him.

"Cleota . . ."

Drawing her to him, he caught a scent of cherries in her hair. The sheer presence of her body in his house astounded him. Only now was he drunk. He lowered his lips to her but was stopped by the surprise in her eyes, a surprise that had something stiff-necked about it, a resistance, a propriety he would have to overcome, and suddenly he felt he wanted to.

His hesitation, like respect, moved her; but he was unnecessary to her now that she could feel his demand. Raising her hand, she tenderly touched his chest, relieved that he wanted her a little. They were accomplices now and she could trust his silence. She straightened before him, and a smile softened her face as she recognized his open need.

He saw a little of her old stance returning, her self-respect, but it was no longer necessary to obey it. He kissed her cheek. But she was less beautiful to him now that her despair was going; she was Cleota again, well-brushed, clear-eyed, and profoundly unapproachable.

"Take care of yourself," he said, meaninglessly, except for the brittle-shelled tone, the bantering voice they both knew so well. But how alive their simulation had become, how much more interesting it was now, this propriety, than it used to be!

"Would you like breakfast?" she asked.

Safe and sound, as on a shore they had finally reached, he said he had to go back to sleep for a while yet.

"Come later then," she said warmly, deeply satisfied.

"Okay."

She went down to her car and got in and drove away with a wave of one hand through the window, already slipping out of her coat with the other. She will be digging in her garden soon, he thought.

He did not go to her later. He lay in bed until the late morning, castigating himself for a coward at one moment, at the next wondering if he ought to be proud that he had been loyal to himself— and, as it turned out, to her as well.

But it never left the back of his mind that every claim to virtue is at least a little false; for was it virtue he had proved, or only fear? Or both! He wanted very much to believe that life could have a virtuous center where conscience might lie down with sensuality in peace, for otherwise everything but sexual advantage was a fraud. He heard her voice again. "What's the matter with you!" It rang. But was there really nothing truthful in her morning voice just now,

so civilized and reserved, inviting him to breakfast? Once again
good order reigned in this countryside. He smiled at a thought—
she would probably welcome Stowey more warmly now that she
had glimpsed a conquest. He was glad for her. So maybe some good
had come of the evening. God! What a ring of fire there always is
around the truth!

He lay a long time listening to the silence in his loveless house.

Alice died toward the end of May, falling asleep in her rocker as she
looked at the valley view while waiting for dinnertime. Joseph heard
of it only accidentally, when he returned after settling his divorce.
He had put his house up for sale and discovered he had no key to the
front door to give the real-estate agent. He removed the lock and
took it to the hardware store to have a key fitted, and the clerk mentioned the old lady's funeral. He wanted to ask how Stowe was but
caught himself. He returned with the key, installed the lock and
closed the place, got into his car and drove off. Before he could
think he found himself on the road to the Rummel house. He
had not seen Stowe since sometime before his trip to Florida, nor
had he seen Cleota since the morning after her fortune was told.

Realizing he was on their road, he reduced speed. In this
fine weather they might be outside and would look up and see
him passing. But what, after all, had he to be ashamed of? He
resolutely resumed speed, aware now that it was Stowe he would
rather not face. Unless, he thought—was this possible too?—
Stowe was dead?

The car traveled the long turn that straightened onto a view of
the Rummel house. Stowe and Cleota were walking idly on the
road, he with a stick knocking the heads off daisies and peering into the weeds every few yards, she at his side watching,
breathing—Joseph could already see—her breaths of fitness and
staring now and then at the newly green valley beyond Stowe's
head. They both turned, hearing the car, and, recognizing it,
stood still and tall. Stowe, seeing Joseph through the window,
nodded, looked at him, as he had the first time they had met many
years ago, with cool and perceptive eyes. Joseph nodded back,

angered by his friend's coolness but smiling, and to both of them said, "How are you?"

"Very well," Cleota said.

Only now could he look directly at her and, strengthened by Stowe's unjust condemnation, he dared hold her in his gaze. She was afraid of him!

"Selling out?" Stowe asked with noticeable contempt.

It dawned that Stowe was condemning him for the divorce; he had always admired Joseph's wife. Only now Joseph realized how correct his estimate of them had been—they were an old-fashioned family underneath, and Stowe despised those who, at the last moment, did not abide by the laws of decency.

"I'm trying to sell it," Joseph said, relaxing in his seat. "But I'll probably be by again before long. Maybe I'll drop in."

Stowe barely nodded.

"Bye," Joseph said. But this time Stowe simply looked at him.

"Have a good summer," Joseph said, turning to Cleota, and he saw, with surprise, that now she was observing him as a stranger, as Stowe was doing. They were joined.

He drove off past them, laughter rising in his heart, a joy at having seen good order closing back over chaos like an ocean that has swallowed a wreck. And he took a deep breath of May, glancing out the side window at the countryside, which seemed now never to have been cold and wet and unendurably dark through so many months.

When his car had gone and it was silent on the road, Stowe swung his stick and clipped a daisy. For a few yards neither spoke, and then he blew his nose and said, "He's not much."

"No," she said, "I suppose he isn't."

"There was always some sneakiness in him, something like that."

"Yes," she said and took his arm and they walked together past his sister's empty house. She kissed his shoulder, and he looked at her, grinning and surprised, for she did not make such displays. He grunted, quite pleased, and she held him tighter, feeling the sun on her back like a blessing, aware once again of Stowe's deep reliability, and her own. Thank God, she thought, for good sense!

Joseph, she remembered, had wanted her very much that morning in his hallway. And she walked in silence, cherishing a rapture, the clear heart of those whose doors are made to hold against the winds of the world.

"Still," she felt the need to say, "it's rather a shame about them."

He shrugged and bent over to part the roadside weeds, reached in and brought out a young toad whose squeaks made him laugh. And suddenly he tossed it to her. She shrieked, reddening with anger, but then she laughed. And as sometimes happened with them, they just stood face to face, laughing down at each other with an enormous heartiness.

[*1961*]

Fame

Seven hundred and fifty thousand dollars—minus the ten percent commission, that left him six hundred and seventy-five thousand, spread over ten years. Coming out of his agent's building onto Madison Avenue, he almost smiled at this slight resentment he felt at having to pay Billy the seventy-five thousand. A gaunt, good-looking woman smiled back at him as she passed; he did not turn, fearing she would stop and begin the conversation that by now was unbearable for him. "I only wanted to tell you that it's really the wisest and funniest play I think I've ever . . ." He kept close to the storefronts as he walked, resolving once again to develop some gracious set of replies to these people, who after all—at least some of them—were sincere. But he knew he would always stand there like an oaf, for some reason ashamed and yet happy.

A rope of pearls lay on black velvet in the window of a jewelry store; he paused. My God, he thought, I could buy that! I could buy the whole window maybe. Even the store! The pearls were suddenly worthless. In the glass he saw his hound's eyes, his round, sad face and narrow beard, his sloping shoulders and wrinkled corduroy lapels; for the King of Broadway, he thought, you still look like a failure. He moved on a few steps, and a hand grasped his forearm with annoying proprietary strength and turned him to an immense chest, a yachtsman's sunburned face with a chic, narrow-brimmed hat on top.

"You wouldn't be Meyer Berkowitz?"

"No. I look like him, though."

The man blushed under his tan, looked offended, and walked away. Meyer Berkowitz approached the corner of Fiftieth Street, feeling the fear of retaliation. What do I want them to do, hate me? On the corner he paused to study his watch. It was only a quarter to six, and the dinner was for seven-fifteen. He tried to remember if there was a movie house in the neighborhood. But there wouldn't be time for a whole movie unless he happened to come in at the beginning. Still, he could afford to pay for half a movie. He turned west on Fiftieth. A couple stared at him as he passed. His eye fell on a rack of magazines next to the corner newsstand. The edge of *Look* showed under *Life*, and he wondered again at all the airplanes, kitchen tables, dentists' offices, and trains where people would be staring at his face on the cover. He thought of shaving his beard. But then, he thought, they won't recognize me. He smiled. I am hooked. So be hooked, he muttered, and, straightening up, he resolved to admit to the next interloper that he was in fact Meyer Berkowitz and happy to meet his public. On a rising tide of honesty, he remembered the years in the Burnside Memorial Chapel, sitting beside the mummified dead, his notebooks spread on the cork floor as he constructed play after play, and the mirror in the men's room where he would look at his morose eyes, wondering when and if they would ever seem as unique as his secret fate kept promising they would someday be. On Fifth Avenue, so clean, gray, and rich, he headed downtown, his hands clasped behind his back. Two blocks west, two blocks to the right of his shoulder, the housemen in two theaters were preparing to turn the lights on over his name; the casts of two plays were at home, checking their watches; in all, maybe thirty-five people, including the stage managers and assistants, had been joined together by him, their lives changed and in a sense commanded by his words. And in his heart, in a hollowed-out place, stood a question mark: Was it possible to write another play? Thankfully he thought of his wealth again, subtracted ten percent commission from the movie purchase price of *I See You* and divided the remainder over ten years, and angrily swept all the dollars out of his head. A cabdriver slowed down beside him and waved and yelled, "Hey, Meyer!" and the two passengers were leaning forward to see him. The cab was keeping pace with him, so he lifted his left hand a few inches in a cripped wave—like a prizefighter, it occurred to him. An unexplainable disgust pressed him toward a sign overhanging the sidewalk a few yards ahead.

He had a vague recollection of eating in Lee Fong's years ago with Billy, who had been trying unsuccessfully to get him a TV assignment ("Meyer, if you would only follow a plotline . . ."). It would probably be empty at this hour, and it wasn't elegant. He pushed open the bright-red lacquered door and thankfully saw that the bar was empty and sat on a stool. Two girls were alone in the restaurant part, talking over teacups. The bartender took his order without any sign of recognizing him. He settled both arms on the bar, purposefully relaxing. The Scotch and soda arrived. He drank, examining his face, which was segmented by the bottles in front of the mirror. Cleanly and like a soft blow on his shoulder, the realization struck him that it was getting harder and harder to remember talking to anyone as he used to last year and all his life before his plays had opened, before he had come on view. Even now in this empty restaurant he was already expecting a stranger's voice behind him, and half wanting it. Crummy. A longing rose up in him to face someone with his mind on something else; someone who would not show that charged, distorted pressure in the eyes which, he knew, meant that the person was seeing his printed face superimposed over his real one. Again he watched himself in the mirror behind the bar: Meyer the Morose, Sam Ugly, but a millionaire with plays running in five countries. Setting his drink down, he noticed the soiled frayed cuffs on his once-tan corduroy jacket, and the shirt cuff sticking out with the button off. With a distant feeling of alarm he realized that he was meeting his director and producer and their wives at the Pavillon and that these clothes, to which he had never given any thought, would set him off as a character who went around like a bum when he had two hits running.

Thank God anyway that he had never married! To come home

to the old wife with this printed new face—not good. But now, how would he ever know whether a woman was looking at him or at "Meyer Berkowitz" in full color on the magazine cover? Strange—in the long memorial chapel nights he had envisaged roomfuls of girls pouring over him when his plays succeeded, and now it was almost inconceivable to make a real connection with any women he knew. He summoned up their faces, and in each he saw calculation, that look of achievement. It was exhausting him, the whole thing. Months had gone by since he had so much as made a note. What he needed was an apartment in Bensonhurst or the upper Bronx somewhere, among people who . . . But they would know him in the Bronx. He sipped his second drink. His stomach was empty and the alcohol went straight to the back of his eyes, and he felt himself lifted up and hanging restfully by the neck over the bar.

The bartender, a thin man with a narrow mustache and only faint signs of Chinese features, stood before him. "I beggin' you pardon. Excuse me?"

Meyer Berkowitz raised his eyes, and before the bartender could speak, he said, "I'm Meyer Berkowitz."

"Ha!" The bartender pointed into his face with a long fingernail. "I know. I recognizin' you! On *Today* show, right?"

"Right."

The bartender now looked over Meyer's head toward someone behind him and, pointing at Meyer, nodded wildly. Then, for some reason whispering into Meyer's ear, he said, "The boss invite you to havin' something on the house."

Meyer turned around and saw a Chinese with sunglasses on standing beside the cash register, bowing and gesturing lavishly toward the expanse of the bar. Meyer smiled, nodded with aristocratic graciousness as he had seen people do in movies, turned back to the bartender and ordered another Scotch, and quickly finished the one in his hand. How fine people really were! How they loved their artists! Shit, man, this is the greatest country in the world.

He stirred the gift Scotch, whose ice cubes seemed just a little clearer than the ones he had paid for. How come his refrigerator never made such clear ice cubes? Vaguely he heard people entering the restaurant behind him. With no warning he was suddenly aware that three or four couples were at the bar alongside him and that in the restaurant part the white linen tablecloths were now alive with moving hands, plates, cigars. He held his watch up to his eyes. The undrunk part of his brain read the time. He'd finish this drink and amble over to the Pavillon. If he only had a pin for his shirt cuff . . .

"Excuse me . . ."

He turned on the stool and faced a small man with very fair skin, wearing a gray-checked overcoat and a gray hat and highly polished black shoes. He was a short, round man, and Meyer realized that he himself was the same size and even the same age, just about, and he was not sure suddenly that he could ever again write a play.

The short man had a manner, it was clear, the stance of a certain amount of money. There was money in his pause and the fit of his coat and a certain ineffable condescension in his blue eyes, and Meyer imagined a woman, no doubt the man's wife, also short, wrapped in mink, waiting a few feet away in the crowd at the bar, with the same smug look.

After the pause, during which Meyer said nothing, the short man asked, "Are you Meyer Berkowitz?"

"That's right," Meyer said, and the alcohol made him sigh for air.

"You don't remember me?" the short man said, a tiny curl of smile on the left edge of his pink mouth.

Meyer sobered. Nothing in the round face stuck to any part of his memory, and yet he knew he was not all this drunk. "I'm afraid not. Who are you?"

"You don't remember me?" the short man asked with genuine surprise.

"Well, who are you?"

The man glanced off, not so much embarrassed as unused to explaining his identity; but swallowing his pride, he looked back at Meyer and said, "You don't remember Bernie Gelfand?"

Whatever suspicion Meyer felt was swept away. Clearly he had known this man somewhere, sometime. He felt the debt of the forgetter. "Bernie Gelfand. I'm awfully sorry, but I can't recall where. Where did I know you?"

"I sat next to you in English four years? De Witt Clinton!"

Meyer's brain had long ago drawn a blind down on all his high-school years. But the name Gelfand did rustle the fallen leaves at the back of his mind. "I remember your name, ya, I think I do."

"Oh, come on, guy, you don't remember Bernie Gelfand with the curly red hair?" With which he raised his gray felt hat to reveal a shiny bald scalp. But no irony showed in his eyes, which were transported back to his famous blazing hair and to the seat he had had next to Meyer Berkowitz in high school. He put his hat back on again.

"Forgive me," Meyer said, "I have a terrible memory. I remember your name, though."

Gelfand, obviously put out, perhaps even angered but still trying to smile, and certainly full of intense sentimental interest, said, "We were best friends."

Meyer laid a beseeching hand on Gelfand's gray coat sleeve. "I'm not doubting you, I just can't place you for the moment. I mean, I believe you." He laughed.

Gelfand seemed assuaged now, nodded, and said, "You don't look much different, you know? I mean, except for the beard, I'd know you in a minute."

"Yeah, well . . ." Meyer said, but still feeling he had offended, he obediently asked, "What do you do?" preparing for a long tale of success.

Gelfand clearly enjoyed this question, and he lifted his eyebrows to a proud peak. "I'm in shoulder pads," he said.

A laugh began to bubble up in Meyer's stomach; Gelfand's coat was in fact stiffly padded at the shoulders. But in an instant he remembered that there was a shoulder-pad industry, and the importance which Gelfand attached to his profession killed the faintest smile on Meyer's face. "Really," he said with appropriate solemnity.

"Oh, yes. I'm general manager, head of everything up to the Mississippi."

"Don't say. Well, that's wonderful." Meyer felt great relief. It would have been awful if Gelfand had been a failure—or in charge of New England only. "I'm glad you've done so well."

Gelfand glanced off to one side, letting his achievement sink deeply into Meyer's mind. When he looked again at Meyer, he could not quite keep his eyes from the frayed cuffs of the corduroy jacket and the limp shirt cuff hanging out. "What do *you* do?" he asked.

Meyer looked into his drink. Nothing occurred to him. He touched his finger against the mahogany bar and still nothing came to him through his shock. His resentment was clamoring in his head; he recognized it and greeted it. Then he looked directly at Gelfand, who in the pause had grown a look of benevolent pity. "I'm a writer," Meyer said, and watched for the publicity-distorted freeze to grip Gelfand's eyeballs.

"That so!" Gelfand said, amused. "What kind of writing you do?"

If I really had any style, Meyer thought, I would shrug and say I write part-time poems after I get home from the post office, and would leave Bernie to enjoy his dinner. On the other hand, I do not work in the post office, and there must be some way to shake this monkey off and get back to where I can talk to people again as if I were real. "I write plays," he said to Gelfand.

"That so!" Gelfand smiled, his amusement enlarging toward open condescension. "Anything I would have . . . heard of?"

"Well, as a matter of fact, one of them is down the street."

"Really? On *Broadway?*" Gelfand's face split into its parts; his mouth still kept its smile, but his eyes showed a certain wild alarm. His head, suddenly, was on straighter, his neck drawn back.

"I wrote *I See You,*" Meyer said, and tasted slime on his tongue.

Gelfand's mouth opened. His skin reddened.

"And *Mostly Florence.*"

The two smash hits seemed to open before Gelfand's face like bursting flags. His finger lifted toward Meyer's chest. "Are you . . . *Meyer Berkowitz?*" he whispered.

"Yes."

Gelfand held out his hand tentatively. "Well, I'm very happy to meet you," he said with utter formality.

Meyer saw distance locking into place between them, and in the instant wished he could take Gelfand in his arms and wipe out the poor man's metaphysical awe, smother his defeat, and somehow retract this very hateful pleasure, which he knew now he could not part with any more. He shook Gelfand's hand and then covered it with his left hand.

"Really," Gelfand went on, withdrawing his hand as though it had already presumed too much. "I . . . I've enjoyed your—excuse me." Meyer's heavy cheeks stirred vaguely toward a smile.

Gelfand closed his coat and quickly turned about and hurried to the little crowd waiting for tables near the red entrance door. He took the arm of a short woman in a mink wrap and turned her toward the door. She seemed surprised as he hurried her out of sight and into the street.

[1966]

Fitter's Night

By four in the afternoon it was almost dark in winter, and this January was one of the coldest on record, so that the night shift filing through the turnstiles at the Navy Yard entrance was somber, huddling in zipper jackets and pulling down earflaps, shifting from foot to foot as the marine guards inspected each tin lunchbox in turn and compared the photographs on identity cards with the squint-eyed, blue-nosed faces that passed through. The former grocery clerks, salesmen, unemployed, students, and the mysteriously incapacitated young men whom the Army and Navy did not want; the elderly skilled machinists come out of retirement, the former truckdrivers, elevator operators, masons, disbarred lawyers, and a few would-be poets, poured off the buses in the blue light of late afternoon and waited their turn at the end of the lines leading to the fresh-faced marines in the booths, who refused to return their quips and dutifully searched for the bomb and the incendiary pencil under the lettuce-and-tomato sandwiches leaking through the waxed paper, against all reason unscrewing the Thermos bottles to peer in at the coffee. With some ten thousand men arriving for each of the three shifts, the law of averages naturally came into play, and it was inevitable that every few minutes someone would put his Thermos back into his lunchbox and say, "What's Roosevelt got against hot coffee?" and the Marines would blink and wave the joker into the Yard.

To the naval architects, the engineers, the yardmaster and his staff, the New York Naval Shipyard was not hard to define; in fact, it had hardly changed since its beginnings in the early 1800s.

The vast drydocks facing the bay were backed by a maze of crooked and curving streets lined with one-story brick machine shops and storehouses. In dark Victorian offices, papers were still speared on sharp steel points, and filing cabinets were of dark oak. Ships of war were never exactly the same, whatever anybody said, and the smith was still in a doorway hammering one-of-a-kind iron fittings, the sparks falling against his floor-length apron; steel bow plates were still sighted by eye regardless of the carefully mapped curves of the drawing, and when a man was injured, a two-wheel pushcart was sent for to bump him along the cobblestones to the infirmary like a side of beef.

It was sure that Someone knew where everything was, and this faith was adopted by every new man. The shipfitter's helper, the burner, the chipper, the welder; painters, carpenters, riggers, drillers, electricians—hundreds of them might spend the first hour of each shift asking one stranger after another where he was supposed to report or what drydock held the destroyer or carrier he had been working on the night before; and there were not a few who spent entire twelve-hour shifts searching for their particular gangs, but the faith never faltered. Someone must know what was supposed to be happening, if only because damaged ships did limp in under tow from the various oceans and after days, weeks, or sometimes months they did sail out under Brooklyn Bridge, ready once again to fight the enemy. There were naturally a sensitive few who, watching these gallant departures, shook their heads with wonder at the mystery of how these happened to have been repaired, but the vast majority accepted this and even felt that they themselves were somehow responsible. It was like a baseball game with five hundred men playing the outfield at the same time, sweeping in a mob toward the high arching ball, which was caught somewhere in the middle of the crowd, by whom no one knew, except that the game was slowly and quite inconceivably being won.

Tony Calabrese, Shipfitter First Class, was one of that core of men who did know where to report once he came through the turnstile at four in the afternoon. In "real life," as the phrase went, he had been a steamfitter in Brooklyn and was not confused by mobs, Marines looking into his sandwiches, or the endless waiting around that was normal in a shipyard. Once through the turnstile, his lunchbox tucked under his arm again, his cap on crooked, he leaned into the wind with his broken nose, notifying oncoming men to clear the way, snug inside his pile zipper jacket and woolen shirt, putting down his feet on the outside edges like a bear, bandy-legged, low-crotched, a graduate of skyscraper construction, brewery repairing, and for eight months the city Department of Water Supply, until it was discovered that he had been sending a substitute on Tuesdays, Wednesdays, and Fridays while he went to the track and made some money.

Tony had never until a year and a half ago seen a ship up close and had no interest in ships, any more than he had had in the water supply, breweries, or skyscrapers. Work was a curse, a misfortune that a married man had to bear, like his missing front tooth, knocked out in a misunderstanding with a bookie. There was no mystery to what the good life was, and he never lived a day without thinking about it, and more and more hopelessly now that he was past forty; it was being like Sinatra, or Luciano, or even one of the neighborhood politicians who wore good suits all day and never bent over, kept two apartments, one for the family, the other for the baloney of the moment. He had put his youth into trying for that kind of life and had failed. Driving the bootleggers' trucks over the Canadian border, even a season as Johnny Peaches's bravo and two months collecting for a longshoremen's local, had put him within reach of a spot, a power position from which he might have retired into an office or apartment and worked through telephones and over restaurant tables. But at the last moment something in his makeup had always defeated him, sent him rolling back into the street and a job and a paycheck, where the future was the same never-get-rich routine. He knew he was simply not smart enough. If he were, he wouldn't be working in the Navy Yard.

His face was as round as a frying pan with a hole in it, a comical face now that the nose was flattened and his front tooth gone, and no neck. He had risen to First in a year and a half, partly because the supervisor, old Charley Mudd, liked a good phone number, which Tony could slip him, and also because Tony could read blueprints quickly, weld, chip, burn, and bulldoze a job to its finish when, as happened occasionally, Charley Mudd had to get a ship back into the war. As Shipfitter First, he was often given difficult and complicated jobs and could call on any of the various trades to come in and burn or weld at his command. But he was not impressed by his standing, when Sinatra could open his mouth and make a grand. More important was that his alliance with Charley Mudd gave him jobs below decks in cold weather and above decks when the sky was clear. If indisposed, he could give Charley Mudd the sign and disappear for the night into a dark corner and a good sleep. But most of the time he enjoyed being on the job, particularly when he was asked how to perform one operation or another by "shipfitters" who could not compute a right angle or measure in smaller units than halves. His usual way of beginning his instruction was always the same and was expected by anyone who asked his help. He would unroll the blueprint, point to a line or figure, and say, "Pay 'tention, shithead," in a voice sludged with the bottom of wine bottles and the Italian cigars he inhaled. No one unable to bear this indignity asked him for help, and those who did knew in advance that they would certainly lose whatever pretensions they thought they had.

But there was another side to Tony, which came out during the waits. Before Pearl Harbor there had been some six thousand men employed in the Yard, and there were now close to sixty thousand. Naturally they would sometimes happen to collect in unmanageable numbers in a single compartment, and the repairs, which had to be done in specific stages, made it impossible for most of them to work and for any to leave. So the waits began; maybe the welder could not begin welding until the chipper finished breaking out the old weld, so he waited, with his helper or partner. The burner could not cut steel until the exhaust hose was brought down by his helper, who could not get hold of one until another burner down the corridor was finished with it, so he waited; a driller could not drill until his point was struck into the steel by the fitter, who was forbidden to strike it until the electricians had removed the electric cables on the other side of the bulkhead through which the hole had to be drilled, so they waited; until the only way out was a crap game, or Tony "enjoying" everybody by doing imitations or picking out somebody to insult and by going into his grin, which, with the open space in his teeth, collapsed the company in hysteria. After these bouts of entertainment Tony always became depressed, reminded again of his real failing, a lack of stern dignity, leadership, force. Luciano would hardly be clowning around in a cruiser compartment, showing how stupid he could look with a tooth missing.

On this January afternoon, already so dark and the wind biting at his eyes, Tony Calabrese, going down the old streets of the Yard, had decided to work below decks tonight, definitely. Even here in the shelter of the Yard streets the wind was miserable—what would it be like on a main deck open to the bay? Besides, he did not want to tire himself this particular shift, when he had a date at half past four in the morning. He went through his mental checklist: Dora would meet him at Baldy's for breakfast; by six a.m. he would be home to change his clothes and take a shower; coffee with the kids at seven before they went to school, then maybe a nap till nine or half past, then pick up Dora and make the first show at the Fox at ten; by twelve to Dora's room, bang-bang, and a good sleep till half past two or three, when he would stop off at home and put on work clothes, and maybe see the kids if they got home early, and into the subway for the Yard. It was a good uncomplicated day in front of him.

Coming out of the end of the street, he saw the cold stars over the harbor, a vast sky stretching out over the bay and beyond to the sea. Clusters of headlights coursed over Brooklyn Bridge, the thickening traffic of the homebound who did not know they were passing over the Yard or the war-broken ships. He picked his way around stacks of steel plate and tarpaulin-shrouded gear piled everywhere, and for a moment was caught in the blasting white glare of the arc lamp focused downward from the top of a traveling crane; slowly, foot by foot, it rolled along the tracks, tall as a four-story building on two straddling legs, its one arm thrust out against the stars, dangling a dull glinting steel plate the width of a bus, and led by a fitter hardly taller than its wheels, who was walking backward between the tracks ahead of it and pointing off to the right in the incandescent whiteness of its one eye. As though intelligent, the crane obediently swiveled its great arm, lowering the swaying plate to a spot pointed at by the fitter, whose face Tony could not make out, shaded as it was by the peak of the cap against the downpouring light of the high white eye. Tony circled wide around the descending plate, trusting no cable or crane operator, and passed into the darkness again toward the cruiser beyond, raised in the drydock, her bow curving high over the roadway on which he walked with his lips pressed together to keep the wind off his teeth. Turning, he moved along her length, head down against the swift river of cold air, welcoming the oncoming clumps of foot-stamping men mounting her along the gangplank— the new shift boarding, the occasional greeting voice still lively in the earliness of the evening. He rocked up the length of the gangplank onto the main deck, with barely a nod passing the young lieutenant in upturned collar who stood hitting his gloved hands together in the tiny temporary guardhouse at the head of the plank. There was the happy smell of burned steel and coffee, the straightforward acridity of the Navy, and the feeling of the hive as he descended a steep stair clogged down its whole length with black welder's cables and four-inch exhaust hoses, the temporary intestine that always followed repair gangs into the patient ships.

His helper, Looey Baldu—where an Italian got a name like Baldu, Tony could not understand, unless a Yugoslav had got into the woodpile or they shortened it—Looey was already waiting for him in the passageway, twenty-three, dignified and superior with his high-school education, in regulation steel-tipped shoes— which Tony steadfastly refused to wear—and giving his resolute but defensive greeting.

"Where's Charley Mudd?"

"I didn't see him yet."

"You blind? There he is."

Tony walked around the surprised Baldu and into a compartment where Charley Mudd, sixty and half asleep, sat on three coils
of electric cable, his eyes shut and a clipboard starting to slide out
of his opening hands. Tony touched the older man's back and bent
to talk softly and put in the fix. Charley nodded, his eyes rolling.
Tony gave him a grateful pat and came out into the passageway,
which was filling with men trying to pass one another in opposite
directions while dragging endless lengths of hose, cable, ladders,
and bulky toolboxes, everybody looking for somebody else, so that
Tony had to raise his voice to Baldu. He always spoke carefully to
the high-school graduate, who never caught on the first time but
was a good boy although his wife, he said, was Jewish. Baldu was
against race prejudism, whatever the hell that meant, and frowned
like a judge when talked to, as though some kind of veil hung before
his face and nothing came through it loud and clear.

"We gonna watertight hatches C Deck," Tony said, and he
turned, hands still clenched inside his slit pockets, and walked.

Baldu had had no time to nod and already felt offended, but he
followed with peaked eyebrows behind his fitter, keeping close so
as not to know the humiliation of being lost again and having to
face Tony's scathing ironies implying incessant masturbation.

They descended to C Deck, a large, open area filled with tiered
bunks in which a few sailors lay, some sleeping, others reading or
writing letters. Tony was pleased at the nearness of the coffee
smell, what with any more than a pound a week almost impossible
for civilians to get except at black-market prices. Without looking
again at his helper, he unzipped his jacket, stowed his lunchbox on
the deck under an empty bunk, took out a blue handkerchief and
blew his nose and wiped his teary eyes, removed his cap and
scratched his head, and finally sat on his heels and ran his fingers
along the slightly raised edge of a hatch opening in the deck,
through which could be seen a ladder going down into dimness.

"Let that there cover come to me, Looey."

Baldu, his full brown-paper lunch bag still in his hand, sprang
to the heavy hatch cover lying on the deck and with one hand

tried to raise it on its hinges. Unwilling to admit that his strength was not enough or that he had made a mistake, he strained with the one hand, and as Tony regarded him with aggravation and lowering lids, he got the hatch cover up on one knee, and only then let his lunch bag down onto the deck and with two hands finally raised the cover toward Tony, whose both hands were poised to stop it from falling shut.

"Hold it, hold it right there."

"Hold it open?"

"Well, what the fuck, you gonna hold it closed? Of course open. What's a-matta wichoo?"

Tony felt with his fingertips along the rubber gasket that ran around the lip of the cover. Then he took hold of it and let it close over the hatch. Bending down until his cheek pressed the cold deck, he squinted to see how closely gasket met steel. Then he got up, and Looey Baldu stood to face him.

"I'm gonna give you a good job, Looey. Git some chalk, rub it on the gasket, then git your marks on the deck. Where the chalk don't show, build it up with some weld, then git a grinder and tell him smooth it nice till she's nice an' even all around. You understand?"

"Sure, I'll do it."

"Just don't get wounded. That's it for tonight, so take it easy."

Baldu's expression was nearly fierce as he concentrated patriotically on the instructions, and now he nodded sternly and started to step back. Tony grabbed him before he tripped over the hatch cover behind him, then let him go and without further remark fled toward the coffee smell.

It was going to be a pretty good night. Dora, whom he had gotten from Hindu, was a little shorter than he would have liked, but she had beautiful white skin, especially her breasts, and lived alone in a room with good heat—no sisters, aunts, mother, nothing. And both times she had brought home fresh bread from Macy's, where she packed nights. Now all he had to do was keep relaxed through the shift so as not to be sleepy when he met her for breakfast at Baldy's. Picking his way along a passage toward the intensifying coffee smell, he felt joyous, and seeing a drunken sailor trying to come down a ladder, he put his shoulder under the boy's seat and gently let him down to the deck, then helped him a few yards along the passage until the boy fell into a bunk. Then he lifted his legs onto it, turned him over, opened his pea jacket and shoelaces, and returned to the search for the source of the coffee smell.

He might have known. There was Hindu, standing over an electric brewer tended by two sailors in T-shirts. Hindu was big, but next to him stood a worker who was a head taller, a giant. Tony sauntered over, and Hindu said to the sailors, "This here's a buddy, how about it?"

A dozen lockers stood against the nearby bulkhead, from one of which a sailor took a clean cup and a five-pound bag of sugar. Tony thanked him as he took the full cup and then moved a foot away as Hindu came over.

"Where you?" Hindu asked.

"C Deck, watertight hatch cover. Where you?"

"I disappeared. They're still settin' up the windbreak on Main Deck."

"Fuck that."

"You know what Washington said when he crossed the Delaware?"

Then both together, "It's fuckin' cold."

They drank coffee. Hindu's skin was so dark he was sometimes taken for an Indian; he made up for it by keeping his thick, wavy hair well combed, his blue beard closely shaved, and his big hands clean.

"I gotta make a phone call," he said quietly, stooping to Tony. "I left her bawlin'. Jesus, I passed him comin' up the stairs."

"Ta hell you stay so long?"

"I coun' help myself." His eyes softened, his mouth worked in pleasurable agony. "She's dri'n' me crazy. We even wen' faw walk."

"You crazy?"

"I coun' help it. If you seen her you drop dead. Byoodiful. I mean it. I'm goin' crazy. I passed him comin' up the stairs, I swear!"

"You'll end up fuckin' a grave, Hindu."

"She touches me, I die. I die. I die, Tony." Hindu shut his eyes and shook his head, memorializing.

Activity behind them turned them about. The big worker, his coffee finished, was pulling on a chain that ran through a set of pulleys hooked to a beam overhead, and a gigantic electric motor was rising up off the deck. Tony, Hindu, and the two sailors watched the massive rigger easily raise the slung motor until it reached the pulleys and could be raised no farther, with three inches yet to go before it could be slid onto a platform suspended from the deck overhead. The rigger drew his gauntlets up tighter, set himself underneath the motor with his hands up under it, and, with knees bent, pushed. The motor rose incredibly until its feet were a fraction above the platform; the rigger pushed and got it hung. Then he came out from under, stood behind it, and shoved it fully onto the platform where it belonged. His face was flushed, and, expanded by the effort, he looked bigger than ever. Slipping off his gauntlets, he looked down to the sailors, who were still sitting on the deck.

"Anybody ever read *Oliver Wiswell*?"

"No."

"You ought to. Gives you a whole new perspective on the American Revolution. You know, there's a school that doesn't think the Revolution was necessary."

Tony was already walking, and Hindu followed slightly behind, asking into his ear, "Maybe I could hang wichoo tonight, Tony. Okay? I ask Cholly, okay?"

"Go ahead."

Hindu patted Tony's back thankfully and hurried up a ladder.

Tony looked at his pocket watch. Five o'clock. He had chopped an hour. It was too early to take a nap. A sense of danger struck him, and he looked ahead up the passage, but there was only a colored worker he did not know fooling with a chipping gun that would not receive its chisel. He turned the other way in time to see a captain and a man in a felt hat and overcoat approaching with blueprints half unrolled in their hands. He caught sight of a chipping-gun air hose, which he followed into a compartment on hands and knees. The two brass went by, and he stood up and walked out of the compartment.

It was turning into one of the slow nights when the clock never moved. The coffee had sharpened him even more, so a nap was out of the question. He moved along passageways at a purposeful pace, up ladders and down, looking for guys he might know, but the ship was not being worked much tonight; why, he did not know and did not care. Probably there was a hurry-up on the two destroyers that had come in last night. One had a bow blasted off, and the other had floated in from the bay listing hard to one side. The poor bastards on the destroyers, with no room to move and some of those kids seasick in bad weather. The worst was when the British ships came in. Good he wasn't on one of those bastards, with the cockroaches so bad you couldn't sit down, let alone stretch out, and their marines a lot of faggos. That was hard to believe the first time he saw it—like last summer with that British cruiser, the captain pacing the deck day and night and the ship in drydock. A real jerked-off Englishman with a monocle and a mustache and a crushed cap, and a little riding crop in his hands clasped behind his back, scowling at everybody and refusing to go off duty even in drydock. And piping whistles blowing every few hours to bring the marines on deck for rifle drill, that bunch of fags screaming through the passageways, goosing each other, and pimples all over their faces. Christ, he hated the English the way they kicked Italy around, sneering. And those stupid officers, in July; walking around in thick blue hairy uniforms, sweating like pigs all over their eyeglasses. You could tell a U.S. ship blindfolded, the smell of coffee and cleanliness, and ice water anywhere you looked. Of course they said the British gunners were better, but who was winning the war, for Christ's sake? Without us they'd have to pack it in and salute the fuckin' Germans. The French had a good ship, that captured *Richelieu*, what paneling in the wardroom, like a fuckin' palace, but something was wrong with the guns, they said, and couldn't hit nothin'.

He found himself in the engine room and looked up through the barrel-like darkness, up and up through the belly of the ship. There was, he knew, a cable passage where he could lie down. Somebody he could barely see high above in the darkness was showering sparks from a welding arc being held too far from the steel, but he pulled up his collar and climbed ladders, moved along the cat- walks until he came to a low door which he opened, went into a hole lined with electric cables, and lay down with his hands clasped under his head. The welding buzz was all he could hear now. Foot- steps would sound on the steel catwalks and give good warning.

Not tired, he closed his eyes to screw the government. Even here in the dark he was making money every minute—every second. With this week's check he would probably have nearly two thou- sand in his account and a hundred and twenty or so in the account Margaret knew about. Jesus, what a dumb woman! Dumb, dumb, dumb. But a good mother, that's for sure. But why not? With only two kids, what else she got to do? He would never sleep with her again and could barely remember the sight of her body. In fact, for the thousandth time in his life, he realized that he had never seen his wife naked, which was as it should be. You could fill a lake with the tears she had shed these fifteen years—an ocean. Good.

He stoked his anger at his wife, the resentment that held his life together. It was his cause, his agony, and his delight to let his mind go and imagine what she must feel, not being touched for eleven— no, twelve, yes, it was twelve last spring—years. This spring it would be thirteen, then fourteen, then twenty, and into her grave without his hand on her. Never, never would he give in. On the bed, when he did sleep at home, with his back to her, he stretched into good sleep, and sometimes her wordless sobs behind him were like soft rain on the roof that made him snug. She had asked for it. He had warned her at the time. He might look funny, but Tony Calabrese was not funny for real. To allow himself to break, to put his hand on her ever again, he would have to forgive what she had done to him. And now, lying in the cable passage with his eyes closed, he went over what she had done, and as always happened when he reached for these memories, the darling face of the balo- ney formed in his darkness, Patty Moran, with genuine red hair, breasts without a crease under them, and lips pink as lipstick. Oh, Jesus! He shook his head in the dark. And where was she now? He did not dare hate his grandfather; the old man was like a storm or an animal that did only what it was supposed to do. He let himself remember what had become for him like a movie whose end he knew and dreaded to see once more, and yet wanted to. It was the only time in his life that had not been random, when each day that had passed in those few months had changed his position and finally sealed him up forever.

From the day he was born, it seemed to him, his mother had kept warning him to watch out for Grampa. If he stole, hit, lied, tore good pants, got in cop trouble, the same promise was made—if Grampa ever came to America he would settle each and every one of Tony's crimes in a daylong, maybe weeklong beating combined with an authoritative spiritual thundering that would straighten out Tony for the rest of his life. For Grampa was gigantic, a sport in the diminutive family, a throwback to some giants of old whose wit and ferocity had made them lords in Calabria, chiefs among the rocks, commanders of fishing boats, capos of the mines. Even Tony's cowed father relied on the absent, never-seen old man for authority and spent every free hour away from work on the BMT tracks playing checkers with his cronies, rather than chastise his sons. Grampa would come one day and settle them all, straighten them out, and besides, if he did come, he would bring his money. He owned fishing boats, the star of the whole family, a rich man who had made it, astoundingly, without ever leaving Calabria, which meant again that he was wily and merciless, brave and just.

The part that was usually hard to remember was hard to remember again, and Tony opened his eyes in the cable passage until, yes, he remembered. How he had ever gotten mixed up with Margaret in the first place, a mewly girl, big-eyed but otherwise blanketed bodily, bodiless, shy, and frightened. It was because he had just come out of the Tombs, and this time Mama was not to be fooled with. She was a fury now as he walked into the tenement, unwilling to listen to the old promises or to be distracted by all his oaths of innocence and frame-up. And this time fate began to step in, that invisible presence entered Tony's life, the Story; his tight time began, when nothing was any longer random and every day changed what he was and what he had to do.

A letter had arrived that nobody could read. They sat around the table, Mama and Papa and Aunt Celia from next door, and Frank and Salvatore, his married cousins. Tony slowly traced the Italian script, speaking it aloud so that Papa could mouth the words and penetrate the underlying thought, which was unbelievable, a marvel that chilled them all. Grampa had sold his holdings, now that Grandma was dead, and was sailing for America for a visit, or, if he approved, to stay the rest of his life.

The cable passage seemed to illuminate with the lightning flashes of the preparations for the arrival—the house scrubbed, walls painted, furniture shined, chairs fixed, and the blackmail begun. Mama, seeing the face of her son and the hope and avidity in his eyes, sat him down in the kitchen. I am going to tell Grampa everything what you done, Tony. Everything. Unless you do what I say. You marry Margaret.

Margaret was a year older than Tony. Somehow, he could not imagine how, now that he knew her, he had come to rest on her stoop from time to time, mainly when just out of jail, when momentarily the strain of bargaining for life and a spot was too much, those moments when, like madness, a vision of respectability overwhelmed him with a quick longing for the clean and untroubled existence. She was like a nervous pony at his approach, and easy to calm. It was the time he was driving booze trucks over the Canadian border for Harry Ox, the last of the twenties, and out of jail it was sweet to spend a half hour staring at the street with Margaret, like a clam thrown up by the moiling sea for a moment. He had been in his first gunfight near Albany and was scared. And this was the first time he had said he would like to take her to the movies. In all the years he had known her, the thought had never crossed his mind to make a date. Home that night, he already heard his mother talking about Margaret's family. The skein was folding over him, and he did not resist. He did not decide either. He let it come

without touching it, let it drape over him like a net. They were
engaged, and nobody had used the word, even, but whenever he
saw Margaret she acted as though she had been waiting for him, as
though he had been missing, and he let it happen, walked a certain
way with her in the street, touching her elbow with his fingertips,
and never took her into the joints, and watched his language.
Benign were the smiles in her house the few times he appeared, but
he could never stay long for the boredom, the thickness of the plot
to strangle his life.

His life was Patty Moran by this time. Once across her threshold over Ox's saloon, everything he saw nearly blinded him. He
had started out with her at three o'clock in the morning in the
back of Ox's borrowed Buick, her ankle ripping the corded rope
off the back of the front seat, and the expanse of her thigh across
the space between the back and front seats was painted in cream
across his brain forever. He walked around the neighborhood
dazed, a wire going from the back of his head to her hard soft
belly. She was not even Harry Ox's girl but a disposable one among
several, and Tony started out knowing that and each day climbed
an agonizing stairway to a vision of her dearness, almost but not
quite imagining her marriageable. The thought of other men with
her was enough to bring his fist down on a table even if he was sitting alone. His nose had not yet been broken; he was small but
quick-looking, sturdy, and black-eyed. She finally convinced him
there was nobody else, she adored his face, his body, his stolen
jokes. And in the same two or three months he was taking Margaret to the movies. He even kissed her now and then. Why? Why!
Grampa was coming as soon as he could clear up his affairs, and
what had begun with Margaret as a purposeless yet pleasant pas-
time had taken on leverage in that it kept Mama pleased and quiet
and would guarantee his respectability in Grampa's eyes—long
enough, anyway, to get his inheritance.

No word of inheritance was written in the old man's letters, but
it was first imagined, then somehow confirmed, that Tony would
get it. And when he did it was off-to-Buffalo, him and the baloney,
maybe even get married someplace where nobody knew her and

they'd make out seriously together. And best of all, Mama knew nothing of the baloney. Nowadays she was treating Tony like the head of the house. He had taken a job longshore, was good as gold, and sat home many an evening, listening to the tock-tick.

The final letter came. Tony read it alone in the bathroom first and announced that Grampa was coming on the tenth, although the letter said the ninth. On the morning of the ninth, Tony said he had to get dressed up because, instead of working, he was going to scout around for a good present for Grampa's arrival tomorrow. Congratulated, kissed, waved off, he rounded the block to Ox's and borrowed three hundred dollars and took a cab to the Manhattan pier.

The man in truth was gigantic. Tony's first glimpse was this green-suited, oddly young old man, a thick black tie at his throat, a black fedora held by a porter beside him, while down the gangway he himself was carrying on his back a small but heavy trunk. Tony understood at once—the money was in the trunk. On the pier Tony tipped the porter for carrying the furry hat, and kissed his six-foot grandfather once he had set the trunk down. Tony shook his hand and felt the power in it, hard as a banister. The old man took one handle of the trunk and Tony the other, and in the cab Tony made his proposal. Before rushing home, why not let him show New York?

Fine. But first Tony wanted to Americanize the clothes; people would get the wrong impression, seeing such a green immigrant suit and the heavy brogans. Grampa allowed it, standing there ravished by the bills Tony peeled off for the new suit, new shoes, and an American tie. Now they toured the town, sinking deeper and deeper into it as Tony graded the joints from the middle-class ones uptown to his hangouts near Canal Street, until the old man was kissing his grandson two and three times an hour and stood up cheering the Minsky girls who bent over the runway toward his upturned face. Tony, at four in the morning, carried the trunk up the stairs of the tenement on his own back, feeling the dead weight inside; then back down and carried Grampa on his back and laid him in his own bed and himself on the floor. He had all he could do to keep from rushing over to Patty Moran to tell her he was in like Flynn, the old man loved him like a son, and they might begin by opening a joint together someplace, like in Queens. But he kept discipline and slept quickly, his face under the old man's hand hanging over the edge of the mattress.

In the cable passage, staring at the dark, he could not clearly recall his wedding, any more than he had been able to an hour after the ceremony. It was something he was doing and not doing. Grampa had emerged from the bedroom with Tony under his armpit; and seeing her father, Mama's face lengthened out as though God or the dead had walked in, especially since she had just finished getting dressed up to meet his boat. The shouting and crying and kissing lasted until afternoon, Grampa's pleasure with his manly grandson gathering the complicated force of a new mission in his life, a proof of his own grandeur at being able to hand on a patrimony to a good man of his blood, a man of style besides.

Papa nodded an uncertain assent, one eye glancing toward the trunk, but as evening came, Mama, Tony saw, was showing two thoughts in her tiny brown eyes, and after the third meal of the day, with the table cleaned off and the old man blinking drowsily, she laid two open hands on the table, smiled deferentially, and said Tony had been in and out of jails since he was twelve.

Grampa woke up.

Tony was hanging with bootleggers, refused until the last couple of months to hold a regular job, and now he was staying with an Irish whore when he had engaged himself to Margaret, the daughter of a good Calabrian family down the block, a girl as pure as a dove, beautiful, sincere, whose reputation was being mangled every day Tony avoided talk of a marriage date. The girl's brothers were growing restive, her father had gotten the look of blood in his eye. Margaret alone could save Tony from the electric chair, which was waiting for him as sure as God had sent Jesus, for he was a boy who would lie as quickly as spit, the proof being his obvious attempt to hoodwink Grampa with a night on the town before any of the family could get to him with the true facts.

It took twenty minutes to convince Grampa; he had had to

stare at Tony for a long time, as though through a telescope that would not adjust. Tony downed his fury, defended his life, denied everything, promised everything, brought out the new alarm clock he had bought for the house out of his own money, and at last sat facing Grampa, dying in his chair as the old man leveled his judgment. Tony, you will marry this fine girl or none of my money goes to you. Not the fruit of my labor to a gangster, no, not to a criminal who will die young in the electric chair. Marry the girl and yes, definitely, I give you what I have.

First days, then weeks—then was it months?—passed after the wedding, but the money failed to be mentioned again. Tony worked the piers dutifully now, and when he did see Patty Moran it was at odd hours only, on his way toward the shape-up or on days when it rained and deck work was called off. He would duck into the doorway next to Ox's saloon and fly up the stairs and live for half an hour, then home again to wait; he dared not simply confront the old man with the question of his reward, knowing that he was being watched for deficiencies. On Sundays he walked like a husband with Margaret, spent the afternoons with the family, and acted happy. The old man was never again as close and trusting and comradely as on that first night off the boat, but neither was he hostile. He was watching, Tony saw, to make sure.

And Tony would make him sure. The only problem was what to do in his apartment once he was alone with Margaret. He had never really hated her and he had never liked her. It was like being alone with an accident, that was all. He spoke to her rarely and quietly, listened to her gossip about the day's events, and read his newspaper. He did not expect her to suddenly stand up in the movies and run out crying, some two months after the wedding, or expect to come home from work one spring evening and find Grampa sitting in the living room with Margaret, looking at him silently as he came through the door.

You don't touch your wife?

Tony could not move from the threshold or lie, suddenly. The old man had short, bristly gray hair that stood up like wire, and he was back to his Italian brogans, a kick from which could make a mule inhale. Margaret dared only glance at Tony, but he saw now that the dove had her beak in his belly and was not going to let go.

You think I'm mentally defective, Tony? A man with spit in the corners of his mouth? Cross-eyed? What do you think I am?

The first new demonstration was, again, at the movies. Grampa sat behind them. After a few minutes Margaret turned her head to him and said, He don't put his arm around me, see?

Put your arm around her.

Tony put his arm around her.

Then after a few more minutes she turned to Grampa. He's only touching the seat, see?

Grampa took hold of Tony's hand and laid it on Margaret's shoulder.

Again, one night, Grampa was waiting for him with Margaret. Okay—he was breaking into English now and then by this time— Okay, I'm going to sleep on the couch.

Tony had never slept in bed with her. He was afraid of Grampa because he knew he could never bring himself to raise a hand to him, and he knew that Grampa could knock him around; but it was not the physical harm, it was the sin he had been committing over and over again of trying to con the old man, whose opinion of him was falling every day, until one day, he foresaw, Grampa would pack up and take the trunk back to Calabria and goodbye. Grampa was no longer astounded by New York, and he still owned his house in Italy, and Tony visualized that house, ready at all times for occupancy, and he was afraid.

He went into the bedroom with Margaret. She sniveled on the pillow beside him. It was still light outside, the early blue of a spring evening. Tony listened for a sound of Grampa through the closed door, but nothing came through. He reached and found her hip and slid up her nightgown. She was soft, too soft, but she was holding her breath. He stretched his neck and rested his mouth on her shoulder. She was breathing at the top of her chest, near her throat, not daring to lay her hand on him, her face upthrust as though praying. He smoothed her hip, waiting for his tension, and nothing was happening to him until—until she began to weep, not withdrawing herself but pressed against him, weeping. His hatred mounted on the disappointed, tattletale sound she was sending into the other room, and suddenly he felt himself hardening and he got to his knees before her, pushed her onto her back and saw her face in the dim light from the window, her eyes shut and spinning out gray teardrops. She opened her eyes then and looked terrified, as though she wanted to call it off and beg his pardon, and he covered her with a baring of his teeth, digging his face into the mattress as though rocks were falling on him from the sky.

"Tony?"

He sat up in the darkness, listening.

"Hey, Tony."

Somebody was half whispering, half calling from outside the cable hole. Tony waited, uncomprehending. Margaret's teardrops were still in his eyes, Grampa was sitting out in the living room. Suddenly he placed the voice. Baldu.

He crawled out onto the catwalk. His helper was dimly lit by a yellow bulb yards away. "Looey?"

Baldu, startled, jerked around and hurried back to him on the catwalk, emergency in his eyes. "Charley Mudd's lookin' for you."

"Wha' for?"

"I don't know. He's lookin' high and low. You better come."

This was rare. Charley never bothered him once he had given the assignment for the shift. Tony hurried down the circular iron stairway, imagining some invasion of brass, a swarm of braid and overcoated men from the Master's office. Last summer they had suddenly halted work to ask for volunteers to burn an opening in the bow of a cruiser that had been towed in from the Pacific; her forward compartments had been sealed against the water that a torpedo had poured into her, trapping nine sailors inside. Tony had refused to face those floating corpses or the bloody water that would surely come rushing out.

In the morning he had seen the blood on the sheets, and Grampa was gone.

On B Deck, scratching his back under his mackinaw and black sweater, Charley Mudd, alarmingly wide awake and alert, was talking to a Protestant with an overcoat on and no hat, a blond engineer he looked like, from some office. Charley reached out to Tony when he came up and held on to him, and even before Charley began to speak Tony knew there was no way out, because the Protestant was looking at Tony with a certain relief in his eyes.

"Here he is. Look, Tony, they got some kind of accident on the North River, some destroyer. So grab a gang and take gas and sledges and see what you can do, will you?"

"Wha' kinda accident, Charley?"

"I don't know. The rails for the depth charges got bent. It ain't much, but they gotta go by four to meet a convoy. This man'll take you to the truck. Step on it, get a gang."

"How do I heat iron? Must be zero outside."

"They got a convoy waiting on the river. Do your best, that's all. Take a sledge and plenty of gas. Go ahead."

Tony saw that Charley was performing for the engineer and he could not spoil his relationship. He found Hindu, sent Baldu for his lunch from under the sailor's bunk, and, cursing the Navy, Margaret, winter, and his life, emerged onto the main deck and felt the whip of a wind made of ice. Followed by Hindu, who struggled with a cylinder of acetylene gas held up at the rear end by Baldu, Tony stamped down the gangplank to the open pickup truck at its foot. A sailor was behind the wheel, racing the engine to keep the heater going hot. He sent Hindu and Baldu back for two more cylinders just in case and extra tips for the burner and one more sledge and a crowbar and sat inside the cab, holding his hands, which were not yet cold, under the heater's blast.

"What happened?" he asked the sailor.

"Don't ask me, I'm only driving. I'm stationed right here in the Yard."

Forever covering his tracks, Tony asked how long the driver had been waiting, but it had been only fifteen minutes, so Charley could not have been looking for him too long. Hindu got in beside Tony, who ordered Looey Baldu onto the open back, and they drove along the donkey-engine tracks, through the dark streets, and finally out the gate into Brooklyn.

Baldu huddled with his back against the cab, feeling the wind coming through his knitted skating cap and his skin hardening. He could not bear to sit on the icy truck bed, and his knees were cramping as he sat on his heels. But the pride he felt was enough to break the cold, the realization that now at last he was suffering, striking his blow at Mussolini's throat, sharing the freezing cold of the Murmansk run, where our ships were pushing supplies to the Russians through swarms of submarines. He had driven a meat truck until the war broke out. His marriage, which had happened to fall the day after Pearl Harbor was attacked, continued to ache like a mortal sin even though he kept reminding himself that it had been planned before he knew America would enter the war, and yet it had saved him for a while from the draft, and a punctured eardrum had, on his examination, put him out of action altogether.

He had gone into the Yard at a slight cut in pay if figured on hourly rates, but with a twelve-hour shift and overtime, he was ahead. This bothered him, but much less than the atmosphere of confusion in the Yard, for when he really thought back over the five months he had been here, he could count on one hand the shifts during which he had exerted himself. Everything was start and stop, go and wait, until he found himself wishing he could dare go to the Yardmaster and tell him that something was terribly wrong. The endless standing around and, worse yet, his having to cover up Tony's naps had turned his working time into a continuous frustration that seemed to be doing something strange to his mind. He had never had so much time to do nothing, and the shifts seemed endless and finally illicit when he, along with the others, had always to watch out for supervisors coming by. It was a lot different than rushing from store to store unloading meat and barely finishing the schedule by the end of the day.

It had never seemed possible to him that he would be thinking so much about sex. He respected and almost worshiped his wife, Hilda, and yet now that she was in Florida with her mother for two weeks, he was strangely running into one stimulation after another. Suddenly Mrs. Curry next door, knowing when he ate breakfast, was taking out her garbage pail at six in the morning with an overcoat on and nothing underneath, and even on very cold mornings stood bent over with the coat open for minutes at a time at the end of the driveway, facing his kitchen window; and every day, every single day now, when he left for work she just happened to be coming out the front door, until he was beginning to wonder if . . . But that was impossible; a fine married woman like her was most likely unaware of what she was doing, especially with her husband in the army, fighting Fascism. Blowing on his heavy woolen gloves, he was held by the vision of her bending over and thrust it furiously out of his mind, only to fall still, again remembering a dream he had had in which he was coming into his own bedroom and there on the bed lay his cousin Lucy, all naked, and suddenly he fell on her, tripped on the rug, and woke up. Why should Lucy have gone to bed in his room?

But now Brooklyn Bridge was unwinding from the tailgate of the truck, and how beautiful it was, how fine to be speeding along like this on a mission for the country, and everybody, even Tony, springing to action for the sake of the war effort. Baldu had to take off his cap and rub the circulation back into his scalp, and finally, feeling shivers trembling in his chest, he looked around and discovered a tarpaulin folded in a corner and covered himself. He sat under it in the darkness, blowing on his gloves.

Tony ate three spinach sandwiches out of his box, swallowing them a half at a time, like wet green cookies. Hindu had fallen silent, signaled by Tony's edgy look. The fitter was combative, turtled into his shoulders. As they crossed Chambers Street, the tall office and bank buildings they saw were dark, the people who worked in them at home, warm and smart and snug. Anybody out tonight was either a cop or a jerk; the defroster could not keep up with the cold, and the windshield was glazed over except for a few inches down near the air exhaust. Every curse Tony knew was welling up into his mouth. On deck tonight! And probably no place to hide either, on a ship whose captain and crew were aboard. *Margaret!* Her name, hated, infuriating, her sneaky face, her tattletale mouth, swirled through the air in front of him, the mouth of his undoing. For she had made Grampa so suspicious of him that he still refused to open the trunk until he had evidence Margaret was pregnant, and even when she got big and bigger and could barely waddle from one corner of the small living room to the other, he refused, until the baby was actually born. Grampa had not earned his reputation for nothing—stupid men did not get rich in Calabria, or men who felt themselves above revenge.

As the last days approached and the three-room apartment was prepared for the baby, the old man started acting funny, coming over after dinner ostensibly to sit and talk to Margaret but really to see, as the three of them well knew, that Tony stayed at home. Nights, for a month or so now, he had followed Tony from bar to bar, knocking glasses out of his hand and, in Ox's, sweeping a dozen bottles to the floor behind the bar to teach Ox never again to serve his grandson, until Tony had to sneak into places where he had never hung before. But even so the old man's reputation had preceded him, until Tony was a pariah in every saloon between Fourteenth Street and Houston. He gave up at last, deciding to go with the hurricane instead of fighting it, and returned from the piers night after night now, to sit in silence while his wife swelled. With about eight or nine days to go, Grampa, one night, failed to show up. The next night he was missing too, and the next.

One night Tony stopped by to see if some new disaster had budded, like the old man's falling ill and dying before he could hand over the money, but Grampa was well enough. It was only his normally hard-faced, suspicious glare that was gone. Now he merely stole glances at Tony and even seemed to have softened toward him, like a man in remorse. Sensing some kind of victory, Tony felt the return of his original filial warmth, for the old man seemed to be huddling against the approach of some kind of holiness, Tony believed, a supernatural and hallowed hour when not only was his first great-grandchild to be born but his life's accomplishment would be handed down and the first shadow of his own death seen. The new atmosphere drew Tony back night after night, and now when he would rise to leave, the old man would lay a hand on Tony's arm as though his strength was in the process of passing from him to a difficult but proud descendant. Even Mama and Papa joined in the silence and deep propriety of these partings.

The pickup truck was turning on the riverfront under the West Side Highway; the sailor bent low to see out of the hand-sized clear space at the bottom of the windshield. Now he slowed and rolled down his window to look at the number on a pier they were passing and quickly shut it again. The cab was instantly refrigerated, a plunge in the temperature that made Hindu groan "Mamma mia" and pull his earflaps even lower. The night of the birth had been like this, in January too, and he had tried to take a walk around the hospital block to waste some time and could only get to the corner for the freezing cold. When he returned and walked back into the lobby, Mama was running to him and gripping him like a little wrestler, gulping out the double news. It was twins, two boys, both healthy and big; no wonder she had looked so enormous, that poor girl. Tony swam out of the hospital not touching the floor, stroked through the icy wind down Seventh Avenue, and floated up the stairs and found Grampa, and with one look he knew, he knew then, he already knew, for the old man's head seemed to be rolling on a broken neck, so frightened was he, so despondent. But Tony held his hand out for the key anyway and kept asking for it until Grampa threw himself on his knees and grasped him around the legs, hawking and coughing and groaning for forgiveness.

The trunk lid opened, Tony saw the brown paper bundle tied with rope, a package the size of half a mattress and deep as the trunk itself. The rope flew off, the brown paper crackled like splintering wood, and he saw the tied packets—Italian lire, of course, the bills covered with wings, paintings of Mussolini, airplanes, and zeros, fives, tens, colorful and tumbling under his searching hands. He knew, he already knew, he had known since the day he was born, but he ran back into the living room and asked. It had been an honest mistake. In Calabria, ask anybody there, you could buy or could have bought, once, once you could have bought, that is, a few years ago, until this thing happened with money all over the world, even here in America, ask Roosevelt why he is talking about closing the banks. There is some kind of sickness in the money and why should Italy be an exception, a poor country once you leave Rome. Hold on to it, maybe it will go up again. I myself did not know until two weeks ago I went to the bank to change it, ask your mother. I took the whole bundle to the National City in good faith, with joy in my heart, realizing that all your sins were the sins of youth, the exuberance of the young man who grows into a blessing for his parents and grandparents, making all his ancestors famous with his courage and manliness. It comes to seventeen hundred and thirty-nine dollars. In dollars that is what it comes to.

I used to make three hundred driving a truck from Toronto to New York, four days' work, Grampa. Seventeen hundred—you know what seventeen hundred is? Seventeen hundred is like if I bought one good suit and a Buick and I wouldn't have what to buy gas, that's seventeen hundred. Seventeen hundred is like if I buy a grocery store I be out on my ass the first bad week. Seventeen hundred is not like you got a right to come to a man and say go tie that girl around your neck and jump in the river you gonna come up rich. That's not nowhere near that kinda money, and twins you gave me in the bargain. *I got two twins, Grampa!*

The red blood washed down off his vision as the truck turned left and into the pier, past the lone light bulb and the night watchman under it listlessly waving a hand and returning to his stove in the shack. Midway down the length of the pier shed, one big door was open, and the sailor coasted the truck up to it and braked to a halt, the springs squeaking in the cold as the nose dipped.

Tony followed Hindu out and walked past him to the gangplank, which extended into the pier from the destroyer's deck, and walked up, glancing right and left at the full length of the ship. Warm lights burned in her midship compartments, and as he stepped onto the steel deck he concluded that they might be stupid enough to be in the Navy but not that stupid—they were all snuggled away inside and nobody was standing watch on deck. But now he saw his mistake; a sailor with a rifle at his shoulder, knitted blue cap pulled down over his ears and a face shield covering his mouth and chin, the high collar of a storm coat standing up behind his head, was pacing back and forth from rail to rail, on guard.

Tony walked toward him, but the sailor, who looked straight at him on his starboard turn, continued across the deck toward port as though in an automatic trance. Tony waited for the sailor to turn again and come toward him and then stood directly in his path until the sailor bumped into his zipper and leaped in fright.

"I'm from the Yard. Where's the duty officer?"

The sailor's rifle started tilting off his shoulder, and Tony reached out and pushed it back.

"Is it about me?"

"Hah?"

The sailor lowered his woolen mask. His face was young, and wan, with staring pop eyes. "I'm supposed to go off sea duty. I get seasick. This ship is terrible, I can't hold any food. But now they're telling me I can't get off until we come back again. Are you connected with—"

"I'm from the Navy Yard. There was an accident, right?"

The sailor glanced at Hindu, standing a little behind Tony, and then at both their costumes and seemed ashamed and worried as he turned away, telling them to wait a minute, and disappeared through a door.

"Wanna look at the rails?" Hindu joked, with a carefully shaped mockery of their order, shifting from one foot to the other and leaning down from his height to Tony's ear.

"Fuck the rails. You can't do nuttn in this weather. They crazy? Feel that wind. Chrissake, it'll go right up your asshole an' put ice on your throat. But keep your mouth shut, I talk to this monkey. What a fuckin' nerve!"

Looey Baldu appeared out of the darkness of the pier, carrying the two sledges. "Where do you want these, Tony?"

"Up your ass, Looey. Put 'em back on the truck."

Baldu, astounded, stood there.

"You want a taxi? Move!"

Baldu, uncomprehending, turned and stomped down the gang-plank with the sledges.

The door into which the sailor had vanished opened, spilling the temptation of warm yellow light across the deck to Tony's feet, and a tall man emerged, ducking, and buttoning up his long overcoat. The chief petty officer, most likely, or maybe even one of the senior lieutenants, although his gangling walk, like a college boy's, and his pants whipping high on his ankles lowered the estimate to ensign. Approaching, he put up his high collar and pulled down his cap and bent over to greet Tony.

"Oh, fine. I'm very much obliged. I'll show you where it is."

"Wait, wait, just a minute, mister."

The officer came back the two steps he had taken toward the fantail, an expression of polite curiosity on his pink face. A new gust sent his hand to his visor, and he tilted his head toward New Jersey, from where the wind was pounding at them across the black river.

"You know the temperature on this here deck?"

"What? Oh. I haven't been out for a while. It has gotten very cold. Yes."

Hindu had stepped back a deferential foot or so, instinctively according Tony the air of rank that a cleared space gives, and now Baldu returned from the truck and halted beside Hindu.

"Could I ask you a little favor?" Tony said, his fists clenched inside his slit pockets, shoulders hunched, eyes squinting against the wind. "Would you please go inside and tell the captain what kinda temperature you got out here?"

"I'm the captain. Stillwater."

"You the captain." Tony stalled while all his previous estimates whirled around in his head. He glanced down at the deck, momentarily helpless. He had never addressed a commanding officer before; the closest he ever came in the Yard was a severe passing nod to one or two in a corridor from time to time. The fact that this one had come out on deck to talk to him must mean that the repair was vital, and Tony found himself losing the normal trucu-lence in his voice.

"Could I give yiz some advice, Captain?"

"Certainly. What is it?"

"We can't do nuttn in this here weather. You don't want a botch job, do ya? Whyn't you take her into the Yard, we give you a brand-new pair rails, and yiz'll be shipshape for duty."

The captain half laughed in surprise at the misunderstanding. "Oh, we couldn't do that. We're joining a convoy at four. Four this morning. I can't delay a convoy."

The easy absoluteness shot fear into Tony's belly. He glanced past the captain's face, groping for a new attack, but the captain was talking again.

"Come, I'll show it to you. Give me that light, Farrow."

The sick watch handed him the flashlight, and the captain loped off toward the fantail. Tony followed behind. He was trapped. The next time he saw Charley Mudd . . .

The flashlight beam shot out and illuminated the two parallel steel rails, extending several feet out over the water from the deck. Two feet in from the end of the portside rail there was a bend.

"Jesus! What happened?"

"We were out there"—the captain flipped up the light toward the river beyond the slip—"and a British ship got a little too close trying to line himself up."

"Them fuckin' British!" Tony exploded, throwing his voice out toward the river where the Englishman must be. Caught by surprise, the captain laughed, but Tony pulled his hands out of his slit pockets and made a pleading gesture, and his face looked serious. "Why don't somebody tell them to stop fuckin' around or get out of the war!"

The captain, unaccustomed to the type, watched Tony with great expectation and amusement.

"I mean it! They the only ones brings cockroaches into the Navy Yard!"

"Cockroaches? How do—"

"Ax anybody! We get French, Norways, Brazils, but you don't see no cockroaches on them ships. Only the British brings cockroaches."

The captain shook his head with commiseration, tightening his smile until it disappeared. "Some of their ships have been at sea a long, long time, you know."

Tony felt a small nudge of hope in his heart. "Uh-huh," he muttered, frowning with solicitude for the English. Some unforeseen understanding with the captain seemed to loom; the man was taking him so seriously, bothering to explain why there were cockroaches, allowing himself to be diverted even for ten seconds from the problem of the rail, and, more promising than anything else, he seemed to be deferring to Tony's opinion about the possibility of working at all tonight. And better yet, he was even going into it further.

"Some of those English ships have been fighting steadily ten and twelve months down around the Indian Ocean. A ship will get awfully bad that long at sea without an overhaul. Don't you think?"

Tony put gravity into his face, an awful deliberation, and then spoke generously. "Oh yeah, sure. I was only sayin'. Which I don't blame them, but you can't sit down on their ships."

Another officer and two more sailors had come out on deck and were watching from a distance as Tony talked to the captain, and he slowly realized that they must all have been waiting hours for him and were now wondering what his opinion was going to be.

With a nod toward the bent rail, the captain asked, "What do you think? Can you straighten it?"

Tony turned to look out at the damaged rail, but his eyes were not seeing clearly. The pleasure and pride of his familiarity with the captain, his sheer irreplaceability on this deck, were shattering his viewpoint. Striving to knit his wits together, he asked the captain if he could have the flashlight for a minute.

"Oh, certainly," the captain said, handing it to him.

Leaning a little over the edge of the deck, he shone the beam onto the bend of the rail. That pimping, motherfuckin' Charley Mudd! Look at the chunks of ice in that water—fall in there it's goodbye forever. In the skyscrapers at his back, men tripled their money every wartime day, butchers were cleaning up with meat so scarce, anybody with a truck in good shape could name his price, and here he stood, God's original patsy, Joe Jerk, without a penny to his name that he hadn't grubbed out by the hour with his two hands.

More than a minute had gone by, but he refused to give up until an idea came to him, and he kept the light shining on the bend as though studying how to repair it. There had to be a way out. It was the same old shit—the right idea at the right moment had never come to him because he was a dumb bastard and there was no way around it and never would be.

"What do you think?"

What he thought? He thought that Charley Mudd should be strung up by his balls. Turning back to the captain now, he was confronted with the man's face, close to his in order to hear better in the wind. Could it be getting even colder?

"Lemme show you supm, Captain. Which I'm tryin' my best to help you out, but this here thing is a son of a bitch. Excuse me. Look."

He pointed out at the bend in the rail. "I gotta hit that rail— you understand?"

"Yes?"

"But where I'm gonna stand? It sticks out over the water. You need skyhooks for this. Which is not even the whole story. I gotta get that steel good and hot. With this here wind you got blowin' here, I don't even know if I can make it hot enough."

"Hmm."

"You understand me? I'm not trying to crap out on ya, but that's the facts."

He watched the captain, who was blinking at the bend, his brows kinked. He was like a kid, innocent. Out in the dark, river foghorns barked, testifying to the weather. Tony saw the sag of disappointment in the captain's face, the sadness coming into it. What the hell was the matter with him? He had a perfect excuse not to have to go to sea and maybe get himself sunk. The German subs were all over the coast of Jersey, waiting for these convoys, and here the man had a perfect chance to lay down in a hotel for a couple of days. Tony saw that the young man needed precise help, his feet placed on the road out.

"Captain, listen to me. Please. Lemme give you piece of advice."

Expressionless, the captain turned to Tony.

"I sympathize wichoo. But what's the crime if you call in that you can't move tonight? That's not your fault."

"I have a position in the convoy. I'm due."

"I know that, Captain, but lemme explain to you. Cut outa here right now, make for the Yard; we puts up a staging and slap in a new rail by tomorrow noon, maybe even by ten o'clock. And you're set."

"No, no, that's too late. Now see here"—the captain pointed a leather-gloved finger toward the bend—"you needn't true it up exactly. If you could just straighten it enough to let the cans roll off, that would be enough."

"Listen, Captain, I would do anything I could do for you, but . . ." An unbelievable blast of iced wind squeezed Tony's cheeks. The captain steadied himself, tilting his head toward the river again, gripping his visor with one hand and holding his collar tight with the other. Tony had heard him gasp at the new depth of cold. What was the matter with these people? The Navy had a million destroyers—why the hell did they need this one, only this one and on this particular night? "I'm right, ain't I? They can't hold it against you, can they? If you're unfit for duty you're unfit for duty, right? Who's gonna blame you, which another ship rammed you in the dark? You were in a position, weren't you? It was his fault, not yours!"

The captain glanced at him, and in that glance Tony saw the man's disappointment, his judgment of him. He could not help reaching out defensively and touching the captain's arm. "Listen a minute. Please. Looka me, my situation. I know my regulations, Captain; nobody can blame me either. I'm not supposed to work unsafe conditions. I coulda took one look here and called the Yard and I'd be back there by now below decks someplace, because if you can't do it safe you not supposed to. The only way I can swing this, if I could swing it, is I tie myself up in a rope and hang over the side to hit that rail. Nobody would kick one minute if I said I can't do such a thing. You understand me?"

The captain, his eyes tearing in the wind, his face squeezing tight against the blast of air, waited for his point.

"What I mean, I mean that . . ." What did he mean? Standing a few inches from the captain's boyish face, he saw for the first time that there was no blame there. No blame and no command either. The man was simply at a loss, in need. And he saw that there was no question of any official blame for the captain either. Suddenly it was as clear and cold as the air freezing them where they stood—that they were both on a par, they were free.

"I'd be very much obliged if you could do it. I see how tough it is, but I'd be very much obliged if you could."

Tony discovered his glove at his mouth and he was blowing into it to spread heat on his cheeks. The captain had become a small point in his vision. For the first time in his life he had a kind of space around him in which to move freely, the first time, it seemed, that it was entirely up to him, with no punishment if he said no, nor even a reward if he said yes. Gain and loss had suddenly collapsed, and what was left standing was a favor asked that would profit nobody. The captain was looking at him, waiting for his answer. He felt shame, not for having hesitated to try, but for a sense of his nakedness. And as he spoke he felt afraid that in fact the repair would turn out to be impossible and he would end by packing up his tools and, unmanned, retreating back to the Yard.

"Man to man, Captain, can I ask you supm?"

"What is it?"

"Which I'm only mentionin'"—he was finding his truculent tone, and it was slowly turning ordinary again with this recollection coming on—"because plenty of times they run to me, 'Tony, quick, the ship's gotta go tonight,' and I bust my balls. And I come back next day and the ship is sittin' there, and even two weeks more it's still sittin', you understand me?"

"The minute you finish I'll be moving out into the river, don't you worry about that."

"What about coffee?" Tony asked, striving to give this madness some air of a transaction.

"Much as you like. I'll tell the men to make some fresh. Just tell the watch whenever you want it." The captain put out his hand. "Thanks very much."

Tony could barely bring his hand forward. He felt the clasping hand around his own. "I need some rope."

"Right."

He wanted to say something, something to equal the captain's speech of thanks. But it was impossible to admit that anything had changed in him. He said, "I don't guarantee nuttn," and the familiar surliness in his tone reassured him.

The captain nodded and went off into the midship section, followed by the other officer and the two sailors who had been looking on. He would be telling them . . . what? That he had conned the fitter?

Hindu and Looey Baldu were coming toward him. What had he agreed to!

"What's the score?" Hindu grinned, waiting for the delicious details of how Tony had outwitted the shithead captain.

"We straighten it out." Tony started past Hindu, who grabbed his arm.

"We straighten what out?"

"I said we straighten it out." He saw the disbelief in Hindu's eyes, the canny air of total refusal, and he felt anger charging into his veins. "Ax a man for a wood saw and a hammer and if they got a wreckin' bar."

"How the fuck you gonna straighten—"

"Don't break my balls, Hindu. Do what I tell you or get your ass off the ship!" He was amazed at his fury. What the hell was he getting so mad about? He heard Baldu's voice behind him, calling, "I'll get it!" and went to the gangplank and down to the pier, no longer understanding anything except the grave feeling that had found him and was holding on to him, like the feeling of insult, the sense that he could quickly find himself fighting somebody, the looseness of violence. Hindu had better not try to make him look like a jerk.

It took minutes for him to see again within the pier, where he walked about in the emptiness, shining the flashlight at random and finding only the bare, corrugated walls. Baldu came hurrying down the hollow-booming gangplank and over to him, carrying the tools. Another idiot. Son of a bitch, what did these guys do with themselves, jerk off instead of learning something, which at least he had done from job to job, not that it meant anything.

The flashlight found a stack of loading trays piled high against the pier wall. Tony climbed up the ten feet to the top tray. "What's this for?" Baldu asked, reaching up to receive it as Tony tipped it over the edge of the stack. He came down without answering and gestured for the wrecking bar. Baldu handed him the saw, blade first, and Tony slapped it away and reached over and picked up the hammer and wrecking bar and set about prying up the boards until the two five-by-five runners underneath were free. "Grab one," he said, and proceeded up the gangplank onto the deck.

He measured the distance between the two rails and sawed the runners to fit. It must be near eleven, maybe later, and the cold would be getting worse and worse. He cut two lengths of rope and ordered Baldu to tie the end of one around his chest, tied the other around himself, and then undid Baldu's crazy knot and made a tight one; he lashed both ropes to a frame at the root of the depth-charge rails, leaving enough slack for him and Baldu to creep out onto the rails. He took one end of a wood runner, Baldu took the other, and they laid themselves prone on the rails, then moved together, with the runner held between them, across the open water. He told Baldu to rest his end inside the L of his rail and to hold it from jarring loose and falling into the water, and he wedged his own end against his rail just behind where the bend began. He told Baldu to inch backward onto the deck, and Hindu to hand Baldu one of the sledges. But the sledges were still on the truck. He told them both to go down to the truck and bring the sledges, bring two tanks of gas, bring the burning torch and tips, and don't get wounded.

Baldu ran. Hindu walked, purposely. Tony sat on his heels, studying the rails. The sick watch paced up and down behind

him in a dream. That fuckin' Charley Mudd, up to the ceiling by
his balls.

"Hey, seasick," he said over his shoulder as the watch approached.
"See if you can get me a tarp, huh?"

"Tarp?"

"Tarpaulin, tarpaulin. And step on it."

Christ, one was dumber than the other, nobody knew nuttn,
everybody's fulla shit with his mouth open. What was the captain
saying now, what was he doing? Had he been conned, really?
Except, what could the captain get out of it except the risk of his
life with all those subs off Jersey? If he had been conned, fuck it,
show the bastard. Show him what?

Suddenly, staring at nothing, he no longer knew why he was
doing this, if he had ever known. And somebody might fall into
the water in the bargain once they started hitting with the sledge.

"Coffee?"

He turned and looked up. The captain was handing him a steaming cup and had two more in his other hand.

"Thanks."

Now Baldu and Hindu were clanking the gas cylinders onto the
deck behind them. Tony drank his coffee, inhaling the good steam.
The captain gave the two cups to the others.

"Whyn't you get off your feet, Captain? Go ahead, git warmed
up."

The captain nodded and went off.

Tony put down his cup. The watch arrived, carrying a folded tarpaulin whose grommets were threaded with quarter-inch rope. Tony
told him to put it down on the deck. He let Baldu drink coffee for a
minute more, then told him to creep out on his rail and steady the
wood runner while Tony hit its other end with the sledge to wedge it
in tight between the two rails. Sliding the sledge ahead of him on his
rail, he crept out over the water. At his left, Baldu, tied again, crept
out wide-eyed. Tony saw that he was afraid of the water below.

Baldu inched along until he reached the runner and held it in
the angle of the L tightly with both hands. Tony stood up carefully on his rail, bent down and picked up the sledge, then edged

farther out on the rail to position for a swing. The water, in the light held by Hindu, was black and littered with floating paper. Tony carefully swung the sledge and hit the runner, and again, and again, and it was tight between the two rails. He told Baldu to back up, and they got the second runner and inched it out with them and wedged it snugly next to the first. Now there would be something to stand on between the two cantilevered rails, although it remained to be seen whether a man could bang the bent rail hard enough with so narrow a perch under him.

He unfolded the tarpaulin and handed one corner to Baldu, took the opposite corner himself, and both inched out over the rails again and tied the tarpaulin on the two runners so that it hung to the windward of the bend and might keep the air blast from cooling the steel. It might not. He backed halfway to the deck and told Hindu to hand him the torch and to grab a sledge and stand on the little bridge he had made and get ready to hit the steel.

"Not me, baby."

"You, you."

"What's the matter with the admiral here?" Hindu asked, indicating Baldu.

"I wanchoo."

"Not me, baby. I don't like heights."

Tony backed off the rail and stood facing Hindu on the deck.

"Don't fuck around, Tony. Nobody's payin' me to get out there. I can't even swim good."

He saw the certain knowledge of regulations in Hindu's mocking eyes. His own brows were lifted, his classic narrow-eyed, showdown look was on his face, and never before would he have let a man sneer at him like that without taking up the challenge, but now, strange as it was to him, he felt only contempt for Hindu, who had it in him to hit the beam much harder than the smaller Baldu could and was refusing. It was a long, long time since he had known the feeling of being let down by anyone; as long as it was since he had expected anything of anyone. He turned away from Hindu and beckoned to Baldu, and in the moment it took for Baldu to come to him, Tony felt sharply the queerness of his pushing on with this job, which, as Hindu's attitude proved, was fit for suckers and, besides, was most probably impossible to accomplish with the wind cooling the steel as fast as it was heated. He bent over and picked up the slender torch.

"You ever work a torch?"

"Well, not exactly, but . . ."

Tony turned to Hindu, his hand extended. "Gimme the sparker." From his jacket pocket Hindu took a spring-driven sparker and handed it to Tony, who took it and, noting the minute grin on Hindu's mouth, said, "Fuck you."

"In spades," Hindu said.

Tony squeezed the sparker as he opened the two valves on the torch. The flame appeared and popped out in the wind. He shielded it with his body and sparked again, and the flame held steady. He took Baldu's hand and put the torch into it. "Now follow me and I show you what to do."

Eagerly Baldu nodded, his big black eyes feverish with service. "Right, okay."

Unnerved by Baldu's alacrity, Tony said, "Do everything slow. Don't move unless you look." And he went to the bent rail and slid the sledge out carefully before him, slowly stretched prone on the rail and inched out over the water. He came to the two runners, from which the tarpaulin hung snapping in the wind, then drew up his legs and sat, and beckoned to Baldu to follow him out.

Baldu, with the torch in his left hand, the wind-bent flame pointed down, laid himself out on the rail and inched toward Tony. But with each thrust forward the torch flame swung up close to his face. "Let the torch hang, Baldu, take slack," Tony called.

Baldu halted, drew in a foot of tubing, and let the torch dangle below him. Now he inched ahead again, and as he neared, Tony held out a hand and pressed it against Baldu's head. "Stop."

Baldu stopped.

"Get the torch in your hand."

Baldu drew up the torch and held it. Tony pointed his finger at the bend. "Point the fire here." Baldu turned the torch, whose flame broke apart against the steel. Tony moved Baldu's hand away from the steel an inch or two and now trained it in a circular motion, then let go, and Baldu continued moving the flame. "That's good."

It must be half-past eleven, maybe later. Tony watched the steel. The paint was blackening, little blisters coming up. Not bad. He raised the tarpaulin to shield the flame better. A light-yellow glow was starting to show on the steel. Not bad. Gusts were nudging his shoulders. He saw the tears dropping out of Baldu's eyes, and the flame was moving off the rail. He slipped off a glove, reached over, and pressed Baldu's eyelids, clearing the tears out, and the flame returned to its right position. He saw that the watch was pacing up and down again across the deck behind Hindu, who was standing with the flashlight, grinning.

The yellow glow was deepening. Not bad. An orange hue was beginning to show in the steel. He took Baldu's hand and moved it in wider circles to expand the heated area. He slipped his glove off again and pressed the tears out of Baldu's eyes, then the other glove, and held his hands near the flame to warm them.

The steel was reddening. Stuffing the gloves into his slit pockets, he drew up one foot and set it on the rail, leaned over to the wooden bridge he had built and brought the other foot under him and slowly stood erect. He bent slowly and took the sledge off the rail and came erect again. He spread his legs, one foot resting on the wood runners, the other on the rail, and, shifting in quarter-inch movements, positioned himself to strike. He raised the hammer and swung, not too hard, to see what it did to his stability, and the rail shuddered but his foot remained steady on it. He brought up the sledge, higher this time, and slammed it down and under against the steel, one eye on the bridge, which might jar loose and send him into the water, but it was still wedged between the rails, resting on the flange of the L. Baldu was wrapping his free arm around the rail, and now he had his ankles locked around it too.

Tony raised the sledge and slammed down. The steel rang, and he heard Baldu grunt with the shock coming into his body. He raised the sledge and put his weight into it, and the steel rang and Baldu coughed as though hit in the chest. Tony felt the wind reaching down his back under his collar and icing his sweat. Pneumonia, son of a bitch. He slammed down and across at the rail and let the sledge rest next to his foot. The bend had straightened a little, maybe half an inch or an inch. His arms were pounding with blood, his thighs ached in the awkward, frightened position. He glanced back at Hindu on the deck.

"Not me, baby."

He felt all alone. Baldu didn't count, being some kind of a screwball, stupid anyway, he went around believing something about everything and meanwhile everybody was laughing at him, a clown who didn't even know it, you couldn't count on Baldu for anything, except he was all right, lying out there and scared as he was.

He was catching his breath, coughing up the residue of tobacco in the top of his chest. He glanced down and a little behind his shoe at the steel. It was deeply red. He pounded the steel rail, all alone—and rested again. It had straightened maybe another half inch. His breath was coming harder, and his back had tightened against the impossible perch, the tension of distributing his weight partly behind the hammer and partly down into his feet, which he dared not move. He was all alone over the water, the beam of the flashlight dying in the black air around him.

He rested a third time, spitting out his phlegm. The son of a bitch was going to straighten out. If he could keep up the hammering, it would. He dared not let Baldu hammer. Baldu would surely end in the water—him with his two left feet, couldn't do nuttn right. Except he wasn't bad with the torch, and the steel against his clothes must be passing the cold into his body. He glanced down at Baldu and saw again the fear in his face with the water looking up at him from below.

He raised the hammer again. Weakness was spreading along his upper arms. He was having to suck in consciously and hold his breath with each blow. Charley Mudd seemed a million miles away. He could barely recall what Dora looked like. If he did decide to go through with the date, he would only fall asleep in her room. It didn't matter. He let the sledge rest next to his foot. Now it was becoming a question of being able to lift it at all. Hindu, to whom he had given a dozen phone numbers, was far away.

Tony licked his lips, and his tongue seemed to touch iron. His hand on the sledge handle seemed carved forever in a circular grip. The wind in his nose shot numbness into his head and throat. He lifted the sledge and felt a jerky buckling in his right knee and stiffened it quickly. This fuckin' iron, this stubborn, idiot iron, lay there bent, refusing his demand. Go back on deck, he thought, and lay down flat for a minute. But with the steel hot now, he would only have to heat it all up again, since he could not pass Baldu, who would also have to back onto the deck; and once having stopped, his muscles would stiffen and make it harder to start again. He swung the hammer, furiously now, throwing his full weight behind it and to hell with his feet—if he fell off, the rope would hold him, and they had plenty of guys to fish him out.

The rail was straightening, although it would still have a little crook in it; but as long as he could spread it far enough from the other one to let the cans pass through and into the sea, some fuckin' German was going to get it from this rail, bammo, and he could see the plates of the sub opening to the sea and the captain watching the water for a sign of oil coming up. He rested the sledge again. He felt he was about to weep, to cry like a baby against his weakness, but he was a son of a bitch if he would call it off and creep back onto the deck and have Hindu looking down at him, both of them knowing that the whole thing had been useless.

He felt all alone; what was Hindu to him? Another guy to trade girls with and buddy with in the bars, knowing all the time that when the time came he'd give you the shaft if it was good for him, like every man Tony had ever known in his life, and every woman, even Mama, the way she told on him to Grampa, which if she hadn't he would never have had to marry Margaret in the first place. He smashed the sledge down against the steel, recklessly, letting his trunk turn freely and to hell with falling in.

"That looks good enough!"

For a moment, the sledge raised halfway to his shoulder, he

could not make out where the voice was coming from, like in a dream, a voice from the air.

"I'm sure that's good enough, fella!"

Carefully turning his upper body, he looked toward the deck. The captain and two other men and the watch were facing him.

"I think you've done it. Come back, huh?"

He tried to speak, but his throat caught. Baldu, prone, looked up at him, and Tony nodded, and Baldu closed the valves and the flame popped out. Baldu inched backward along the rail. A sailor reached out from the edge of the deck and grabbed the back of his jacket, holding on to him until he slid safely onto the deck and then helping him to stand.

Out on the rail, the sledge hanging from his hand unfelt, Tony stood motionless, trying to educate his knees to bend so that he could get down on the rail and inch back onto the deck. His head was on crooked, nothing in his body was working right. Slowly now, he realized that he must not lie down anyway, or he would have to slide his body over the part of the rail that was probably still hot enough to scorch him. Experimentally he forced one foot half an inch along the rail but swayed, the forgotten weight of the sledge unbalancing him toward his right side. He looked down at his grasping hand and ordered it to open. The sledge slipped straight down and splashed, disappearing under the black water. The captain and the crewmen and Baldu stood helplessly in a tight group, watching the small man perched with slightly spread arms on the outthrust spine of steel, the rope looping from around his chest to the framework on the deck where it was lashed. Tony looked down at his feet and sidled, inch after inch, toward the deck. Joyfully he felt the grip of a hand on his arm now and let his tension flow out as he stepped off the rail and onto the deck. His knee buckled as he came down on it, and he was caught and stood straight. The captain was turning away. Two sailors held him under the arms and walked him for a few steps like a drunk, but the motion eased him and he freed himself. A few yards ahead, the captain slowed and, glancing back, made a small inviting gesture toward the midships section, and pushed by the wind went through a doorway.

He and Baldu and Hindu drank the coffee and ate the buns. Tony saw the serious smiles of respect in the sailors' faces, and he saw the easy charm with which Hindu traded jokes with them, and he saw the captain, uncapped now, the blond hair and the way he looked at him with love in his eyes, saying hardly anything but personally filling Tony's cup and standing by and listening to Hindu with no attention but merely politeness. Then Tony stood up, his lips warm again and the ice gone out of his sweat, and they all said good night. As Tony went through the door onto the deck, the captain touched him on the shoulder with his hand.

When Hindu and Baldu had loaded the gas tanks onto the truck with the sledges, Tony indicated for Baldu to get into the cab, and the helper climbed in beside the sailor, who was racing the engine. Tony got in and pulled the door shut and through the corners of his eyes saw Hindu standing out there, unsmiling, his brows raised, insulted. "It's only midnight, baby," Tony said, hardly glancing at Hindu. "We got four more hours. Git on the back."

Hindu stood there for twenty seconds, long enough to register his narrow-eyed affront, then climbed onto the open back of the truck.

Outside the pier the sailor braked for a moment, glancing right and left for traffic, and as he turned downtown Tony at the side window saw sailors coming down the gangplank of the destroyer. They were already casting off. The truck sped through the cold and empty streets toward Chambers and Brooklyn Bridge, leaving it all behind. In half an hour the destroyer would be back in its position alongside the cargo ships lined up in the river. The captain would be where he belonged. Stillwater. Captain Stillwater. He knew him. Right now it felt like the captain was the only man in the world he knew.

In the Yard, Tony made the driver take them up to the drydock where the cruiser lay on which they had been working. He went aboard with Baldu, without waiting for Hindu to get off the back, and found Charley Mudd and woke him up, cursing the job he had given him and refusing to listen to Charley's thanks and explanations, and without waiting for permission made his way through the ship to the engine room. Overhead somebody was still welding with the arc too far from the steel, and he raised his collar against the sparks and climbed up to the dark catwalk and found the cable passage and crawled in, spreading himself out on the steel deck. His body felt knotted, rheumatic. His smell was powerful. He went over the solutions he had found for the job and felt good about having thought of taking the runners off the loading tray. That was a damn good idea. And Baldu was all right. He visualized the kink that remained in the rail and regretted it, wishing it had been possible to make it perfectly straight, but it would work. Now the face of the captain emerged behind his closed eyes, the face uncapped as it had been when they were standing around having coffee, the blond hair lit, the collar still raised, and the look in his eyes when he had poured Tony's coffee, his closeness and his fine inability to speak. That lit face hung alone in an endless darkness.

[1966]

A Search for a Future

I read where Faulkner, just before he died, was having dinner in a restaurant and said, "It all tastes the same." Maybe I am dying. But I feel good.

I was pasting on my beard. My mind was going back through the mirror to all the other beards, and I counted this as number nine in my life. I used to like beard parts when I was younger because they made me look mature and more sure of myself. But I don't like them so much now that I'm older. No matter how I try I can't help acting philosophical on stage with a beard, and in this part I'm a loud farmer.

That night I looked at my makeup jars, the sponge, the towel, the eye pencil, and I had a strong feeling all of a sudden: that it had always been the same jars, the same sponge, the same towel stained with pink pancake, exactly like this one is; that I had not gotten up from this dressing table for thirty-five years; and that I had spent my whole life motionless, twenty minutes before curtain. That everything tasted the same. Actually I feel I am optimistic. But for quite a lengthened-out minute there I felt that I had never done anything but make myself up for a part I never got to play. Part of it is, I suppose, that all dressing rooms are the same. The other part is that I have been waiting to hear that my father has died. I don't mean that I think of him all the time, but quite often when I hear a phone go off I think, There it is, they are going to tell me the news.

The stage-door man came in. I thought he was going to announce ten minutes (ten minutes to curtain), but instead he said that somebody was asking to see me. I was surprised. People never

visit before a show. I thought it might be somebody from the nursing home. I felt frightened. But I wanted to know immediately, and
the stage-door man hurried out to get the visitor.

I never married, although I have been engaged several times—
but always to a gentile girl, and I didn't want to break my mother's
heart. I have since learned that I was too attached to her but I don't
feel sure about that. I love nothing more than children, family life.
But at the last minute a certain idea would always come to me and
stick in my brain. The idea that this marriage was not absolutely
necessary. It gave me a false heart, and I never went ahead with it.
There are many times when I wish I had been born in Europe, in
my father's village, where they arranged marriages and you never
even saw the bride's face under the veil until after the ceremony. I
would have been a faithful husband and a good father, I think. It's
a mystery. I miss a wife and children that I never had.

I was surprised to see a boy walk in, although he might have
been twenty-two or -three. But he was short, with curly hair and
a pink complexion that looked as though he never had to shave.
Maybe, I thought, it is the son of the owner of the nursing home.
He had a sweet expression, a twinkle in his eyes.

"I just wanted to remind you about midnight," he said.

About midnight? What about midnight? I was completely lost.
For a minute there I even thought, My father has died and I have
forgotten about it, and there is some kind of procedure or a ceremony at midnight.

"The meeting," he said.

Then I remembered. I had agreed to sit on the platform at a
meeting, "Broadway for Peace." I had agreed in Sardi's because
Donald Frost challenged me. My dresser's nephew, a musician
twenty-one years old, had just had his eyes shot out in Vietnam
somewhere, and I was very, very sick about it. I still haven't seen
my dresser, Roy Delcampo. He doesn't even call me up since it
happened. I know he'll show up one of these nights, but so far
there is no sign of him. To tell the truth, I do not know who is
right about this war, but I know that nobody is going to remember ten years from now what it was all for. Just as I so often sit

here at my dressing table, where I am writing this, and it sometimes seems that I have never even gotten up to play, and I have
had forty-three shows, forty-three openings, and who can even
remember the casts, the exact kind of battles we had in production, let alone the reviews or even most of the titles? I know it all
kept me alive, that's about all. But it is even hard to remember the
kind of actor I had wanted to be. It wasn't this kind is all I know.

Suddenly, though, I was a little nervous about this meeting. I
have always respected actors with convictions, the people in the
old days who were Leftists and so on. Whatever people might say,
those guys and girls had wonderful friendships between them.
But I never felt it was really necessary for me to put my name on
anything political. I never felt it would make a difference of any
kind if I put my name or I didn't.

Besides, I felt nervous about a public appearance. But I looked
at this boy and he looked at me, and I could see once again how
my generation used to look way back there, that this meeting was
more than a meeting, it was to stop the world from ending. Which
I didn't believe, but for him it wasn't all the same, for him—and I
could see he was an actor—each new show was some kind of new
beginning. I could see that he still remembered every single thing
that had ever happened to him, that he was on his way up, up.
Actually I was quite frightened about the meeting, but I couldn't
bear to say to him that it was not going to make any difference if
I appeared or not. So we shook hands, and he even grasped my
arm as though we were in league, or even to indicate that he felt
especially good that an older man was going to be with them.
Something of that kind.

When he turned around and walked out I saw that the seat of
his overcoat was worn—it was a much lighter color than the rest
of the coat. An actor notices such things. It means that he sits a
lot in his overcoat, and on rough places, like the concrete bases of
the columns in front of the Forty-second Street Library, or even
park benches, or some of the broken chairs in producers' outer
offices. And here he is spending his time with meetings. I thought
to myself, I cannot imagine anything I would sit and wait for, and

I wished I had something like that. I ended up a little glad that I was going to be at the meeting. Exactly why, I don't know.

I think I acted better that night, not that anyone else would notice, but I found myself really looking at my fellow actors as though I had never seen them before. Suddenly it was remarkable to me, the whole idea of a play, of being able to forget everything else so that we were really angry up there, or really laughing, or really drinking the cider we were supposed to drink, which is actually tea, and coughing as though it were bitter. Toward the end of Act II some man got up from the third row and walked out, and I usually feel upset about a walkout, but this night it went through my mind that it was his role to walk out, that the whole audience was acting too; after all, the whole idea of so many people sitting together, facing in the same direction, not talking, is a kind of acting. Except that some of us very soon are actually going to die.

That thought came to me also—it was just as the man was walking out—that really the only difference offstage is that you don't get up after the death scene. Even the President gets made up now for his TV talks. Everybody, every morning, gets into costume. Except that I, instead of actually marrying, stop short at the last moment every time.

As we were taking the curtain calls I thought, Maybe I never got married because it would make my life real, it would rip me off the stage somehow.

The next morning I went to visit my father at the nursing home. I had been there only four or five days before, but I woke up and tried to read the scripts that had been sent to me, and I made a few phone calls, but I felt pulled. So I went.

It was a very windy day in October, a clear blue sky over New York. My father always liked strong wind and cold weather. He would put up his coat collar and say, "Ahhh," and even as a little boy I imitated the way he exhaled and enjoyed facing into a cold wind. He would look down at me and laugh. "This is not a hot day, boy."

The old man is in a cage. But the bars are so close to his face he cannot see them, so he keeps moving a step this way and a step that way. And finally he knows, for the hundredth time every day, that he is not free. But he does not know why. He feels someone knows, and whoever it is means him harm. Something is going to happen when the time comes. Someone is keeping him here for a time, temporarily, as you might say.

The room is freshly painted and smells it—a light blue color over many coats of paint so that the shiny surface is lumpy. A string hangs from the middle of the ceiling with a fluorescent plastic tassel on the end of it. His head strikes it whenever he moves about the room. In the dark at night he lies on his bed and goes to sleep with the bluish glow of this tassel on his retina. In the afternoons he can pull the string and make the ceiling light go on. He has never been at ease with machinery, so when he pulls the string he looks up at the ceiling fixture, a little surprised that the light goes on. Sometimes after his head has hit the tassel he scratches the spot lightly as though a fly had sat on his skin. The word "stroke" is very right, like a touch on the brain, just enough.

The nursing home is an old converted apartment house, but an extremely narrow one. The corridors on each floor are hardly wider than a man. You come in and on the right is an office where a fat woman is always looking into a thick registry book. On the left is a slow elevator. Up one flight is my father's floor. There is always a mattress or a spring standing on edge in the corridor; someone has been moved out or died. Rooms open off the corridor, most of them occupied by old women. They sit motionlessly facing their beds, some asleep in their chairs. There is no sound in the place; they are all dozing, like thin, white-haired birds that do not thrive in captivity. All their eyes seem blue.

A zoo smell is always in the air as soon as you walk into the building, and it gets thicker upstairs. But it is not a filthy smell. It is like earth, humid but not diseased. At my first visit I was repelled by it, as by sewage. But after a while, if you allow yourself to breathe in deeply and normally, you realize it is the odor of earth and you respect it.

The old man's room is the last one on the corridor. Opposite his door is a widened space where the nurses have a desk. They do not look up when I open his door. Nobody is going to steal anything here or do any harm. Everyone is so old that there cannot be an emergency.

He is usually asleep on his bed whatever time I come. I am already twenty years older than he was at my birth. I am an older man than the one I looked up at during the windy walks. My hair is gray at the sides. Mother has been dead a long, long time. All of his brothers and sister are dead, everyone he knew and played cards with. I have also lost many friends. It turns out that he is not really too much older than I am, than I am becoming.

I stood there looking down at him and recalled the meeting the night before. About fifteen others were sitting on a row of chairs on the stage. Donald Frost was the chairman and introduced us in turn. For some reason, when I stood up, there seemed to be heavier applause, probably because it was the first time I had ever come out for such a thing, and also because I have been quite a hit in this current play and they knew my face. But when I stood up and the applause continued, Donald waved for me to come up to the microphone. I was frightened that the newspapers would pick up what I might say, and I had no idea what to say. So I came to the microphone. There was a really good silence. The theater was packed. They said that people were jammed up outside trying to get in. I bent over to the microphone and heard my own voice saying, "Someone went blind that I knew." Then I realized that I did not actually know the boy who had been blinded, and I stopped. I realized that it sounded crazy. I realized that I was frightened, that someday there might be investigations and I could be blamed for being at such a meeting. I said, "I wish the war would stop. I don't understand this war." Then I went back to my chair. There was terrific applause. I didn't understand why. I wondered what I had really said that made them so enthusiastic. It was like an opening night when a line you never had thought about very much gets a big reaction. But I felt happy and I didn't know why. Maybe it was only the applause, which I didn't understand either, but I felt a happiness, and I thought suddenly that it had been a terrible, terrible mistake not to have gotten married.

"Pop?" I said softly, so as not to shock him. He opened his eyes and raised his head, blinking at me.

He always smiles now when he is awakened, and the lower part of his long face pulls down at his eyes to open them wider. It isn't clear whether or not he knows who you are as he smiles at you. I always slip in my identification before I say anything. "I'm Harry," I say, but I make it sound casual, as though I am saying it only because he hasn't got his glasses on. His fingers dance nervously along his lower lip. He is touching himself, I think, because he is no longer certain what is real and what is dream, when people he is not sure he knows suddenly appear and disappear every day. He immediately insists on getting out of bed. He is fully dressed under the blankets, sometimes even with his shoes on. But today he has only socks. "My slippers."

I got his slippers from the metal closet and helped him into them. He stood on the floor, tucking in his shirt, saying, "And uh, and uh," as though a conversation had been going on.

There are no immense emotions here but deep currents without light. He is bent a little and stiff-kneed, and he plucks at his clothes to be sure everything is on. He is very interested that someone is here but he knows that nothing, absolutely nothing, will come of it. But he wants to lengthen it out anyway, just in case something might happen to free him. He is afraid of the end of the visit suddenly being announced so he tries to be quick about everything. He says, "Sit down, sit down," not only to make you comfortable but to stall off the end. Then he sits in the one armchair, the fire escape behind him and a patch of city sky, and I sit on the edge of the bed facing him.

"I hear you went for a walk today with the nurse?"

"Ya. Awd the river. Doom days deen unden, but this here's a beautiful day. Some day."

"Yes. It's a beautiful day," I repeat so that he'll know I understand what he is talking about, although it doesn't make much difference to him. Some things he says, though, he is very anxious should be understood, and then it all gets terrible. But I am not sure he knows he is mostly incomprehensible.

He wanders his arm vaguely toward the night table. "My glasses." I open the drawer and hand him one of the two pairs he keeps in there.

"Are these the ones?"

He puts on the wobbly frames, which his incapable hands have bent out of shape. The lenses are coated with his fingerprints. "Ya," he says, blinking around. Then he says, "No," and roots around in the drawer. I give him the other pair, and he takes off the first pair, opens the second, and puts the first one on again and looks at me.

I realize as he is looking at me that he feels friendship between us and that he is glad to see me, but that he is not sure who I am. "I'm Harry," I say.

He smiles. He is still a big man even though he is very thin now; but his head is massive and his teeth are good and strong and there is some kind of force lying in pieces inside of him, the force of a man who at least has not at all settled for this kind of room and this kind of life. For him, as for me and everybody else, it is all some kind of mistake. He has a future. I suppose I still go to see him for that reason.

I never realized before that his ears stick out, that they face front. I think I was always so busy looking into his eyes that I never really saw his ears. Because there is nothing more to listen to from him or to fear, I have time to look at his body now.

His left leg is quite bowed out, more than I ever noticed. His hands are very slender and even artistic. His feet are long and narrow. He has strangely high, almost Slavic cheekbones, which I never noticed when his face was fuller. The top of his head is flatter, and the back of his neck. It was less than five years ago that I first realized he was an old man, an aged man. I happened to meet him walking on Broadway one afternoon and I had to walk very slowly beside him. A little breeze on his face made his eyes tear.

But I felt then that it was not something very sad; I felt that after all he had lived a long time.

But this day I felt that it was different because he had not given up his future. In fact, he was reaching toward his future even more energetically than I was toward mine. He really wanted something.

"Linnen, I ah gedda hew orthing. Very important."

"You want something?"

"No-no. I ah gedda hew orthing."

He waited for me to reply. "I don't understand what you're saying but keep talking, maybe I'll understand."

He reached over toward the door and tested that it was shut. Now as he spoke he kept glancing with widened eyes toward the corridor outside, as though interlopers were out there who meant him no good. Then he clamped his jaw angrily and shook his head. "I never in my life. Never."

"What's the matter?"

"He maug lee me ounigh."

"They won't let you out?"

He nodded, scandalized, angry. "Hew maug lee me ounigh."

"But you went out with the nurse, didn't you?"

"Linnen. Hew linnen?" He was impatient.

"Yes, Pop, I'm listening. What do you want?"

Something politic came over him as he prepared to speak again, something calculating. He was positioning himself for a deal. His lips, without sound, flicked in and out like a chimpanzee's as he practiced an important message. Then he crossed his legs and leaned over the arm of the chair toward me.

"Naw hen my money."

"Your money?"

"Naw hen. Yesterday she said sure. Today, naw hen."

"The lady downstairs?"

"Ya."

"She asked you for money?"

"Naw hen my money."

"She wouldn't give you your money?"

He nodded. "Naw hen. Fifty thousand dollars."

"You asked her for fifty thousand dollars?"

"For my money hen."

He was leaning toward me, cross-legged, just as I had seen him do with businessmen, that same way of talking in a hotel lobby or in a Pullman, a rather handsome posture and full of grace. Of course he had no fifty thousand dollars, he had nothing any more, but I did not realize at the time what he really had in his mind even though he was telling it to me clearly.

"Well, you don't need money here, Pop."

He gave me a suspicious look with a little wise smile. I too was not on his side.

"Linnen."

"I'm listening."

"I could go home," he said with sudden clarity. He had no home either; his wife was dead eight years now, and even his hotel room had been given up. "I wouldn't even talk," he said.

"It's better for you here, Pop."

"Better!" He looked at me with open anger.

"You need nursing," I explained.

He listened with no attention while I explained how much better off he was here than at home, his eyes glancing at the door. But his anger passed. Then he said, "I could live."

I nodded.

"I could live," he repeated.

Now came the silence, which is always the worst part. I could find nothing to say any more, and he no longer had a way to enlist my help. Or maybe he was expecting me to start packing his things and getting him out. All we had in the room was his low-burning pleasure that someone was here with him, even though he did not know for sure who it was, except that it was someone familiar; and for me there was only the knowledge that he had this pleasure.

He would look at me now and then with various expressions. Once it would be with narrowed eyes, an estimating look, as though he were about to say some searching sentence. Then he would blink ahead again and test his lips. After a few moments he would look at me, this time with the promise of his warm, open smile, and once again go into a stare.

Finally he raised his finger as though to draw my attention, a stranger's attention, and, tilting back his head as though recalling, he said, "Did you St. Louis?"

"Yes, I'm back now. I was there and now I'm back." I had been in St. Louis with a show nine or ten years ago. One of his factories had been in St. Louis forty years ago.

He broke into a pleased smile. He loved cities; he had enjoyed entering them and leaving them, being well served in hotels; he had loved to recall buildings that had been demolished, the marvelous ups and downs of enterprises and business careers. I knew what he was smiling at. He had once brought me a toy bus from St. Louis, with a whole band on top that moved its arms when the bus moved, and inside it was a phonograph record that played "The Stars and Stripes Forever." He had come home just as I had gotten up from my nap. In his arms were gift boxes. This bus, and I remember a long pair of beige kid gloves for my mother. He always brought fresh air into the house with him, the wind, his pink face and his reedy laugh.

"Well, I have to go now, Pop."

"Ya, ya."

He hastened to stand, hiking his pants up where his belly used to be, plucking at his brown sweater to keep it properly placed on his shoulders. He even enjoyed the goodbye, thinking I had important work to do, appointments, the world's business with which no one had a right to interfere. We shook hands. I opened the door, and he insisted on escorting me to the elevator. "This way, this way," he said in a proprietary manner, as though he could not help being in charge. He walked ahead of me down the narrow corridor, bent, heavily favoring his bowed left leg, his face very much averted from the open rooms we passed where the old ladies sat motionless. He had never liked old women.

Outside the wind was even faster than before, but the sky was turning gray. I had some time so I walked for a while, thinking of him turning back and re-entering his room, lying down on the bed, probably exhausted, and the plastic thing on the light string swaying overhead.

It was fine to walk without a limp. I resolved again to stop smoking. I have wide hands and feet. I am not built like him at all. I crossed from Riverside Drive to the Park and caught a bus to Harlem, where I was born. But as soon as I got out I knew I had lost the feeling I had started with, and it was impossible to feel what I had felt there in my youth forty years ago.

There was only one moment that held me; I found myself facing a dry-cleaning store, which had once been one of the best restaurants in New York. On Sundays the old man would take my mother and me for dinner. There had been a balcony where a baker in a tall white hat baked fresh rolls, and whenever a customer entered he would put in a fresh batch. I could smell the rolls through the odor of benzine on Lenox Avenue. I could see the manager, who always sat down with us while we ate. He had some disease, I suppose, because the right side of his face was swollen out like a balloon, but he always wore a hard wing collar and a white tie and never seemed sick.

A Negro with a mustache was looking through the store window at me. For a moment I had the urge to go inside and tell him what I remembered, to describe this avenue when no garbage cans were on the street, when the Daimlers and Minervas and Locomobiles had cruised by and the cop on the corner threw back the ball when it got through the outfield on 114th Street. I did not go into the store, or even toward our house. Any claim to anything had slipped. I went downtown instead and sat in my dressing room trying to read.

I was just opening my pancake can when I thought of something I still don't altogether understand: that the old man is the only one who is not an actor. I am, the President is, and Donald Frost is even though his convictions are very sincere; but on the platform last night I could tell, probably because I am an actor, that he was listening to his modulations, that he was doing what he was doing because he had told himself to do it. But he is not desperate enough, not like the old man is desperate. The old man does not know enough to listen to his own voice or to ask himself what he ought to do; he just speaks from his heart, and he has even lost his hold on the language so all that is left is the sound, you might say, of his gut, which is not acting. I wondered about the young, pink-cheeked boy who had come to remind me about the meeting—whether he also was acting. Maybe in his case, with the draft grabbing for him, it was real.

I started pasting on my beard, and I thought again of my not being married. It was like all this agitation now, like everything I saw and knew about, it was a lack of some necessity. Nobody seems to have to do anything, and the ones who say they do have to, who say that something is absolutely necessary for them, may only be the best actors. Because that is what a really good actor does; he manages to make his feelings necessary, so that suddenly there is no longer the slightest choice for him. He has to scream or die, laugh or die, cry real tears or die. And at the same time he knows that he is not going to die, and this thought makes him happy while he is screaming or crying, and it may be what makes the audience happy to cry too.

I was just taking off my clothes in my bedroom that night when the phone rang. And it frightened me, as it usually does these days. It really was the fat woman in the nursing home this time; the old man had escaped. He had slipped out not long after I had left, and here it was nearly two in the morning and the police had a missing persons alarm out, but there was no sign of him yet. The worst thing was that he had gone out without his overcoat, and it was raining and blowing like hell. There was nothing more to be done now, as long as the police had an eye out for him, but I couldn't go back to sleep. I couldn't help feeling proud of him and hoping they would never find him, that he would just disappear. I have always admired his willfulness, his blind push toward what he has to have. I have admired his not being an actor, I suppose, and he was not acting tonight, not out there in that rain and wind. I couldn't sleep, but there was nothing I could do. The clock was inching up to three by this time. I got dressed and went out.

I had walked only a block when I felt my socks getting wet so I stepped into a doorway, trying to think what to do. It was somehow strange that both of us were walking around in the same rain. But whom was he looking for? Or what? I half didn't want to find him. In fact, for moments I had visions of him crossing the river to the West, just getting the hell out of here, out of the world. But how would he talk to anybody? Would he know enough to get onto a bus? Did he have any money? Naturally I ended up being worried about him, and after a while I saw a taxi and got in.

I joke with cabdrivers but I never talk with them, but this time I had to explain myself for wanting to cruise around, and I told the driver that I was looking for my father. Cabdrivers never seem to believe anything, but he believed me—it seemed perfectly natural to him. Maybe it happens quite often like this. I don't even remember what he looked like, even whether he was white or Negro. I remember the rain pouring over the windshield and the side windows because I was trying to see through them. It was getting on toward half-past four by the time I got home again, and the rain was coming down stiff. I got into my bedroom and undressed and lay down and looked toward my window, which was running with water. I felt as though the whole city were crying.

They found him next morning at about ten o'clock, and the police phoned me. They had already returned him to the nursing home so I hurried up there. The rain was over, and once again the sky was clear, a good sharp, sunny October day. He was asleep on his bed, wrapped in his flannel robe. A bandage was plastered over his nose, and he seemed to have a black eye coming on. His knuckles were scraped and painted with Mercurochrome. He badly needed a shave.

I went downstairs and talked with the fat woman in the office. She was wary and cautious because they can probably be sued, but I finally got the story out of her. He had been found in Harlem. He had gone into a luncheonette and ordered some food, but the counterman had probably realized that he was not quite right and asked for the money in advance. The old man had a dollar but would not pay in advance, and they went looking for a cop to take care of him. When he realized they were looking for a cop he got up and tried to leave and stumbled and fell on his face.

I went up again and sat in the armchair, waiting for him to

wake up. But after a while one of the nurses came in and said they had given him a sedative that would keep him under for several hours. I left and came back just before my show, and he was sitting in the armchair, eating some chicken. He looked up at me, very surprised, and felt his lips with rapid fingers.

I smiled at him. "I'm Harry," I said.

He looked at me without much recognition, except as before, only knowing that there was something of a past between us. I sat on the bed and watched him eat. I talked at length about the good day we were having and how hard it had rained last night. I kept wishing and wishing that even for one split second he would look at me clearly and laugh—just one shrewd laugh between us to celebrate his outing. But he sat there eating, glancing at me with a little warmth and a little suspicion, and finally I grinned and said, "I hear you went for a walk last night."

He stopped eating and looked at me with surprise. He shook his head. "No. Oh, no."

"Don't you remember the rain?"

"The rain?"

"You went to Harlem, Pa. Were you going home?"

A new attention crossed his eyes, and a sharpened interest. "I en home raro." He spoke the sounds with an attempt to convince me. He had one finger raised.

"You're going home tomorrow?"

"Ya." Then he glanced toward the closed door and returned to the chicken.

Every night, sitting here putting on my beard, I keep expecting a phone call or a visitor, a stranger, and I feel I am about to be afraid.

He was trying to reach home, where ages ago he had entered so many times, carrying presents. He has a future that they will never be able to rip away from him. He will close his eyes for the last time thinking of it. He does not have to teach himself or remind himself of it. As long as he can actually walk they are going to have trouble with him, keeping him from going where he wants to go and has to go.

I'm not sure how to go about it, but I have a terrific desire to live differently. Maybe it is even possible to find something honorable about acting, some way of putting my soul back into my body. I think my father is like a man in love, or at least the organism inside him is. For moments, just for moments, it makes me feel as I used to when I started, when I thought that to be a great actor was like making some kind of a gift to the people.

[*1966*]

HOMELY GIRL,
A LIFE

Homely Girl, A Life

I

A cold wind seemed to blow on her as she surfaced from a deep sleep. Yesterday had been warm in Central Park, and it was June. Opening her eyes as usual toward him, she saw how strangely blanched his face was. Although what she called his sleeping smile was still there, and the usual suggestion of happiness at the curled corners of his mouth, he seemed heavier on the mattress. And she knew immediately and with dread raised her hand and touched his cheek—the end of the long story. Her first thought, like an appeal against a mistake: But he is only sixty-eight!

Fright but no tears, not outside. Just the thump on the back of her neck. Life had a fist.

"Ah!" she pitied aloud, and bringing palms together, she touched fingers to her lips. "Ah!" She bent to him, her silky hair touching his face. But he wasn't there. "Ah, Charles!" A little anger soon dispersed by reason. And wonder.

The wonder remained—that after all her life had amounted to a little something, had given her this man, this man who had never seen her. He was awesome now, lying there.

Oh, if one more time she could have spoken with him, asked or told him . . . what? The thing in her heart, the wonder. That he had loved her and had never seen her in the fourteen years of their life. There was always, despite everything, something in her trying to move itself into his line of vision, as though with one

split-second glimpse of her his fluttering eyes would wake from
their eternal sleep.

Now what do I do? Oh, Charles dear, what do I do with the
rest of it?

Something was not finished. But I suppose, she said to herself,
nothing ever is except in movies when the lights come on, leaving
you squinting on the sidewalk.

Once more, she moved to touch him, but already he was not
there, not hers, not anything, and she withdrew her hand and sat
there with one leg hanging over the mattress.

She hated her face as a girl but knew she had style and at least
once a day settled for that and her very good compact body and a
terrific long neck. And yes, her irony. She was and wanted to be a
snob. She knew how to slip a slight, witty rotation into her hips
when she walked, although she had no illusions it made up for a
pulled look to her cheeks, as if alum had tightened her skin, and
an elongated upper lip. A little like Disraeli, she thought once,
coming on his picture in a high-school text. And a too-high forehead (she refused to overlook anything negative). She wondered if
she'd been drawn out of the womb and lengthened, or her mother
startled by a giraffe. At parties she had many a time noticed how
men coming up behind her were caught surprised when she turned
to face them. But she had learned to shake out the straight silky
light-brown hair and flick the ironic defensive grin, silent pardon
for their inevitable fade. She had a tonic charm and it was almost
enough, although not quite, of course, not since childhood when
her mother held up a *Cosmopolitan* Ivory ad to her face and so
warmly and lovingly exclaimed, "Now that's beauty!" as though
by staring at it hard enough she could be made to look like one of
those girls. She felt blamed then. Still, at fifteen she believed that
between her ankles and her breasts she was as luscious as Betty
Grable, or almost. And she had a soft, provocative lisp that men
who had an interest in mouths seemed to like. At sixteen, she'd
been told by Aunt Ida, visiting from Egypt, "You've got an Egyptian look; Egyptian women are hot." Recalling that oddity would

make her laugh and would raise her spirits even into her sixties, after Charles had died.

A number of memories involved lying in bed on a Sunday morning, listening thankfully to muffled New York outside. "I was just thinking, apropos of nothing," she whispered into Charles's ear one time, "that for at least a year after Sam and I had separated, I was terribly embarrassed to say we had. And even after you and I married, whenever I had to refer to 'my first husband' it curdled something inside me. Like a disgrace or a defeat. What a simple-minded generation we were!"

Sam was beneath her in some indefinite class sense, but that was part of his attraction to the thirties, when to have been born to money was shameful, a guarantee of futility. People her age, early twenties then, wanted to signify by doing good, attended emergency meetings a couple of times a week in downtown lofts or sympathizers' West End Avenue living rooms to raise money for the new National Maritime Union or buying ambulances for the Spanish Republicans, and they were moved to genuine outrage by Fascism, which was somehow a parents' system and the rape of the mind; the Socialist hope was for the young, for her, and no parent could help but fear its subversive beauty. So political talk was mostly avoided at home. Anyway, hers were hopelessly silly people, Jews putting on the dog with a new, absurd name endowed by the Immigration inspectors back in the other century because Great-grandpa's original Russian one was unpronounceable by their Irish tongues. So they were Sessions.

But Sam was Fink, which she rather relished as a taunt to her father, long a widower and very ill now but still being consulted on the phone as an authority on utilities by the time of her marriage, dying as he read that Hitler had walked into Vienna. "But he won't last," he whispered scoffingly across the cancer in his throat. "The Germans are too intelligent for this idiot." But of course by now she knew better, knew a world was ending, and would not be surprised to see American storm troopers with chin straps on Broadway one evening. It was already scary to go walking around in Yorkville on the Upper East Side, where the Germans were rallying on the street corners to bait Jews and praise Hitler on summertime Saturday nights. She was not particularly Semitic-looking, but she feared the fear of the prey as she passed thick-necked men on Eighty-sixth Street.

In her teens, she wondered: I am never going to be beautiful or even a genius. What am I supposed to expect then? She felt surrounded by too much space and longed for a wall to have to climb over.

A stylish man, her father, with a long, noble head and an out-moded mind, or so she thought of him in the flush of her newfound revolutionary independence. Stroking his cold hand in the gloom of the West End Avenue apartment, she thanked her luck, or rather her own perceptive intelligence, which had helped turn her away from all this heavy European silverware, the overstuffed chairs and the immense expanse of Oriental carpet, the sheer doomed weight of their tea service and the laughable confidence it had once expressed. If not beautiful, she was at least strong, free of Papa's powerful illusions. But now that he was weak and his eyes closed most of the time, she could let herself admit that she shared his arrogant style, caring a lot and pretending not to, unlike her mother, who'd screamingly pretended to care and hadn't cared at all. But of course Papa accepted the injustice in the world as natural as trees. Outwardly a conventional man, he was quickly bored by predictable people, and this had conspiratorially linked her to him. She delighted in his covert mockery of uniformity, which fueled her rebellion against her mother. A day before he died, he smiled at her and said, "Don't worry, Janice, you're pretty enough, you'll be okay, you've got the guts." If only okay could ever be enough.

The rabbi's brief ceremony must have been developed for these bankrupt times; people were scanting even rote funerary farewells to get back to their gnawing make-a-living worries. Following the prayer, the funeral chapel man, looking like H. L. Mencken, with hair parted in the middle, shot his starched cuffs and picked up the small cardboard box of ashes, handing it to her fat brother, Herman, who in his surprise looked at it as if it were a ticking ex-plosive. Then they went out into the hot sunlit street and walked downtown together. Herman's butterball wife, Edna, kept falling behind to look into an occasional shoe store window, one of the few shops still occupied in whole blocks of vacancies along Broadway. Half of New York seemed to be for rent, with permanent "Vacancy" signs bolted to nearly every apartment house entrance. Now, eight years after the Crash, the heads of the bolts were beginning to rust. Herman walked flopping his feet down like a seal and sucked for breath. "Look at it, the whole block," he said with a wave of his hand.

"Real estate doesn't interest me right now," Janice said.

"Oh, it doesn't? Maybe eating does, 'cause this is where Papa put a lot of your money, baby." They entered a darkened Irish bar on Eighty-fourth Street facing Broadway and sat with an electric fan blowing into their faces. "Did you hear? Roosevelt's supposed to have syph."

"I'm trying to drink this, please." Defying ritual and capitalist superstition, she wore a beige skirt and a shiny white silk blouse and high-heeled tan shoes. Sam had to be in Syracuse to bid on an important library being auctioned. "You must be the last Republican Jew in New York," she said.

Herman wheezed, absently moving the little box around on the bar like the final beleaguered piece in a lost chess game, a futile three inches in one direction and then in the other. He sipped his beer and talked about Hitler, the remorseless heat that summer, and real estate.

"These refugees are coming over and buying up Amsterdam Avenue."

"So what difference does that make?"

"Well, they're supposed to be so downtrodden."

"You want them more downtrodden? Don't you understand anything? Now that Franco's won, Hitler's going to attack Russia, there's going to be a tremendous war. And all you can think of is real estate."

"So what if he attacks Russia?"

"Oh God, I'm going home." Disgust flowed up her back, and glancing at the little box, she drank her second martini fast; how

really weird, a whole man fitting into a four-by-six-inch carton
hardly big enough for a few muffins.

"If you'd throw some of your share in with mine, we could pick
up buildings for next to nothing. This Depression won't last forever, and we could clean up someday."

"You really know how to pick a time to talk about business."

"Did you read? No rain in Oklahoma; it's starting to blow
away again."

He had all Papa's greed but none of his charm, with a baby face
and pudgy hands. Slipping off her stool, smiling angrily, she gave
him a monitory bop on the head with her purse, kissed Edna's plump
cheek, and with heels clacking walked into the street, Herman
behind her defending his right to be interested in real estate.

She was halfway home in the taxi when she recalled that at some
point he had bequeathed the ashes to her. Had he remembered to
take them from the bar? She called him. Scandalized, he piped,
"You mean you lost them?" She hung up, cutting him off, scared.
She had left Papa on the bar. She went weak in the thighs with
some superstitious fear that she had to force out of her mind. After
all, she thought, what is the body? Only the *idea* of a person matters, and Papa's in my heart. Running a bath and flowing toward
transcendence again in the remnants of her yellow martini haze,
she glimpsed her unchangeable face in the steamy mirror and the
body mattered again. Yet at the same time it didn't. She tried to
recall a classical philosopher who might have reconciled the two
truths, but tired of the effort. Then, realizing she had bathed only
a few hours earlier, she shut off the tap and began to dress again.

She found she was hurrying and knew she had to get the ashes
back; she had done an awful thing, leaving them there, something
like sin. For a moment her father lived, reprimanding her with a
sad look. But why, despite everything, was there something funny
in the whole business? How tasteless she was!

The bartender, a thin, long-armed man, recalled no such box.
He asked if there was anything valuable in it, and she said, "Well,
no." Then the guilt butted her like a goat. "My father. His ashes."

"Holy Jesus!" The man's eyes widened at this omen of bad luck.

His flaring emotion startled her into weeping. It was the first time, and she felt grateful to him and also ashamed that he might feel more about Papa than she did. He touched her back with his hand and guided her to the dismal ladies' room in the rear, but looking around, she found nothing. The man was odorless, like Vaseline, and for a split instant she wondered if this was all a dream. She stared down at the toilet. Oh God, what if someone sprinkled Papa down there! Returning to the bar, she touched the man's thick tattooed forearm. "It doesn't matter," she reassured him. He insisted on giving her a drink and she had a martini, and they talked about different kinds of death, sudden and drawn out, the deaths of the very young and the old. Her eyes were red-rimmed. Two gas company workers at the bar listened in their brutal solemnity from a respectful distance. It had always been more relaxing for her to be among strange men than with women she didn't know. The bartender came around the bar to see her to the door, and before she could think, she kissed him on the cheek. "Thank you," she said. Sam had never really pursued her, she thought now; she had more or less granted herself to him. She walked down Broadway, angering at their marriage, and by the time she reached the corner loved, or at least pitied, him again.

And so Papa was gone. After a few blocks she felt relieved as she sensed the gift of mourning in her, that illusion of connection with a past; but how strange that the emotion should have been given her by a probably right-wing Catholic Irishman who no doubt was a supporter of Franco and couldn't stand Jews. Everything was feeling, nothing was clear. But she rejected that idea at once. "If feeling is everything, I might as well settle for being my mother." Too awful. Somehow, in this sudden, unexpected collision with the barman's direct feeling, she saw that she really must stop waiting to become someone else: she was Janice forever. What an exciting idea if she could only follow it; maybe it would lead her to solid ground. This endless waiting-to-become was like the Depression itself—everybody kept waiting for it to lift and forgot how to live in the meantime, but supposing it went on forever? She must start living! And Sam had to start thinking of something else than Fascism and organizing unions and the rest of the endlessly repetitive radical agenda. But she mustn't think that way, she guiltily corrected herself.

She smiled, perversely reminded of her new liberation. No parents! I am an orphan. In a few minutes, walking down Broadway, she saw something amusing in so formal and fastidious a man as Dave Sessions being left in a box on a bar: she could see him trapped in there, tiny, outraged, and red-faced, banging on the lid to be let out. A strange thought struck her—that the body was more of an abstraction than the soul, which never disappeared.

Sam Fink had a warming smile, an arched bony nose, which, as he said, he had been years learning to love. He was just about Janice's five feet seven, and standing face-to-face with him sometimes brought to mind her mother's nastily repeated warning, "Never marry a handsome man," a barely disguised jab not only at beautiful Papa's vanity but at her daughter's looks. But unhandsome Sam, absolutely devoted to her, had a different beauty, the excitement of the possessed. His Communist commitment turned her to the future and away from what she regarded as her nemesis, triviality, the bourgeois obsession with things.

Nevertheless, it was painful to look at pictures in museums with him at her side—she had majored in art history at Hunter—and to hear nothing about Picasso but his conversion to the Party, or about the secret anti-monarchical codes buried in Titian's painting or the class-struggle metaphor in Rembrandt. "They are not necessarily conscious of it, of course, but the great ones were always in a struggle with the ruling class."

"But, darling, all that has nothing to do with painting."

And, spoken with a teacher's gently superior grin toward a child—and incipient violence buried deep in his eyes: "Except that it has everything to do with painting; their convictions were what raised them above the others, the 'painters.' You have to learn this, Janice: conviction matters."

She felt love in his voice, and so she was somehow reassured by what she did not quite believe. Tucking her arm under his as they walked, she supposed most people married not out of overwhelming

love but to find justification in one another, and why not? Glancing
at his powerful nose and neat, nearly bald head, she felt elevated by
his moral nature and safe in his militancy. But it was not always
possible to banish the vision of an empty space surrounding them, a
lightless gloom out of which something horrible could suddenly
pounce one day. Unconsciously, she began waiting for its appearance, a rending explosion from below.

It was his amazing knowledge of books that helped quiet her
doubts. Sam, unusual among book dealers, read or at least
skimmed what he was selling, and could pick out of the air the
names of authorities on a couple of hundred of subjects from
Chess to China, as he snappily put it to his awed customers, who
forgave his arrogance for the research it saved them from having
to do. He knew the locations of dozens of old mansions all over
New York State, Connecticut, Massachusetts, and New Jersey
where expiring old families still had sizable libraries to get rid of
on the death of some final aunt, uncle, or inheriting retainer. A
couple of times a month, he would drive into the country in his
green stiff-sprung Nash for a day or two and return with trunk
and back seat packed with sets of Twain, Fenimore Cooper, Emer-
son, Dickens, Poe, Thackeray, Melville, Hawthorne, and Shakespeare, and armfuls of arcane, mouse-nibbled miscellany—*John
Keats' Secret*, an 1868 *Survey of Literature of the Womb*, a 1905
Manual of Chinese Enamelware, Lasting Irish Melodies of 1884,
Annals of Ophthalmology, or *A Speculation on Ancient Egyptian Surgery*. Janice would sit with Sam on the floor of their dark
East Thirty-second Street living room, she imagining the silent,
sealed-up life of the family in some upper Monroe County house-
hold from whose privacy these books had been ripped, books that
must once have brought news of the great world out and beyond
their lilac doorways.

Watching him thumb through his finds, she thought he had the
ethereal look of a cute monk, including the innocent round tonsure. Was it his sheer goodness that annoyed her? There was
something monkish in his pretense of not noticing—when she
leaned back resting on her elbows, one leg tucked under and her

skirt midway up her thigh—that she was asking to be taken there on the floor. When she saw him flush and shift to some explication of the day's news, a fury flashed and died away within her, and she despaired for herself. Still, with Britain and France secretly flirting with Fascism, she could hardly ask him to set her greedy desire ahead of serious things.

But his plain love for his books and his work stirred her love for him. With the proprietary self-congratulation of an author, he would read choice passages to her, from Trollope especially, or Henry James or Virginia Woolf, or Communist Louis Aragon and the young Richard Wright. He was snobbish like her but, unlike her, denied it.

Alone at least two evenings a week, when Sam went to Party meetings, she walked across the dead East Side over to slummy Sixth with its tenements and dusty Irish bars under the el and came home tired to listen to Benny Goodman records and smoke too many Chesterfields until she was tensed and angry at the walls. When Sam came home explicating Stalin's latest utterances on how the Socialist future, bearing goodness at last, was moving as inexorably toward them as an ocean wave, she nearly drowned in her own ingratitude and was only restored for the moment by the vision of justice that he was guarding, along with the nameless army of civilized comrades spread out across every country in the world.

On another Sunday morning in bed with Charles, forever trying to visualize herself, she said, "I can never figure out what got me; it was about four years after being married; we'd usually come home from a French or Russian movie on Irving Place and go to bed, and that was that. This time I decided to make myself a martini and then sat on the couch listening to records, you know, like Benny Goodman's 'A Train' or the Billie Holiday things or Ledbetter, or maybe Woody Guthrie, I think, was coming on at that time, and after twenty minutes Sam came out of the bedroom in his pajamas. He was really shy but he wasn't a coward, and he stood there, poor man, with that tense grin, leaning on the bedroom doorjamb like Humphrey Bogart, and he said, 'Sleeptime.'"

"That's when it just fell out of my mouth. 'Fuck the future,' I said."

Charles's eyes fluttered and he laughed with her and pressed his hand on the inside of her thigh.

"He laughed, but blushing—you know, that I'd said that word. And he said, 'What does that mean?'"

"Just fuck the future." She heard her own tinkling giggle and would always remember the free-falling feeling in her chest.

"It must have a meaning."

"It means that there must be something happening now that is interesting and worth thinking about. And now means now."

"Now always means now." He grinned against apprehension.

"No, it mostly means pretty soon, or someday. But now it means tonight."

Angered, he blushed deeper, right up his high forehead, into his hair. She opened the dark oak cabinet and made another martini and giggling at some secret joke got into bed and drank it to the bottom. Feeling left out, he could only go on idealistically grinning, brave man, elbow on the pillow, trying hard to get a grasp on her spinning mind.

"Papa and I once lived in this Portuguese beach house for a month after Mama died, and I used to watch this peasant cook we had when she'd come over the sand dunes carrying fresh vegetables and a fish in a basket for me to inspect so she could cook it for us. She'd take forever trudging in the sand till she got to me, and then all it was was this fish, which was still damp from the ocean."

"What about it?"

"Well, that's it—you wait and wait and watch it coming, and it's a damp fish." She had laughed and laughed, helplessly nearing hysteria, then brushed a dismissive kiss on Sam's wrist and fell into a separate sleep, smiling with some uncertain air of victory.

Now she ran a finger lightly along Charles's nose. "Did any of that mean anything to you—the Left?"

"I was studying music in the thirties."

"How wonderful. Just studying music."

"I had enough to do just organizing my days. But I was always sympathetic. But what could I have done about anything? Some friends took me out to a picket line at Columbia once. I can't recall the issue, but I was more of a nuisance to them than anything else; my dog hated walking around and around." He turned and kissed her nose. "You make it all sound such a waste. Was it, you think?"

"I don't know yet. When I think of the writers we all thought were so important, and no one knows their names any more. I mean the militant people. That whole literature simply dribbled away. Gone."

"It was a style, wasn't it? Most styles crack up and disappear."

"And why is that, do you think?"

"It depends. When the occasion dominates, the work tends to vanish with the occasion."

"What should dominate, then?"

"The feelings that the occasion roused in the artist. I personally believe that what lasts is what art itself causes to exist in the artist—I mean the sounds that create other sounds, or the phrases that generate new phrases. Bach wrote some wonderful piano pieces that were really meant as piano lessons, but we listen now to their spiritual qualities, now that the occasion is forgotten. The work created its own spirituality, in a sense, and this lasts."

"What are you trying to tell me?" she asked, kissing his earlobe.

"You seem to have a need to mock yourself as you were then. I don't think you should. A lot of the past is always embarrassing— if you have any sensitivity."

"Not for you, though."

"Oh, I've had plenty of moments."

"That you're ashamed of?"

He hesitated. "For a while I tried to act as though I had sight. For a long time I refused to concede. I did some boorish things. With women especially. It was terrible."

She felt she was blushing for him and could not press him. She did not want his nobility marred. Someday he might tell her. What she imagined was that he may have, in effect, blackmailed girls with his handsome blindness, pressed himself on them as a debt they owed. That would certainly embarrass him now. In fact, she was aware of how really little she knew of his life—as little as he knew of her face. "Radicals," she said, "think they want truth, but what they really long for is high-minded characters to look up to."

"Not only radicals, Janice. People have to believe in goodness." His eyelids fluttered faster when he was excited, and they did now, like birds' wings. "They're disappointed most of the time, but in some part of his beliefs every person is naïve. Even the most cynical. And memories of one's naïveté are always painful. But so what? Would you rather have had no beliefs at all?"

She buried her face in his flesh. His acceptance of her, she thought, was like a tide. She had lived a life of waiting, she thought now, and the waiting had ended, the thirst for a future was not in her any more, she was there. With a man who had never seen her. It was wonderfully odd.

With Charles she would often think back with wonder at what now seemed like thirty years of waiting. Or had the war stalled life for everyone? Nowadays there seemed to be no future at all any more, but it was all there was in the old days. One of her permanent stinging memories was of the day she had been shopping on Thirty-fourth Street for shoes and was walking home in new high heels, pleasured by how they sensualized the shape of her legs, when her eye fell on a corner candy store newsstand with the immense headline slashed across the *Times* front page: STALIN AND HITLER IN PACT. Fink usually brought the paper home at night, and when she handed the vendor her three pennies he said, "Sam bought one this morning."

"I know. I want one."

The man shared Fink's politics. "I thought he was going to faint," he confided. "His face went white."

With her old shoes in the box under her arm, she walked down Madison to Thirty-first Street, stopping in the middle of the sidewalk to read the incredible again and again. Simply unthinkable. Stalin so much as uttering Hitler's name without snarling was like a god being discovered screwing on the floor, or farting. Yet she felt she had to find some way to continue believing in the Soviets, which after all were still the only imaginable opposite of West End Avenue, carpets, silverware, and things.

"How can it have happened?" she asked Fink over dinner at a place called Barclay's on Eighth Street, where a meal was ninety cents rather than the sixty-five next door in the University Inn. The Village was stunned. She could feel it in the restaurant. Bud Goff, the owner, normally pumped Fink for inside political information; he believed the Party had some secret key to future events. But tonight he had merely nodded when they entered, as though at a wake.

With a wink and a canny grin, Fink tapped the side of his nose, but she knew how raked his spirit was. "Don't worry, Stalin knows what he's doing; and he's not helping Hitler—he'll never supply Germany."

"But I think he is, isn't he?"

"He is not. He's just refusing to pull the French and British chestnuts out of the fire. He's been pleading with them for a pact against Hitler for five years now, and they've stalled, hoping Hitler would attack Russia. Well, he's turned the chess game around."

She quickly agreed; in some secret windblown room in her mind, she sensed that her connection to Sam depended somehow on her keeping the faith with the Soviets—they had made Russia literate and turned her lights on. To discard the Revolution meant living without the future, meant merely living now, a frighteningly bereft feeling. In that parched year-and-a-half interval, she had seen Sam Fink straining to justify the pact to her and to their friends. And when it was no longer deniable that Russian wheat and oil were actually being shipped to a Germany that was now invading France, something within her came to a halt and stood motionless behind her eyes.

Soon after, she would happen to be in Times Square the day France capitulated to the Nazis. An immense crowd had halted on Broadway and stood reading the moving headline around the Times Building. Shame gripped her heart. Fink had explained that it was an imperialist war and that Germany, now a Soviet ally, was no worse than France, and she had tried to take that to heart, but a man standing beside her, a middle-aged round fellow in his sixties, had begun to weep into his handkerchief. It was weird how she had walked from him to the corner of Forty-second and Broadway, where a front-page photo looked up at her from a newsstand, of a round-faced middle-aged man standing on the Champs Élysées, watching the Nazi cavalry parading by as it entered Paris after the French defeat, and his eyes were flooding with tears, like a beaten child's.

Trained to reason or think her way toward hope, she put things aside, neither denied nor affirmed. She lived in waiting as though for some verdict that had not yet been announced.

Suddenly she could wait no more. "Frankly, I am almost ashamed sometimes of saying I'm not anti-Soviet," she dared to declare one night at dinner.

"My darling, you don't know what the hell you are talking about." He grinned paternally.

"But, Sam, they are helping Hitler."

"The story hasn't ended yet."

Twenty-five years on, she would look back at this, one of her emblematic conversations, aware that she had known at the time that she was losing respect for Sam's leadership; and how odd that it should have come about because of a pact made ten thousand miles away!

"But shouldn't we object? Shouldn't you?" she asked.

His mouth formed a smile that to her seemed smug, and he shook his head with unshakable pity. That was when it happened, the first cut of hatred for him, the first sense of personal insult. But of course she hung on, as one did in those times, and even pretended—not only to him but to herself—that she had absorbed another of his far-seeing lessons.

She felt paralyzed. They went coolly to bed, with the winds of the world crossing their faces. They knew they did not like one another that night. But how she could love him if he could only admit how wounded he was! Still, maybe a marriage could more easily sustain both parties lying rather than one. This must be a chapter for us, she thought. Maybe now it will all change. She reached to his shoulder, but he seemed happily asleep. Closing her

eyes, she invited Cary Grant to lean over her and speak ironically
as he undid his incredible bow tie and slipped out of his clothes.

But a year and a half later, when Hitler finally broke the pact
and attacked Russia, the Village was relaxed again, with Fascism
again the enemy. The Russians were heroic, and Janice felt part of
America once more, no longer so dreadfully ashamed of a part-
nership with Hitler.

Sam Fink presented himself at the 90 Church Street navy
recruitment office a week after Pearl Harbor, but with his name
and his nose, he was not naval officer material—the grin on the
amused face of the blond examiner, a lieutenant senior grade, was
not lost on Sam, nor was its irony in this anti-Fascist war—and so
he enlisted in the more democratic army. The rebuff was embarrassing but not unexpected under capitalism, when for years now
so many Jewish students had been having to go to Scottish and
British medical schools, turned away by the *numerus clausus* of
American institutions. Sam trained first in Kentucky, then in the
officers' school in Fort Sill, Oklahoma, while Janice waited in
broiling-hot wooden rooming houses off-base. The war might last
eight or ten years, they were saying. But of course she must not
complain, considering the bombing of London and the crucifix-
ion of Yugoslavia. Desperately fighting loneliness, she taught herself shorthand and typing just in case she never landed the
editorial job she had begun to apply for at magazine offices and
publishing houses, which were losing men to the war.

By now she was twenty-eight, and on bad nights her bored face—
the face of a trim, small horse, she had decided—could bring her
close to tears. Then she would take a notebook and try to write out
her feelings. "It isn't that I feel positively unattractive—I know better. But that somehow I am being kept from anything miraculous
happening to me, ever."

With the dimming of her love for Sam, time moved in detached
patches, and she could no longer find reasons to do or not do anything. A saving miracle was becoming a less than silly idea.
"Somehow, when I look at myself, the miraculous seems to be
more and more possible. Or is this hot room driving me crazy?"

Here in Oklahoma, deep in America, she understood that secretly she was part of nothing larger than herself, a ridiculous person. At night, awakened by a line of tanks roaring past, she would go out on the front stoop of their cottage and wave to the officers, whose upper bodies, like centaurs, stuck up out of the top portholes. The thought of the familiar faces of the ones she knew being blown apart astonished her all over again. She had never understood life, and now it was death that bewildered her. All she was sure of was that America was beautiful for fighting the wrong! When the tanks were gone, leaving behind a rain of dust sparkling in the moon rays, she stood there wondering: "Did we huddle together with one another because we each felt unwanted?" This hateful self-affront would send her more and more gratefully and often to the bottle, and with a couple of drinks she would force the worst to her lips: "He makes love like mailing a letter." And then she would flush one more of what she called her "whorish notes" down the ever-obliging toilet.

Her rage, like everything else in this wartime, was on hold for the duration. Drunk, she saw more broadly; saw herself in a sort of a secret American consensus to conceal the vileness of their true needs. The whole apple-cheeked country, was it a gigantic fraud? Or was it only the homely ones who, when all was said and done, were—had to be—unhappy and full of hate? Back inside the cottage, she sat on the lumpy mattress and thought guiltily of poor Sam on bivouac, sleeping on the wet ground out there in the dripping pinewoods, his alien self in a swamp of Deep South accents. "What an ungrateful bitch I am," she said aloud. And falling back onto the damp pillow: "That bastard Hitler!" and swung out into sleep on her anger. Would she ever be allotted time for anything but goodness?

II

Recalling it all later, her collision with Lionel Mayer, in all its painful ordinariness, had sent her flying off the track of her old life. He and his wife, Sylvia, a left-wing organizer for the Newspaper Guild, had been their friends for years by this time, and by some miracle he had been assigned as press officer in Sam's division. That fall, ordered out on a five-day bivouac, Sam, giving up pretending that his wife was happy hanging around army camps, asked Lionel to invite her to dinner in Loveock. Janice was vaguely unnerved at the date; Lionel, with his thick black curly hair, powerful hands, and juicy sense of the outrageous—he had acting ambitions—had always seemed to be inviting her curiosity about him; she had noticed how he lost himself staring at women, and it was easy to set him to performing for her with his impudent stories and jokes. Gradually, she had realized, with some amusement, that she had some kind of control over him. With Sam gone, he invited her to dinner, and she knew at once that he wanted to make love to her. The idea sent an exciting charge of power into her, along with a deep curiosity about how he reconciled his principled nature and his shyness with his wife with this hot interest in her—until she thought of her own behavior.

She had never been alone with him in a strange place, and he was a different man over dinner, holding her hand on the table, all but offering himself in his gaze. Calculating the risk, she thought it seemed low; he would clearly not want the undoing of his marriage any more than she did hers.

"You have gray eyes," he said, with a certain hunger she found absurd and necessary.

"Two of them, yes."

He burst out laughing, relieved that ploys were no longer necessary. Walking back to the bus stop from the restaurant, they saw the Loveock Rice Hotel sign overhead, and he simply grasped her hand and steered her into the lobby. The room clerk, a stout woman listening to a radio play and eating hard-boiled eggs out of a waxed-paper wrapper, seemed to recognize Lionel, or at least to be less than surprised to see him, and absently handed him a key after hardly any talk between them. Janice's insides caved in like sand before the notion of his experience. She was delighted. If she was recognized going up the broad mahogany stairway with him, then so be it; she numbly resolved not to stop the force that was carrying her forward and out of a dead life. Lionel descended on her like an ocean wave, tumbling her, invading her, pounding her past to bits. She had forgotten what stings of pleasure lay asleep in her groin, what lifts of feeling could swamp her brain. As they rested, a sentence spread before her mind: "The key to the present is always pleasure." In the bungalow afterward, sliding back down to the bottom of her pit, she studied her sated face in the bathroom mirror and saw how slyly feminine she really was, how somber and untruthful, and she happily and sadly winked. It flickered across her mind that she felt free once more, as she had when her father died.

Kissing Sam Fink goodbye the night he sailed for England, she thought he had never looked so handsome in his uniform and his shoulder bars and his fine double-breasted trench coat. But with the holy cause so nobly glowing in his face, his eyes, his manly grin, she mournfully knew she could not go on with him for life; even at his best it would not be enough. She was a real stinker, a total fraud. He insisted she stay behind in the apartment and not accompany him to the ship. A novel gravity was in his look now: "I know I'm not right for you, but . . ."

Guilt smashed her in the face. "Oh, but you are, you are!" What a thing to say, when he might be going to his death!

"Well, maybe we'll figure it out when I come back."

"Oh, my darling . . ." She clutched him closer than she had ever wanted to before, and he kissed her hard on the mouth in a way he'd never done.

It was still difficult for him to speak, even though it might be their last moment together. "I don't want you to think I don't know what's been happening." He glanced at a wall to escape her eyes. "I just haven't taken us seriously enough—I mean in a certain sense—and I regret it . . ."

"I understand."

"Maybe not altogether." He looked straight at her now with his valorous warm smile. "I guess I've thought of you as a partner in the Revolution, or something like that. And I've left out everything else, or almost everything. Because my one obsession has

been Fascism, it's taken up all my thinking." No, dear, it's sexual
fear that's done that. "But America is on the line now, not just
people like me, and Hitler is finished. So if I do come back I want
to start over as a couple. I mean I want to start listening to you."
He grinned, blushing. "The idea of that excites the hell out of
me." Appalled at herself, she knew it was hopeless with them—he
was sweet and dear, but nothing would stop him from going to
meetings the rest of his life, and she could not bear to be good any
more; she wanted glory. She drew his head to her lips, kissing his
brow like a benediction. In death's shadow, she thought, we part
in love. He let her hand slide out of his fingers and moved to the
door, where he turned to look back at her one last time; romantic!
She stood in their doorway watching him as he waited in the corridor for the elevator. When its door clanked open, she raised a
hand and wiggled her fingers, giving him her smile and her irony.
"Proud of you, soldier!" He threw her a kiss and backed into the
elevator. Would he die? She threw herself onto their bed, dry-
eyed, wondering who in the world she was as she filled up with
love for this noble man.

He might be gone a year. Maybe two. No one knew. She registered at Hunter as a graduate student in art history. It was perfect;
her good husband off to the war in the best imaginable cause, and
she in New York and not some godforsaken army camp, taking
courses with Professor Oscar Kalkofsky.

The war continued its unrelenting grip on time. The "duration"
calcified most decisions; nothing long-term could be started until
peace came, in probably five or six years, it was thought now.
Frustration was mitigated by the solace of having a ready excuse
for everything undone or put off—like confronting Sam Fink
with a divorce when he was off fighting in Germany and might
well be sent to the Pacific for the assault on Japan.

But suddenly the Bomb settled that and everyone was coming
home. But where would she find the strength to tell Sam Fink that
she could not be with him any more? She must find a job, an independence from which to address him. She walked endlessly in
Manhattan, tensed, half angry, half afraid, trying to conjure up a

possible career for herself, and finally one day went to see Professor Kalkofsky, to talk not about art but about her life.

Months earlier, tired of walking, she stopped by the Argosy store on lower Fifth Avenue, to get off her feet and look for something new to read, and was talking to Peter Berger, the owner's son and Sam's immediate boss, when the professor came in. Almost immediately his quiet, self-mocking smile and wry fatalism drew her in, an affectation of weariness so patently flirtatious that it amused her. And his gaze kept flicking to her calves, her best feature.

A gentle, platinum-haired giant, he sat with European academic propriety in his office one afternoon, both enormous shoes set on the floor, his pipe smoldering in his right hand, whose two crooked fingers, broken by a Nazi torturer, spoke to her of a reality the Atlantic Ocean had sterilized before it reached America. She was sure he not only was taken with her but had no thought of a future relationship; his witty eyes and unsmiling mouth, some adamance in his unspoken demand on her, and his quiet speech that day—it all seemed to be solemnly taking charge of her body. Despite his muscled bulk, there was something womanly about him; maybe, she thought, because unlike most men, he was obviously unafraid of sex.

"Is not very complicated, Mrs. Fink." She liked his not using her first name yet and hoped, if they made love, he would continue calling her Mrs. Fink in bed. "After war like this, will be necessary to combine two contradictory drives. First, how to glamorize, as you say, cooperative modes in new society; at same time, incorporate pleasure ethic which certainly must sweep world after so much deprivation. That means following: to take what is offered, ask for it if it is not offered, regret nothing. The regret element is main thing; once you accept that you have chosen to be as you are, incredible as that seems, then regret is impossible. We have been slaves to this war and to Fascism. If Communism is brought to Poland and Europe, it will never last long in countries of the Renaissance. So now we are free, the slavery is finished, or will soon be. We are going to have to learn how to select self, and so to be free."

She had read existentialist philosophy but had never been seduced by it before, armed as she was by the decade of puritanical Marxism that followed the disgraced Jazz Age of her father. But there was another fascination: Europeans liked talking about submerged connecting themes rather than mere disjointed events, and she loved this, thinking she might figure herself out if she could only generalize with precision. But it never quite happened. As though she had known him a long time—which in a way she had—she began telling about her life. "I realize I don't have any kind of standard look, but . . ." He did not interrupt with a reassuring false compliment, and this meant he accepted her exactly as she was. This thrilled her with sudden possibilities. "But I . . . I forgot what I was starting to say." She laughed, her head full of lights, admitting a hunger for something to happen between them beyond speech.

"I think what you are saying is that you don't feel you have ever really made a choice in life."

Of course! How could he possibly have known that? She was drifting with no real goal . . . She felt her hair, suddenly believing it must be tangled.

And he said, "I know it because I see how much expectation there is in you." Yes, that was it! "Almost any suffering is tolerable provided you have chosen it. I was in London when they attacked Poland, but I knew I must go back, and I also knew the danger if I did. When he broke my fingers, I understood why the Church was so strong—it was built by men who had chosen to suffer for it. My pain was also chosen, and that dimension of choice, you see, made it significant; it was not wasted, not nothing."

Then he simply reached out over the arm of his chair and gripped her hand and drew her to him and meditatively kissed her lips, closing his eyes as though she symbolized something for him and his wise European suffering. She immediately knew what the years-long aching in her really was—simply that she had never truly chosen Sam, he had kind of happened to her because—yes, because she had never thought of herself like this, as a woman of value choosing to grant herself. He slipped his hand into her clothing, and even the cynicism of his cool expertise pleased her with its brazen consciousness.

She looked down at him kneeling on the floor, with his face buried between her thighs. "I love knowing what I'm doing, don't you?" she said, and laughed.

His face was broad and very white, its bones thick and strong. He looked up at her and, making a wry mouth, said, "The postwar era begins." But he kept it wry, just this side of laughter. What delight that, as she knew now, she meant nothing to him!

III

After Sam's return in September, whole guilty months passed before she could dare to tell him that she could no longer bear her life with him. It came about by accident.

Bringing it up had been difficult because he behaved once again as though they had never had a problem; and it didn't help that somewhere in him he was taking a substantial amount of credit for destroying Fascism. His prophetic Marxism had proved itself in Russia's new postwar power and Fascism's extinction and set him consciously as a participant in history, and nobly at that. A new note, something close to arrogance, a quality she had formerly wished for him, irritated her now that their spirits had parted. But what set her off was his implying one evening that he had forced himself on a German farm woman who had given him shelter in a rainstorm one night.

She grinned, fascinated. "Tell me about it. Was she married?"

"Oh, sure. The husband was gone; she thought he'd been captured or killed at Stalingrad."

"How old was she—young?"

"About thirty, thirty-two."

"Good-looking?"

"Well, kind of heavy." In his gruff laugh she saw that he had probably decided not to be obsequious with her any more. His lovemaking since his return had been markedly overbearing but no less inept than before; he was better at handling her body, but her feelings seemed to have no space in his mind.

"And what happened? Tell me."

"Well, Bavaria . . . We were stuck in this half-bombed-out town hall with the wind blowing through the windows, and I had a cold that was killing me. Coming into town, I'd noticed this house half a mile or so off down the road, and it'd looked tight and had smoke coming out of the chimney. So I went over. She gave me some soup. She was too stupid to hide the Nazi flag hanging over her husband's picture. And it got late and I . . ." He pursed his lips cutely, stretched out his legs, and clasped his hands behind his head. "You really want to hear this?"

"Come on, dear, you know you want to tell it."

"Okay. I said I wanted to spend the night, and she showed me to this tiny cold room near the kitchen. And I said, 'Look, you Nazi bitch, I am sleeping in the best bed in this house . . .'"

She laughed excitedly. "That's wonderful. And what did she do?"

"Well, she let me have her and her husband's bedroom." He left it at that.

She sensed the gap and grinned broadly. "And? Come on, what happened!" He was blushing, but pridefully. "Was she hot stuff or what? Come on! She grab for you?"

"Not at all. She was a real Nazi."

"You mean you raped her?"

"I don't know if you'd call it rape," he said, clearly hoping she would.

"Well, did she want to or not?"

"What's the difference? It wasn't all that bad."

"And how long'd you stay with her?"

"Just two nights, till we pulled out."

"And was she anti-Nazi by then?" She grinned at him.

"I didn't ask."

His pride in it filled her with wonder, and release. "And did she have blond braids and a dirndl?"

"Not a dirndl."

"But blond braids?"

"As a matter of fact, yes."

"And big breasts?"

"Well, it was Bavaria," he said before he could catch himself, and they both burst out laughing. At the moment she did not know why, but suddenly now she was free, free of him, free of her past, of the Revolution, of every last unwilling obligation. She felt a happiness as she got up and walked to his chair and bent over and kissed his tonsure. He looked up at her with love and pride in his having scaled an inhibition, and she felt pain for his awkwardness, which she saw would never leave him. He was completed now, would not go beyond his present bounds.

"I'm leaving you, Sam," she said, a touch of humor still in her voice. Suddenly she no longer had to reach down to sustain him. He would be all right.

After his disbelief, his shock and anger, she said, "You'll be fine, dear." She made a martini and crossed her legs under her on the couch as though for a nice chat. How excellent not to need anyone any more, not to feel either pulled or repulsed; suddenly there was time simply to be interested in him.

"But where will you go?" Truly, it was as though with a face like hers he was her only harbor in the world.

The insult was even worse because he was unaware of it, and she instantly raged at the time she had wasted with him. She had developed a way of chuckling softly when hurt, tucking in her chin and looking up at her opponent with raised eyebrows, and then unwinding her ironies as off a spool of wire. "Well, now that you mention it, it would hardly matter where I went, since to all intents and purposes I am nowhere now." She waited an instant. "Don't you think so, Sam?"

IV

In its seedy Parisian ornateness, the Crosby Hotel on Seventy-first off Broadway was still fairly decent then, at the end of the war, and it was wonderful to have a room with nothing in it of her own.

How great to have no future! Free again. It reminded her a little of the Voltaire on the quay in '36, with her father in the next room tapping on the wall to wake her for breakfast. She dared to call Lionel Mayer—"I wondered if you needed any typing done"—and bantered with him on the phone like a teenager, dangling herself before him and taking it all back when pressed; clearly, with no war to direct his life, he was as lost as she was, a deeply unhappy young man posing as a *paterfamilias*, and soon he was standing with crotch pressed against her head as she sat typing an article he had written for *Collier's* on his Philippine experiences. But she had no illusions, or the merest inevitable ones that lasted only while he was in her, and when she was alone her emptiness ached and she felt fear for herself, passing thirty now, with no one at all.

Herman came one afternoon to see how she lived. He had lost some weight. "No more trains; I fly now. I'm buying in Chicago— you can pick up half the city for beans." He sat glancing out disapprovingly at upper Broadway. "This is a dump, sister; you picked a real good dump to waste your life in. What was wrong with Sam, too intellectual? I thought you liked intellectuals. Why don't you come in with me? We form a company, the cities are full of great buys, we can put down ten, fifteen percent and own a building, get mortgages to fix it up, raise the rents as high as you want, and walk away with fifty percent on your money."

"And what happens to the people living in those buildings?"

"They start paying a decent rent or go where they can afford. It's economics, Janice. The country is off welfare, we're moving into the biggest boom there ever was, 1920s all over again. Get on board and get out of this dump." He had eyeglasses now, when he remembered to wear them. He put them on to show her. "I'm turning thirty-six, baby, but I feel terrific. How about you?"

"I expect to feel happy, but I'm not terrific yet. But you can't have my money to throw people out on the street. Sorry, dear." She wanted to change stockings, still wore silk despite the new nylons, which felt clammy to her. Starting to open a drawer in the old dresser, she felt the pull come off in her hand.

"How can you live in this dump, everything falling apart?"

"I like everything falling apart; it's less competition for when I start falling apart."

"By the way, you never found those ashes, did you."

"What brings that up?"

"I don't know, I was just reminded because it was his birthday last August." He scratched his heavy leg and glanced again out the window. "He'd have given you the same advice. People with heads are going to be millionaires in the next five years. Real estate in New York is undervalued, and there's thousands walking around looking for decent apartments. I need somebody with me I can trust. By the way, what do you do all day? I mean it, you have a funny look to me, Janice. You look like your mind is not concentrated any more. Am I wrong?"

She rolled a stocking up her leg, careful to keep the seam straight. "I don't want my mind concentrated, I want it receptive to what's around me. Does that seem odd or dishonorable? I'm trying to find out what I have to do to live like a person. I read books, I read philosophical novels like Camus and Sartre, and I read dead poets like Emily Dickinson and Edna St. Vincent Millay, and I also—"

"It doesn't look to me like you have any friends. Do you?"

"Why? Do friends leave traces? Maybe I'm not ready to have friends. Maybe I'm not fully born yet. Hindus believe that, you know—they think we go on being born and reborn right through life, or something like that. Life is very painful to me, Herman."

Tears had flowed into her eyes. This ridiculous person was her brother, the last one in the world she would think of confiding in, yet she trusted him more than anyone she had known, as ludicrous and overweight as he still was. She sat on the bed and saw him by the slanting gray light through the dirty window, a young blob full of plans and greed's happiness.

"I love this city," she said, with no special point in mind. "I know there are ways to be happy in it, but I haven't found any. But I know they're there." She went to the other front window and parted the dusty lace curtain and looked down at Broadway. She could smell the soot on the window. A light drizzle had begun to fall.

"I'm buying a new Cadillac."

"Aren't they awfully big? How can you drive them?"

"Like silk. You float. They're fantastic. We're trying to have a baby again; I don't want a car that joggles her belly."

"Are you really as confident as you seem?"

"Absolutely. Come in with me."

"I don't think I want to be that rich."

"I think you're still Communistic."

"I guess so. There's something wrong, living for money. I don't want to start."

"At least get out of those bonds and get into the market. You're literally losing money every hour."

"Am I? Well, I don't feel it, so the hell with it."

He heaved up onto his feet and buttoned his blue jacket, pulled his tie down, picked his topcoat off the back of a chair. "I will never understand you, Janice."

"That makes two of us, Herman."

"What are you going to do the rest of the day? I mean just as an instance."

"An instance of what?"

"Of what you do with your days."

"They play old movies on Seventy-second Street; I may go there. There's a Garbo, I think."

"In the middle of a working day."

"I love being in the movies when it's drizzling out."

"You want to come home with me for dinner?"

"No, dear. It might jiggle her belly." She laughed and quickly kissed him to take the sting out of that remark, which she had been as unprepared for as he. But in truth she did not want children, ever.

"What do you want out of life, do you know?"

"Of course I know."

"What?"

"A good time."

He shook his head, baffled. "Don't get in trouble," he said as he left.

V

She adored Garbo, anything she played in, could sit through two showings of even the most wooden of her films, which released her irony. She loved to be set afloat and pushed out to sea by these creakingly factitious Graustarkian tales, and their hilarious swan-shaped bathtubs and eagle-head faucets, their dripping Baroque doors and windows and drapes. Nowadays their glorious vileness of taste cheered her to the point of levitation, of hysteria, cut her free of all her education, rejoined her with her country. It made her want to stand on a roof and scream happily at the stars when the actress emerged from a noble white Rolls without ever catching a heel on a filmy long dress. And how unspeakably glorious Garbo's languorous "relaxing" on a chaise, the world-weariness of her yard-long pauses as she moodily jousted with her leading men— Janice sometimes had to cover her face so as not to look as Garbo gave her ceramic eyelids permission to pleasurably close at Barry-more's long-delayed kiss. And of course Garbo's cheekbones and the fabulous reflectiveness of her perfect white skin, the carved planes of her face—the woman was proof of God. Janice could lie for half an hour on her hotel bed, facing the ceiling, hardly blinking as the Garbo face hung over her eyes. She could stand before her dressing table mirrors, which cut her off at the neck, and find her body surprisingly ready and alive with a certain flow, especially from a side view, which emphasized her good thighs.

VI

The creaky elevator door opened one afternoon and she saw standing before it a handsome man in his forties, or possibly his early fifties, with a walking stick in one hand and a briefcase in the other. With an oddly straight-backed walk, he entered the elevator, and Janice only realized he was blind when he stopped hardly six inches from her and then turned himself to face the door by lifting his feet slightly instead of simply swiveling about. There was a shaving cut on his chin.

"Going down, aren't we?"

"Yes, down." Her chest contracted. A freedom close by, a liberation swept her up as for one instant he stared sightless into her face.

At the lobby, he walked straight out and across the tiled floor to the glass doors to the street. She hung on behind him and quickly came around to push the doors open for him. "May I help you?"

"Don't bother. But thanks very much."

He walked into the street, turning directly right toward Broadway, and she hurried to come up alongside him. "Do you go to the subway? I mean, that's where I'm going, if you'd like me to stay with you."

"Oh, that'd be fine, yes. Thank you, although I can make it myself."

"But as long as I'm going too . . ."

She walked beside him, surprised by his good pace. What life in his fluttering eyelids! It was like walking with a sighted man, but the freedom she felt alongside him was bringing tears of happiness to her eyes. She found herself pouring all her feeling into her voice, which suddenly flew out of her mouth with all the open innocence of a young girl's.

His voice had a dry flatness, as though not often used. "Have you lived in the hotel long?"

"Since March." And added without a qualm, "Since my divorce." He nodded. "And you?"

"Oh, I've been there for five years now. The walls on the twelfth floor are just about soundproof, you know."

"You play an instrument?"

"The piano. I'm with Decca, in the Classical division; I listen to a lot of recordings at home."

"That's very interesting." She felt his pleasure in this nice conversation without tension, she could sense his gratitude for her company as they walked. He must be lonely. People probably avoided him or were too formal or apologetic. But she had never felt more sure of herself or as free in dealing with a strange person, and for a moment she celebrated her instinct.

At the top of the subway steps she took his arm with a light grasp, as though he were a bird she might scare off. He did not resist and at the turnstile insisted on paying her fare out of a handful of nickels he had ready. She had no idea where he was going or where she could pretend to be going.

"How do you know where to get off?"

"I count the stops."

"Oh, of course; how stupid."

"I go to Fifty-seventh."

"That's where I'm going."

"You work around there?"

"Actually, I'm kind of still settling in. But I'm on the lookout for something."

"Well, you shouldn't have a problem; you seem very young."

"Actually, I wasn't really going anywhere. I just wanted to help you."

"Really."

"Yes."

"What's your name?"

"Janice Sessions. What's yours?"

"Charles Buckman."

She wanted to ask if he was married, but clearly he couldn't be, must not be; something about him was deeply self-organized and not hostage to anything or anyone.

Out on the street, he halted at the curb facing uptown. "I go to the Athletic Club on Fifty-ninth."

"May I walk with you?"

"Certainly. I work out for an hour before the office."

"You look very fit."

"You should do it. Although I think you're fit too."

"Can you tell?"

"The way you put your feet down."

"Really!"

"Oh yes, that tells a lot. Let me have your hand."

She quickly put her left hand in his right. He pressed her palm with his index and middle fingers, then pressed the heel of her thumb, and let her hand go. "You're in pretty good shape, but it would be a good thing to swim; your wind isn't very great."

She felt embraced by the sweep of his uncanny knowledge of her. "Maybe I will." She hated exercise but vowed to begin as soon as she could. Under the gray canopy of the Athletic Club, he slowed to a halt and faced her, and for the first time she could look for more than an instant past his flickering lids directly into his brown eyes. She felt she would choke with amazed gratitude, for he was smiling slightly as though pleased to be seen looking so intimately at her in this very public place. She felt herself standing more erectly than she ever had since she was born.

"I'm in 1214 if you'd like to come up for a drink."

"I'd love it." She laughed at her instantaneous acceptance. "I must tell you," she said, and heard herself with a terror of embarrassment but resolved not to quail before the need exploding in herself. "You've made me incredibly happy."

"Happy? Why?"

He was beginning to blush. It amazed her that embarrassment could penetrate his nearly immobile face.

"I don't know why. You just have. I feel you know me better than anyone ever has. I'm sorry I'm being so silly."

"No, no. Please, be sure to come tonight."

"Oh, I will."

She felt she could stretch up and kiss his lips and that he wouldn't mind, because she was beautiful. Or her hand was.

"You can turn off the light, if you like."

"I don't know. Maybe I'd rather leave it on."

He slipped out of his shorts and felt for the bed with his shin and lay down beside her as she stared into his sightless face. His hand discovered her good happy body. It was pure touch, pure truth beyond speech, everything she was was moving through his hand like water unfrozen. She was free of her whole life and kissed him hard and tenderly, praying that there was a God who would keep her from error with him, and moved his hands where she wished them to be, mastering him and enslaving herself to his slightest movements.

In a respite, he ran his fingers over her face and she held her breath, hearing his breaths suspending as he felt the curve of her nose, her long upper lip and forehead, lightly pressed her cheekbones—discovering, she was sure, that they lacked distinction and were buried in a rounded yet tightened face.

"I am not beautiful," she asked more than stated.

"You are, where it matters to me."

"Can you picture me?"

"Very well, yes."

"Is it really all right?"

"What earthly difference can it possibly make to me?" He rolled over on top of her, placing his mouth on hers, then, moving over her face, he read it with his lips. His pleasure poured into her again.

"I will die here, my heart will stop right here under you, because I don't need any more than this and I can't bear it."

"I like your lisp."

"Do you? It doesn't sound childish?"

"It does; that's why I like it. What color is your hair?"

"Can you imagine colors?"

"I think I can imagine black; is it black?"

"No, it's kind of chestnut, slightly reddish chestnut, and very straight. It falls almost to my shoulders. My head is large and my mouth is on the large side too and slightly prognathous. But I walk nicely, maybe beautifully if you ask some people. I love to walk in a sexy way."

"Your ass is wonderfully shaped."

"Yes, I forgot to mention that."

"It thrilled me to hold it."

"I'm glad." Then she added, "I'm really dumbfoundedly glad."

"And how do I look to you?"

"I think you're a splendidly handsome man. You have darkish skin and brown hair parted on the left, and a nicely shaped strong chin. Your face is kind of rectangular, I guess, kind of reassuring and silent. You are about three or four inches taller than me and your body is slim but not skinny. I think you are spectacular-looking."

He chuckled and rolled off her. She held his penis. "And this is perfection." He laughed and kissed her lightly. Then quietly he fell asleep. She lay beside him not daring to stir and wake him to life and its dangers.

In the late seventies, living in the Village, she read in the papers that the Crosby Hotel was being demolished for a new apartment house. She was working as a volunteer now for a civil rights organization, monitoring violations East and West, and decided to take an extra hour after lunch and go uptown to see the old hotel once more before it vanished. She was into her sixties now, and Charles had died in his sleep a little more than a year earlier. She came out of the subway and walked down the side street and found that the top floor, the twelfth, was already gone. Comically gone, as a matter of fact; the cube where Charles had carefully judged Mozart, Schubert, and Beethoven recordings was now open blue sky. She leaned against a building up the street from the hotel and watched the men prizing apart the brick walls with surprising ease. So it was more or less only gravity that held buildings up! She could see inside rooms, the different colors people had so carefully selected to paint the walls, what care had been taken to select the right shade! With each falling chunk of masonry, billowing bursts of dust rushed upward into the air. Each generation takes part of the city away, like ants tugging twigs. Soon they would be reaching her old room. An empty amazement crept over her. Out of sixty-one years of life, she had had twenty good ones. Not bad.

She thought of the dozens of recitals and concerts, the dinners in restaurants, the utterness of Charles's love and reliance on her, who had become his eyes. In a way he had turned her inside out, so that she looked out at the world instead of holding her breath for the world to look at her and disapprove. She walked up closer to the front doors of the hotel and stood there across the street, catching the haunted earth-cold smell of a dying building, trying to recapture that first time she had walked out with him into the street and then down to the subway, the last day of her homeliness. She had bought a new perfume, and it floated up to her through the dusty air and pleased her.

She turned back to Broadway and strolled past the fruit stands and the debris of collisions lying on the curbs, the broken pizza crusts of the city's eaters-in-the-streets, fruit peels and cores, a lost boot and a rotted tie, a woman sitting on the sidewalk combing her hair, the black boys ranting after a basketball, the implosion of causes, emergencies, purposes that had swept her up and which she could no longer find the strength to call back from the quickly disappearing past. And Charles, arm in arm with her, walking imperturbably through it all with his hat flat straight on his head and his crimson muffler wrapped neatly around his throat and whistling softly yet so strongly the mighty main theme of *Harold in Italy*. "Oh Death, oh Death," she said almost aloud, waiting on the corner for the light to change as a teenage drug dealer slowly rolled his new BMW past with its rap music defiantly blasting her face. She crossed as the light turned green, filling with wonder at her fortune at having lived into beauty.

PRESENCE

Bulldog

He saw this tiny ad in the paper: "Black Brindle Bull puppies, $3.00 each." He had something like ten dollars from his house-painting job, which he hadn't deposited yet, but they had never had a dog in the house. His father was taking a long nap when the idea crested in his mind, and his mother, in the middle of a bridge game when he asked her if it would be all right, shrugged absently and threw a card. He walked around the house trying to decide, and the feeling spread through him that he'd better hurry, before somebody else got the puppy first. In his mind, there was already one particular puppy that belonged to him—it was his puppy and the puppy knew it. He had no idea what a brindle bull looked like, but it sounded tough and wonderful. And he had the three dollars, though it soured him to think of spending it when they had such bad money worries, with his father gone bankrupt again. The tiny ad hadn't mentioned how many puppies there were. Maybe there were only two or three, which might be bought by this time.

The address was on Schermerhorn Street, which he had never heard of. He called, and a woman with a husky voice explained how to get there and on which line. He was coming from the Midwood section, and the elevated Culver line, so he would have to change at Church Avenue. He wrote everything down and read it all back to her. She still had the puppies, thank God. It took more than an hour, but the train was almost empty, this being Sunday, and with a breeze from its open wood-framed windows it was cooler than down in the street. Below in empty lots he could see old Italian women, their heads covered with red bandannas, bent over and loading their aprons with dandelions. His Italian school friends said they were for wine and salads. He remembered trying to eat one once when he was playing left field in the lot near his house, but it was bitter and salty as tears. The old wooden train, practically unloaded, rocked and clattered lightly through the hot afternoon. He passed above a block where men were standing in driveways watering their cars as though they were hot elephants. Dust floated pleasantly through the air.

The Schermerhorn Street neighborhood was a surprise, totally different from his own, in Midwood. The houses here were made of brownstone, and were not at all like the clapboard ones on his block, which had been put up only a few years before or, in the earliest cases, in the twenties. Even the sidewalks looked old, with big squares of stone instead of cement, and bits of grass growing in the cracks between them. He could tell that Jews didn't live here, maybe because it was so quiet and unenergetic and not a soul was sitting outside to enjoy the sun. Lots of windows were wide open, with expressionless people leaning on their elbows and staring out, and cats stretched out on some of the sills, many of the women in their bras and the men in underwear trying to catch a breeze. Trickles of sweat were creeping down his back, not only from the heat but also because he realized now that he was the only one who wanted the dog, since his parents hadn't really had an opinion and his brother, who was older, had said, "What are you, crazy, spending your few dollars on a puppy? Who knows if it will be any good? And what are you going to feed it?" He thought bones, and his brother, who always knew what was right or wrong, yelled, "Bones! They have no teeth yet!" Well, maybe soup, he had mumbled. "Soup! You going to feed a puppy *soup*?" Suddenly he saw that he had arrived at the address. Standing there, he felt the bottom falling out, and he knew it was all a mistake, like one of his dreams or a lie that he had stupidly tried to defend as being real. His heart sped up and he felt he was blushing and walked on for half a block or so. He was the only one out, and people in a few of the windows were watching him on the empty street. But how could he go home after he had come so far? It seemed he'd been traveling for weeks or a year. And now to get back on the subway with nothing? Maybe he ought at least to get a look at the puppy, if the woman would let him. He had looked it up in the *Book of Knowledge*, where they had two full pages of dog pictures, and there had been a white English bulldog with bent front legs and teeth that stuck out from its lower jaw, and a little black-and-white Boston bull, and a long-nosed pit bull, but they had no picture of a brindle bull. When you came down to it, all he really knew about brindle bulls was that they would cost three dollars. But he had to at least get a look at him, his puppy, so he went back down the block and rang the basement doorbell, as the woman had told him to do. The sound was so loud it startled him, but he felt if he ran away and she came out in time to see him it would be even more embarrassing, so he stood there with sweat running down over his lip.

An inner door under the stoop opened, and a woman came out and looked at him through the dusty iron bars of the gate. She wore some kind of gown, light-pink silk, which she held together with one hand, and she had long black hair down to her shoulders. He didn't dare look directly into her face, so he couldn't tell exactly what she looked like, but he could feel her tension as she stood there behind her closed gate. He felt she could not imagine what he was doing ringing her bell and he quickly asked if she was the one who'd put the ad in. Oh! Her manner changed right away, and she unlatched the gate and pulled it open. She was shorter than he and had a peculiar smell, like a mixture of milk and stale air. He followed her into the apartment, which was so dark he could hardly make out anything, but he could hear the high yapping of puppies. She had to yell to ask him where he lived and how old he was, and when he told her thirteen she clapped a hand over her mouth and said that he was very tall for his age, but he couldn't understand why this seemed to embarrass her, except that she may have thought he was fifteen, which people sometimes did. But even so. He followed her into the kitchen, at the back of the apartment, where finally he could see around him, now that he'd been out of the sun for a few minutes. In a large cardboard box that had been unevenly cut down to make it shallower he saw three puppies and their mother, who sat looking up at him with her tail moving slowly back and forth. He didn't think she looked like a bulldog, but he didn't dare say so. She was just a brown dog with flecks of black and a few stripes here and there, and the puppies were the same. He did like the way their little ears drooped, but he said to the woman that he had wanted to see the puppies but hadn't made up his mind yet. He really didn't know what to do next, so, in order not to seem as though he didn't appreciate the puppies, he asked if she would mind if he held one. She said that was all right and reached down into the box and lifted out two puppies and set them down on the blue linoleum. They didn't look like any bulldogs he had ever seen, but he was embarrassed to tell her that he didn't really want one. She picked one up and said, "Here," and put it on his lap.

He had never held a dog before and was afraid it would slide off, so he cradled it in his arms. It was hot on his skin and very soft and kind of disgusting in a thrilling way. It had gray eyes like tiny buttons. It troubled him that the *Book of Knowledge* hadn't had a picture of this kind of dog. A real bulldog was kind of tough and dangerous, but these were just brown dogs. He sat there on the arm of the green upholstered chair with the puppy on his lap, not knowing what to do next. The woman, meanwhile, had put herself next to him, and it felt like she had given his hair a pat, but he wasn't sure because he had very thick hair. The more seconds that ticked away the less sure he was of what to do. Then she asked if he would like some water, and he said he would, and she went to the faucet and ran water, which gave him a chance to stand up and set the puppy back in the box. She came back to him holding the glass and as he took it she let her gown fall open, showing her breasts like half-filled balloons, saying she couldn't believe he was only thirteen. He gulped the water and started to hand her back the glass, and she suddenly drew his head to her and kissed him. In all this time, for some reason, he hadn't been able to look into her face, and when he tried to now he couldn't see anything but a blur and hair. She reached down to him and a shivering started in the backs of his legs. It got sharper, until it was almost like the time he touched the live rim of a light socket while trying to remove a broken bulb. He would never be able to remember getting down on the carpet—he felt like a waterfall was smashing down on top of his head. He remembered getting inside her heat and his head banging and banging against the leg of her couch. He was almost at Church Avenue, where he had to change for the elevated Culver line, before realizing she hadn't taken his three dollars, and he couldn't recall agreeing to it but he had this small cardboard box on his lap with a puppy mewling inside. The scraping of nails on the cardboard sent chills up his back. The woman, as he remembered now, had cut two holes into the top of the box, and the puppy kept sticking his nose through them.

His mother jumped back when he untied the cord and the puppy pushed up and scrambled out, yapping. "What is he doing?" she yelled, with her hands in the air as though she were about to be attacked. By this time, he'd lost his fear of the puppy and held him in his arms and let him lick his face, and seeing this his mother calmed down a bit. "Is he hungry?" she asked, and stood with her mouth slightly open, ready for anything, as he put the puppy on the floor again. He said the puppy might be hungry, but he thought he could eat only soft things, although his little teeth were as sharp as pins. She got out some soft cream cheese and put a little piece of it on the floor, but the puppy only sniffed at it and peed. "My God in Heaven!" she yelled, and quickly got a piece of newspaper to blot it up with. When she bent over that way, he thought of the woman's heat and was ashamed and shook his head. Suddenly her name came to him—Lucille—which she had told him when they were on the floor. Just as he was slipping in, she had opened her eyes and said, "My name is Lucille." His mother brought out a bowl of last night's noodles and set it on the floor. The puppy raised his little paw and tipped the bowl over, spilling some of the chicken soup at the bottom. This he began to lick hungrily off the linoleum. "He likes chicken soup!" his mother yelled happily, and immediately decided he would most likely enjoy an egg and so put water on to boil. Somehow the puppy knew that she was the one to follow and walked behind her, back and forth, from the stove to the refrigerator. "He follows me!" his mother said, laughing happily.

On his way home from school the next day, he stopped at the hardware store and bought a puppy collar for seventy-five cents, and Mr. Schweckert threw in a piece of clothesline as a leash. Every night as he fell asleep, he brought out Lucille like something from a secret treasure box and wondered if he could dare phone her and maybe be with her again. The puppy, which he had named Rover, seemed to grow noticeably bigger every day, although he still showed no signs of looking like any bulldog. The boy's father thought Rover should live in the cellar, but it was very lonely down there and he would never stop yapping. "He misses his mother," his mother said, so every night the boy started him off on some rags in an old wash basket down there, and when he'd yapped enough the boy was allowed to bring him up and let him sleep on some rags in the kitchen, and everybody was thankful for the quiet. His mother tried to walk the puppy in the quiet street they lived on, but he kept tangling the rope around her ankles, and because she was afraid to hurt him she exhausted herself following him in all his zigzags. It didn't always happen, but many times when the boy looked at Rover he'd think of Lucille and could almost feel the heat again. He would sit on the porch steps stroking the puppy and think of her, the insides of her thighs. He still couldn't imagine her face, just her long black hair and her strong neck.

One day, his mother baked a chocolate cake and set it to cool on the kitchen table. It was at least eight inches thick, and he knew it would be delicious. He was drawing a lot in those days, pictures of spoons and forks or cigarette packages or, occasionally, his mother's Chinese vase with the dragon on it, anything that had an interesting shape. So he put the cake on a chair next to the table and drew for a while and then got up and went outside for some reason and got involved with the tulips he had planted the previous fall that were just now showing their tips. Then he decided to go look for a practically new baseball he had mislaid the previous summer and which he was sure, or pretty sure, must be down in the cellar in a cardboard box. He had never really got down to the bottom of that box, because he was always distracted by finding something he'd forgotten he had put in there. He had started down into the cellar from the outside entrance, under the back porch, when he noticed that the pear tree, which he had planted two years before, had what looked like a blossom on one of its slender branches. It amazed him, and he felt proud and successful. He had paid thirty-five cents for the tree on Court Street and thirty cents for an apple tree, which he planted about seven feet away, so as to be able to hang a hammock between them someday. They were still too thin and young, but maybe next year. He always loved to stare at the two trees, because he had planted them, and he felt they somehow knew he was looking at them, and even that they were looking back at him. The back yard ended at a ten-foot-high wooden fence that surrounded Erasmus Field, where the semi-pro and sandlot teams played on weekends, teams like the House of David and the Black Yankees and the one with Satchel Paige, who was famous as one of the country's greatest pitchers except he was a Negro and couldn't play in the big leagues, obviously. The House of Davids all had long beards—he'd never understood why, but maybe they were Orthodox Jews, although they didn't look it. An extremely long foul shot over right field could drop a ball into the yard, and that was the ball it had occurred to him to search for, now that spring had come and the weather was warming up. In the basement, he found the box and was immediately surprised at how sharp his ice skates were, and recalled that he had once had a vise to clamp the skates side by side so that a stone could be rubbed on the blades. He pushed aside a torn fielder's glove, a hockey goalie's glove whose mate he knew had been lost, some pencil stubs and a package of crayons, and a little wooden man whose arms flapped up and down when you pulled a string. Then he heard the puppy yapping over his head, but it was not his usual sound—it was continuous

and very sharp and loud. He ran upstairs and saw his mother
coming down into the living room from the second floor, her
dressing gown flying out behind her, a look of fear on her face. He
could hear the scraping of the puppy's nails on the linoleum, and
he rushed into the kitchen. The puppy was running around and
around in a circle and sort of screaming, and the boy could see at
once that his belly was swollen. The cake was on the floor, and
most of it was gone. "My cake!" his mother screamed, and picked
up the dish with the remains on it and held it up high as though to
save it from the puppy, even though practically nothing was left.
The boy tried to catch Rover, but he slipped away into the living
room. His mother was behind him yelling "The carpet!" Rover
kept running, in wider circles now that he had more space, and
foam was forming on his muzzle. "Call the police!" his mother
yelled. Suddenly, the puppy fell and lay on his side, gasping and
making little squeaks with each breath. Since they had never had
a dog and knew nothing about veterinarians, he looked in the
phone book and found the A.S.P.C.A. number and called them.
Now he was afraid to touch Rover, because the puppy snapped at
his hand when it got close and he had this foam on his mouth.
When the van drew up in front of the house, the boy went outside
and saw a young guy removing a little cage from the back. He
told him that the dog had eaten practically a whole cake, but the
man had no interest and came into the house and stood for a
moment looking down at Rover, who was making little yips now
but was still down on his side. The man dropped some netting
over him and when he slipped him into the cage, the puppy tried
to get up and run. "What do you think is the matter with him?"
his mother asked, her mouth turned down in revulsion, which the
boy now felt in himself. "What's the matter with him is he ate a
cake," the man said. Then he carried the cage out and slid it
through the back door into the darkness of the van. "What will
you do with him?" the boy asked. "You want him?" the man
snapped. His mother was standing on the stoop now and over-
heard them. "We can't have him here," she called over, with fright
and definiteness in her voice, and approached the young man.

"We don't know how to keep a dog. Maybe somebody who knows how to keep him would want him." The young man nodded with no interest either way, got behind the wheel, and drove off.

The boy and his mother watched the van until it disappeared around the corner. Inside, the house was dead quiet again. He didn't have to worry any more about Rover doing something on the carpets or chewing the furniture, or whether he had water or needed to eat. Rover had been the first thing he'd looked for on returning from school every day and on waking in the morning, and he had always worried that the dog might have done something to displease his mother or father. Now all that anxiety was gone and, with it, the pleasure, and it was silent in the house.

He went back to the kitchen table and tried to think of something he could draw. A newspaper lay on one of the chairs, and he opened it and inside saw a Saks stocking ad showing a woman with a gown pulled aside to display her leg. He started copying it and thought of Lucille again. Could he possibly call her, he wondered, and do what they had done again? Except that she would surely ask about Rover, and he couldn't do anything but lie to her. He remembered how she had cuddled Rover in her arms and even kissed his nose. She had really loved that puppy. How could he tell her he was gone? Just sitting and thinking of her he was hardening up like a broom handle and he suddenly thought what if he called her and said his family were thinking of having a second puppy to keep Rover company? But then he would have to pretend he still had Rover, which would mean two lies, and that was a little frightening. Not the lies so much as trying to remember, first, that he still had Rover, second, that he was serious about a second puppy, and, third, the worst thing, that when he got up off Lucille he would have to say that unfortunately he couldn't actually take another puppy because . . . Why? The thought of all that lying exhausted him. Then he visualized being in her heat again and he thought his head would explode, and the idea came that when it was over she might insist on his taking another puppy. Force it on him. After all, she had not accepted his three dollars and Rover had been a sort of gift, he thought. It would be embarrassing to refuse another puppy, especially when he had supposedly come back to her for exactly that reason. He didn't dare go through all that and gave up the whole idea. But then the thought crept back again of her spreading apart on the floor the way she had, and he returned to searching for some reason he could give for not taking another puppy after he had supposedly come all the way across Brooklyn to get one. He could just see the look on her face on his turning down a puppy, the puzzlement or, worse, anger. Yes, she could very possibly get angry and see through him, realizing that all he had come for was to get into her and the rest of it was nonsense, and she might feel insulted. Maybe even slap him. What would he do then? He couldn't fight a grown woman. Then again, it now occurred to him that by this time she might well have sold the other two puppies, which at three dollars were pretty inexpensive. Then what? He began to wonder, suppose he just called her up and said he'd like to come over again and see her, without mentioning any puppies? He would have to tell only one lie, that he still had Rover and that the family all loved him and so on. He could easily remember that much. He went to the piano and played some chords, mostly in the dark bass, to calm himself. He didn't really know how to play, but he loved inventing chords and letting the vibrations shoot up his arms. He played, feeling as though something inside him had sort of shaken loose or collapsed altogether. He was different than he had ever been, not empty and clear any more but weighted with secrets and his lies, some told and some untold, but all of it disgusting enough to set him slightly outside his family, in a place where he could watch them now, and watch himself with them. He tried to invent a melody with the right hand and find matching chords with the left. By sheer luck, he was hitting some beauties. It was really amazing how his chords were just slightly off, with a discordant edge but still in some way talking to the right-hand melody. His mother came into the room full of surprise and pleasure. "What's happening?" she called out in delight. She could play and sight-read music and had tried and failed to teach him, because, she believed, his ear was too good and he'd rather play what he heard than do the labor of reading notes. She came over to the piano and stood beside him, watching his hands. Amazed, wishing as always that he could be a genius, she laughed. "Are you making this up?" she almost yelled, as though they were side by side on a roller coaster. He could only nod, not daring to speak and maybe lose what he had somehow snatched out of the air, and he laughed with her because he was so completely happy that he had secretly changed, and unsure at the same time that he would ever be able to play like this again.

The Performance

Harold May would have been about thirty-five when I met him. With his blondish hair parted in the exact middle, and his horn-rimmed glasses and remarkably round boyish eyes, he resembled Harold Lloyd, the famous bespectacled movie comic with the surprised look. When I think of May, I see a man with rosy cheeks, in a gray suit with white pinstripes and a red-and-blue striped bow tie—a dancer, slender, snugly built, light on his feet, and, like a lot of dancers, wrapped up (mummified, you might say) in his art. So he seemed at first, anyway. I see us in a midtown drugstore, the kind that at that time, the forties, had tables where people could sit around for an unemployed hour with their sodas and sundaes. May was wanting to tell a long and involved story, and I wasn't sure why he was bothering but I gradually caught on that it was to interest me in doing a feature about him. My old friend Ralph Barton (né Berkowitz) brought him to me thinking I might make use of his weird story, even though he knew that I had left journalism by then and was no longer sitting around in drugstores and bars, having become sufficiently known as a writer to be embarrassed by strangers accosting me in restaurants or on the street. This was probably in the spring, only two years after the end of the war.

As Harold May told it that afternoon, he had been employed only fitfully back in the mid-thirties, having built a tap-dance act that had played the Palace twice. While he almost always got excited *Variety* notices, he could never really escape the devoted but small audiences in places like Queens, Toledo, Ohio, and Erie or Tonawanda, New York. "If they know how to fit things together they tend to like watching tap," he said, and it pleased him that steelworkers particularly loved the act, as well as machinists, glassblowers—almost anybody who appreciated skills. By '36, though, Harold, convinced that his head was bumping the ceiling of his career, was so depressed that when an offer came to work in Hungary he snapped it up, although uncertain where that country might be located. He soon learned that a so-called vaudeville wheel existed in Budapest, Bucharest, Athens, and half a dozen other East European cities, with Vienna the big prestige booking that would give him lots of publicity. Once established, an act could work almost year-round, returning again and again to the same clubs. "They like things not to change much," he said. Tap, however, was a real novelty, a purely American dance unknown in Europe, invented as it had been by Negroes in the South, and a lot of Europeans were charmed by what they took to be its amusingly optimistic American ambience.

Harold worked the wheel, he explained to me over the white-marble-topped table, for some six or eight months. "The work was steady, the money was decent, and in some places, like Bulgaria, we were practically stars. Got to go to dinners in a couple of castles, with women falling all over us, and great wine. I was as happy as I was ever going to get," he said.

With his little troupe of two men and a woman and himself plus a pickup piano player or, in some places, a small band, he had a mobile and efficient business. Still young and unmarried, with his whole short life concentrated on his legs, his shoes, and persisting dreams of glory, he surprised himself now by enjoying sightseeing in the cities of the wheel and picking up odd bits about European history and art. He had only a high-school diploma from Evander Childs and had never had time to think about much beyond his next gig, so Europe opened his eyes to a past that he had hardly imagined existed.

In Budapest one night, contentedly removing his makeup in his decrepit La Babalu Club dressing room, he was surprised by the appearance in his doorway of a tall, well-dressed gentleman who bowed slightly from the waist and in German-accented English introduced himself and asked deferentially if he could have a few minutes of May's precious time. Harold invited the German to have a seat on a shredded pink-satin chair.

The German, about forty-five, had gleaming, beautifully coiffed silver hair and wore a fine, greenish, heavyweight suit and black high-top shoes. His name was Damian Fugler, he said, and he had come in his official capacity as Cultural Attaché of the German Embassy in Budapest. His English, though accented, was flawlessly exact.

"I have had the pleasure of attending three of your performances now," Fugler began in a rolling baritone, "and first of all wish to pay my respects to you as a fine artist." Nobody had ever called Harold an artist.

"Well, thanks," he managed to say. "I appreciate the compliment." I could imagine the inflation he must have felt, this pink-cheeked young guy out of Berea, Ohio, taking praise from this elegant European with his high-top shoes.

"I myself have performed with the Stuttgart Opera, although not as a singer, of course, but a 'spear-carrier,' as we call it. That was quite a time ago, when I was much younger." Fugler permitted himself a forgiving smile at his youthful pranks. "But I will get down to business—I have been authorized to invite you, Mr. May, to perform in Berlin. My department is prepared to pay your transportation costs as well as hotel expenses."

The breathtaking idea of a government—any government—having an interest in tap-dancing was, of course, way beyond imagining for Harold, and it took a moment to digest or even to believe.

"Well, I really don't know what to say. Like where do I play, a club or what?"

"It would be in the Kick Club. You must have heard of it?"

Harold had heard of the Kick Club as one of Berlin's classiest. His heart was banging. But his booking experience warned him to circle around the proposal. "And how long an engagement would this be?" he asked.

"Most probably one performance."

"One?"

"We would require only one, but you would be free to arrange more with the management, provided, of course, they wish you to continue. We are prepared to pay you two thousand dollars for the evening, if that would be satisfactory."

Two thousand for one night! This was practically a normal year's take. Harold's head was spinning. He knew he ought to be asking questions, but which? "And you? Excuse me, but you are what again?"

Fugler removed a beautiful black leather card case from his breast pocket and handed Harold a card, which he tried unsuccessfully to focus on once he glimpsed the sharply embossed eagle clutching a swastika, which flew up like a dart into his brain.

"Could I let you know tomorrow?" he began, but Fugler's mellow baritone voice quickly cut him off.

"I'm afraid you would have to leave sometime tomorrow. I have arranged with the management here to free you from your contract, should you find that agreeable."

Free him from his contract! "I felt," he said to me over his half-empty chocolate-soda glass, "that unbeknownst to me people had been discussing me in some high office somewhere. It was scary, but you can't help feeling important," he said, and laughed like a wicked adolescent.

"May I ask why so soon?" he asked Fugler.

"I'm afraid I am not at liberty to say more than that my superiors will not have the time to see your performance after Thursday, at least not for several weeks or possibly months." Suddenly the man was leaning forward over Harold's knees, his face nearly touching Harold's hand, his voice lowered to a whisper. "This may change your life, Mr. May. You cannot possibly hesitate."

With two grand dangling before him, Harold heard himself saying, "All right." The whole encounter was so weird that he immediately began to backtrack and ask for more time to decide, but the German was gone. In his hand he saw a five-hundred-dollar bill and vaguely recalled the accented baritone voice saying, "As a deposit. Berlin then! *Auf Wiedersehen.*"

"He'd never even offered me a contract," Harold told us, "just left the money."

He barely slept that night, castigating himself. "You like to think you're in charge of yourself, but this Fugler was like a hurricane." What particularly bothered him now, he said, was his having agreed to the single performance. What was that about? "Over the months, I'd gotten used to not bothering to understand what was going on around me—I mean, I didn't know a word of Hungarian, Romanian, Bulgarian, German—but a single performance? I couldn't figure out what it could mean."

And why the big hurry? "I was stumped," he said. "I wished to God I'd never taken the money. At the same time, I couldn't help being curious."

His mind was somewhat eased by the troupe's delight at getting out of the Balkans, and at his sharing some of his advance among them, and on the train north they were jounced with life and this cockeyed adventure. The prospect of playing Berlin—the capital of Europe, second only to Paris—was like going to a party. Harold ordered champagne and steaks and tried to relax among his dancers and smooth out his anxieties. As the train clanked northward, he contrasted his luck with his probable situation had he stayed in New York, with its lines of unemployed and the unbroken grip of the American slump.

When the train stopped at the German border, an officer opened the door of his compartment, which Harold shared with Benny Worth, who had been with him the longest, and two Romanians, who slept almost continuously, but did waken occasionally, smile briefly, and return to their dreams. The officer, Harold thought, scowled at him as he opened his passport. He had been scowled at by border guards any number of times on this tour, but this German's scowl touched something very deep in his body. It was more than his suddenly remembering that he was Jewish; he had never really had a problem with being Jewish, especially since his blond hair, blue eyes, and generally happy nature had never invited the usual reactions of the era. It was, rather, that until now he had managed to erase almost totally the stories he had read a year or so earlier about the young German government's having staged rallies against Jews, driving them out of businesses and professions, closing synagogues, and forcing many to emigrate. On the other hand, Benny Worth, who called himself a Communist and had all kinds of information that never appeared in regular papers like *The New York Times*, had told him that the Nazis had been tamping down on the anti-Jewish stuff this year so as not to look nasty for the Olympic tourists. In any case, none of this had applied to him personally. "I'd heard some bad stories of Romanian incidents, too, but I never saw anything, so I could never keep them in my head," he explained. I could understand this; after all, he'd had no verbal contact with his audiences and could not read local papers, so that a certain remoteness was wrapped around anything real going on in the cities he had been playing.

In fact, he said, his one distinct impression of Hitler had come from a newsreel that showed him walking out of the Olympics a few months earlier when Jesse Owens, the Negro runner, mounted the platform to accept his fourth gold medal. "Which was pretty bad sportsmanship," he said, "but let's face it, something like that could have happened in lots of places." The truth was, Harold had a hard time concentrating on politics at all. His life was tap, nailing his next gig, keeping edible food on his table and his troupe from splitting up and forcing him to train new people in his routines. And, of course, with his American passport in his pocket, he could always pick up and pull out and go back to the Balkans or even home, if worst came to worst.

They arrived in Berlin on Tuesday evening and were met as they stepped down from the train by two men, one in a suit resembling Fugler's but blue instead of green, and the other in a black uniform with white piping down the edges of the lapels. "Mr. Fugler is awaiting you," the uniformed one said, and Harold caught his own importance in this and could hardly control the thrill it gave him; normally he and his troupe emerged from trains hauling their heavy leather luggage while struggling with some idiotic foreign language to direct porters and hail cabs, usually in the rain. Here, they were led into a Mercedes, which gravely proceeded to the Adlon Hotel, the best in Berlin and maybe in all Europe. By the time he was finishing his dinner of oysters, osso buco, potato pancakes, and Riesling alone in his room, Harold had buried his qualms in imaginings of what he might do with his newfound money and he was ready to go to work.

Fugler showed up at breakfast next morning and sat down in his room for a few minutes. They would perform at midnight, he said, and would have the club for rehearsals until eight that evening, when the regular show started. This was a slightly more excited Fugler; "He looked like he'd throw his arms around me any minute," Harold said.

"I was getting along so good with Fugler," Harold said, "that I figured it was time to ask who we were supposed to be dancing for. But he just smiled and said security considerations forbade that kind of information and he hoped I'd understand. Frankly, Benny Worth had mentioned that the Duke of Windsor was in town, so we wondered if maybe it was him, seeing he was pretty snug with Hitler."

Breakfast done, they were driven to the club, where they confronted the six-piece house band, whose only member under fifty was Mohammed the Syrian pianist, a sharp young sport with fantastically long brown fingers covered with rings, who knew some English and translated Harold's remarks to the rest of the band. Relishing his new authority, Mohammed proceeded to take revenge on the other players, all Germans, whom he had been trying for months, unsuccessfully, to bring up to tempo. They knew "Swanee River," so Harold had them try that as an accompaniment, but they were hopelessly slack, so he managed to drive off the violinist and the accordionist as diplomatically as possible and worked with the drum and piano and it was tolerable. Waiters and kitchen help started arriving at noon, and he had an amazed audience standing around polishing silver as he went through the troupe's stuff. To dance before applauding waiters was a new experience, and the troupe began to feel golden. They were served a broiled-trout lunch in the empty room, another first, with wine, freshly baked hard rolls, and chocolate cake with marvellous coffee, and by half-past two were sharp on their feet but sleepy. A car brought them back to the Adlon for a nap. They would have dinner at the club, free, of course.

Harold for a long time lay motionless in a six-foot marble tub in his habitual pre-performance hot bath. "The faucets were gold-plated, the towels were yards long." It was the waiters' unprecedented near-reverence for him and the troupe that forced him to suspect that his audience tonight had to be some very high-level Nazi political people. Hitler? He prayed not. His own stupidity at having failed to insist on knowing appalled him. He should have deduced this problem the moment Fugler had said it was to be a single performance. Once again, what I imagined must have been his lifelong curse of timidity soured Harold's mind. Sliding down the bath until his head was underwater, he said, he tried to drown but finally decided otherwise. What if they discovered he was Jewish? The images of persecution, which he had seen in newspapers earlier this year, marched out of the locked closet hidden in a recess of his mind. But they couldn't possibly do something to an *American.* Blessing his passport, he got out of the tub and, dripping wet, fear in his belly, he checked that it was still in his jacket pocket. The plush towel on his skin somehow made it even more absurd that he should be feeling anxiety rather than happy anticipation as a command performance neared. Standing at a tall, satin-draped window, tying his bow tie, he stared down at the busy thoroughfare, at this very modern city with nicely dressed people pausing at store windows, greeting each other, tipping hats, and waiting for traffic lights to change, and felt the craziness of his position—he was like a scared cat chased up a tree by some spectre of danger it had glimpsed which might have been only an awning snapping in the breeze. "Still, I remembered Benny Worth's saying the Nazis' days were numbered because the workers would soon be knocking them out of office—so all hope wasn't lost."

He decided to gather the troupe in his dressing room. Paul Garner and Benny Worth stood in their tuxedos and Carol Conway in her blazing-red filmy number, all of them a little edgy since there was no precedent for Harold's summoning them before a show. "I'm not guaranteeing this, but I have an idea we are dancing for Mr. Hitler tonight." They nearly swelled with the pleasure of their success. Benny Worth, a born team player, his gravelly voice burgeoning through his cigar smoke, clenched his heavy right fist, flashing a diamond ring with which he had more than once wounded interlopers, and said, "Don't worry about that son of a bitch."

Carol, always a quick weeper, looked at Harold with waters threatening her eyes. "But do they know you're—"

"No," he cut her off. "But we'll get out of here tomorrow and go back to Budapest. I just didn't want you to be thrown off—in case you see him sitting there. Just play it the same as usual, and tomorrow we're back on the train."

A massive chandelier hung over the nightclub's circular stage, a blaze of twinkling lights which irritated Harold, who distrusted anything hanging over his head when he danced. The pink walls had a Moorish motif, the tabletops were grass green. They watched through peepholes from behind the orchestra as, promptly at midnight, Herr Bix, the manager, stopped the band, stood center stage, and apologized to the packed room for interrupting the dance, assured the customers of his gratitude for their having come this evening, and announced that it was his "duty" to request everyone to leave. Since normal closing time was around two, everyone imagined an emergency of some sort, and the use of the word "duty" suggested that this emergency involved the regime, so that with only a murmur of surprise the several hundred patrons gathered up their things and filed out into the street.

Some strolled off, others entered cabs, and the stragglers halted at the curb to watch, awed, as the famous long Mercedes appeared and turned in to the alley next to the club, preceded and followed by three or four black cars filled with men.

Through the peepholes, Harold and the troupe watched, amazed, as twenty or so uniformed officers spread out around the Leader, whose table had been moved to within a dozen feet of the

stage. With him sat the enormously fat and easily recognized Göring, and another officer, and Fugler. "In fact, they were almost all
enormous men; at least, they looked enormous in their uniforms,"
Harold said. Waiters were filling all their glasses with water,
reminding Harold, also practically a non-drinker, of Hitler's
reported vegetarianism. Bix, the Kick manager, who had scurried
around backstage, now touched Harold's shoulder. Mohammed,
no longer in his usual spineless slope over the keyboard but bolt
upright, caught the signal from Bix and, with his ringed fingers
and with the drummer backing up with his brush, went into "Tea
for Two," and Harold was on. The shape of the number could not
have been simpler; Harold soloed soft-shoe, went into the shuffle,
then, on the third chorus, Worth and Garner cakewalked in from
left and right, and finally Carol, as happy temptress, swooned pli-
ably around the formations that were made and unmade and
made again. Within a minute, it was obvious to the astonished
Harold as he glanced at Hitler's dreaded face that the man was
experiencing some profound kind of wild astonishment. The
troupe went into the stomp, shoes drumming the stage floor, and
Hitler seemed transfixed now, swept up in the booming rhythms,
both clenched fists pressing down on the tabletop, his neck
stretched taut, his mouth slightly agape. "I thought we were looking at an orgasm," Harold said. Göring, who "began to look like
a big fat baby," was lightly tapping the table with his palm and
occasionally laughing delightedly in his condescending fashion.
And, of course, their retinue, cued by their superiors' clear approval
of the performers, was unleashed, ho-ho-ing in competition over
who would show the most unmitigated enjoyment. Harold, helplessly enjoying his own triumph, was flying off the tips of his shoes.
After so much trepidation, this surprising flow of brutal appreciation blew away his last restraint and his art's power took absolute
command of his soul.

"You couldn't help feeling terrific," Harold said, and a curiously mixed look of embarrassment and victorious pleasure
flushed his face. "I mean, once you saw Hitler in the throes, he
was like . . . I don't know . . . a girl. I know it sounds crazy, but

he almost looked delicate, in a kind of monstrous way." I thought he was dissatisfied with this explanation, but he broke off and said, "Anyway, we had them all in the palm of our hands and it felt goddam wonderful, after being scared half to death." And he gave a little empty laugh that I couldn't quite interpret.

The routines, repeated three times at the order of the more and more involved Leader, took close to two hours to finish. As the troupe took bows, Hitler, eyes shining, rose from his chair and gave them a two-inch nod, his accolade, then sat, his chaste authority descending upon him again. Fugler and he now busily whispered together. The room fell silent. No one knew what to do. The retinue picked at the tablecloths and sipped water, staring about aimlessly. On the stage, the troupe stood, shifting from hip to hip. Worth, after several minutes, started to walk away in a silent show of defiance, but Bix rushed to him and led him back to the others. Hitler was clearly impassioned with Fugler, time and again pointing at Harold, who stood waiting with the troupe a few feet away. The dancers' hands were clasped behind their backs. Carol Conway, terrified, kept defensively nodding, coquettishly lifting and lowering her eyebrows toward the uniformed men, who gallantly smiled back.

More than ten minutes had gone by when Fugler gestured to Harold to join them at the table. Fugler's hand was trembling, his lips cracked with dryness, his eyes stared like a sleepwalker's; Harold saw in the man's tremendous success tonight the volcanic power Hitler wielded, and once again was touched by fear and pride at having tamed it. "You could laugh at him from a distance," Harold said of Hitler, "but up close, let me tell you, you felt a lot better off if he liked you." In his adolescent face I began to see something like anguish as he smiled at his remark.

Fugler cleared his throat and faced Harold, his manner distinctly formal. "We shall speak further in the morning, but Herr Hitler wishes to propose to you that . . ." Fugler paused, said Harold, to compose the Leader's message carefully in his mind. Hitler, slipping on a pair of soft brown leather gloves, watched him with a certain excited intensity. "In principle, he wishes you to create a school here in Berlin to teach German people how to tap-dance. This school, as he envisions it, would be set up under a new government department which he hopes you will take charge of until you have trained someone to take your place. Your dancing has deeply impressed him. He believes that the combination it offers of vigorous healthy exercise, strict discipline, and simplicity would be excellent for the well-being of the population. He foresees that hundreds, perhaps thousands, of Germans could be dancing together at the same time, in halls or stadiums, all over the country. This would be inspiring. It would strengthen the iron bonds that unify the German people while raising up their health standards. There are other details, but this is the gist of the Leader's message."

With which Fugler, with military sternness, indicated to Hitler that he had finished, and Hitler stood and offered his gloved hand to Harold, who scrambled to his feet, too nervous to say anything at all. Hitler took a step away from the table, but then, with a sudden bird-like snap of his head, turned back to Harold, and with pursed lips smiled at him and left, his small army behind him, their boots thrumming on the wooden floor.

Telling this, Harold May was, of course, laughing at times, but at other times one could see that he still had not quite shed the awesome distinction implicit in the story. Hitler at the time of the telling was only two years dead, and his menace, which had hung over us all for more than a decade, had not completely disappeared. His victims, so to speak, were still in fresh graves. Repulsive as he had been, and grateful as all of us were for his death, his presence was like a disease we had had to focus on for too long for it to heal and vanish so quickly. That he had been human enough to lose himself in Harold's performance, and had even had artistic aspirations, was not a comfortable thought, and I listened with a certain uneasiness as Harold pushed on with the tale. He looked different now than he had at the start, seeming almost to have aged in the telling of the story.

"Fugler showed up for breakfast again next morning," Harold said, "a totally changed man. The fucking Führer had offered me a *department*! In *person*! And my hit had also raised Fugler a couple of notches in the hierarchy, because the whole audition had been his idea. So the both of us were super *hoch*, big shots. He had a hard time staying in his seat as we went over the next steps. I would have the pick of Berlin spaces for the school, since my authority came directly from the top, and somebody from some other department would shortly be coming by to discuss my salary, but he thought at least fifteen thousand a year was possible. I nearly fell over. A Cadillac was around a thousand in those days. Fifteen was immense money. I had blasted the ball out of the park."

With a school and immense money on offer, he was handed a dilemma, he went on. He could, of course, simply leave the country. But that would mean tossing away enough money to buy himself a house and a car and maybe seriously think about finding a girl and marrying. He now began trying to explain himself more deeply. "I've always had a hard time with major decisions," he said to me, "and of course Hitler'd been in office only a few years and the real truth about the camps and all hadn't hit us yet, although what was already known was bad enough. Not that I'm excusing myself, but I just couldn't honestly say yes or no. I mean, going back to the Balkans wasn't exactly Hollywood, and knocking around in the States again was something I didn't want to think about."

"You mean you accepted the offer?" I asked, smiling in embarrassment.

"I didn't do anything for a couple of days except walk a lot in the city. And nobody was bothering me. My people were enjoying Berlin and, I don't know, I guess I was busy full time trying to figure myself out. I mean, if you were walking around in Berlin just then nothing was happening. It was no different from London or Paris except that it was cleaner. And maybe you'd notice a few more uniformed men here and there." He looked directly at me. "I mean, that's just how it was," he said.

"I understand," I said. But Hitler was too horrible a figure; I couldn't appreciate even the most perverse attraction to him or his Berlin. And it could be that that thought was what made me ask myself for the first time whether Harold had done something utterly outrageous, like . . . falling in love with the monster?

Harold stared out at the street through the drugstore window. I had the feeling that he hadn't quite realized how the story would sound to others. It was partly the particular character of the late forties; for some, but by no means for everyone, there was still an echo of wartime anti-Fascist heroism in the air; on Paris street corners, stone tablets were still being cemented into buildings, commemorating the heroism of some anti-Nazi Frenchman or -woman who had been shot on the spot by Germans. But of course most people, Harold probably among them, were oblivious of these ceremonies and their moral and political significance.

"Go ahead," I said. "What happened next? It's a great story." I reassured him as warmly as I could.

He seemed to open a bit to my acceptance. "Well," he said, "about four or five days later, Fugler showed up again."

Fugler was still in the glow. Talks were proceeding about how and where to set up the school. "Then," said Harold, "without making anything much of it, he told me that of course part of the routine was that every man in an executive cultural position had to pass a 'racial certification program.'" Returning to his ironical grin, Harold said, "I had to get measured for Aryan." He was to accompany Fugler to a Professor Martin Ziegler's laboratory for a routine check.

With this news, Harold found himself drifting into an even more uncomfortable position. "It's hard to explain; I'd ended up in this deal where I knew I'd be having to leave Germany. Exactly when and how I wasn't sure. But being examined seemed to put me in a different position. Because I'd be deceiving them. I mean, they could cook that into a stew, claiming that I was an enemy and they had to do something about me, passport or no passport. I'd gotten so I could smell violence in the air."

But he did not flee. "I don't know," he replied when I asked him why. "I guess I was just waiting to see what would happen. And, look, I don't deny it, the money'd dug itself into my head. Although—" Again he broke off, dissatisfied with that explanation.

In any case, as he got into Fugler's car he began to fear that he might be even more vulnerable because he had come to Hitler's personal and affectionate notice. "It was almost like . . . I don't know, like he was watching me. Maybe because we'd met, I'd shaken his actual hand," he said, suggesting that he also had a vague feeling of obligation to Hitler, who, after all, was his would-be benefactor— whom he had misled.

Watching Harold now, I found things simplified; there was certainly a bewildering mix of feelings in him, but I thought I saw a clear straight line underneath—Hitler had esteemed him so feelingly, in a sense had loved him or at least his talent, and more ardently than anyone anywhere else had ever come close to equalling. I wondered if that performance had been the high point of his art, perhaps of his life, a hook he had swallowed that he could still not cough up. After all, he had never become a star and probably would never again feel the burning heat of that magical light upon his face.

In the car, sitting beside Fugler on the way to his exam, and looking through the window at the great city and the ordinary things people did on the street, Harold felt that everything he saw seemed to signify, was suddenly like a painting, as though it were all supposed to *mean* something. But what? "You had to wonder," he said, "did they all feel like this? Like they were in a fishbowl and up above there was somebody looking down who *cared*?"

I couldn't believe my ears—Hitler *cared*?

Harold's eyes now were filled. He said that when he looked at Fugler sitting comfortably beside him smoking his English cigarette, and then at the people on the streets, "everything was so fucking *normal*. Maybe that's what was so frightening about it. Like you're drowning in a dream and people are playing cards on the beach a few yards away. I mean, here I'm in a car going to have my nose measured or something, or my cock inspected, and this was absolutely normal, too. I mean, these were not some fucking moon people, these people had *refrigerators*!"

Anger seemed to speak in him for the first time, but not, I thought, at the Germans particularly. It was, rather, at some transcendent situation that was beyond defining. Of course, his nose was small, a pug nose, and circumcision had become common among Germans by that time, so he had little to fear from a physical examination. And, as though reading my thought, he added, "Not that I was afraid of an exam, but . . . I don't know . . . that I was *involved* with this kind of shit—" He broke off again, again dissatisfied with his explanation, I thought.

The walls of Eugenics Professor Ziegler's inner office, in a modern building, were loaded with heavy medical volumes and plaster casts of heads—Chinese, African, European—on shelves behind sliding glass. Glancing around, Harold felt surrounded by an audience that had died. The Professor himself was on the tiny side, a nearsighted, rather obsequious scholar, hardly up to Harold's armpits, who hurriedly ushered him to a chair while Fugler waited in the outer office. The Professor tick-tacked around on the white linoleum floor gathering notebook, pencils, and fountain pen, while assuring Harold, "Only a few minutes and we can finish. Indeed, this is quite exciting, your school."

Now, sitting down on a high stool facing Harold, notebook on his lap, the Professor noted the satisfactory blue of his eyes and the blond hair, turned his palms up, apparently looking for a telltale sign of something, and finally announced, "We shall take some measurements, please." Drawing a large pair of brass calipers out of his desk drawer, he held one side under Harold's chin and the other on the crown of his head, and noted down the distance between them. The same with the width of his cheekbones, the height of his forehead from the bridge of his nose, the width of his mouth and jaws, the length of his nose and ears, and their positions relative to the tip of his nose and crown of his head. Each span was carefully plotted in a leather-bound notebook, as Harold sat trying to think of how to get hold of a railroad timetable without being noticed, and how to create an unobjectionable reason for having to go to Paris that very evening.

The whole session had taken about an hour, including an inspection of his penis, which, though circumcised, was of little interest to the Professor, who, with one eyebrow critically raised, had bent forward to look at the member for a moment, "like a bird with a worm in front of him." Harold laughed. Finally, looking up from the notes spread out on his desk, the Professor announced with a decided clink of professional self-appreciation in his voice, "I am concluding zat you are a very strong and distinct type of the Aryan race, and I wish to offer you my best wishes for suczess."

Fugler, of course, had never had any doubts on this score, especially not now, when he was being credited by the regime as the creator of this astonishing program. Imitating Fugler's smooth accent, Harold told how, on the way back in the car, he had become rhapsodic about tap's promising to "transform Germany into a community not only of producers and soldiers but artists, the noblest and most eternal spirits of humanity," and so on. Turning to Harold beside him, he said, "I must tell you—but may I call you Harold now?"

"Yes. Sure."

"Harold, this adventure—if I may call it so—coming to such a triumphant conclusion, suggests to me what an artist must feel when finishing a composition or painting or any work of art. That he has immortalized himself. I hope I am not embarrassing you."

"No—no. I see what you mean," Harold said, his mind distinctly elsewhere.

Back in the hotel, Harold greeted the members of his troupe who had gathered in his room. He was quite pale and frightened. He sat the three dancers down and said, "We're getting out."

Conway said, "Are you all right? You look white."

"Pack. There's a train at five tonight. We have an hour and a half. My mother is very ill in Paris."

Benny Worth's eyebrows went up. "Your mother's in *Paris*?" Then he caught Harold's look, and the three dancers rose and without a word hurried out to their rooms to pack.

As Harold expected, Fugler was not giving up that easily. "The desk clerk must have called him," Harold said, "because we had hardly turned in our keys when there he was, looking around at our luggage with disaster in his face."

"What are you doing? You can't possibly be leaving," Fugler said. "What has happened? There is a definite possibility of a dinner with the Führer. This is not to be declined!"

Conway, who happened to be standing nearby, stepped over to Fugler. Fright had raised her voice half an octave. "Can't you see? He's terrified of his mother's passing away. She's not an old woman, so something terrible must have happened."

"I can call the Paris embassy. They will send someone. You must stay! This is impossible! What is her address? Please, you must give me her address, and I will see that doctors attend to her. This cannot happen, Mr. May! Herr Hitler has never before in his life expressed such . . ."

"I'm Jewish," Harold said.

"What did he say?" I asked, astonished.

Harold looked up, caught up in my excitement. I wondered then if this was the point of the story—to describe his escape not only from Germany but from his relation to Hitler, such was the pleasure spreading over his grinning boy's face, right up to the part in the middle of his hair.

"Fugler said, 'How do you do?'"

"How do you do!" I almost yelled, totally flummoxed.

"That's what he said. 'How do you do?' He took half a step back like a shot of compressed air had hit him in the chest, and said, 'How do you do?' and stuck out his hand. His mouth fell open. He went white. I thought he was going to faint or shit. I felt a little sorry for him . . . I even shook his hand. And I saw he was scared, like he'd seen a ghost."

"What did he mean, 'How do you do'?" I demanded.

"I've never been sure," Harold said, seriously now. "I've thought about it a lot. He had an expression like I'd dropped down from the ceiling in front of him. And definitely scared. Definitely. I mean badly scared. Which I could understand, because he'd brought a Jew in front of Hitler. Jews to them were like a disease, which is something I didn't really understand till later. But I think it could have been something else that had him frightened, too."

He paused for a moment, staring at his empty soda glass. Through the window I saw office workers starting to crowd the sidewalk; the day was ending. "Thinking back to when we met in Budapest and all, I wonder if maybe he'd gotten to, you know, feel pretty close to me. I don't mean sex, I mean like I'd been his ticket to that face-to-face with Hitler, which only important people ever got to have, and on top of that I know he had a top spot in the new school marked out for himself. I mean, I'd gotten hold of the power in a certain way, which I'd begun to notice when I was taken to the Professor to be certified and in the car Fugler began treating me as though I were higher up than him. And when the Professor came out and told him I was kosher, he was already turning into a different man, like he was under me. It was sort of pathetic.

"Mind you," Harold went on, "this was before we knew much about the camps and all," and then he stopped.

"What do you mean?" I asked.

"Nothing. Just that I . . ." He broke off. After a moment, he looked at me and said, "To tell the truth, he wasn't really such a bad guy, Fugler. Just crazy. Badly crazy. They all were. The whole country. Maybe all countries, frankly. In a way. When I look at Berlin bombed to shit now, everything on the ground, and I remember it when there wasn't a candy wrapper on the sidewalks, and you ask yourself, How is this possible? What did it to them? Something did it. What was it?"

He paused again. "I'm not excusing them in any way, but when he said, 'How do you do?' as though he'd never seen me before, I thought, These people are absolutely in a dream. And suddenly here's this Jew who he'd thought was a person. I guess you could say it was a dream that killed forty million people, but it was still a dream. To tell the truth, I think we all are—in a dream, I mean. I've kept thinking that ever since I left Germany. It's over ten years since I got home, and I'm still wondering about it. I mean, no people love nuts and bolts like Germans. Practical people down to their shoelaces. But they still dreamed themselves into this rubble."

He glanced out at the street. "You can't help wondering, when you walk around in the city. Are we any different? Maybe we're also caught in some dream." And, gesturing toward the crowd moving along the street, he said, "The things in their heads, the things they believe. Who knows how real it is? To me now we're like walking songs, walking novels, and the only time it gets to seem real is when somebody kills somebody." No one spoke for a moment; then I asked, "So you got out all right?"

"Oh, no problem. They were probably glad to see us go without bad publicity. We went back to Budapest and then we worked the wheel till the Germans marched into Prague, and after that we came home." He sat back in his chair, preparing to stand. It struck me how deceptively young and unmarked he had seemed a half hour earlier, when we first met, like a guy fresh out of the Corn Belt, while in fact failure had wrinkled the flesh around his eyes. He stuck out his hand, and I shook it. "Use it if you like," he said. "I want people to know. Maybe you'll figure it out—be my guest." Then he got up and went out into the street.

I never saw him again, but the story has visited me a hundred times over the past fifty years, and for some reason I keep pushing it under again. Maybe I would much rather think of positive, hopeful things. Which could also be a way of dreaming, of course. Still, I like to think that a lot of good things have come out of dreaming.

Beavers

The pond, normally as silent as a glass of water, now gave up a sound, a splash at the man's approach. A heavy splash far weightier than a frog or leaping fish could make. And then spread itself flat as the mirror it usually was. The man waited but there was only silence. He walked the shoreline watching for signs, stood still listening. His eye caught the tree stump at the far end of the pond. Coming upon it, he saw the fallen poplar and its gnawed tip and the gnawed stump as well. He had beavers. Strangers thieving his privacy. Now, scanning the shore, he counted six trees felled during the single night. In another twenty-four hours the slope above the pond would begin to look like wasteland. Another couple of days and a bulldozer would seem to have gone through it, knocking over what was a lovely wood that had nestled the pond through the years. Long ago he had marveled at the wreckage of a wood on Whittlesy's place, at least ten acres looking like the Argonne Forest after a World War I shelling. The green woods at his back were his to defend.

He turned back to the water in time to see the flattened rodent head moving across the water. Watched motionless as the beast arrived at the narrow end of the pond and sounded, its flat leathery tail, with a parting slap on the water, flashing toward the sky as it slipped down and disappeared. Stepping closer to the shoreline, the man now made out, just below the surface of the clear, sky-reflecting water, the outline of the lodge. Incredible. They must have built it overnight, since he had been swimming right there the day before and there had been nothing. Amazement chilled his spine, the sheer appropriation. He recalled reading, long ago, that beaver shit was toxic. He and Louisa could no longer swim here as they had for thirty years, exulting in the water's purity, which had once tested potable, cleansed by its passage upward through sand and clay.

He hurried up to the house and found his shotgun and a box of shells and hurried back down the hill to the pond and circled around it to the lodge. With the sun lower he could make out its structure, a wall woven of thin branches the beaver had cut from the trees it had felled and then plastered with mud from the pond's bottom. Most likely the animal was resting on the shelf it had built inside the structure. The man aimed, careful to miss the lodge, and fired into the water's surface, which answered with a resonating boom and a peppering of light. The man waited. In a few minutes the head appeared. Expecting a confrontation, he reloaded and waited, hoping not to kill the beast but to introduce it to enough uncertainty to make it go away. He fired again. The flat tail arched up and sounded. The man waited. In a few minutes the head reappeared. The beaver swam, possibly worried but showing full confidence as it headed in a straight line across the pond to the fourteen-inch steel overflow pipe that stood five or six feet in from the opposite shore. There, defiantly—or was it some other emotion?—the beast pulled down a hazel bush growing at the shoreline and swam with it in its jaws and, raising up, pushed the whole plant into the pipe. Then it dived and emerged again with a tangle of grass and mud in its grasp and shoved that load into the pipe on top of the hazel bush. He was intending to stop the overflow. He wanted to raise the water level of the pond.

Perplexed, the man, standing across the pond from this intense work, sat on his heels to think about the enigma before him. The conventional analysis was that beaver dam building had as its purpose the blocking of a small stream with a dam in order to create a pond in which the beaver could build its lodge and raise its family, safe from predators. The project would deforest large areas that provided thin branches for lodge building, and cellulose from the felled tree stems on which the animal lived. *But this fellow already had a deep pond in which to build its lodge.* Indeed, it had already built one. Why did it need to stuff the pipe, stop the overflow, and raise the pond level? The whole effort was somehow admirable for its engineering skill and, in this case, thoroughly pointless. Watching the beast working, the man recognized his feeling of unhappiness with what he was witnessing and wondered, after a few minutes, whether he had somehow come to rely on nature as an ultimate source of steady logic and order, which only senseless humans betrayed with their greed and frivolous stupidity. This beaver was behaving like an idiot, imagining he was creating a pond where a perfect one already existed. The man aimed close enough to the beast to remind him once again of his unwelcome, fired, saw the tail rise and slap the water, and the idiot was gone. In a few minutes he had surfaced and returned to stuffing the pipe. The man felt himself weakening before this persistence, this absolute dedication that was so unlike his own endlessly doubting nature, his fractured convictions. He would need some expert advice; one way or another the beast had to go.

Carl Mellencamp, the druggist's son, was the man he needed. He had known Carl since his infancy, watched him grow enormous until now, in his late twenties, when he stood over six feet tall, weighing probably well over two hundred, with a rocking gait, thick archer's fists, a steady mason's gaze, and a certain straw hat with curled-up brim that he had worn cocked to the left side in heat and snow for at least the last ten years or maybe more. Carl lived to lay up stone walls, install verandas and garden paths, and hunt with gun or bow. When he arrived in his white Dodge truck late in the afternoon, the man felt the heavy cloak of responsibility passing off his shoulders and onto Carl's.

They went first to inspect the pipe, Carl carrying his rifle. Through the clear water they saw, with some amazement, that the beast had piled up a cone of mud around it reaching up to its lip. "He's got in mind to seal that pipe good and solid."

"But why the hell is he doing it? He's already got a pond," the man said.

"You might ask him next time you see him. We're going to have to kill him. And his wife."

The man stood there on the top of the dam shaking his head. "Isn't there some way to scare him off? . . . And I haven't seen a wife."

"She's around," Carl said. "They're juveniles, probably, that got thrown out of the tribe in Whittlesy's pond. Maybe two or three years old. They go forth to start a new family. They mean to stay." And waving his arm toward a stand of pines at the far end of the pond that the man had planted as seedlings four decades earlier, he said, "You can kiss a lot of those trees goodbye."

"I'd hate to kill them," the man said.

"I don't like it either," Carl said, and stood there squinting down at the water. Then he straightened up and said, "Let me try pissing."

The sun was almost down, long shadows stretched toward the pond, the sky's blue was darkening. Carl set off down the length of the dam to where the lodge was and stood pissing on the ground near it. Then he returned to the man and stood shaking his head. "I doubt it'll work. They've got too much invested in that lodge." They heard the splash and saw, down at the end of the pond, that the beast—or one of them—was climbing up out of the water and making his way a few feet from where Carl had pissed, undeterred by the scent of man.

"So much for that," Carl whispered. "I'd like to get him when he's out of the water, OK?"

The man nodded. The hateful stabbing joy of the kill moved into him. "Incidentally," he asked with an ironical smile, "are we legal?"

"As of this year," Carl said. "They've finally decided they're pests."

"What about trapping them?"

"I don't have traps. And what would we do with them? Nobody wants them. I know a guy would take the pelt, but they're not protected any more."

"Well, okay," the man agreed.

"Don't move," Carl whispered, and lowered himself to one knee, raising the rifle to his shoulder and cocking it as he aimed at the beast climbing up the side of the dam. Suddenly it turned and scurried down the slope it had been climbing and slid into the water. Carl stood up again.

"How'd he know?" the man asked.

"Oh, they know," Carl said with some odd hunter's pride in the beaver's wit. "Stay here and try not to move." He spoke quietly, conspiratorially. "I don't want to hit him in the water or we'll lose him if he sinks," he said. Then he took off down the length of the dam, to the far end, where the lodge was, setting his feet down flat lest he kick a stone and alarm the beasts, the rifle balanced tenderly in his hand.

Facing the lodge there was a dense clump of reeds at the water's edge, some of them rooted under the water. Carl carefully slipped himself into their midst and sat on his heels, the rifle butt resting on his thigh. The man stood watching from the center of the dam, fifty yards away, wondering how Carl could know that the beast would emerge. Carl, he was somehow glad to have learned, had not really wished to kill.

Minutes passed. The man stood watching. Now Carl, he saw through the reeds, was raising his gun very slowly. The shot's reverberations boomed across the water. Carl quickly stepped into the shallow water and lifted the beast, carrying it out of the reeds by the tail. The man hurried to see it. Carl, holding his rifle in his right hand, held the dead thing up to him with his left and then, suddenly dropping it onto the grass, turned back toward the pond, raised his gun and fired toward the opposite shore. "That was the lady," he said, and, handing his gun to the man, hurried down the dam and around the end of the pond and halfway up the other side, where he reached down into the water and lifted out the beaver's mate.

In the driveway, with the two dead things on the bed of the truck, the man watched Carl stroking the fur of one of them. "My friend's going to make something out of these. They're beauties."

"I don't understand what they had in mind, do you?"

Carl liked leaning on things and raised a foot to rest it on the hub of a rear wheel, removing his beloved straw hat to scratch his perspiring scalp. "They had some idea, I guess. It's like people, you know. Animals are. They have imaginations. These probably had some imaginary idea."

"He already had a pond. What was the point?" the man asked.

Carl did not seem overly concerned about the question. He did not seem to think it was up to him to find a solution to it.

The man pressed on. "I wonder if he was just reacting to the sound of running water coming out of the pipe."

Amused, Carl said, "Hey. Could be." But he obviously did not believe this.

"In other words," the man said, "maybe there was no connection between stuffing the pipe and raising the pond level."

"Could be," Carl said, seriously now. "Specially when he'd already built his lodge. That is peculiar."

"Maybe running water irritates them. They don't like the sound. Maybe it hurts their ears."

"That would be funny, wouldn't it. And us thinking they do it for a purpose." He was beginning to take to the idea.

"Maybe they don't have any purpose," the man said, excited by the prospect. "They just stop up the sound, and then turn around and see that the water is rising. But in their minds there's no connection between one thing and the other. They just see the pond rising and that gives them the idea of building a lodge in it."

"Or maybe they just don't have anything to do, so they stuff a pipe."

"Right." They both laughed.

"They do one thing," Carl said, "and that leads them to do the next thing."

"Right."

"Sounds good to me," Carl said, and opened the truck door and heaved his bulk into the cab. He looked down at the man through the side window. "Story of my life," he said, and laughed. "I started out to be a teacher, you know."

"I remember," the man said.

"Then I fell in love with cement. And next thing you know I'm heaving rocks all over the place."

The man laughed. Carl drove off, waving back through the window. On his truck bed the two beasts' bodies wobbled under their fur.

The man returned to the pond. It was his again, undisturbed. Moonlight was spreading over its silent face like a pale salve. Tomorrow he would have to somehow drag the debris up out of the pipe and get somebody with a backhoe with a long enough reach to extend from the shore over the water and lift the lodge out of the mud it was anchored in.

He sat on the wooden bench he had built long ago beside the little sandy beach where they always entered for a swim. He could hear the water trickling over the drainpipe's edge through the debris the beast had stuffed it with.

What had been in its mind? The question was like a hangnail. Or did it have a mind? Was it merely a question of irritated eardrums? If it had a mind it could imagine a future. It might have had happy feelings, feelings of accomplishment when stuffing the pipe, picturing a rising level of water resulting from its efforts.

But what useless, foolish work! It seemed a contradiction of Nature's economy, which did not allow for silliness, any more than, let's say, a priest or a rabbi or a president or a pope. These types did not take time out to tap-dance or whistle tunes. Nature was serious, he thought, not comical or ironical. After all, a sufficiently deep pond was already there. How could the beast have ignored this? And why, he wondered, was it so disturbing to think about; was it its parallel with his sense of human futility? The more he thought about it the more likely it seemed that the beast had had emotions, a personality, even ideas, not merely blind overpowering instincts that drove it to an act that had completely lost its point.

Or was there some hidden logic here that he was too literal-minded to grasp? Could the beast have had a completely different impulse than the raising of the water level? But what? What could it have been?

Or could he have had nothing in his mind at all except a muscular happiness at being young and easily able to do what millions of years had trained his mind to do? Beavers, he knew, were extremely social. Once having stuffed the pipe, he may have imagined returning to his mate asleep in the lodge to signal that he had caused the water level to rise. She may have expressed some appreciation. It was something she had always wanted from him for her greater safety. Nor would it occur to her, any more than it had to him, that the water level was already deep enough. The important thing was the idea itself. Of love perhaps. Animals did love. Could he have been stuffing the pipe for love? Real love had no purpose, after all, beyond itself.

Or was it all much simpler: did he simply wake one morning and with infinite pleasure start swimming through the clear water when, quite by chance, he heard the trickling of the overflow and, steering himself over to it, was filled with desire to capture the lovely wet sound, for he adored water above all things and wished somehow to become part of it, if only by capturing its tinkle?

And the rest, as it turned out, was unforeseen death. He had not believed in his death. The shots fired into the water had not caused him to flee but merely to dive and surface again a couple of minutes later. He was young and immortal to himself.

The man, unsatisfied, lingered by the water, tiring of the whole dilemma. Relieved that his woods would not be ravaged nor his water poisoned by beaver crap, he knew he did not regret the killings, sad as they were, despite the animals' complexity and a certain beauty. But he would really have been grateful had he been able to find some clean purpose to the stuffing of the overflow. Anything like that seemed not to exist now, unless its secret had died with the beavers, an idea that oppressed him. And he fantasized about how much more pleasantly things would have turned out had there been not a finished pond to start with but the traditional narrow meandering brook that the beast, in its wisdom, had dammed up in order to create a broad pond deep enough for the construction of its lodge. Then, with the whole thing's utility lending it some daylight sense, one might even have been able to look upon the inevitable devastation of the surrounding trees with a more or less tranquil soul, and somehow mourning him would have been a much more straightforward matter, even as one arranged to shoot him dead. Would something at least feel finished then, completely comprehended and somehow simpler to forget?

The Bare Manuscript

Carol Mundt lay on the desk, propped up on her elbows, reading a cooking article in *You*. She was six feet tall and a hundred and sixty pounds of muscle, bone, and sinew, with only a slightly bulging belly. In Saskatchewan she had not stood out for her size, but here in New York it was a different story. She shifted to take the pressure off her pelvis. Clement said, "Please," and she went still again. She could hear his speeded-up breathing over the back of her head and now and then a soft little sniffing.

"You can sit up now if you like," Clement said. She rolled onto her side and swivelled up to a sitting position, her legs dangling. "I need a few minutes," he said, and added jokingly, "I have to digest this," and laughed sweetly. Then he went over to his red leather armchair, which faced the dormer window that looked uptown as far as Twenty-third Street. Sighing, getting comfortable in his chair, he stared over the sunny rooftops. The house was the last remaining brownstone on a block of old converted warehouses and newish apartment houses. Carol let her head hang forward to relax, sensing that she was not to speak at such moments, then slid off the desk, her buttocks making a zipping sound as they came unstuck from the wood, and crossed the large study to the tiny bathroom, where she sat studying a recipe in the *Times* for meat loaf. Three or four minutes later, she heard "Okay!" through the thin bathroom door, and hurried back to the desk, where she stretched out prone, this time resting her cheek on the back of one hand, and closed her eyes. In a moment, she felt the gentle movement of the marker on the back of her thigh and tried to imagine the words it was making. He started on her left buttock, making short grunts that conveyed his rising excitement, and she kept herself perfectly still to avoid distracting him, as if he were operating on her. He began writing faster and faster, and the periods and the dots over the "i"s pushed deep into her flesh. His breathing was louder, reminding her again what a privilege it was to serve genius in this way, to help a writer who, according to his book jacket, had won so many prizes before he was even thirty and was possibly rich, although the furniture didn't match and had a worn look. She felt the power of his mind like the big hand pressing down on her back, like a real object with weight and size, and she felt honored and successful and congratulated herself for having dared answer his ad.

Clement was now writing on the back of her calf. "You can read, if you like," he whispered.

"I'm just resting. Is everything okay?"

"Yes, great. Don't move."

He was down around her ankle when the marker came to a halt. "Please turn over," he said.

She rolled onto her back and lay looking up at him.

He stared down at her body, noting the little smile of embarrassment on her face. "You feeling all right about this?"

"Oh, yes," she said, in this position nearly choking on her high automatic laugh.

"Good. You're helping me a lot. I'll start here, okay?" He touched just below her solid round breasts.

"Wherever," she said.

Clement pushed up his wire-rimmed glasses. He was half a head shorter than this giantess, whose affectionate guffaws, he supposed, were her way of hiding her shyness. But her empty optimism and that damned Midwestern affliction of regular-fella good will annoyed him, especially in a woman—it masculinized her. He respected decisive women, but from a distance, much preferring the inexplicit kind, like his wife, Lena. Or, rather, like Lena as she once was. He would love to be able to tell this one on his desk to relax and let her bewildered side show, for he had grasped her basic tomboy story and her dating dilemmas the moment she'd mentioned how she'd had her own rifle up home and adored hunting deer with her brothers Wally and George. And now, he surmised, with her thirties racing toward her, the joke was over but the camouflaging guffaws remained, like a shell abandoned by some animal.

With his left hand, he slightly stretched the skin under her breast so that the marker could glide over it, and his touch raised her eyebrows and produced a slightly surprised smile. Humanity was a pitiful thing. An inchoate, uncertain joy was creeping into him now; he had not felt this kind of effortless shaping in his sentences since his first novel, his best, which had absolutely written itself and made his name. Something was happening in him that had not happened in years: he was writing from the groin.

Self-awareness had gnawed away at his early lyricism. His reigning suspicion was simply that his vanishing youth had taken his talent with it. He had been young a very long time. Even now his being young was practically his profession, so that youthfulness had become something he despised and could not live without. Maybe he could no longer find a style of his own because he was afraid of his fear, and so instead of brave sentences that were genuinely his own he was helplessly writing hollow imitation sentences that could have belonged to anybody. Long ago he had been able to almost touch the characters his imagining had provided, but slowly these had been replaced by a kind of empty white surface like cold, glowing granite or a gessoed canvas. He often thought of himself as having lost a gift, almost a holiness. At twenty-two, winner of the Neiman-Felker Award, and, soon after, the Boston Prize, he had quietly enjoyed an anointment that, among other blessings, would prevent him, in effect, from ever growing old. After some ten years of marriage, he began groping around for that blessing in women's company, sometimes in their bodies. His boyish manner and full head of hair and compact build and ready laughter, but mainly his unthreatening vagueness, moved some women to adopt him for a night, for a week, sometimes for months, until he or they wandered off, distracted. Sex revived him, but only until he was staring down at a blank sheet of paper, when once again he knew death's silence.

To save the marriage, Lena had pointed him toward psychoanalysis, but his artist's aversion to prying into his own mind and risking the replacement of his magic blindness with everyday common sense kept him off the couch. Nevertheless, he had gradually given way to Lena's insistence—her degree had been in social psychology—that his father might have injured him far more profoundly than he had ever dared admit. A chicken farmer in a depressed area near Peekskill, on the Hudson, Max Zorn had a fanatical need to discipline his son and four daughters. Clement at nine, having accidentally beheaded a chicken by shutting a door on its neck, was locked in a windowless potato cellar for a whole night, and for the rest of his life had been unable to sleep without a light on. He had also had to get up to pee two or three times a night, no doubt as a consequence of his terror of peeing on potatoes in the dark. Emerging into the morning light with the open blue sky over his head, he asked his father's pardon. A smile grew on his father's stubbled face, and he burst out laughing as he saw that Clement was pissing in his pants. Clement ran into the woods, his body shaking with chills, his teeth chattering despite the warm spring morning. He lay down on a broken hay bale that was being warmed by the sun and covered himself with the stalks. The experience was in principle more or less parallel to that of his youngest sister, Margie, who in her teens took to staying out past midnight, defying her father. Returning from a date one night, she reached up to the cord hanging from the overhead light fixture in the entrance hall and grasped a still warm dead rat that her father had hung there to teach her a lesson.

But none of this entered Clement's first story, which he expanded into his signature novel. Instead, the book described his faintly disguised mother's adoration of him, and pictured his father as a basically well-meaning, if sad, man who had some difficulty with expressing affection, nothing more. Clement, in general, would always find it hard to condemn; Lena thought that for him the levelling of judgment in itself was a challenge to confront his father and symbolically invited a second entombment. And so his writing was romantically left-wing, a note of wistful protest always trembling in it somewhere, and if this quality of innocence was attractive in his first book it seemed predictably formulaic thereafter. In fact, he would join the sixties' anarchic revolt against forms with enormous relief, having come to despair of structure itself as the enemy of the poetic; but structure in art—so Lena told him—implied inevitability, which threatened to turn him toward murder, the logical response to his father's terrifying crimes. This news was too unpleasant to take seriously, and so in the end he remained a rather lyrical and winningly cheerful fellow, if privately unhappy with his unbudging harmlessness.

Lena understood him; it was easy, since she shared his traits. "We are charter members of the broken-wing society," she said late one night while cleaning up after one of their parties. For a while in their late twenties and thirties, a party seemed to coagulate every weekend in their Brooklyn Heights living room. People simply showed up and were gladly welcomed to smoke their cigarettes, from which Lena snipped off the filters, to flop on the carpet and sprawl on the worn furniture, to drink the wine they'd brought and talk about the new play or movie or novel or poem; also to lament Eisenhower's collapsed syntax, the blacklisting of writers in radio and Hollywood, the mystifying new hostility of blacks toward Jews, their traditional allies, the State Department's lifting of suspect radicals' passports, the perplexing irrational silence that they felt closing in on the country as its new conservatism went about scooping out and flipping away its very memory of the previous thirty years, of the Depression and the New Deal, even changing the war's Nazi enemy into a kind of defender against the formerly allied Russians. Some were refreshed by the Zorns' hospitality and went into the night either newly joined or alone but, either way, under the influence of a forlorn time of lost valor: they saw themselves as a lucid minority in a country where ignorance of the world's revolution was bliss, money was getting easier to make, the psychoanalyst the ultimate authority, and an uncommitted personal detachment the prime virtue.

In due time, Lena, uncertain about everything except that she was lost, analyzed matters and saw that she, like his sentences, was no longer his, and that their life had become what he took to saying his writing had become: an imitation. They went on living together, now in a lower-Manhattan brownstone on permanent loan by the homosexual heir of a steel fortune, who believed Clement was another Keats. But Clement often slept on the third floor these days and Lena on the first. The gift of the house was only the largest of many gifts that people dropped on them: a camel's-hair coat came from a doctor friend who found that he needed a larger size; the use of a cottage on Cape Cod year after year from a couple who went off to Europe every summer, and with it an old but well-maintained Buick. Fate also provided. Walking along a dark street one night, Clement kicked something metallic, which turned out to be a can of anchovies. Bringing it home, he found that it needed a special key and put it in a cupboard. More than a month later, on a different street, he once again kicked metal—the key to the can. He and Lena, both anchovy lovers, instantly broke out some crackers and sat down and ate the whole thing.

They still had some laughs together, but mostly they shared a low-level pain that neither of them had the strength to bring to a head, both feeling they had let the other down. "We even have an imitation divorce," she said, and he laughed and agreed, and they went on anyway with nothing changed except that she cut her long wavy blond hair and took a job as a child counsellor. Despite their never having been able to decide to have a child, she understood children instinctively, and he saw with some dismay that her work was making her happy. At least for a while, she seemed to perk up with some sort of self-discovery, and this threatened to leave him behind. But in less than a year she quit, announcing, "I simply cannot go to the same place every day." This was the return of the old crazy lyrical Lena, and it pleased him despite his alarm at the loss of her salary. They were beginning to need more money than he could make, with the sales of his books falling to near nothing. As for sex, it was hard for her to recall when it had meant very much to her. Gradually, it was a four- or five-times-a-year indulgence, if that. His affairs, which she suspected but refused to confirm, relieved her of a burden even as they gnawed at what was left of her self-regard. His view was that a man had to *go* somewhere with his erection, while a woman felt she *was* somewhere. A big difference. But in a cruel moment he admitted to himself that she was too unhappy to be happily screwed, a condition he blamed on her background.

Then one summer afternoon, while smoking his pipe on the rickety step of their donated beach cottage, he saw a girl walking all alone by the lip of the sea, looking totally immersed in her thoughts, with the sun flashing across her hips, and he imagined how it would be if he could get her naked and write on her. His soul quickened. It had been a long, long time since he had had any vision of himself that brought such a lift of joy. This picture of himself writing on a woman's body was somehow wholesome and healthful, like holding a loaf of fresh bread.

He might never have placed the ad at all had Lena not finally erupted. He was up in his third-floor workroom, reading Melville, trying to cleanse his mind, when he heard screaming from downstairs. Lena, when he rushed into the living room, was sitting on the couch pouring herself into the air. He held her in his arms until she was exhausted. There was no need to talk; she was simply dying of inchoate outrage at her life, the relentless lack of money, and his failure to provide some kind of lead. He held her hand, and could hardly bear to look at her ravaged face.

She grew quiet. He brought her a glass of water. They sat together on the couch, waiting for nothing. She took a Chesterfield from a pack on the coffee table, snipped off its filter with her fingernail, and lay back inhaling defiantly, Dr. Saltz having seriously warned her twice now. She was having an affair with Chesterfields, Clement thought.

"I'm thinking of writing something autobiographical," he said, somehow implying that this would bring in money.

"My mother . . ." she said, and went silent, staring.

"Yes?"

This obscure mention of her mother reminded him of the first time she had openly revealed the guilt she felt. They were sitting at Lena's rooming-house window overlooking a splendid street lined with trees in full leaf, with students idling past and the placid quiet of a Midwestern campus sequestering them from the real world, while back in Connecticut, she said, her mother was rising before five every morning to board the first streetcar for her eight-hour day in the Peerless Steam Laundry. Imagine! Noble Christa Vanetzki ironing strangers' shirts so she could send her daughter the twenty dollars a month for room and board, meanwhile refusing to let her daughter work, as most students did. Lena had to shut her eyes and squeeze her unworthiness out of her mind. To make her mother happy, she had to succeed, success would cure everything—maybe a job in social psychology with a city agency.

She was wearing her white angora sweater. "That sweater makes you glow like a spirit in this crazy light," Clement said. They went out for a walk, holding hands along the winding paths through shadows so black they seemed solid. The clarity of the moon that windless night brought it unnervingly near. "It's got to be closer than usual, or something," he said, squinting up at its light. He loved the poetry of science, but the details were too mathematical. In this amazing glare his cheekbones were more prominent and his manly jaw sculpted. They were exactly the same height. She had always known he adored her, but alone with him she could sense his body's demand. Suddenly he drew her into a clearing beneath some bushes and gently pulled her to the ground. They kissed, he fondled her breasts, and then stretched out and pressed against her to spread her legs. She felt his hardness and tensed with the fear of embarrassment. "I can't, Clement," she said, and kissed him apologetically. She had never given even this much of herself to anyone before, and she wanted her gift forgotten.

"One of these days we have to." He rolled off her.

"Why!" She laughed nervously.

"Because! Look what I bought."

He held up a condom for her to see. She took it from him and felt the smooth rubber with her thumb. She tried not to think that all his verses about her—the sonnets, the villanelles, the haiku—were merely ploys to prepare her for this ridiculous rubber balloon. She raised it to her eye like a monocle and looked up at the sky. "I can almost see the moon through it."

"What the hell are you doing!" He laughed and sat up. "The mad Vanetzkis." She sat up giggling and returned the condom to him. "What is it, your mother?" he asked.

She was dead serious. "Maybe you ought to find somebody else. We could still be friends." And then she added, "I really don't understand why I'm alive." Clement had always been moved by these quick mood changes—"the Polish depths," he called them. She had a baffling connection with some mystery across the Atlantic in the dark Polish middle of Europe, a place neither he nor she had ever been.

"Is there a poem about anything like this?"

"Like what?"

"A girl who can't find out what she thinks."

"Probably Emily Dickinson, but I can't think of a particular one. Every love poem I know ends with glory or death."

He wrapped his arms around his raised knees and stared up at the moon. "I've never seen it like this before. This must be how it makes wolves howl."

"And women go mad," she added. "Why is it always women the moon makes mad?"

"Well, they've got such a head start."

She bent forward to clear a branch from her line of sight, narrowing her gaze against the glare. "I really think it could make me crazy." In a distant way, she actually was afraid of insanity. Her father's mad death had never left her. "How close it seems, like an eye in Heaven. I can see it frightening people. You'd think it would be warm with this brightness, but it's cold light, isn't it?

Like the light of death." Her dear, childlike curiosity chilled him with anticipation of her body, which he still hoped to have someday. Was she blond down there? At the same time, she was holy and rare. Her only defect was her cheekbones, slightly too prominent but not fatally so, and the too broad Polish nose. But he was past comparing her to perfection. He opened her hand and pressed her palm to his lips. "Cathleen ni Houlihan, Elizabeth Barrett Browning, Queen Mab"—now he had her giggling pityingly— "Betty Grable . . . who else?"

"The Karamazov woman?"

"Ah, yes, Grushenka. And who else? Peter Paul Mounds, Baby Ruth, Cleopatra . . ." She grasped him by the head and crushed her mouth on his. She hated disappointing him like this, but the more physical she tried to become the less she felt. Maybe if they did do it, some spring would uncoil inside her. He was certainly gentle and lovable, and if anyone was to enter her before she found a husband it might as well be Clement. Or maybe not. She was certain of nothing. She let his tongue slide over hers. Her welcoming mouth surprised him, and he rolled her back and lay on her and began pumping, but she slid out from under him, got up, and walked out onto the path, and he caught up with her and had started to apologize when he saw her intense concentration. Her frustrating mood changes dangled above him like a bright-colored toy over a baby's crib. They walked in a nearly mournful silence to the road and then to her rooming house, where they stood below the deep Victorian porch, the brightness of the moon stretching their giant inky silhouettes across the grass.

"I wouldn't know how to do it."

"I could teach you."

"I'll be embarrassed."

"Only for a minute or two. It's easy." They both burst out laughing. He loved to kiss her laughing mouth. She touched his lips with her fingertips.

He stood on the sidewalk watching her incredible form going up the path to the house—her round ass, the full thighs. She turned in the doorway and waved and vanished.

He had to marry her, crazy as that sounded. But how? He had nothing, not even prospects, unless he could win another prize or be taken on as a faculty assistant. But there were hundreds with degrees higher than his looking for jobs. He was most likely going to lose her. An erection was stirring as he stood there on the moon-flooded sidewalk, a hundred feet from where she was undressing.

"Why do you bother with her?" Mrs. Vanetzki asked Clement. Clyde, the white-and-black mutt, lay stretched out in the shade, dozing at her feet. It was a hot mill-town Sunday afternoon, the last day of spring break. Even the rushing Winship River looked oily and warm below the house, and in the still air shreds of the smoke of a long-departed train hung over the railroad tracks along the riverbank.

"I don't know," Clement said. "I figure she might get rich someday."

"Her? Ha!" For Clement's visit, Mrs. Vanetzki wore a carefully ironed blue cotton dress with lace trim around the collar, and white oxfords. Her reddish hair was swept up to a white comb at the top of her head, emphasizing both her height—she was half a head taller than her daughter—and, somehow, the breadth of her cheekbones and forehead. Beneath her defiant banter, Clement felt the scary force of the majestically defeated, something he could not reconcile with his hopes. A framed tinted photo in the living room showed her only ten years earlier, standing proud beside her husband, with his Byronic foulard and flowing hair, a fedora hanging from his hand. His misunderstanding of America's sometimes lethal contempt for foreignness had not yet strapped him to the stretcher and made him into a paranoid, raving in Polish to the walls of an ambulance, cursing his wife as a whore and the human race as murderers. Only Lena was left her now. The responsible one, "the only one who got herself a brain in her head." Lena's sister Patsy, the middle child, had had two abortions with different men, one of whose surnames she admitted she didn't know. She had a wild loud whine of a voice and helter-skelter in her eyes. A sweet girl, really, with a big heart, but simply barren in the head. Patsy had once heavily intimated to Clement that she knew Lena was not letting him in and that she would not mind substituting herself "a couple of times." There had been no envy or spite in this offer, simply the fact of it and no hard feelings whichever way he decided. "Hey, Clement, how about me if she won't?" Kidding, of course, except for the undeniable light in her eye.

There was also Steve, the last-born, but for her he somehow hardly counted. He was dull and sweet and heavy-footed, the peasant side of the family. Steve was like Patsy, swimming around like a carp at the bottom of the pond, but at least he wasn't sex-mad. Hamilton Propeller liked him, amazingly enough. They knew they had a serious worker, and had advanced him into calibration technology after his first six months—Steve, who was only nineteen, with but two years of high school. He would be all right, although his recent shenanigans troubled her.

"Steve does a lot of walking in his sleep, you know. Lately." Mrs. Vanetzki addressed this to Lena with an implicit request for her college-educated interpretation.

"Maybe he needs a girl," Lena ventured. Clement was astonished and amused at the irony of her speaking so easily about sex.

"Trouble is there are no whores in this town," Mrs. Vanetzki said, scratching her belly. "Patsy keeps telling him to go to Hartford for a weekend, but he doesn't understand what she's talking about. How about you, Clement?"

"Me?" Clement flushed, imagining she would be asking next if he'd slept with Lena.

"Maybe you could tell him about the birds and bees. I don't think he knows it." Lena and Clement laughed, and Mrs. Vanetzki allowed herself a suppressed grin. "I really don't think he's even heard of it, but what can be done?"

"Well, somebody has to teach him!" Lena exclaimed, worried by her brother's persisting childishness. Clement was baffled that she could apply this level of energy to making her family face their dilemmas when she was fleeing her own.

"He seems to have bent Patsy's old bicycle," Mrs. Vanetzki said, mystified.

"Bent her bicycle!"

"When we were all asleep. He seems to have been sleepwalking in the night and gone outside and bent the front fork in his two hands. It's some kind of force in him." She turned to Clement. "Maybe you could talk to him about going to Hartford some weekend."

But before Clement could reply Mrs. Vanetzki waved him down. "Ah, you men, you never know what to do when it comes to practical."

Lena quickly defended him. "He'd be glad to talk to Steve. Wouldn't you, Clement?"

"Sure, I'd be glad to talk to him."

"But do you know anything about sex?"

"Mama!" Lena went red and screamed with laughter, but her mother barely smiled.

"Oh, I know a thing or two." Clement tried to brush off the woman's bewildering near contempt for him.

"Now, you be nice to Clement, Mama," Lena said, and went and sat on the glider beside her mother.

"Oh, he knows not to be upset. I just say things." But she had pinned inadequacy to his nature. She pushed her heel against the floor and made the glider swing.

Nobody spoke. The glider squeaked intimately. Beyond the porch the street was silent. Mrs. Vanetzki finally turned to Clement. "The main thing that puts people's lives to ruin is sex."

"Oh, come on—even if you love somebody? I love this crazy girl," Clement said.

"Ah, love."

Lena nervously giggled through her cigarette smoke.

"Isn't there such a thing?" Clement asked.

"Whoever is not realistic, America kills," Mrs. Vanetzki said. "You are an educated young man. You are handsome. My daughter is a mixed-up person. She will never change. Nobody changes. Only more and more is let out, that's all, the way a ball of string unwinds. Do yourself a favor—forget about her, or be friends, but don't marry. You should find a smart woman with a practical mind and clear thoughts. Marriage is a thing forever, but a wife is only good if she is practical. This girl has no idea of practical. She is a dreamer, like her poor father. The man comes to this country expecting some respect, at least for his name. Nobody respects a Polack. What did they know of Vanetzkis, who go back to the Lithuanian dukes? He went crazy for a little respect, a man with engineer training. They kept wanting to make friends with him, the kind of people he wouldn't have spoken to in the old country, except maybe to get his shoes shined. So he comes to Akron and Detroit and then here looking for a cultured circle. This is the nature of Lena's father. He didn't know that here you are either a failure or a success, not a human being with a name. So he went raving to his grave. Don't talk about marriage. Please, for both your sakes, leave her to herself. Our Patsy, yes—she should be married. Only marriage can save her, and even that I doubt. But not this one." She turned now to look at her elder daughter, who had giggled in loving embarrassment through all her remarks. "Have you told him how lost you are?"

"Yes," Lena said, uncomfortably. "He knows."

Mrs. Vanetzki sighed, pressed a hand against her own perspiring cheek, and rocked slightly from side to side. She was in touch with what time was to bring to her, Clement thought, and he was moved by this transcendency in her nature, even if it was excessively tragic for his taste.

"What are you going to do for a living? Because I can tell you now she will never amount to anything financially."

"Mama!" Lena protested, delighted by the implied female revolt in her mother's candor. "Oh, Mama, I'm not that bad!"

"Oh, you're getting there," Mrs. Vanetzki said. She repeated her question to Clement. "What are you going to live on?"

"Well, I don't know yet."

"Yet? Don't you know that every day costs money? 'Yet'? Economics does not wait for 'yet.' You have to know what you are going to live on. But I see you are like her—the world is not real to you, either. Isn't there something in Shakespeare about this?"

"Shakespeare?" Clement asked.

"You tell me everything is in Shakespeare. Tell me how a hopeless beautiful girl's supposed to marry a poet who hasn't got a job.

My God, you are regular children!" And she laughed, shaking her head helplessly. Clement and Lena, relieved that she was no longer judging them, joined her, delighted that she was sharing their dilemma in this crazy life.

"But it's not going to happen right away, Mother. I've got to graduate first, and then if I can get a job . . ."

"She'll get a job—she's got perfect grades," Clement said, with complete confidence.

"What about you? Is there a job for poets? Why don't you try to be famous? Is there a famous poet in America?"

"Sure, there are famous American poets, but you probably wouldn't have heard of them."

"That's what you call famous, people that nobody's ever heard of?"

"They're famous among other poets and people interested in poetry."

"Write some kind of story—then you'll be famous. Not this poetry. Then maybe they'd make a moving picture out of your story."

"That's not the kind of writing he does, Mama."

"I know, you don't have to tell me that."

Patsy appeared behind the screen door in her bra and panties. "Ma, you seen my other bra?" She sounded persecuted.

"Hangin' up in the bathroom. Why don't you look sometime instead of 'Ma, Ma, Ma'?"

"I did look."

"Well, look again with your eyes open. And when you goin' to wash your own stuff?"

Patsy opened the screen door and came out barefoot on the porch, her arms crossed over her big breasts in deference to Clement. A towel was wrapped like a turban over her wet hair. In the fading daylight, he saw grandeur in her powerful thighs and her broad back and deep chest. On an impulse Patsy grasped her mother's face between her hands and kissed her. "I love you, Mama!"

"There's a man here and you walking around naked like that? Go inside, you crazy thing!"

"It's only Clement. Clement don't mind!" She turned her back on her mother and sister and faced Clement, whose heart swelled at the sight of her outthrust breasts, barely cupped by the under-sized bra. With her taunting whine of a laugh, she asked, "You mind me, Clement?"

"No, I don't mind."

Mrs. Vanetzki leaned forward and smacked her daughter's ass hard with the flat of her hand and then laughed.

"Ow! You hurt me!" Patsy ran into the house, gripping her buttock.

It was almost dark now. A freight train clanked along in the near distance. Lena lit a cigarette and leaned back into the glider cushion.

"He's going to write a play for the stage, Ma."

"Him?"

"He can do it."

"That's good," Mrs. Vanetzki said, as if it were a joke. Before her black mood of disbelief, everyone fell silent.

Later, they went for a walk. It was a neighborhood of bunga-lows and four-story wooden apartment houses, workers' homes.

"She's right, I guess," Clement said, hoping Lena would contra-dict him.

"About getting married?"

"It'd be silly for us."

"Probably," she agreed, relieved. A decision decisively put off was as comforting as one that had been made, and she grasped his hand, lifted by this concretizing of the indefinite.

He could not get up the courage to place the ad. He was beginning to wonder if it might be thought perverse. But it gradually loomed like a duty to himself. One day, he picked up a copy of the *Village Voice* and stood on the corner of Prince and Broadway perusing the personal columns: page after page of randy invitations, pleas for a companion, offers of psychic discovery and physical improvement—like an ice field, he thought, with human voices calling for rescue from deep crevasses. Dante. He took the paper home to his barren desk, trying to think of some strategy, and finally decided on a direct approach: "Large woman wanted for harmless experiment, age immaterial but skin must be firm. Photos."

After five false starts—immensely blubbery nude women photographed from either end—he knew the moment he saw the photo that Carol Mundt was perfect: head thrown back as if in a laughing fit. When she appeared at his door—in her yellow miniskirt and white beret and black blouse, six inches taller than he, and touching in a corny way with that shy, brave grin—he wanted to throw his arms around her, instantly certain that she was going to validate his concept. At last he had done something about his emptiness.

Snuggling into his armchair, she made a desultory attempt to draw down her skirt while trying to look skeptically game, as if they were strangers at a bar. She jingled the heavy bracelets and chains around her neck, and neighed—horse laughter, irritating his sensitive hearing. In fact, there was something virginal about her that she might be working to cover up, maybe extra-virginal, like the best olive oil, a line he resolved to remember to use sometime. "So what's this about? Or am I wide enough?" she asked.

"It's very simple. I'm a novelist."

"Ah-huh." She nodded doubtfully.

He took down one of his books from the shelf and handed it to her. She glanced at his photo on the dust jacket, and her suspicions collapsed. "Well, now, say . . ."

"You will have to be naked, of course."

"Ah-huh." She seemed excited, as if steeling herself for the challenge.

He pressed on. "And I want to be able to write anywhere on you, because, you see, the story I have in mind will need all your space. Although I could be overestimating. I'm not sure yet, but it might be the first chapter of a novel." Then he explained about his block and his hope that writing on her skin would deliver him from its grip. Her eyes widened with fascination and sympathy, and he saw that she was proud to be his confidante. "It may not work—I don't know . . ."

"Well, it's worth a try, right? I mean, if you don't try you don't fly."

Vamping for time, he moved a small box of paper clips off his

desk and a leather-bordered blotter, a long-ago Christmas present
from Lena. How to tell her to undress? The madness of the scheme
came roaring at him like a wave, threatening to fling him back
into his impotence. Scrambling, he said, "Undress, please?"—
something he had never actually dared say to a woman, at least
not standing up. With what seemed a mere shrug and a wriggle,
she was standing before him naked but for her white panties. His
eye went down to them and she asked, "Panties?"

"Well, if you don't mind, could you? It's kind of less—I don't
know—stimulating with them off, you know? And I want to use
that area."

She slid out of her panties and sat on the desk. "Which way?"
she asked. Clearly, she had been having compunctions and now in
overcoming them had been left in uncertainty, a mental state he
practically owned. And so their familiarity deepened.

"On your stomach first. Would you like a sheet?"

"This is all right," she said, and lowered herself onto the desk-
top. The broad expanse of her tanned back and global white buttocks was in violent contrast, it seemed now, to his desk's former
devastated dryness. An engraved silver urn, one of his old prizes,
held a dozen felt-tipped pens, one of which he now took in hand.
Something in him was quivering with fear. What was he doing?
Had he finally lost his mind?

"You okay?" she asked.

"Yes! I'm just thinking."

There had been a story—it was months ago now, maybe a
year—which he had begun several times. Then, suddenly and
simply, it occurred to him that he had outlived his gift and he had
no belief in himself any more. And now, with this waiting flesh
under his hand, he had committed himself to believe again.

"You sure you're okay?" she repeated.

It hadn't been a great story, or even a very good one, but it held
the image of how he had first met his wife, under a wave that had
knocked them both down and sent them tumbling together
toward the beach. As he got to his feet, yanking up his nearly
stripped-away trunks while she staggered up as well, pulling her

tank suit up over a breast that had popped out in the churning water, he saw them as fated, like Greeks rising from the ocean in some myth of drowning and being reborn.

He was a naïve poet then, and she worshiped Emily Dickinson and burning the candle at both ends. "The sea tried to strip you," he said. "The Minotaur." Her eyes, he saw, were glazed, which pleased him, for he was reassured by vague people, as it soon turned out that she was. Disgorged by the sea—as he saw the scene for years afterward—they instinctively glimpsed in each other the same anguish, the same desire to escape the definite. "Death by the Definite," he would write, a paean to the fog as creative force.

Now, holding the black felt-tipped pen in his right hand, he lowered his left onto Carol's shoulder. The warmth of her firm skin was a shock. Not often had his fantasy turned real, and that she was willing to do this for him, a stranger, threatened tears. The goodness of humanity. He had sensed that she had needed all her courage to respond to his ad, but something kept him from inquiring too deeply about her life. As long as she wasn't crazy. A little weird, maybe, but who wasn't? "Thank you, Carol."

"It's okay. Take your time."

He felt himself beginning to swell. The way it used to happen long, long ago when he wrote. A man wrote with it, his aptly named organ, and a gallon of extra blood seemed to expand his veins. He leaned over Carol's back, his left hand pressing down more confidently on her shoulder now, and slowly wrote: "The wave gathered itself higher and higher far out where the sand shelf dropped down into the depths as the man and the woman tried to swim against the undertow that was sweeping them, strangers to each other, out toward their fate." Astonished, he saw with clarity fragments of days of his youth and young manhood, and, arcing over them like a rainbow, his unquestioning faith in life and its all but forgotten promise. He could smell Carol's flesh as she responded to the pressure of his hand, a green-tinted fecund sea scent that somehow taunted him with his desiccated strength. How to describe the sheer aching he felt in his heart?

And Lena's face rose before him as she had looked more than

twenty years before, her eyes slightly bloodshot from the salt water, her swirling blond hair plastered across her laughing face, the fullness of her young body as she stepped upward across the sand and collapsed breathlessly laughing, and himself already in love with her form and both of them somehow familiar and unwary after their shared battering. It seemed that these were the first images he'd experienced in many years, and his pen moved down Carol's back to her buttocks and then down her left thigh and then the right, and, turning her over, it continued onto her chest and belly and then back down her thighs and onto her ankle, where, miraculously, the story, barely disguised, of his first betrayal of his wife came to its graceful end. He felt he had miraculously committed truth to this woman's flesh. But was it a story or the beginning of a novel? Oddly, it didn't matter, but he must show it to his editor right away.

"I finished on your ankle!" he called, surprised by a boyishness in the tone of his voice.

"Isn't that great! Now what?" She sat up, hands childishly spread out in the air so as not to smudge herself.

It struck him how strange it was that she was as ignorant of what had been written on her as a sheet of paper. "I could get you scanned, but I don't have a scanner. Otherwise, I could copy it on my laptop, but it'll take a while—I'm not a fast typist. I just hadn't thought of this . . . unless I put you in a cab to my publisher," he joked. "But I'm only kidding. He might want some cuts."

They solved the problem by him standing behind her reading her back aloud while she sat typing on his laptop. They burst into laughter at the procedure from time to time. For the text on her front, she thought of having a full-length mirror to read from, but it would all be reversed. So he sat down in front of her and typed while she held the machine on her lap. When he had read down to her thighs, she had to stand so he could continue—until he was on the floor reading her calves and ankles.

Then he stood up and they looked deeply into each other's eyes for the first time. Then, possibly because they had done something so intimate, and so unthought-of, they had no idea what to do next, and started to giggle and then collapsed from laughing, an infectious hysteria heaving their diaphragms until they had to lean their foreheads on the edge of the desk and not look at one another. Finally, he was able to say, "You're welcome to shower, if you like." And this for some reason rendered them screeching again, falling around with delicious helplessness.

Gasping, they slid to the floor and their laughter subsided. They lay side by side, filled with some unexpected childish knowledge of one another. Now they were quiet, still panting, lying face-to-face on his Oriental carpet.

"I guess I'll go, right?" she asked.

"How will you wash it off?" he asked, feeling an incomprehensible anxiety.

"Take a bath, I guess."

"But your back . . ."

"I know somebody who'll wash it."

"Who, a man?"

"No, a girl down the hall."

"But I'd rather nobody read it yet. I'm not really sure it's ready to publish, you know? Or for somebody to read it. I mean . . ." He was lurching about, looking for some reason to fend off the curiosity of this unknown back-washing girlfriend; or perhaps it was to preserve the privacy of his creation—God knew why, but he felt her body was still too personal for any stranger to look at. He raised himself up on one elbow. Her hair had spread out over the carpet. It was almost as if they had made love. "I can't let you out this way," he said.

"What do you mean?" There was a hopeful note in her voice.

"People who know us will recognize things about my wife in it. I'm not ready for that."

"Why'd you write it, then?"

"I just put it down raw and then I'd change some of it later. You can't go this way. I'll take a shower with you and scrub your back, okay?"

"Okay, sure. But I didn't intend for anybody to read it," she said.

"I know, but I'll feel better if it's gone."

In the small metal shower stall, she seemed so immense that he started to tire after scrubbing her for a few minutes with his back brush. Carol washed her front, but he did the backs of her thighs, calves, and ankles. And when she was clean, the water coursing down over her shoulders, he drew her to him. There was solid power in her body.

"Feeling better now?" she asked. He went abstract before this woman, the last vestiges of his brain slipping out of his skull and down into his groin.

Later, he wondered why making love to her under the stream of water was so easy and straightforward, while earlier, covered as she was with his words, the very thought of it was like penetrating thick brush and thorns. He wished he could have discussed this riddle with Lena. But of course that was out of the question, although he was not convinced it should be.

After he had helped dry Carol off, she slipped into her panties, bra, and blouse and yanked up her skirt while he sat at the desk and opened a drawer and took out a checkbook. But she immediately touched his wrist.

"It's all right," she said. Her damp hair bespoke their intimacy, the fact that he had changed her.

"But I want to pay you."

"Not this time." An open shyness passed over her face at this perhaps unintended suggestion of her wish to return. "Maybe next time, if you want me again." And then she seemed alarmed by a new thought. "Or will you? I mean, you've done it, right?" Her earlier brashness was returning. "I guess you can't have a first time twice, right?" She laughed softly, but her eyes were imploring.

He stood up and moved in to kiss her goodbye, but she turned away slightly and he landed on her cheek. "I guess you're right," he said.

A certain hardness surfaced in her face now. "Then, look, maybe I'd better take the money."

"Right," he said. Reality is always such a relief, he thought, but why must it come with anger? He sat down and wrote a check and, with a twinge of shame, handed it to her.

She folded the check and stuck it in her purse. "This has been quite a day, hasn't it!" she yelled, and let out one of her horselaughs, startling him, for she had left off laughing like that since their initial moments as strangers. She's gone back to hunting deer now, he thought, and slogging through the tundra. After peeking out of concealment for a self-confident moment, she had scurried back in.

With Carol gone, he sat at his desk with his manuscript before him. Eighteen pages. His unfocused stare, his freshly washed body and spent force seemed to clarify and elevate him. He laid his palm on the pile of paper, thinking, I have dipped my toe over sanity's edge, so this had better be good. He rubbed his eyes and began to read his story when from far down below he heard the front door slam shut. Lena was home. Home with her face deeply wrinkled like a desiccated overripe pepper, her mouth drawn down, her breasts flat, the hateful brown nicotine smell on her breath. He was getting angry again, filling up with hate for her stubborn self-destruction.

Turning to his story, reading and rereading it, he felt a terrible amazement that its sweet flood of sympathy and love for her was thriving in him even now, almost as though a very young and unmarked man had written it, a man imprisoned inside him, a free-singing poet whose spirit was as real and convincing as the waves of the sea. What if he tried to turn the story into a kind of paean to her as she once had been—would she recognize herself and be reconciled? As he read, he saw how perfectly beautiful and poetic she still was in some buried center of his mind, and remembered how merely waking with her in the mornings had once filled him with happiness and purpose. Looking up from the manuscript to stare out across the barren rooftops, he felt a pang for Carol, whose brutally young presence was still vibrating in the room, and he wanted her to return maybe one more time so that he could write on her tight skin again and perhaps dredge up some other innocent thing that might be shivering in the darkness inside him, some remnant of love so terrified of coming out that it seemed to have disappeared—taking with it his art.

The Turpentine Still

I

That winter in the early fifties was unusually cold in New York, or at least seemed so to Levin. Unless at thirty-nine he had prematurely aged, an idea he secretly rather liked. For the first time in his life he really longed to get away to the sun, so when Jimmy P. returned all tanned from Haiti he listened with more than sociological interest to his rapturous report of a new democratic wind blowing through the country. Levin, rather ahead of his time, had come to doubt that politics ever really changed human behavior for the better, and apart from his business, had turned his mind to his music and a few exemplary books. But even in his more political past he had never quite trusted Jimmy's enthusiasms, although he felt warmed by Jimmy's naïve respect. A former Colgate wrestler with a flattened nose and sloping shoulders and a lisp, Jimmy was a sentimental Communist who idolized talented people, some of whom he represented as a publicity man, as well as Stalin and any individual who showed signs of flaunting whatever respectable rule happened to be in play at the moment. Rebellion to Jimmy was poetic. The day of his seventh birthday his heroic father had kissed the top of his head and left to join a revolution in Bolivia, and he never really returned except for some unexpected visits lasting a couple of weeks until he disappeared forever. But a fossilized shred of expectancy of the man's reappearance may still have lurked in Jimmy's mind, feeding his idolatrous bent. What he admired in Mark Levin was his courage in

having quit his job at the *Tribune* to take over his father's boring
leather business rather than editorialize with the new anti-Russian
bellicosity demanded of him. The truth, however, was that Levin's
mind was on Marcel Proust. During the past year or so Proust's
books had crowded very nearly everything else out of his thoughts
except for his music, his cherished combative wife Adele, and a
comforting hypochondria.

Haiti, for Levin and Adele, was the dark side of the moon. What
they knew of the place had been gleaned from their dentist's
*National Geographic*s and the Carnival photos of wild-looking
women, some strikingly beautiful, dancing in the streets, and Voodoo. But according to Jimmy, an inexplicably sophisticated outbreak of remarkable painting and writing was taking place now,
exploding like a suppressed force of nature in a country ruled for
generations by knife and gun. Jimmy's old friend, former *New
York Post* columnist Lilly O'Dwyer, would be eager to welcome
the Levins; she had moved down there to live with her expatriate
mother and knew everybody, especially the new young painters
and intellectuals who were trying to insinuate leftist democratic
reforms before being murdered or run out of the country. In the
last election, the opposition candidate, his wife, and their four
children had been hatcheted to death in their street-level parlor by
parties unknown.

The Levins were eager to go. Their last winter vacation—an
endless five days on a Caribbean beach—had sworn them off such
brainless self-indulgence, but this promised to be different. The
Levins were serious people; in an era before foreign films were
shown in New York, they joined a society devoted to showing
them in living rooms, and Mark especially was full of passion
about the French and Italians. He and his wife were both accom-
plished classical pianists and in fact had first met at their piano
teacher's home, she arriving for her lesson as he was leaving, and
were immediately drawn to each other's unusual height. Mark
was six four, Adele an even six feet; their pairing had normalized
what they had borne as a kind of deformation, even if it still
sprinkled a defensive irony over their conversations. Mark would

say, "I've finally found a girl into whose eyes I can look without sitting down."

"Yes," she would add, "and one of these days he's going to decide to look at me."

Adele's face under her bangs and short-cropped hair had an almost Oriental cast, her black eyes and wide cheekbones squinching up her gaze, and Mark had a long, horsey face and dense kinky hair and a shyly reluctant laugh, except for the days when, muttering in despair, he once again believed that his stomach had tragically dropped or that his heart had shifted slightly toward the center of his chest. Still, beneath a guarded irony they could be naïve enough to be swept up, at least at a discreet distance, in one or another idealistic scheme for social improvement. Eating lunch in his Long Island City office, he read *The New Republic* with an occasional dutiful glance at *The New Masses* and drank his milk sometimes coursing over *Remembrance of Things Past* in the French he loved only a little less than his music. They flew to Port-au-Prince in the roaring cabin of a Pan American Constellation, both of them fending off the premonition that the trip was fated to be one more bead on the string of their mistakes.

The O'Dwyer house, finished the year before, hung like a rambling concrete nest over Port-au-Prince's harbor. Designed by Mrs. Pat O'Dwyer and son-in-law, Vincent Breede, in her version of the Frank Lloyd Wright spirit, the house induced breezes to blow freely through its wide rooms and windows. Mrs. Pat was at the moment in deep concentration in a poker game with Episcopal Bishop Tunnel, Commander Banz of the United States heavy cruiser anchored in mid-harbor, and the Chief of Police, Henri Ladrun. Around them a vast Oriental carpet spread out to white walls covered with a Klee, a Leger, and a half-dozen brightly colored Haitian paintings, the latter testimony to Mrs. Pat's taste and acumen, their prices having skyrocketed since she had bought them well before Haitian painters had begun to sell. She had quickly taken a liking to Adele this evening, sharing anger at right-wing Congressmen and Republicans in general for instigating the current hunt for Reds in government, a specious slandering of liberal New Dealers in her view, and for being the party of the infamous Senator McCarthy.

Jimmy P. had primed the Levins about Mrs. Pat before they left New York. Starting out as a social worker in Providence, Rhode Island, she had early on concluded that what her mainly Catholic clients needed most were condoms, which at the time were under-the-counter items where they weren't illegal. Carrying boxes of them up from New York where she bought them on consignment, she graduated into becoming a distributor and finally opened a plant to manufacture them, ultimately acquiring great wealth. On vacation in Haiti, she perceived an even greater need for her product here and started another factory, this time donating the largest part of the production to nonprofit organizations. Nearing eighty now, handsome as ever with flowing silver hair and a blue-eyed gaze as placid as a pond, Mrs. Pat had a life that consisted of trying to make people get to the point. Impatience had converted her from Catholicism to the Christian Science that she interpreted as a faith in self-reliance, thus expressing her personal entrepreneurship and, in its larger application, her goal of a socialist, caring society.

Stretched out on a chaise near the card table reading her three-day-old *Times*, her daughter, Lilly said, "Jean Cours saw Charles Lebaye on the street yesterday." Defeated in her battle with weight, Lilly wore flowing white gowns and negligees. Locally made tin bracelets tinkled on her arms. Her eye had caught the entry of her eleven-year-old Peter, child of her first marriage to an alcoholic New York theatre critic, and she couldn't help thinking he had his father's dreaded black Irish moodiness and handsome elegance. Peter, in dirty tan shorts and barefoot, was stuffing his mouth with cherries out of a fruit bowl and not deigning to acknowledge her greeting, taunting her, she thought, for depriving him of his father.

Mrs. Pat hardly glanced up from her hand. "Saw Lebaye the Commissioner?"

"Yes."

"But I thought he died a week or so ago."

"He did." The card game stopped. Vincent and Levin came in

from the balcony to hear, and all the players turned to Lilly. "Cours saw him in his casket and attended the burial."

"How could he know it was Lebaye?"

"He's known him all his life. He says he went up to him on the street but he walked right past him. He's been turned into a zombie, he says."

"What's a zombie?" Adele asked, turning to Vincent, who as a black Jamaican was likely to know.

Vincent said, "A kind of slave. They claim to resurrect a dead person and draw out his spirit so he does whatever the capturer wants."

"But what is it really?" Levin asked, towering over the card table and feeling his carotid artery with his index finger to test his pulse.

"I don't know, I think they possibly drug the victim and pretend to bury him . . ."

"Cours swears he saw him going into the ground," Lilly said.

"He may have seen a casket going in, dear, but . . ." Vincent said.

"Some very strange things do happen," the bishop interrupted. All turned to him as the most experienced with Haitians, having converted a few as well as promoting the new painting and writing in the country. The whitewashed interior of his large church was covered with fresh pictures. With his melon-shaped pink face he had a pleasantly incompetent air, but he had sheltered revolutionaries and duped men with guns looking for them. "I'm not at all sure drugs are involved," he said. "They have a way of getting at the core of things, you know. I mean it's more like a kind of deep hypnotism that gets them to the center of a person."

"But they couldn't have actually buried the man," Commander Banz said, "he'd have suffocated." Black-haired, with a flawless profile, his white naval uniform with its standup collar perfectly fitted around his neck, he looked more the militant priest than the overweight bishop. Patriotically disagreeing with everything Mrs. Pat believed about U.S. imperial skulduggery, Banz found her a superior woman, an elegant mystery waiting to be solved. In any case, this house was the only place on the whole island where he felt welcome.

"Unless they had a way of slowing down his metabolism," Vincent said, "but I don't believe any of it."

Chief Ladrun, a short two-hundred-and-ninety-pounder whose belly seemed to start below his chin, was the only Haitian in the room. With a contented laugh he said, "It's all nonsense. Lots of people resemble one another. Voodoo is a religion like all the others, except there is more magic of course. But recall the loaves and fishes and the walking on water."

The conversation turned to magic, the game picked up again, and Lilly went back to her paper. Vincent and Levin returned to the balcony, where they sat side by side facing the harbor. Vincent, the only black man Levin had had the chance to talk to since his basket-shooting afternoons at college, was impressive to Levin. He knew by now that starting out as a poor, powerfully built Jamaican, Vincent held degrees from Oxford and a Swedish university and was in charge of the UN agency for reforestation of the Caribbean area. And Levin felt rather pleased by Vincent's open interest in him and his fascination with Proust.

"Is Voodoo serious?" Levin asked.

"Well, you know the saying—Haiti is ninety percent Catholic and a hundred percent Voodoo. My personal view is that it's more of a nuisance than anything else, but I think all religion at bottom is a means of social control, so I can't take its spiritual side too seriously. This country needs scientists and clear thinkers, not magicians. But I suppose like anything else it has its good uses. In fact, I've used it myself." He tended to excuse any assertion with a chuckle.

He had arranged for a planting, he explained, of several thousand fast-growing trees, charcoal being the basic fuel here. Hardly a year later the small seedlings had all been cut down and carted off for burning. "After I finished being outraged," he said, "I happened to be at my barber's one day and he suggested I look up the local *houngan*, who might help. I found the guy; for a donation he arranged a ceremony to make the planting area sacred. A big crowd showed up to watch the planting, and nobody bothered the sacred trees for three years until they were properly harvested. I must say I hated the idea but it did work." After a moment's silence he asked, "Why are you interested in Haiti?"

"I didn't know I was," Levin said, "but there's some kind of atmospheric attraction, a kind of secrecy, maybe. I really don't know."

He looked at the black man's face in the glow of yellow light from the living room, and with the dark waters of the harbor beyond him and the sparse lights of the impoverished city below, the strangeness of his being here struck him, and with it an apprehension, like finding himself over his head swimming in the sea. He enjoyed his safety but longed for the risks of an artist rather than the waste of his daily wrangle with business. "I hop along solidly on one foot, the other suspended over a cliff," he once said to Adele after they had finished a Schubert duet that had moved him almost to tears.

"Would you and your wife like to see more of the country? I have to go up into the pine forest tomorrow." Vincent faced him, a thick-shouldered man in his thirties, infinitely confident and at ease in this black country.

Eager to see into this strange place, Levin instantly agreed, surprised by the shock of anticipation he had almost forgotten was still alive in him. Proust's beloved face flashed across his mind, *like a dead flower*, he thought.

II

When Adele saw the tiny Austin in the driveway of the Gustafson Hotel she begged off, preferring to spend the day sightseeing in town rather than sitting sideways for hours in its backseat. Actually, she planned to wander around the hotel for a while; its unremodeled French colonial style reminded her of a sunken relic. Through its tall, gauzy curtained windows she could imagine Joseph Conrad passing by or sitting in one of the lobby's enormous rattan chairs, and there must be some shops that Mark would have no patience for. She waved happily at the departing little car.

As the Austin moved past her, the early sun was still low enough to flood her amused face under her wide-brimmed, black straw hat; it was a soft light that seemed to elevate and suspend her in space, and Levin reprimanded himself for not making love to her more often. What was it now, a week? Maybe longer. A quiet alarm sounded in him. Tossing their ironies and sage observations back and forth was no substitute for horned clashes such as he had in business, and he resolved to begin trying to get to know Adele again. Seven years into their marriage, and they had lost a lot of curiosity. He had to stop hiding himself. He had to start listening again.

Vincent threaded the car down the town's main streets and around telephone poles that drooped broken wires, some of them planted like distracted afterthoughts in the middle of streets or a few feet from a curb, some on the sidewalks. Overhanging second stories shaded the interiors of shops open to the street, in most of which men seemed to be repairing pots, car fenders, broken furniture. An enormous store on one corner sold tires, stoves, refrigerators, meat, fish, dresses, boots, kerosene, gas. The bank's windows were spotless, and through them Levin saw young women cashiers in starched white blouses working solemnly at what were no doubt the best jobs in town. A couple of neatly dressed, unsmiling businessmen stood on the sidewalk, hands clasped in a dignified morning handshake. There was still time for everything here.

Vincent tugged at the steering wheel around turns. "English steering," he laughed, "tight but accurate. This thing is built to improve character—I think I've pushed it more than I've driven it. If there's a rumor of a distant mist the thing won't start."

The town thinned out and the surprisingly good blacktop road wound through clusters of shacks and tiny gardens, almost always worked by a woman while the man sat nearby talking to her or a friend. "The men don't seem to do anything much," Levin observed.

"Africa," Vincent said. "The man hunted and the woman did the house and the planting. Of course, there's nothing here left to hunt. Some of them do work hard, but they need education. It's desperate. This country is waiting to start existing."

"What can they export?" Levin asked. Every cluster of shacks

seemed to have a hand-lettered sign advertising *reparations pneu.*
"Aside from repairs?"

"Bauxite. The ore to make aluminum. There used to be gold.
Not much, but it's long gone."

Levin found himself trying to imagine improving things. "And
what could they do with more education? Aside from emigrating?"

"Get a decent government, to start with. That would be a great
thing." Vincent's grave intensity deepened his voice. He had suddenly stopped kidding; Levin was surprised. It reminded him of
his own frantic political arguments in college, so long ago.

The car had been climbing for half an hour past deepening
pine growth, and the air smelled cool and fresh now. "Who owns
all this?"

"The State. But the politicians are stealing it away."

"How?"

"Fiddling the books."

"Is it being replanted?"

"No. That's what I'm trying to get done. It's doomed, the whole
forest, but public office is a license to steal," Vincent said.

Levin's body tightened with a kind of combativeness that he
instantly recognized as absurd—it wasn't his forest, and anyway,
what could he do about it?

A lone woman suddenly appeared out of the forest leading a
stubborn goat by a rope. Her long body moved like an effortless
dream figure that hardly touched the earth, and the tail of a long
crimson bandanna was wound around her head and streamed
over her breast like a wound. She held out one gracefully waving
arm for balance, like a dancer.

"A lot of them are very beautiful," Levin said.

"That's the pity of it, yes."

The road leveled out and, in a clearing, Levin saw an Alpine-
style log cabin with a steeply pitched roof and deep eaves, here
where it never snowed.

"I have to pay respects to the manager," Vincent said as he got
out and disappeared into the building. Levin got out of the car
and stretched, going up on his toes. The silence was like a soft

stroke on his flesh. At that moment, his standing on this particular spot on the earth was somehow miraculous. What was he doing here? In the car Vincent had mentioned a man he would have to talk to today. He had laughed about the fellow, a onetime Madison Avenue ad executive who had gone native up here. He had said more but the noise from the transmission had garbled it. Now he emerged from the building, laughing along with a black man who hung back and was waving goodbye.

"One of the lesser crooks," Vincent said as he drove away. In a few minutes, they were off the road altogether, following an earthen trail through the woods. Trees were much larger here, harder to get at and fell than the ones at the periphery of the forest. Presently they came to a simple log bungalow. Newspaper was stuffed into a broken window and a spavined red Ford pickup sat alongside it. Metal parts of some machine were scattered over the weedy clearing, along with bald tires, a large awning, window frames, a rusted hand pump, and a forlorn outhouse leaning against a tree. Everything seemed to be leaning. The porch steps were warped. A clothesline stretched between two trees with a single bra hanging from it. Vincent turned off the engine but remained behind the wheel. His chuckling ironies had disappeared, and Levin thought he saw some tension around his eyes.

"Who's this again? I didn't quite catch . . ."

"Douglas. It's a ticklish problem," he said, for the first time looking uncertain. "I shouldn't have allowed myself to get into it, but at the time I didn't think he'd ever get this far."

"You've lost me. What are you talking about?" Vincent had evidently forgotten that not everyone was up on this situation.

He settled back in his seat, his eyes on the house with only an occasional glance toward Levin. "I like the man but he's very odd. Good-hearted, you know, but . . . well, I guess you could call him silly. Quit an important job a couple of years ago with BBD&O on Madison Avenue to cruise around with his family on a surplus Navy boat, showing films to people on the various islands." Now he laughed, but the tension stayed in his face. "Actually thought he could make a living selling tickets to the natives! And of course there weren't enough customers with a quarter in their pockets, not in the Caribbean. So he arrived here, probably looking for something he could do with his boat, I think. And—God knows where the idea came from, I've never understood that part of it—but I think it was when he saw this gigantic tank near the dock he'd tied up at. It may have come off some large wreck. It could hold, I don't know, probably a few thousand gallons. And there it lay doing nothing. He hung around, living on the boat with his family, filling himself up with frustration about the tank."

"Because it wasn't doing anything."

"Of course! Yes!" He laughed again. "We're all forever saving Haiti. You seem to have some of that feeling yourself."

"Well, not really, although I guess I can understand it. Maybe it's the people; they seem so . . ."

"Sweet, yes. And so full of imag*ination*," he gave the word a celebratory Jamaican lilt. "Anyway, he heard of the forest and came up here one day, and the thought hit him that with all this pine he could harvest the resin for turpentine and set up a distillation process. Turpentine's a big thing in Haiti; they use it for everything from rheumatism to chest and sex problems and a dozen other things. So he had the tank and suddenly here was a terrific use for it." He burst out laughing, but the concern was still there in his eyes. "Not only have a use for the tank but help protect the forest, and create maybe a couple of dozen good jobs for people. It had a lot of different virtues, like turpentine itself."

He paused, still staring at the house. His lips had dried, and he wet them with his tongue. "I really didn't mean to, but I guess I inadvertently encouraged him. I was the only one around with some scientific background, although what he really needed was engineering advice. He had some friends at the ad agency send him literature about distillation technology, and he pumped me for the chemistry I barely remembered, and he was off. First thing, he'd learned that the tank had to lie at a specific angle—I've forgotten exactly what degree that was—but he got hold of some surveyor's stuff and went about up here until he'd found a grade with precisely the incline he needed, and hired a couple of men to set up concrete pillows to support the tank. Of course the thing was far too large to be trucked up here so I unfortunately found him a welder I knew down in the port, and he had the thing cut into sections, brought it up piece by piece in his pickup and welded it back into shape again. The whole thing was so absurd that I . . ." He broke off, dead serious now. "I guess I feel somewhat responsible, although I tried to discourage him. Even so . . ." He paused again, confused. "I don't know, maybe I encouraged him too, in the sense that I was glad that *somebody* was enthusiastic about this country's possibilities. I simply—I don't know, I think I should have taken it more seriously. The danger, I mean."

"How long has he been at this?"

"It must be at least eight months, maybe a year. It's crazy—if you need a nail there's nothing between here and the port, so he or his wife had to be running up and down the mountain to fetch the least little thing."

"But what's worrying you? It all seems harmless enough," Levin said.

"He's ready to light the fire."

"And?"

"That tank will fill with vapor. He's got some kind of relief valve on the top, but Christ, I don't know if it's the right one; it's just some damned thing he picked up in the port. Valves like this have different capacities and I know nothing about them, any more than he does." A nervous high-pitched laugh escaped him now: "The steam pressure has to be around a hundred seventy pounds per square inch and all his equipment is secondhand or improvised. That's a lot of pressure for equipment that's been rewelded, with welds on top of welds, and fiddled around with. God knows, he could blow off the top of this mountain or set fire to the forest and kill himself in the bargain!"

"When is this supposed to happen?"

"Today."

"You'd better steal his matches and get us the hell out of here." Both men burst out laughing. "What *are* you going to do?"

"Well, I'm certainly going to try to talk him out of it. He's got to get some professional engineering advice."

"You'd think he'd have done that a long time ago."

Suddenly, out of the corner of his eye, Levin saw a face looking in at his window, but the instant he turned it was gone. It had seemed the face of a child.

"That's Catty," Vincent said, slipping out of his seat. As they walked up to the house he continued, "There's also Richard, who's seven, I think, and she's about nine. Listen." He halted, facing Levin. "I wish you'd ask him where the kids go to school. Because I don't think they have in all the time they've been up here, they're just running wild with the local kids. He won't listen to me, thinks I'm one of these over-conventional niggers. Could you do that?"

A woman appeared on the narrow porch, her arm in a white sling. "Vincent! How nice!" With a careful glance down at a broken step, she hurried across the weeds to them with her good hand extended like a hostess at some elegant lunch. Denise was small and vivacious, in her mid-forties. A wild distraction flared in her eager eyes, and her fair hair was twisted and knotted, probably, Levin thought, because she couldn't wash it with one hand. She never ceased to smile, but "Please rescue" was like a lit sign hanging over her head.

"What happened?" Vincent asked, indicating the sling.

"Oh Vincent," she began, and grasped his upper arm for more than physical support, a wan look on her face now. "I was unloading one of the fifty-five-gallon drums, and it slipped and hit me. I'm healing but it was awful for a while, the truck wouldn't start and the children were off somewhere and Douglas was over at the tanks. So I had to walk holding it together . . ."

Vincent, Levin saw, was clearly her savior, her one hope of escaping whatever it was that had an obviously upper-class woman grappling fifty-five-gallon drums. She must have felt she was dreaming until it cracked her bone. "Come, come inside, he'll be so glad to see you." Levin was only now introduced as they entered the house, but she hardly glanced at him, her whole attention fixed on Vincent.

The room they entered had a dank smell. In one wall was an

immense fireplace made of round boulders with a mantel on which four or five tattered books stood. There were no chairs or tables, only a few scattered wooden boxes, on one of which lay the unwashed dishes of a recent meal. A dusty filigreed pump organ stood against one wall, and on one of the boxes sat a perspiring man in work boots, torn jeans and T-shirt, and an oil-stained Yankees cap, studying blueprints spread out on his lap and around the floor, his tongue sticking out between his lips. One lens of his small wire-rimmed glasses was cracked, and the misshapen frame had a temple piece missing, replaced by a white string looped around his ear. Several days' growth of beard had been shaved in spots, as though absentmindedly, leaving graying tufts. There was a darkness in the room despite the sunny day; the windows set high in the walls under the broad eaves of the roof seemed to admit shadow rather than light.

"Vincent's here, darling!" the woman fairly shrieked as they entered.

It took Douglas a good half minute to come out of his rapt concentration. Then he sprang up and threw his arms around Vincent, still clutching the blueprint, and quickly shook hands with Levin without looking at him. His oil-stained hand was rough as sandpaper. Douglas was tall and politely stooped, and Levin recognized the Ivy League as soon as he began to speak.

"Son of a gun, where've you been, I've been waiting for you all week!" Three children—two white, one black—flicked past the screen door and disappeared as quick as deer.

"Would you like a tea before we go?" he asked, his arm lingering on Vincent's shoulder, a comradely gesture from which Vincent seemed to shrink. "I think we have tea, don't we, darling?" He looked around for his wife but she had vanished, and he called toward the back of the house, "Is there tea, darling?"

When no answer came back Vincent suggested, "Why don't we sit down for a minute first, Doug?"

"Of course, yes, sorry." Douglas leaped up and pulled another box over, his gait rocking, bear-like. At this point Vincent, aware that Douglas had not really taken in Levin's presence, introduced him again; Douglas turned to him with surprise, as though he had dropped through the ceiling. "Yes! Very nice to meet you. Sorry for the accommodations," he chuckled and turned back to Vincent, who had sat down facing him. His wife reappeared and sat on a box, her good hand resting protectively on the cast. She had managed to brush out her hair and change into fresh jeans and a peach blouse which sketched out her breasts, and this attempt at renewal touched Levin. He sensed in her high nervousness the culmination of some struggle which had determined her to enlist Vincent on her side.

But Douglas seemed oblivious. "I've been ready to go since last weekend." Despite his smile a touch of complaint was in his tone. "What's happened? Where have you been?"

Vincent set himself for a second or two and began, "I've been busy. But I really have to remind you, Doug, that I've never set myself up as . . . I mean I don't feel I have a particular responsibility for this."

"Of course not. I never expected that. But I did think you had an *interest*."

"I do, but I may as well be candid with you, Doug, I don't really feel confident in the whole process. As far as I can understand it anyway. As I told you last time I was here—I've asked around concerning the type of tree we have up here—"

"I'm aware of that," Douglas interrupted.

"*Pinus sylvestris* is the right kind—"

"Well, it's the best kind, yes, but there's plenty of resin in these too."

"Doug, I have to ask you to listen to me." Vincent's voice had risen and the hard core in it struck Levin for the first time. Douglas kept quiet but the effort showed. "They apparently call for a live steam temperature of around a hundred degrees centigrade in the melter—"

"Eighty-five to a hundred."

"Apparently that depends on the quality of the resin, and the kind you have here is poor. My point, Doug, is this: you've got rewelded tanks, and I've noticed some rust—"

"That's entirely superficial."

"But how sure are you of that? The pressure can go to 150 psi and the temperature to 170. All I'm trying to tell you, Doug, is that—"

"The thing is perfectly safe!" Douglas stood up. "Where did you get your information?"

"I talked to Commander Banz."

"Off that *battleship*? What could he possibly know about turpentine?"

"He comes from Alabama. They do a lot of it there and his family was involved—"

"Gawwd!" Douglas turned his face toward a deaf heaven, "a *Navy guy* spouting off about turpentine!" He tramped around snapping his cap on his thigh like a thwarted boy. "I've been in command, Vincent, you know that. Sixteen months on a fucking tin-can destroyer, and I'm here to tell you that no Navy guy knows piss about turpentine. He's thinking of his goddamn boilers, which are a whole different story."

Levin had a hard time keeping a serious look on his face. But a certain genuineness nevertheless reached him in Douglas's anguish, an authentic outcry such as he had never met with, at least not in a cultivated man. Neither he nor anyone he knew, he suddenly realized, had ever cared this much and this openly. But all for the sake of turpentine? Levin doubted that money lay behind it all— turpentine was too inexpensive, he reasoned. What was it then?

"Darling, you really need to at least listen to Vincent," Denise said.

"Well, are you proposing something?" Douglas asked.

Vincent paused for a moment, then spoke: "I have nothing but respect, Doug, for what you've been trying to accomplish up here—"

"God's sake, Vince, you'd have jobs up here, you'd have self-respect for once, there'd be people working and preventing all this theft. This country is *dying*, Vincent!"

His eyes were filled with pain, the sight of which repelled Levin, who promptly damned himself for insensitivity. A kind of undirected disgust lingered around the edges of his mind as the two men and Denise agreed to drive over to the still and have a look at things. Levin found it incredible that despite all the uncertainty Douglas was apparently still determined to start up the process.

Vincent and Levin rode in the Austin, with Douglas and Denise following in the pickup. Vincent's temper had surfaced and he kept plunging the car ahead and braking. "This is really not my business, you know." For some reason he was apologizing to Levin, who himself felt some unnamable responsibility, why and for what he could not begin to explain to himself.

"He's put together a lot of junk. It's junk! I'm certainly not going to hang around if he lights it up."

"What about their kids?"

"I don't know. I just don't know."

Levin saw steel cups on some of the tree trunks, and Vincent explained they caught the resin flowing from cuts in the cambium layer above them. The air here was almost cold, like Northern Europe. Odd that a few miles down the mountain was the warm sea. "Of course, they're the wrong kind of pine. But don't ask me why. This is not my expertise."

"What is it with him?" Levin asked. "Vanity? I mean he can't be expecting to make a lot of money for himself, or can he?"

"Possibly, if he had a number of stills, but he only has this one. I'm not sure it's vanity, though. He does love the country, although I think she's just about had it here."

"I forgot to ask him about the children's schooling."

"Doesn't matter, I know what he'd answer: he'll point to those books on the mantel. A history of the world as of 1925 or something, a chemistry textbook from around 1910, a Kipling collection of stories, and one other I can't recall . . . oh yes, a world atlas. Which still has India colored British pink."

"What about her? Isn't she concerned?"

"You saw his stubbornness." He paused for a moment. "He's in love, you see."

"With?"

"I don't know how to put it. With the idea, maybe. Of . . ." He struggled for the word, then seemed to give up. "You see, he was after German subs in the area during the war and fell in love. With the sun and that marvelous sea. That was before the tourists, of course, or anything like a technological civilization. There

were horse carriages in the port, and the beaches were like vir-
gins, he said to me once. It was all terribly poor but hadn't got
spoiled yet. So he dreamed about living down here and cooked up
this idea of showing movies on that boat. I sometimes wonder if
it's really very simple—he just wanted to *start* something. We all
do, I guess, but for some people it's absolutely necessary. To be
the germ of something, the inventor, the one who begins it. I say
that because he had a very good spot in New York and the house
in Greenwich, the whole pot. But he wasn't *starting* anything. In
a way he was looking for a fight, I guess." He laughed, shook his
head. "And this is the place, if that's what you want."

"He wants to do good, you think?"

"Oh yes, he wants that, but I've come to think that's maybe not
the main thing."

"To kind of invent himself. To create something."

"I think so."

Levin stared at the dirt path ahead, the holes and boulders. He
had no children and had come to believe that his low sperm count
was lucky. He just wasn't a father, certainly not now that he was
approaching forty. For one thing he had all the time he wanted for
piano, and Adele did too. No regrets about that. Or would she
agree? Bumping along in the tiny car, his knees up to the dashboard,
he wondered whether Adele was really as content with childlessness
as she made out. He thought of painful hints, gestures, a tear he had
once noticed in her eye when looking into the cradle of a friend's
infant son. He inwardly groaned at these memories. What was he
doing in Haiti, in this nonsensical place where he understood nothing? He felt bereft, abandoned, and suddenly he wondered whether
Adele loved him, even whether her quick decision to stay in town
today had some other purpose. A ridiculous thought—she would
never betray him. But there it was. And instantly the idea effloresced
into bloom: she had waited till the last minute when it would be too
late for him to cancel the trip, leaving her free to move into that
unknowable city, a white woman alone. . . .

They were on the highway for no more than half a mile when
Vincent turned off again onto a path, and they came on it suddenly

in a clearing: the black tank lay up against the mountain at an angle like a resting monster, connected by a tangle of piping to several smaller tanks placed at various heights beside and above it. A massive pile of pine logs twice a man's height stood nearby, as well as a cement mixer, barrels, steel drums, sleeping dogs, and half-a-dozen men moving about drinking water, laughing together or staring into space.

Levin got out of the car as Denise approached. Vincent walked over to the tanks with Douglas, who was explaining something. Denise said in a rather conspiratorial hush, "We have an organ, you know."

"Yes, I noticed it."

"Perhaps you could play for us."

"Oh. Well . . ." How did she know he played? Unanswered questions were exhausting him. He wasn't even sure he'd told Vincent that he and Adele played, and then Vincent's voice turned him toward the tanks.

"You're just going to have to listen to me, Douglas!" he was yelling. And Douglas was literally writhing as he tried to interrupt his friend, twisting his head toward the sky and stamping one foot. "I know what this means to you, Douglas, but it's all a mistake, you can't possibly start this up without a professional inspection."

"You—"

"No!" Vincent yelled, a pleading tone in his voice, "I'm not competent, I've told you a hundred times, and I will not be held responsible—"

"But the pressures aren't—"

"I don't know that and you don't either! I ask you to wait! Just wait, for God's sake, until you can find someone who—"

"I can't wait," Douglas said quietly.

It would always strike Levin that at this instant, when Douglas had stopped shouting and became quiet, a very distant chain saw went silent. As though the whole world was listening in on this.

"Why can't you wait?" Vincent asked, curiosity overtaking his anger.

"I'm ill," Douglas said.

"What do you mean?"

"I have a cancer."

Vincent instinctively reached out and grasped his friend's wrist. The workers were all beyond earshot at the moment, standing around waiting for Douglas's orders. "I must see it working before I go," Douglas said.

"Yes," Vincent agreed. Denise had gone over to her husband and was clasping his arm. Levin saw how in love they were, she so unfitted for this life, sacrificing even her children's education so Douglas could live out his necessary fantasy. "I'm returning to the port this afternoon. Let me make some calls," Vincent said. "I'm sure I can get someone, if necessary, from our Miami office. There must be people there who'd know whom to bring down, somebody who could give us an expert opinion." The *us* seemed to melt Douglas's stiff defensive posture; at last they were in this together, at least to an extent that validated the thing, making it real. Douglas gripped Vincent's neck and drew him close; Denise stretched forward and kissed Vincent's cheek. The relief playing over Vincent's face astonished Levin, who felt grateful that nothing terrible had exploded between the two friends, but unlike Vincent, he wasn't quite taken in by the outbreak of hopefulness on all sides. After all, nothing about the tanks or the process had been resolved; an air of doom still hung undisturbed over the project. Nothing had really happened except that the three of them had been joined in some passion of mutual reconciliation.

Back at the bungalow, Douglas and Denise stood waving goodbye as Vincent backed the car to make the turn onto the path. They were strikingly happy, Levin thought, at peace, where only a couple of hours ago tensions were flying about all over the place. The car negotiated the holes and boulders. Levin wondered what he had missed that would explain why everything had changed, especially in Vincent. And all he could come up with was the obvious—that Vincent had at long last accepted, however inadvertently, if not a responsibility for the project then a kind of participation in it by offering to bring in expertise from abroad. To that extent he had identified himself with Douglas's dream.

"Will you be calling Miami?" Levin asked, unable to strip the ironical coating from his voice.

Vincent glanced at him. "Certainly. Why do you ask?" He seemed almost offended by Levin's tone.

"Just that . . ." Levin broke off. The whole event was so tangled in his mind that he didn't know where to grasp one of its threads. "You suddenly seemed to, I don't know, believe in the process. I'd had the idea you didn't at all."

"I don't think I said I didn't believe in it, but I still don't know if I do or don't. I was just glad he showed a willingness to put off firing the thing up."

"I see," Levin said.

They fell silent. In other words, Levin reasoned, for the sake of peace Vincent was pretending to believe in the reality of the process while Douglas was similarly pretending that someone beside himself was sharing responsibility for what could turn out a catastrophe. The two of them were creating a kind of fantasy of shared belief. Levin felt a certain pleasure rising in himself, the pleasure of clarity, and his mind inevitably turned to Proust. But now he saw the great author differently; Proust, he said to himself, was also a pretender. He pretended to an absolute accuracy in describing towns, streets, smells, people, but after all he was describing nothing but his fantasy.

They'd stayed longer on the mountain than Levin realized. They lunched late by the roadside on sandwiches Vincent had brought, and by the time they reached the lower edges of the forest, it was dark. Levin had taken over the wheel to relieve Vincent, and as they chatted, Levin had to strain to make out the winding, tilted road. The headlights, he realized, were penetrating the darkness less and less, until abruptly they went out and the engine died. He coasted over to the side of the road and kicked the starter button on the floor, with no result. "The battery's died," he said. Vincent found a flashlight in the glove compartment, and they got out of the car and lifted the hood. Levin wiggled the battery cable and tried the starter again, but it was dead. The two men stood in the total dark, in the silence.

"What now?" Levin asked. "Are there people around, you suppose?"

"They're watching us right now."

"Where?" Levin turned toward the roadsides.

"Everywhere."

"Why?"

"Waiting to see what happens." Vincent laughed appreciatively.

"You mean they're actually sitting out there in the dark?"

"That's right." Vincent sat down on the front bumper and leaned forward.

Levin cocked his ears toward the dark roadsides. "Can't hear them."

"You won't." Vincent giggled.

"And what would you say their mood was?"

"Curious."

Levin sat on the bumper next to Vincent. He could hear his friend's breathing, but in the absence of any nightshine he could barely define his head. Even the sky was lightless. Could there be people out there watching from the dark? What were they thinking? Would they decide to rob us? Or were we like two performers, he wondered, whom they enjoyed watching from their theater in the overgrowth?

"Suppose we let her coast down? We might find a village, don't you think?"

"Ssh."

Levin listened, and soon registered the noise of a distant motor. Both men stood and looked toward the sound, toward the mountaintop where they had come from. Headlights were moving up there in the remote distance, and presently the truck appeared out of the night, an open flatbed packed with a crowd of people standing in the back. Vincent and Levin waved down the truck, and Vincent explained to the driver in Creole that their battery had quit. The driver opened the door and hopped down. He was young and trim and spoke surprisingly good English. "I think there may be a helpful thing here," he said as he walked to the back of the truck, where he lowered the tailgate and shouted at the passengers to jump down. They poured off the truck without complaint. This was interesting for them. The driver leaped onto the bed and wrestled a tarpaulin off a dim pile of junk, speaking English all the while to impress *les blancs*, no doubt. "I believe is here something possibly . . . Ha!" His passengers burst into triumphant laughter with him as he danced off the truck bed and onto the road, where he handed a car battery to Levin. He hurried around to the truck's cabin and pulled some wrenches from under the seat, returned to the car, disconnected the battery, dropped the fresh one in, and clamped the cables. Levin squirmed into the car, turned the key, and the engine screamed to life and the headlights came on. He slid out and stood laughing along with the driver and the delighted Vincent.

"Let us pay you," he said, "*s'il vous plaît, permettez . . .*" He pulled out his wallet before the Austin's thankfully bright light beams.

"No-no," the driver said, holding up a palm. Then he spoke Creole to Vincent, who translated for Levin.

"He says we should simply return the battery to him in the next few days."

"But what's his address?" Levin asked. The driver was already climbing back into his truck.

"He just said to deliver it to one of the piers and ask for Joseph. Everybody knows him, he says."

"But which pier?"

"I have no idea," Vincent said as they got back into the car and started down the mountain.

Levin drove again, struggling now with amazement at their salvation, and beyond that, the trusting generosity of the driver. And even more impenetrable, the absence of surprise among the onlookers. Was it all simply another scene in the ongoing fantasy of their life, the sudden appearance of these *blancs* on the dark road, the appearance of this battery from under the tarpaulin? And how did the battery happen to be the right size for the Austin? And charged too?

"What do you suppose they made of all this?" Levin asked.

"Of what just happened?"

"Yes. Us suddenly being there, and him having the battery and all."

Vincent chuckled. "God knows. Probably that it was inevitable. Like everything else."

"They wouldn't think it odd that he didn't even want money from us? And trusted us to return the battery?"

"I doubt they'd think that very strange. Because in a way *everything* is so strange. This was just one more thing, I imagine. Most of what they live through can't be easily explained. It's all one wide flow of . . . whatever. Of time, I suppose." He fell silent except to indicate to Levin which turns to make through the streets. The town slept in darkness except for an occasional store, no more than a counter open to the street where people sat with soft drinks under orange lights, and children played at the edge of the dark, and a tethered donkey munched in a garbage pile.

III

Thirty years passed. Thirty-three to be exact, as Mark Levin tried to be concerning time, "the last items in the inventory," as he called the passing hours and weeks. He was becoming obsessed by time, he told himself, not necessarily a good thing. Past seventy now, he was dropping tulip bulbs into holes he had punched in the small garden alongside the front door of his house. As Adele had had him do every fall so long ago, but this time he mused on whether he would see the flowers. Everything now, as in some dreams, took forever to get done. He could hear the bumbling of waves in the near distance, felt a certain empty gratitude to the ocean for being there. The net bag empty, he covered the bulbs and stamped down the thin, sandy soil, took the digging tool to the garage and then went through his basement, up the stairs, and into his kitchen. The *Times* lay flat and virginal on the kitchen table, its news already outdated, and he wondered how many tons of *Times* he had read in his life and whether it had really mattered at all. He had seen the few good movies in surrounding towns and had no interest in television. The piano, which he hadn't touched in more than two months, remonstrated in its black silence. The light was dying fast outside on the sandy street. What to do with his evening and his night, aside from confronting self-pity and fending it off?

He had played less and less in the six years since Adele's death, gradually realizing that he had been playing for her approval, to a degree anyway, so that now it had lost some of its point. In any case he had finally agreed with himself that he would never reach the level he had once dreamed of, most certainly not alone. He was sitting at the kitchen counter where he had landed. There was no pain in his healthy body, but a practiced inner eye still supervised the beating of his heart and the positioning of his stomach. The question before him, he said to himself, was whether and why to get up and where to move to: the living room, his bedroom, the guest bedroom, or perhaps a walk in the empty street. He was a free man. But freedom without obligations, as it turned out, was something else. In such stasis his thoughts usually coursed over the ranks of the dead, of his small circle of friends, the last of whom he had recently survived, which left him wondering, with some flicker of pride, why he had been so chosen. But all the main questions were answerless.

Call Marie? Have a lover-like conversation with that dear person, only to remain unchanged by the dialing of her number, still more than twice her age, still and forever her mere friend? How stupid, how awful, to be the friend of the person one loves. "But if I made love to you," she'd said, "it would wall me off from someone else." Yes, someone of her generation. Time again. But the selfish bastard inside him howled before going agreeably silent. Better not to call her but to launch himself in some potent direction. He would be a free man until he fell to his knees.

And inevitably his mind, like a circling bird, landed on Adele, returning again and again to that worn but still glamorous vision of her from the Austin, standing before the Gustafson Hotel in her black straw, wide-brimmed hat, and the low morning sun holding her suspended in its yellowish light, fixed there, as it turned out, forever. How really beautiful she had looked then! How he wished to have shown her more of his love! But maybe he had; who knew? He got up, slipped into a light jacket that hung beside the front door, and went into the street where the fall chill braced him.

The sun would be setting. He walked, his steps shorter than in time past, down the street and onto the beach, where he stood in the sand watching the sun slipping down to the horizon. Stiffly he lowered himself to sit on the cool sand. Soft waves made way for an occasional boomer. The beach was empty, as were most of the houses behind him now that October was looming. He thought of Douglas up there in the pine forest. Probably dead now. As poor Vincent was, after the local doctor had given him a mistaken injection of some kind the year after their short acquaintance.

Did anyone but him remember Vincent, he wondered? (And how could it have been thirty-three years ago when in his mind it was all so fresh?) Levin recalled now, staring at the waves, that Jimmy P., also dead, had once mentioned that the turpentine still had never been lit. Out of fear, Levin wondered, or for some business reason? Or had Jimmy gotten it wrong? But the main questions were always answerless.

He hated his loneliness, it was like a rank closet, a damp towel, loose shoes. Then why not offer marriage to the girl, make her his heir? But money had no meaning to her, and he had so little life to promise. But this endless string of days that threatened to unroll emptily before him was intolerable. Why not a trip to Haiti? Try to see how it all turned out. The thought, absurd as it seemed, quickened him, drove off his weariness. But who would he look up? Mrs. Pat was surely gone by now, and probably her daughter too. It was so odd that he alone might be carrying the pictures of these people in his mind. Except for him keeping them alive in the soft knot of tissue under his skull they might have no existence. And of them all, it was Douglas who returned most vividly to Levin, especially his Yankees cap and throaty voice; he could still hear him shouting, "This country is *dying*, Vincent!" The anguish in that man! The longing he must have had to . . . to what? What was he about?

Staring at the gray sea, the darkening sky, it was suddenly

obvious to Levin that for Douglas the turpentine still must have been his work of art. Douglas was sacrificing himself, his career, his wife and children, to the creation of a vision of some beauty in his mind. Unlike me, Levin said to himself, or most people who never get to intercept that invisible beam which stirs them with its power to imagine something new. So what matters, he thought, was creation, the creation of what has not yet been. "And this I could never do," he said aloud, chilled now and tramping excitedly up the beach toward his house.

He stood still for a moment in the middle of his living room, struck by the question of whether—what was his name? The young son of—what was her name again? Yes, Lilly O'Dwyer. Peter! Yes, it was Peter. Could he still be there? He'd only be in his forties now. For the first time in memory, Levin felt life surging into him again. How glorious to be here, standing upright on the earth! To be free to think! To ride one's imaginings! He clapped his hands together and quickly found Adele's old address book in the drawer under the phone, and searched for their travel agent's number. Kendall Travel. Mrs. Kendall, yes. A very helpful woman.

"Kendall Travel, can I help you?"

She was alive! He recognized the voice. A wave of self-pity engulfed him as he realized he was going to Haiti, but alone. Then anguish all over again for his extinguished wife. And finally in the plane, wondering why he was doing this, going to a country that by all accounts had sunk into the abyss. What was behind it, he wondered? Could it be simply that he was an idle old man who needed something to do?

Peter O'Dwyer remembered him, an amazement to Levin who, however, had recognized him the moment he entered his small chaotic office on the pier. Two prefab metal windows looked out on the harbor with its half-sunk derelicts and a rusting freighter whose deck showed no sign of life. A dozen or so black workers were assembling and packing chairs in the corrugated steel warehouse through which Levin had passed to get here.

Peter was still the dark-skinned, barefoot child Levin recalled eating all the cherries on their first evening, only big now, almost his height, and powerfully built. There was something like meanness in his face, or just toughness, it was hard to tell, but he had remarkable water-gray eyes, like Weimaraner dogs.

"We make chairs for export, woven raffia," Peter replied to Levin's questions. "What brings you to Haiti? And how'd you know to find me?"

"The Gustafson manager."

"Right. Phil. What can I do for you?" There was something punished in his eyes.

"I won't take your time—"

"I remember you playing that night, a duet with your wife."

"I'd forgotten that."

"It was the first time anyone had gotten real music out of that piano."

"I hadn't thought of that in years. In fact, now that you mention it, I think it was a Schubert piece."

"I don't know that kind of music but it was really terrific." Peter's open admiration surprised Levin and helped launch him now. "You still playing?"

"No, not seriously. My wife died, for one thing."

"Oh, sorry. So what can I do for you?" he repeated, with some insistence this time.

"I've been wondering about that turpentine still up in the pine forest."

"The what?"

"The still that man Douglas put together up there. He was a good friend of Vincent's."

"Vincent died, you know."

"I heard. You didn't know Douglas?"

Peter shook his head.

Levin felt stymied; he'd assumed that in this small country with so few whites they would all know everything about one another. He felt alarm, and as he took in Peter's honest vacant look, the question crossed his mind whether (impossible, of course) Douglas had ever really existed.

Levin smiled, and making light of Douglas said, "He was kind of a whacko. Lived up there in the forest in a kind of wrecked bungalow with his family."

Peter shook his head. "Never heard of him. Did my mother know him?"

"I don't think so, but I'm pretty sure she knew *about* him. Is she . . . ?"

"She's gone. And Grandma."

"Sorry to hear that."

"What'd you want with him?" Peter's interest at least had been captured, but confronted with the bald question Levin was at a loss. What *did* he want with Douglas? "I guess I . . . well, I'm curious whether he ever started up that still. Because Vincent was very concerned, you know, about an explosion." The explanation seemed ludicrous to Levin. An explosion thirty years ago had brought him here now? So to keep things real he reached for something business-like. "He was going to use the resin from the pines. He thought there was a big market for turpentine here."

To his surprise, Peter's expression changed to one of sympathetic curiosity. "From those pines, really?" Something had apparently caught his imagination.

Relieved now that he was not being thought mad, Levin pressed further into the hard realities. "It wasn't the best resin but good enough, according to Vincent. But the whole contraption was improvised and stuck together from odd parts, and the pressures were very high. I've wondered if it blew up or what."

"And that's why you came?" Peter asked, more intrigued than critical, which gave Levin the sense that maybe they shared some need, still undefined, or a view of some kind, a feeling. And with the relief of the confessor he laughed and said, "I wanted to find some way to get back up there, although it's probably gone by now. But maybe not."

"How do you plan to get up there?"

"I don't know. I thought I'd rent a car, if that's still possible. It's all pretty chaotic here, I understand."

"I'd take you up."

"Would you? That would be fantastic. I'm ready any time."

"How's tomorrow? I'll have to tend to some things around here first." Peter stood. Levin rose and offered his grateful hand, and feeling the power in Peter's grip, it seemed as if he'd crossed from water to land.

The Land Rover truck rode hard, its diesel engine sounding like a rolling barrel of bearings. Peter was wearing a tan shirt and white duck trousers, along with thick, well-worn work boots and a base-ball cap with a Texaco logo. The sleeves of his shirt were neatly rolled up, exposing thick, tanned forearms as tight as the cheeks of a horse. Behind the front seat stretched a full-sized mattress covered with a red plaid blanket and two pillows at the forward end. The manager of the Gustafson, chatting with Levin at the hotel's entrance, had grinned on seeing this vehicle pulling up, and smil-ing wickedly, had said something about there having "been a lot of living on that mattress." And Peter was handsome with his clean, tanned face. He seemed eager, less guarded than on their meeting yesterday. As they left the city behind and climbed toward the pine forest he sounded happy, as if he welcomed the outing. "I haven't been up here since I was a kid," he said.

"Is there another road going up?"

"No. Why?"

"It doesn't look like I remember it. Wasn't there forest here?"

"Probably."

Peter had shifted out of fourth to third to make the climb and in places had to go down to second. On both sides of the road, bare soil dissolving to dust and sand stretched away into the distance. Levin's memory still held the image of the trees. Before them lay a beige-white expanse of bedrock where the pavement vanished.

"How far is it to the top?"

"At least an hour, maybe more on this road."

"Vincent had said they were stealing the forest."

"Yes, everything," Peter said.

"I can't believe this." Levin waved at the blasted landscape.

Peter merely nodded. It was hard to tell what he was feeling. He braked to a halt, estimating a gulley a couple of feet deep that cut across the road. Then proceeded into it and climbed back out, the truck's stiff frame groaning.

"Jesus, I remember a good road here."

"Erosion. With all the trees gone the last hurricanes really wiped things out."

"Looks lost forever."

Peter nodded slightly.

"It's like they ate the country and shat it out."

Peter glanced at him, and Levin regretted his outburst; things were so far gone here that indignation had to border on self-indulgence.

In fact, Levin's indignation reminded Peter of people he had known as a boy. His father and then grandma and his mother used to sound like this, like there was something to be done about things. The idea interested him, like old-time jazz, distantly. He liked the beat but the words were silly and ancient.

The bedrock was tilted here. Peter had to hold on to the door handle to keep from falling on Levin, who gripped the dashboard. Levin remembered nothing like this. Now, off to the right, there were people and what looked like tables set out on the ground. Peter headed across the rocky desert and stopped the truck. There were shanties clustered beyond the tables, a small village. The scene seemed as novel to Peter as to himself, Levin thought.

They were mostly women in rags, each hovering around her own table on which she had set out her wares, incongruous out here beyond any buyers. Peter and Levin moved among the tables, nodding to the women who barely acknowledged their greetings. On the tables were old combs, mismatched tableware, knives and spoons and forks—some of them rusted—and on one table old pop bottles made opaque by sun and rain, bottle caps, pencils and pencil stubs, worn-out shoes, and everywhere hunger-bloated children underfoot, some of them under a year old, mouthing dust. Peter picked up a small spoon engraved with unreadable writing and gave the woman money. Finally they came to a halt, looking around. People pretended not to be looking at them.

"Why do they do this, where would customers come from?"

Peter shrugged, and seemed annoyed by the question, as though Levin had spoken too loudly at a graveside. They went back to the truck.

The semblance of road was indicated by a few feet of snipped-off restraining cable that had once marked its edges. "Am I wrong?" Levin asked. "This *was* all forest, wasn't it?"

"I don't know. Probably. But the island had eighty percent of its surface in forest a hundred years ago, and it's less than three percent now." After a moment he said, "You say you met this Douglas guy?"

"Yes. Just briefly. I was only up here one day."

"What was he up to?"

"It's hard to describe. He was almost in a fever. Vincent thought he was slightly cracked, but that he wanted to do something for the country as well as for himself. Start a little industry and create some jobs, give the people some dignity. I heard him say that."

"Is that why you're interested?" There was no ironical inflection, no mockery in Peter's voice.

"I'm not sure," Levin said. "In a sense, I suppose, yes."

"In what sense?"

"I'm not sure how to put it exactly. I guess it was his conviction. It impressed me. In his crazy way I think he loved this place."

Peter turned abruptly to Levin, then back to the road. "What'd he love about it?" he asked. The question seemed important to him.

"Well, I don't know," Levin laughed, "now that you ask." After a moment he said, "You never heard of Douglas at all?" The truck was pitching wildly from side to side.

"No. But I was running around all over the place in those days, didn't stop to listen much." After a moment he asked rather shyly, "You came all the way down here for this?"

Levin was embarrassed. "Well, I don't have much to do. My wife is gone, practically all my friends. I'm not sure why, but the guy keeps coming back to me. I think about him a lot. And frankly," he tried to chuckle, "sometimes it seems like something I dreamed. And now, I come down here," he did laugh now, "and there are no witnesses left!"

Peter drove in silence, edging cautiously around the big holes. They'd begun to pass patches of surviving pines and the air had cooled. Levin continued, "To be perfectly frank about it, I really don't know why I came down. Except that I felt I had to. It's almost a question of," he laughed again, "sanity."

Peter glanced at him.

"I'd really like to find that still, if it's possible. Just to see it again."

"I understand," Peter said. And then he added, "I'd like to see it too."

They were grinding up out of a draw, and reaching the top, they saw a hundred yards ahead another Land Rover parked on the wasteland with half-a-dozen people seated around it. Peter pulled up and got out, and Levin followed him over to the vehicle, a taxi, which was listing sharply to the right. A man was lying underneath it—the driver, Levin gathered, trying to make a repair. The onlookers were an odd collection: a somber young woman in a short red dress with black net stockings and high heels and large brass earrings and hair piled high on her head was sitting on a newspaper on the dry ground; and beside her sat a short, large-bellied man with a pistol on his hip who occasionally eyed her like a dog guarding a sheep. A skeletal woman sat on a flat stone clutching a baby, and two others, a pair of young peasants, stood smoking, while another young man sat with his head between his knees.

No one spoke as Peter bent to see under the chassis. He had not greeted the people or taken any notice of them. Now he spoke Creole to the taxi driver, who ceased working and replied in soft tones to Peter's questions. Levin heard a clattering at his back and turned to see a brown, white-faced horse and rider galloping across the waste toward him. The horse was small but beautifully formed with an Arab head and slender, nervous legs which, when he was pulled up by the rider, never went still, its hooves constantly clacking against loose stones. Around the horse's neck a rope as thick as a hawser was neatly wound up to its jaws. The rider had long dreadlocks and a perky smile. "God's blessing on you all!" he called cheerfully. "Think of the sufferings of this world and thank your heaven for health and good spirits! I greet you, brothers and sisters, with all the good will in the creation!"

The group had turned to listen to him without reacting. Peter stood and walked up close to the rider and said, "They have a problem."

"Yes, I see," said the rider, "but we must have no doubt it could be much worse."

"I would like to buy the rope." Peter pointed at the rope wound around the horse's neck.

"Oh, I regret that is impossible. I need to tie him or he will run off when I get down."

"I would pay and you could find another rope."

"But how then could I get down?"

"You might find someone to hold him while you buy the rope."

"No-no."

"I will pay you a dollar American for the rope."

"No-no."

"Then two dollars."

"For this rope?" He seemed to be reconsidering.

"Yes."

"No-no," the rider said. The horse, its eyes rolling, suddenly danced a complete circle and faced Peter again. Unaccountably, the rider unknotted the rope, unwound it and let it fall into Peter's hand. Peter reached back for his wallet, but the rider, fighting to hold the reins and having to turn himself left and right to keep facing Peter and the group, lifted one arm and called out, "Remember God!" then crouched low to keep his seat as the horse flew off, its hooves sending loose stones clattering down the bare slope.

The unexpected gift of the battery thirty years ago crossed Levin's mind, and his back chilled. Peter crouched beside the truck and instructed the driver on where to place the jack under the frame. A U-bolt had broken, releasing the spring from the frame link. His commands seemed brutally brief, impatient, sometimes scornful. "No! To the left, the left, don't you know left from right? Hold it in place and pump it up. Good. Now come out." The driver squirmed out from under the truck, and Peter lay on the ground and slid in with the rope. The group watched without commenting, interested but keeping clear. Everyone waited in silence while Peter worked. Presently he slid out from under the vehicle and accepted with a nod—not quite of thanks but mute acknowledgment—a large blue bandanna from the man with the pistol with which to wipe his hands. The driver, exhausted, bone-thin, stood before Peter saluting.

Peter said, "Go slow. It won't hold very long. Very slow."

The group filed into the Land Rover. Levin brushed soil off the back of Peter's shirt. The man with the pistol shepherded the woman in the red dress, his hand hovering around her lower back. The man kept nodding obsequiously to Peter, who returned him his kerchief and gestured toward the revolver on his hip.

"You need that here?"

"The bad types are starting to come down out of the trees," the man said.

"No army up here? *Gendarmerie?*"

The man threw his head back with a silent laugh, saluted, and got into the Land Rover behind his woman.

Peter said nothing as he drove on, seemed angry. Levin felt responsible for his dirtied shirt, for the threatening pointlessness of the trip itself, even for the ugliness of the wasteland through which they had to pass.

"Strange thing, his giving you that rope for free," he said, trying to cheer Peter up. He then told him about the man lending the battery thirty years ago in very nearly this same place.

"What about it?" Peter asked.

"I don't know, it just seems unusual. Or do they normally help out strangers that way?"

Peter thought for a moment. "I don't think so. But I don't understand what gets into people anyway. I guess he just wanted to do it."

It occurred to Levin that Peter had stopped to repair the taxi with no thought of any kind of reward for himself. He felt ashamed, then stupid as he struggled and failed to understand the man beside him, just as he couldn't understand the horseman's gift, or the truck driver's so many years ago. Maybe what was so bewildering was Peter's lack of any sentimentality or enthusiasm about the people he was helping. There had even been a tone close to contempt in the way he'd ordered the driver around. Why had he bothered?

Scraggly pines were appearing now on both sides of the road, with numerous stumps between the trees. The road was blacktop again here. Peter glanced at Levin and said, "We should be getting closer. You recognize any of this?"

"They lived in a bungalow off a side road. It wasn't far from the manager's office, if I recall. It came in from the right, I think, but it's hard to recognize it with the trees gone."

"I think the office would be a bit further up ahead, maybe we could ask there." But suddenly Levin recognized a pile of white stones beside a dirt road leading off to the right. "Here!" he cried, and Peter swerved the truck into the narrow road. And there, a hundred yards in, stood the bungalow.

Levin said, "Last time I saw this was thirty-three years ago." Peter pulled up before the porch. The screen was ripped and the door hung open, windows were broken, the place looked sullen. Levin got out and went onto the hollow-sounding porch, Peter behind him, and paused to look around at the junk still in the yard, the weeds, the dead bushes. He hadn't dreamed it, after all; he could see Douglas scanning his blueprints and yelling for tea, and his wife appearing in her pink blouse and sling. They were going to beat the system, cruise the sea showing movies, lie on deck at night licking the stars. Then turpentine, be useful to the people, trying to *matter*. He walked into the living room. The four disintegrating books were still on the mantelpiece, and two long-cold carbonized logs lay half-burnt in the fireplace. The organ still stood against the wall. Douglas's wife had once invited him to play; now he would never learn how she'd known he could. He went to the organ. His steps seemed to echo. The ivory had been picked off the keys. He sat on a box and pumped, but the rotted bellows wheezed. He remembered her coming out in her pink blouse, her hand held protectively over the cast. He looked around. The room was as he remembered; there was nothing here to steal, and their dream and their wonderings were vanished with them. To be useful, he supposed, was the idea that had captured them and Vincent as well, but something else had won out in the end.

"I have a feeling I could find the still. We drove to it from here that day," Levin said as they walked outside. Peter seemed softened; "Was it like this before?" he asked. The romance of the search seemed to have entered him, and he liked it; Levin judged that it might be the profitlessness of it all that appealed to him, the romantic's natural attraction to lost things. Perhaps, Levin speculated, because his mother had chosen a new man to replace his father. Like Levin himself, Peter seemed to live with one foot over the edge searching for the cloud he could stand on.

Peter drove the truck onto the paved road and proceeded slowly, Levin watching the roadside tangles of vines and bushes for a sign. Peter slowed as they passed the manager's Alpine office, but there was no car parked in front, probably nobody inside. "Anyway, I'd rather not get the government involved," Levin said. Not since she died had he felt Adele's absence like this. He wanted her now, in the truck, saw her as she'd looked in her twenties, forty years before her death, with her flesh firm and her full arms around him. *I guess I'm also looking for what was lost,* he thought, and the idea seemed to illuminate his return to this place. It made him smile—*then it's her I'm looking for?*—he almost said aloud, and then he thought, *well, it's as good a reason as any.*

They continued on for a half mile. When Levin said he didn't recall the still having been this far from the office, they stopped and instantly heard a chain saw starting up nearby. They got out and found a narrow footpath into the brush, and after a short walk, came on four men hacking at a fallen pine, with a pile of stems nearby in a clearing. On seeing the strangers the men immediately stopped, waiting for the *blancs* to speak. They were all young, in their twenties, except for a bent, old, silver-haired man in a ragged overcoat, with a machete hanging from one hand and a stick for a cane in the other. He was catching his breath. Toward

him Peter walked, and after a touch to his cap and a rather formal, quiet greeting, he asked him if he had worked around the
area very long. The man said he had, all his life. The other men
watched, alert as trespassers.

"There was once a *blanc* living over there in that bungalow
with his wife and two children, he operated a machine to make
turpentine. Did you ever hear of him?"

"I worked for him," the old man said, "when I was young."

"And is the machinery still to be found?"

"It's that way," the old man said, and pointed in the direction
Peter and Levin had come from.

With the old man, whose name was Octavus, sitting between
them they drove back along the paved road. He held the machete
point down between his legs. He had tiny eyes in a flattened face,
and his dank old man's smell filled the cab. "He smells like old
iron, if that could smell," Peter said toward Levin. Then to Octavus
he asked in Creole, "Papa, are we getting closer or further away?"

"*Près, près,*" the old man said, pointing ahead.

"*Près* could mean a couple of miles," Peter said. Just then the
old man jabbed his finger toward the brush, croaking, "*V'la,
v'la,*" and laughing like they'd been playing a game.

Stiff as he was, Octavus had to slide himself across the seat and
onto the ground like a board. Peter grasped his elbow as he moved
unsteadily into the brush, parting it with his machete and straightening up to shield his face. He walks like he's parting the sea,
Levin thought. The spiky vines snatched at their shirts and trousers as if defending a space. Levin, coming up behind, felt short of
breath and recalled the altitude here, or was this his long-awaited
heart attack? His slight struggling for air reminded him of Jimmy
P.'s broken nose and how he would snort like a boxer whenever he
exerted, the image reminding him that Jimmy must be dead some
twenty-five years. And what happened to Jimmy's abject faith in
the Russians, in the built-in virtue of the working class and the
inevitable unspooling of history into benevolent socialism? Belief
that profound almost deserved having dimension and weight
enough to be buried; a national holiday might be good, perhaps,

when people could visit their dead convictions. Funny, how it was easier to accept Jimmy's disappearance from the earth than that of his passion and all the mix of love and vengeance that had gone into it. What was more dispiriting than the waste of devotion that leaves behind the vanishing footsteps of the people it has misled? Or was there some other point to all the striving, he wondered.

They stepped into a clearing filled with stumps and weeds. The old man stopped with Peter still touching his elbow, prepared to catch him if he toppled, and he pointed to the right, to a low butte with a dense mass of spiky vines at its base. The three men approached and peered through the vines, and once their eyes had adjusted to the dimness of the thicket, they saw deep within it a tall dark object, a black tube some six feet wide and maybe fifteen feet high. The thing leaned at an angle with its head raised against the butte as though it were resting, exhausted.

"I'll be damned," Peter whispered, "he really did it." And then laughed at its outrageousness, but his eyes were serious.

"Amazing, isn't it?" Levin said, glad now that Peter had found some excitement to make up for the troubles on the trip, and relieved also that the thing had turned out to be real. "He dragged it all the way up from the port!" He laughed, and in his happiness he couldn't help confessing to Peter, "You know, I was getting to where I wasn't sure I'd dreamed the whole thing, like I'd invented an obsession of some sort. I'm really relieved, though I still don't understand it."

"Well, you'd have to see it to believe it. I gotta get a closer look," Peter said, and he borrowed Octavus's machete and attacked the tank's vine barrier. Levin helped, dragging away the cut vines. "It's like a leopard's hideaway," he said, breathing hard. "We saw one once in Africa, my wife and I. Leopards are very secretive, live in the middle of thorn bushes, a lot like this." When they pulled away a dense eucalyptus the main tank was bared to the sunlight with a phalanx of smaller tanks piped together. Some pipes that must have connected to other tanks were amputated and ended in midair. The whole apparatus stood over them like a snake-armed god, Levin thought, a presence, a mute intention asking to be read.

And it was much grander than it had seemed at first, maybe twenty feet tall by eight or ten wide.

"Christ!" Peter exhaled, "he really *meant* it, dragging all this up here!"

"I'd love to know if he ever lit it," Levin said.

Peter turned to Octavus and asked in Creole whether they had ever operated the still. The old man sighed and lowered himself onto a stump. Peter sat on the ground in an easy descent and translated as he spoke. Levin bent in a crouch and tumbled back onto the ground. The old man's voice was hoarse and cracked.

Mister Douglas had lit the fire and Octavus and three others had milked the pines, and he recalled Vincent the Jamaican who had supervised the process for only one day and then never came back. They had made turpentine, which was like a miracle coming from the pines, and everyone was given a liter to keep from the first draw, and barrels of it were trucked down to the port. And then sick people had begun showing up but they had nothing to pay for turpentine so Mister Douglas would give a cup or two to some of them for their bowels and skin troubles and mouth sores and the babies until in the end there were crowds of people some days, hoping for a cure of their sicknesses. Douglas would even examine them like a doctor, and his wife was like a nurse. "Some people paid with bits of goat meat or garden beans, but he needed more money to operate, as I understood," Octavus said, "because my family has always run a store and I know about business. So Mister Douglas went down to the bank at the port and they sent people up to look at the thing, but they said it was not the right kind of pine and they wouldn't give him anything."

"We worked like this for five or six months," Octavus went on, "until one morning when we started to work he came and told us to stop and said he had no more money to pay us. We all sat down and talked about this but there was nothing anybody could think of doing, and so we went away and never came back. But my place is near so every few days I would stop by just to look around and see if maybe he was going to start up again, and one morning I found him bent over on the ground before the main tank like he was at prayer, but he was not moving and I touched him and he looked up at me, his face was only bone. His wife, I should mention, her arm had swelled up and she went back to the States for an operation and took the children and we never saw her again. But Douglas held my hand and we sat together on the ground for a long time. He spoke very good Creole so I remember it well. He said that he was dying now and thanked me for my work—I never allowed slacking on the job, and I was the responsible one over the others, you see. And he said that I should be the owner now, and handed me a paper from his shirt pocket which I couldn't read as it was in English. But the priest could read it and it said that I was the man inheriting. But where would I get the money to pay the workers? And so it ended."

"Was that the last you saw of him?" Peter asked.

"No, after a while I went to his house to see how he was faring now that I knew how sick he was, and he was alone there with one of the old women giving him goat's milk and so forth. He was glad to see me again and held my hand and then he wrote some words on a paper and gave it to me. I always keep it as I never saw him alive again."

He reached under his arm to a worn kid sack and brought out a yellowed patch of note paper with Douglas's name elegantly engraved on the top. Peter read it and handed it to Levin. *If the idea goes let it go, but if you can keep it, do so and it will surely lift you up one day.* It was signed, *Douglas Brown.*

Peter watched the old man intensely and now asked, "What idea did he mean?" Levin caught the tone of longing in Peter's voice.

The old man's head was square as a block; at one time he must have been very strong. He shook his head gravely and said, "I don't know. I never understood. The tanks . . ."

He broke off, turning to the tanks, staring at them for a long time, trying, it seemed, to bring something to the surface. Levin thought it must all seem like a dream to him too after so many years. The old man seemed on the verge of speaking but gave up, shaking his head, his small eyes blinking, and Levin thought, *And*

now it will all slide into oblivion, all that life and all that caring,
and all that hope, as incoherent as it was.

As they made their way out to the road, Levin saw a shiny bolt
lying in the weeds. He picked it up and put it in his pocket, wondering what metal could have kept its shine after so many years.
Levin, once inside the truck, saw that the old man was moved and
looked satisfied. "He looks happier now," he said.

"Well, he passed it on," Peter said.

Swaying and thudding on its unforgiving springs, the Land Rover
shouldered down the devastated mountain, the diesel grinding
against the crazy tilts of the all but vanished roadbed. Staring out
the window, Levin said, "They really destroyed the whole landscape. I would never have believed it was possible. And there was
a pretty good road up here, you know."

Peter merely nodded. His silences, Levin understood now, were
a kind of mourning for something far greater than his own life;
the whole country was a surround of suffocating greed, inex-
pressible in the face of his hopelessness about changing anything.
In the silence between them, Levin remembered once again how
the last descent so long ago had brought him back with Vincent,
dead Vincent now, to Mrs. Pat's house and to Adele to whom he
had told the whole adventure that evening, and even how they
had rediscovered their bodies that night in the broad beams of
moonlight flowing into the room at the hotel, and it was once
again inconceivable that she was no more, not to be found anywhere. They were two giants in bed, four feet sticking out from
under the covers. How he had loved to *rely* on her body, feeling
small sometimes on top of her. All gone. Pitching back and forth
now between the unlined truck door and Peter's shoulder, the
remorselessness of his loneliness astonished him. Douglas, he saw,
had been driven crazy by hope. Hope on this mountain which
even then, thirty years back, was being stripped of its life down to
dead stone. Who could feel the quality of that hope any more? Or
was it illusion? But what was not? Up here he had caught a whiff

of it again; blundering Douglas may have touched something almost sacred, having wanted to make a Madison Avenue life mean something and not knowing how except to do something so absurd. *And maybe that was why his image, after so short a time in his presence, stayed on in my mind,* Levin thought. It seemed now it would never leave him, even if he could only partially grasp its connection to himself.

He turned to Peter, whom, after all, he had known since he was a boy stuffing his mouth with cherries. "What do you make of it, Peter?" he asked.

"Make of what?"

"All this," Levin said, gesturing out the window. "Everything."

"Did you know my mother in New York?"

"Your mother? No, we met here. Why?"

Peter shrugged, but decided to continue. "They all thought they had the answer here. The political answer. Did you think that way?"

"Me? You mean some kind of socialism."

"Yes."

"I did, for a while."

"What happened to all that?"

"Well, the Russians, for one thing. The camps and the backwardness and so on soured people on it. And American prosperity."

"So it's all gone."

"Seems so, yes."

They rode in silence for a while. Here and there a lone man could be seen standing in the open, staring in surprise at them going by, his face dust-covered. "It's the end here, you know," Peter said.

Levin heard the depth of the loss in him, even though Peter's tone was dry and controlled. "You think you'll be staying on here indefinitely or . . . ?" He broke off, realizing that Peter must love this country, and why prick at the pain of leaving it?

"I might go to the States, but I don't really know. My girl wants to get married, but I just don't know."

"I'm curious, Peter—what are your feelings about Douglas?"

"I don't know. He was a damned fool, I guess."

"Because?"

"Well, he could have checked out the kind of pine he had here before he got that far into it. And Christ, not getting his technical information beforehand. That was stupid." He thought for a moment. "But you'd have a hard time working with these people no matter what you did."

"Why, what's wrong with them?"

"Their heads are someplace else. They see things we don't. Hear things we can't."

"You have Haitian friends?"

"Oh sure, I was raised here. But most of them just fuck up sooner or later."

"But they seem to have a sweetness," Levin said, thinking of Octavus.

"Oh yes. Some." Then after a moment, "There's some very bad people around now, and they're armed. With CIA help, they say. Killings all the time."

"What will you do?"

"I doubt they'll bother me. If they did, probably because they'd want a cut of my business. I'd have to close down and get out if it's too much."

They were passing the small huddled shacks, the tiny gardens again. Levin turned the question over in his mind for a few minutes, and finally said, "I thought the way you got that taxi going again was pretty terrific, Peter."

"I just tied the spring back on, that's all."

"I have to admit I was surprised you stopped and did that for them."

Peter seemed not to like where this was going and frowned. "I knew that guy."

"The driver?"

"Uh-huh."

"You didn't seem to from the way you talked."

"He's stupid. He shouldn't even be driving. He'd never have got that car going, didn't even know where to place the jack. He was trying to raise the car up instead of the spring, exactly the opposite of what he should have been doing. He's an idiot. Worked for me for a while till I had to can him."

"I see," Levin said. Then Peter had not been moved so much by some disinterested compassion or some knightly noblesse as by a kind of elegant impatience with the stupid driver and a pride in his own ability to make the repair? So the rescue was not as noble an act as he had imagined? Unless knights too had egos to massage. All Levin knew for sure was that he himself would probably not have stopped even if he'd known how to fix the taxi spring. Was it because he lacked Peter's love for these people? Or did he lack the wish to be anyone's seigneur?

He grinned to himself, thinking, *But if there'd been a piano out there on that waste I think I'd have been happy to sit and play for them while that driver bungled around and the people died of hunger and thirst waiting for someone to show up and save them. Chacun à son ego.* But then he thought again of the still, the size of the great main tank and the labor it must have taken to drag it up from the port and through the forest, plus the welder and his generator, and then of Douglas's frantic appeal to Vincent, his cracked and dirty eyeglasses crooked on his nose, and his outcry, "This country is *dying*, Vincent!"

Peter left him off at the hotel saying he would come by to pick him up for dinner that evening, clearly pleased to have new company. Levin waved goodbye and went up to his room. After a shower he lay naked on the bed, perhaps the same one he had shared with Adele. A car horn drifted through the shutters, which he recalled Adele had admired, and then a voice on the street in the chirping baby-talk language, then a roaring motorbike. He thought again of the tank and how it still looked in good condition, only a little rust along the welds. It could probably last a thousand years out there. In some sense it was like a kind of work of art that transcended the pettiness of its maker, even his egotism and foolishness. He felt glad he had come back here. Not that it meant anything, but he had inadvertently paid some kind of homage to Douglas's aspiration, an idea that he felt now had gone from the world, at least the world he knew. He loved Douglas and wished he could have been as careless with himself. He longed to play Schubert with Adele. He was falling asleep. There might be a piano in the hotel which he could imagine sharing with her beside him, he must ask the clerk. He could smell her scent. Odd, that she would never see the tank.

Presence

He wakes at quarter to six, sun in his face, still tight about being criticized for not doing enough for women, slips into walking shorts and sandals with a glance toward her exposed arm, and thirsty for the morning fog steps out into the chill, walks toward the beach road in the swirling mist, grateful even to the dimmed sun for its uncomplicated touch of warmth on his back. The row of sleeping beachfront houses and their dozing cars alongside the road, his sandals whispering, he searches for the public path down to the beach and at last finds it alongside the last house in the row. On the brow of the path before it descends he pauses for his first glimpse of the sterling ocean, his hallowed homewater from so long past in childhood, when it loved him and scared him into sparkling and foamy white on top and dark below with live things in its holy depths. Once he had nearly drowned, at six, seven. Another step now descending upon the tippy, blanched gray planks, and through the long spear grass alongside him a white body suddenly, a man in his black T-shirt seen from his overhead vantage, fucking. He halts to watch. Slowly back and forth, a young body, tight and tanned, on his knees in hard control, but the crouched woman all but hidden behind a hummock of sand and grass. Without deciding to he finds himself turning back up the path and halts witless beside the road. There is no other way to the beach, he will have to wait. He parades in his loose sandals past the beach houses not really too surprised that he is not aroused himself. Possibly because there is something mute and controlled and therefore remote about this lovemaking, or maybe it is his own repression. Whatever, it merely leaves him with the restraint of courtesy. Which is soon superseded by resentment at being barred from entering the beach; what an idea, to do it ten feet from the public pathway! On the other hand, they couldn't have expected anyone to come by at this hour. Still, though, a few people must. Sure they must be finished, he returns to the path and starts down again, managing to utter a warning cough, certain they must be lying side by side this time, probably covered by a blanket. At the dune's brow he halts, seeing the man below him still fucking but a little faster now, absolutely demanding, dominating, a Pan fucking earth itself for all one could tell. A feather of something like fear now at the sight, something sanctified in such power, the primordial exchange of domination for submission. The man was now lunging in quicker and longer and silently controlled strokes. He turned, his mind confused, and walked back toward the road before impending outcry, fearful of it now, not wishing to witness its absurdly sacred thunder, as though in watching it he would make it obscene, perhaps, or some challenge was there he would rather decline.

Another stroll, longer this time, nearly the whole block to the house where he and his wife were guests, and finally turning back in a last attempt to enter the beach, he mounted the dune and descended. Fog had given way to pure Atlantic blue sky. Beside the path lay the form of the man buried like a larva inside a khaki sleeping bag, the woman gone. The ocean rolled softly, at peace with itself, the scalloped spume washing the gentle beige slope of packed sand. No one in the virgin water, but now, off to the right, a woman in black shorts and a white T-shirt, standing up to her ankles in the margins of the receding surf, bending over to thrash her open hands in the restlessly churning suds. From his distance he could not tell what she looked like excepting that her thighs were full and beautiful, but her hair seemed to stand up in stiff, wiry kinks. He watched her staring out to sea, saw her climbing up the incline and crossing to the soft sand. She saw him but did not let her gaze linger and trudged back to their dune and spread out a blanket and sat beside the hidden man curled up on his side. A space of a foot or two separated them. She turned to look at the pupa-like shape beside her. Then she looked at the sea again. She wiped her hands dry on the blanket, then seemed to sigh and lay down with her knees raised. After a few moments she turned on her side, her back to the sleeping bag.

He walked to the edge of the sea, whose sibilant suck and push had, he realized, been the sounds he had heard through it all. Without a plan, he idled along the edge of the water away from the pair. The sheer thoughtfulness of the ocean depths stirred him; nothing in life was as dense with feeling, as wise and deceitfully pleasing with its soothing strokes, while its murderous temper was gathering hate. Breakfast hunger; starting back toward the path to the street, he was halted after a few steps by the sight of them lying there some hundred feet away, the pupa shell and the woman curled up with her back to it, and he sat on the sand and stared. Why did he assume, he wondered, that she must feel deserted and unhappy now? Why could the guy not have been a stud with whom she wanted nothing more to do? Perhaps she had hunted him down, landed him, and now lay there the victor, resting before her next conquest. Mute as apes, he thought. Two of them in a cage with their silence and surfeit. And the sun. The sea's waves are the spin of the earth made visible. The young woman sat up, the man remaining inert in his shroud, having done what could be done with his earlier taunting of death. She was staring toward the sea, the length of beach still altogether empty. They must have slept the night there. It could have been their second fuck. She slowly turned now and looked across the light at him. He lowered his gaze deferentially, touched for some reason by guilt of his knowledge of her, then resolved to return her stare. She slid upward onto her feet and came walking over to him. As she approached, he saw the round of her hips and the bloom of her breasts. She was short. As she came closer he saw that her rigidly kinky hair had been only his illusion brought on somehow by mist and sunlight; she actually had heavy brown hair bobbed to the nape and round cheeks and dark-brown eyes. A widow's peak and orange coral earrings the size of half dollars. A Band-Aid around her left thumb; maybe she spent a lot of time on the beach with its broken bottles and splintery wood. She halted, standing over him where he sat cross-legged.

"Do you have the time?"

"No, but it's about half-past six."

"Thanks."

She glanced full of indecision out at the sea behind him. "Do you have a house here?"

"No, I'm visiting for the weekend."

"Uh." She nodded deeply several times like a philosopher, but pretentious or not he began to feel she included him in her vision of things, whatever that was. She seemed to accept as inevitable his sitting there, the only one on the beach besides her lover and herself. She stood at her ease, pressing a loose edge of her bandage down on her skin. Then she turned from her thumb to him, her head tilted down to inspect him, take him in, a soft and slack smile broadening her mouth as though expecting some admission to come from him. He felt he was blushing. Then she sighed peacefully and looked once more out at the water, her uplifted chin lending her a certain nobility. He recognized the absurdity of his thought now that it was she who was in charge of the beach.

Something had happened. Uncomprehending, he realized with fear and unhappiness that he had made a link, was not alone, and resolved not to speak again unless to some purpose. Thirty years ago he had made love on this beach. There were fewer houses here then. It could have been in the grass on the same dune, although the one he remembered doing it on seemed higher. She was dead now, a skeleton by this time, he supposed. But they had not done it in absolute silence. And it had been in darkness, and he remembered the moon path shining on the water like a road, its light continuing into her black hair.

Was she not going to speak? He tried to seem amused but fear was mixed in him as he looked up at her. A quick glance told him that the sack had not moved, as though her partner had left for another world. But she was not sleepy. She might still be throbbing. Thoughts crossed the screen of her brow, her lowered eyes. From his angle her planted legs were like pillars rising from the sand.

"You watched us."

His breath caught but he clung to his right. "I had no idea you were there. . . ."

"I know, I saw you."

"Really? I didn't see you. You were hidden by the grass."

"I could see you, though. Did we look great?"

"Pretty great."

She turned and glanced toward the sack, shaking her head as though marveling at something. But letting herself down on the sand, she looked back over her shoulder again, apparently to make sure that he would not yet stir. Then she pulled her ankle under her thigh and sat almost facing him in a half-lotus position, her back straight. Now she seemed to have an almost Eastern visage, with her round cheeks pressing up her eyes into a narrowed gaze. "You came back once, didn't you?"

"Well, I thought you'd be finished."

"I couldn't actually see you, you know; but I felt you were there."

"How do you mean?"

"Some people have a presence."

Sitting in silence and staring at him, she seemed to be waiting for some agreed-upon thing to happen. He did not want to say or do something that might embarrass him or send him away. He turned out to the sea for a moment, pretending to relax with no necessity for them to speak because they were so secure in a shared silence. But she rose on oiled joints and walked yards into the water. He flushed with the beginnings of shame at losing her, then decided to follow and walked into the water behind her despite recalling the fine penknife in his pocket, his wife's birthday gift, which would be ruined by salt water. She slipped under a soft wave. The water was repellently cold, but he let himself into it and swam beside her. They treaded water facing each other, then she floated closer to him and laid a hand on his shoulder. He drew her in by the waist and then felt her legs opening and forking him. A wave lapped over their heads and they coughed and laughed, and she grasped his hips and pulled him to her and kissed him, her lips cold, then she slipped off and swam away and walked out of the water onto the beach, continuing up toward her lover who had still not moved.

Emerging, he reached into his pocket and drew out the penknife and opened the four blades, wiping them with his damp fingers and blowing moisture out of its nested interior, then sat on the sand. He had no towel but the sun was warming up. The fresh air in his lungs made him light-headed, and he threw his head back with his eyes closed to absorb everything in relaxation. There must be something he should do. He turned and looked up across the beach and found her staring at him where she sat on the blanket, and they held the stare like two ends of a long silken thread. Now he would lose her. Familiar aches were returning to his hips. Stretching out, he lay on his back with his small victory at having touched her body and somehow her spirit, and closed his eyes. Surprisingly, sleep's fingers began to creep into the backs of his closed eyes; a swim in the sea sometimes left him as relaxed as after sex, and he felt he could doze off now if he wished. A dreamscape began to form but the sun was rapidly heating up and would burn him, so he sat up and, starting to his feet, he glanced once more across the beach toward her protective dune and his heart chilled. They had gone. The shock flew into his stomach, threatened vomit. How was it possible so quickly? They would have to have folded her blanket and the man's sleeping bag and packed away some other things lying around. He hurried over to the dune where they had been but there was nothing, and the sand here was too loose to retain footsteps. A lump of fear swelled in his chest and turned him in all directions, but there was only the sea and the empty beach. He hurried over to the slatted path, hoping to reach the street before they disappeared, then halted, seeing a white T-shirt suspended on points of spear grass. Reaching down he took it in his hands and felt a very slight body warmth in the cotton. Or had it been forgotten by previous lovers and was only warmed now by the heat of the sun? A fear of having stepped over some restraining edge into utter loss. But at the same dark moment, a tremendous joy was flowing into him that was no longer connected to anything. He climbed the path to the street and turned up the road toward the house where he was staying. How strange, he thought, that it mattered so little whether or not they were actually here if what he had seen had left him so happy?